Sign up for our newsletter to hear
about new and upcoming releases.

www.ylva-publishing.com

OTHER BOOKS BY JAE

Backwards to Oregon

A HISTORICAL ROMANCE

JAE

Acknowledgments

First and foremost, I want to thank my readers. You are the reason I get to live my dream—writing full-time.

A very special thank-you goes to my beta readers, especially to Pam, who has been incredibly helpful and supportive since the very beginning. I also want to thank Erin, Marion, Melanie, Patty, Peggy, RJ Nolan, Sheryl, Sue, and Susanne for their time and their excellent beta-reading skills.

Thank you to Astrid and to Ylva Publishing for providing *Backwards to Oregon* with a loving home.

Map: Oregon Trail 1851

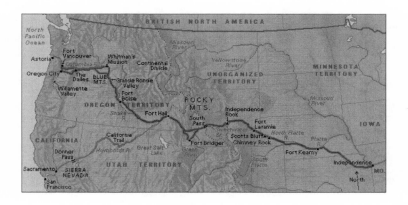

INDEPENDENCE, MISSOURI, JUNE 1846

Tess Swenson inwardly cursed the smoke-filled, dimly lit room and the tinny clanking of the piano. She strained to keep a watchful eye and ear on her girls and their customers lounging in secluded alcoves, sitting on sofas, or leaning against the long mahogany bar.

"Damn." Charlie, her bartender, narrowed his eyes at the stream of soldiers filtering in. "And here I thought we'd get some peace and quiet once all the trappers and emigrants headed west."

"It's the war," Tess said. She leaned her back against the bar and scanned each customer for signs of trouble. "They all want to spend one last night with a woman before they go off to war."

All around her, soldiers were laughing, fighting for the attention of the girls, and gulping down whiskey as if there were no tomorrow. *For some of them, there might not be.* Tomorrow they would march south, with orders to conquer New Mexico. The fear generated by the upcoming war was a powerful stimulant for Tess's business, but it also made their work more dangerous. Charlie poured a whiskey for a customer and a glass of cold tea for the girl hanging on the customer's arm. "Some of them are barely more than boys. Look at him." He pointed at a young soldier whose comrades pushed and pulled him into the parlor. The other men were eager to enter the brothel, but he dragged his feet and stalled by stopping at the door to knock the mud off his boots. He waved his friends away and leaned against the bar, facing the rest of the room.

One of Tess's girls wandered over and seductively trailed one hand over the young soldier's shoulder.

He gazed at her without returning her smile. Under the pretense of reaching for his shot of whiskey, he broke the physical contact between them.

The girl stepped closer, but he shook his head and said something that made the girl shrug and walk away.

Tess had seen the skittish behavior of first-time visitors before, but something about the young man told her that he wasn't merely shy. She stepped away from the bar to study him without him noticing.

Neither his stature nor his worn uniform or scuffed boots set him apart from his comrades. He wasn't unusually tall, and compared to the burly build of his friends, his lean frame didn't seem impressive, but something about him made her take notice nonetheless.

The insignia on the sleeve of his navy-blue uniform coat told her he was a sergeant. He was young to hold that rank, but in times of war, it wasn't that unusual.

What set the young man apart was the way he carried himself. When he crossed the room and settled down at one of the corner tables, he moved with the smooth stride of a cat, a combination of strength and unconscious grace where Tess had expected the gangly awkwardness of someone barely out of puberty.

He leaned back in his chair, nursing his whiskey, and watched the other men with a stoic expression. Everything about him showed calm confidence—everything but the way he worried the forage cap on his lap between his long, slender fingers.

Angry voices from the bar made Tess turn around. A red-faced soldier grabbed one of her girls by the throat and shook her.

"Let go of her! Now!" Tess rushed back to the bar.

The angry soldier let go of the girl. Roaring like a grizzly bear, he whirled around and backhanded Tess.

Pain exploded in her face. She crashed into the bar. For a moment, she couldn't breathe. Out of the corner of her eye she saw Charlie reach for the revolver he kept behind the bar.

Before the situation could escalate further, someone grabbed the soldier by his uniform lapel, whirled him around, and forced him away from Tess and the gasping girl.

The drunken soldier swung up his fists.

A jab threw back his opponent's head.

Tess's eyes widened. Her savior was none other than the young man from the corner table. He was half a head shorter and weighed considerably less than his drunken foe, but he didn't back down. He stepped forward and threw a punch.

The bigger man lowered his head and charged him like a furious bull.

One of her girls cried out. A few of the men shouted encouragements at the fighters, hastily betting money on how long the smaller man would last under the iron fists of his opponent.

Tess reached for the small revolver hidden in one of her garters. She swung up the weapon, but the big soldier was already standing still, looking down the barrel of the boy's revolver.

"You better sober up real quick, Corporal, before I spare the Mexicans the work and shoot you right here, right now." The boy's voice was low and quiet, yet left no doubt about his determination.

The corporal brought up a trembling hand and wiped blood off his lip without looking away from the boy. The silent battle of wills went on for a few seconds before he lowered his gaze and let out a breath. "All right, all right, I'm sober."

The boy put away his revolver, but his sharp gaze remained fixed on his opponent. "I think you owe these ladies an apology, Corporal."

"What?" The soldier stared at him. "But they ain't no la—"

"Was that a 'Yes, sir'?" the boy asked, his eyes narrowed.

The corporal's teeth ground against each other. "Yes, sir."

The boy gestured toward Tess.

After hesitating for a few more seconds, the corporal turned around and faced her. "I... apologize."

"An apology won't pay for the glasses you broke when you threw me against the bar," Tess said, the small revolver still in her hand. As the brothel's madam, she had learned to be a charming hostess, a motherly figure for her girls, and most of all a tough businesswoman.

"Pay her," the boy said, his gray eyes like steel.

Grumbling, the soldier threw some coins on the bar and stormed out of the brothel.

The boy watched him leave, then laid another coin on the bar and turned to follow him.

"Wait!" Tess hurried after him.

The young man reluctantly turned back around. His gaze flickered to the door as if he wanted to disappear through it as quickly as possible. "Yes, ma'am?"

"Your nose." Tess pointed. "It's bleeding. Come with me to my room, and let me tend to it." She extended her hand.

The boy didn't take it. "That's not necessary, ma'am. It'll stop soon enough."

"It'll stop sooner if I tend to it. I have a lot of experience with patching up victims of a brawl."

"Come on, Luke," one of the boy's comrades shouted. "No man in his right mind says no when Miss Tess invites him up to her room. Be a man and go with her."

The corner of the boy's mouth twitched, hinting at an almost smile, the first Tess had seen from him. Before he could refuse once more, Tess took his hand and led him upstairs, ignoring the cheers from the rest of his company.

"Sit down." Tess patted the bed that took up most of her room. "It doesn't bite—and neither do I."

He cautiously sank down on the very edge of the bed, holding on to his forage cap with both hands. He looked like a schoolboy on a detention bench. It was hard to believe that this was the fearless fighter who had stood toe to toe with a much bigger man just minutes ago.

Tess turned to her crystal decanter and poured him a shot of whiskey.

He shook his head. "No, thank you, ma'am."

"It's on the house," she said.

He took the glass from her but held it without drinking.

"Drink up." Tess searched for a clean cloth. "This ain't gonna be pleasant." The cloth in hand, she stepped between his legs and bent to take a closer look at his nose. She dabbed at it with the cloth, wiping away the blood, and laid a gentle hand on his neck to guide his head to one side. "I think it's broken."

He trembled against her.

For a second, she attributed it to the pain of a broken nose, but then she saw the look in his eyes. Tess smiled. She had been in this job long enough to know that it was not the pain that darkened his gray eyes; it was her physical closeness, her half-bared bosom pressing against his shoulder. She slid the hand resting on his neck around and touched his still smooth cheek. "How old are you, soldier?"

The boy turned his face away from her touch and scrambled back until the headrest stopped him. "Old enough to go to war."

Tess looked down at him. He was very young, but the weary look in his eyes told her he had seen more things in his life than most men twice his age. This was not a naïve boy, but something about him made her believe he had never been with a woman.

This is gonna be a nice change. He was so different from most of her other customers—polite, clean, and sober. "Old enough for this?" She stepped close again, pressed him down on the bed, and lowered her lips to his.

Slender but strong hands closing around her wrists stopped her. "No."

"No?" Tess couldn't remember the last time she had heard that word from a man. "If you're worried about money, I don't intend to take any from you. This is my way of saying thank you for your help with that drunken bastard."

The boy still held her roaming hands captive. "No, no. I… This is not what you think. I…I'm…"

Tess smiled at him. "Relax, I know what you are." It wasn't difficult to guess the boy was a virgin.

His eyes widened. "You…you know? How…?"

"I have enough experience with men to know these things."

The boy stared at her. "And you invited me up to your room anyway?"

"Sure." What was so surprising about that? Every whore knew that virginal customers were easily earned money.

"And you tried to kiss me even though you knew what I am?"

Tess studied him. *Does he really think he's the first virgin in my bed? A whore doesn't go to bed with the men who can give her the most pleasure, but the ones with the most money.* "And I would kiss you if you let go of my hands."

The grip around her wrists wavered for a moment. "You…you like…women?"

"What?"

For a second, they stared at each other, then the boy—the girl, Tess realized—jumped up with a curse and fled to the door.

"Wait!" Tess hurried after her mysterious visitor and laid a hand against the door to prevent it from opening. "Wait a minute. What's going on here? Who are you?"

The girl slowly turned back around. She looked at Tess without answering. The muscles in her jaw clenched.

Tess studied the slender, yet muscular body and the boyishly handsome face. The girl was taller than most women. Even now that Tess knew, she couldn't detect any signs of feminine curves. "Who are you?"

"Luke Hamilton." Her guest extended his—her—hand.

Tess took her hand, noticing the strong grip of the calloused fingers. Everything she saw, heard, and felt made her believe she was dealing with a young man. She couldn't stop staring at her guest. "That's not the name your parents gave you, though, is it?"

The girl hesitated. "No," she finally said, "it's not."

For a second, Tess wanted to ask her real name but then thought better of it. The girl had no reason to trust her with her biggest secret, and she already looked as if she wanted to bolt. "Come back and sit." Tess patted the bed.

The girl remained right next to the door. "I need to go."

"Your friends in the parlor wouldn't be very impressed if your visit up here only lasted for three minutes," Tess said with a smile. "So come sit and tell me how a girl ended up becoming a dragoon sergeant."

The girl shuffled her feet. "That's a long story. And I would appreciate it if you wouldn't refer to me as a girl. The life I live is that of a man."

Tess leaned back on the bed with a seductive grin. "Every aspect of it?"

A hint of a blush spread across the tan face. "Almost."

"So you don't want me to thank you, huh?" Tess nodded down at her low-cut bodice.

Luke blinked. "I'm… You know what I am. It's not possible to… Is it?"

"Oh, it's very possible, I assure you, sweetheart." Tess stood and circled her visitor with seductive sways of her hips. "Do you want me to demonstrate?"

She had expected another blush, but this time, the young woman looked her straight in the eyes. "I don't approve of prostitution. No man—or woman—should take advantage of women who have been forced to sell their bodies to survive."

Tess stared into the young woman's eyes. There was no judgment, no contempt, only a simple honesty. Tess was charmed. "You don't believe in prostitution. Do you believe in friendship?"

Dark lashes blinked rapidly. Obviously, it was the last thing Luke had expected from her.

"Do you?" Tess asked when Luke remained silent.

"I don't know. I don't have many friends."

"Well, if you want, you've got one now." Tess paused. "Unless you don't want to be seen in the company of a lady of negotiable affections."

A small grin flitted across Luke's reserved face. "I guess to be seen with you could only help my reputation."

With a laugh, Tess lifted up on her tiptoes and kissed the smooth cheek. "All right, friend. Then let's get that nose taken care of. We wouldn't want it to mar that handsome face of yours." She laughed at Luke's blush and pulled her back to the bed.

Independence, Missouri, April 27th, 1851

Rough laughter and the thumping of booted feet across the boardwalk made Tess look up.

"Soldiers." Fleur groaned next to her before the first of them had even entered. In the three years that the young woman had worked for Tess, she had learned a lot about men— even identifying their profession by their footfalls.

"Don't sound so snide, girl," Tess said. "Last time, they left you a nice tip."

"Last time, they also left me a nice black eye."

True. After long months of living in the shabby barracks of a secluded fort, with no break from their monotonous duties and bad food, soldiers tended to go a little wild on payday. "I'll keep an eye on them," Tess said.

The door swung open. Loud voices and fresh air drifted into the brothel's parlor, and for a moment, the smoke dispersed.

Tess stepped forward to extend a flirtatious greeting, but her well-practiced business smile gave way to a delighted laugh when she saw the last man being dragged in by his comrades.

Luke Hamilton was no longer the girl she had been five years ago. She had returned from Mexico after fighting for more than a year, wounded, commissioned on the battlefield to the rank of lieutenant, and more reserved than ever. The war had changed her. Tess had fought hard to break through that shield of bitter aloofness, and though Luke had shared her bed in the aftermath of the war, she had never really shared her thoughts and emotions.

"Well, well, well, if it isn't Lieutenant Luke Hamilton, visiting a house of ill repute," Tess said. "Finally gotten lonely, soldier?"

Her visitor took off a wide-brimmed hat and smiled down at Tess. "I'm no longer a soldier."

"What?" For the first time, Tess noticed that Luke's navy-blue uniform had been replaced by worn civilian clothes.

"I've resigned my commission," Luke said. "My soldiering days are over."

Tess blinked. "How long have you been planning that?"

Luke looked down, studying the tips of her scuffed boots. "A while."

She hadn't mentioned anything on her last payday, and for a moment, that hurt, but then Tess reminded herself of her role. She was Luke's friend and occasional lover, nothing more.

"So what are you gonna do now?" Tess asked. "You got a position in town somewhere?"

Luke shook her head. "I'm gonna be my own man now."

It was no longer strange for Tess to hear Luke refer to herself as a man.

"I'll head west in a few days," Luke said.

"West? Don't tell me you've contracted that gold fever?"

Luke smiled. "Lord, no. I prefer working with horses to digging in the mud. The Donation Land Claim Act grants one hundred and sixty acres of land to every male citizen," she grinned at Tess, "and I hear the Oregon Territory would be a good place for a horse ranch."

"So you're leaving for good?" Tess bit her lip. She was sad to see Luke go because she was a friend and one of very few people who had always treated her like a respectable woman.

"Yes. As soon as the grass grows long enough that the oxen won't starve on the way. Some of the boys dragged me in here for a memorable good-bye. I was wondering if you might be free tonight." Luke looked up at her through dark lashes. A rare shy smile appeared on Luke's lips.

Tess rubbed her forehead and sighed. "No, I'm not."

"Oh. All right." Luke was fast to hide her disappointment, as reluctant as ever to show her feelings.

Tess touched her hand to establish some kind of contact and prevent her younger friend from pulling away. "I'm sorry. If I could somehow—"

"No." Luke squeezed her hand for a second. "You've got nothing to apologize for. You need to make a living. I know that."

Suppressing another sigh, Tess signaled Charlie to pour Luke a whiskey. "I have to go and play the charming hostess now, but I'll make sure to see you before you leave, all right?" Tess made her way to the back of the room, greeting customers left and right. She stopped when she felt some gold dollars being shoved into her hand. "I'm sorry, but I'm already otherwise engaged tonight. Why don't you—?"

The bearded soldier laughed. "I wasn't asking for myself. I want the services of your best girl for my friend over there." He pointed to the bar. "He's leaving town in a few days, and I want him to have a memorable send-off."

Tess looked down at the money in her hand. "Must be some friend," she said with her well-practiced flirtatious smile.

"He saved my life twice. So, you'll arrange it?"

Tess nodded. "Just point him out, and I'll see to it."

The soldier turned and indicated—Luke Hamilton.

Great. Tess mentally rolled her eyes. *How do I get you out of this one, my friend?* She was the only one Luke had ever trusted with her body and her secret, so she couldn't very well send her off with one of her girls. But she also couldn't ignore the bearded soldier's request. Every unmarried man in town would jump at the chance to spend a few hours with a working girl for free, especially if it would be months until he saw another available woman. Refusing the generous offer would make Luke's friends suspicious and could blow her cover. *And I want to give her a memorable send-off too.* She nodded at the bearded soldier. "I'll make sure he has a good time."

"Thank you." The soldier walked away.

The question is just how. Deeply in thought, Tess looked up—and right into the forest green eyes of a girl passing by. *That's it.* "Fleur," she called.

Out of the twelve girls working for her, Fleur was the one Tess trusted the most. At twenty, Fleur was only ten years younger than Tess, but she was like a daughter nonetheless. With her flaming red hair and her pretty, innocent face, she was popular with the men and brought in a lot of money for the establishment, but Tess hoped that she'd one day leave to begin a new life. She genuinely liked the young woman.

Fleur casually disengaged herself from the man she had been leading toward the bar and stopped in front of Tess. "Yes?"

"Are you about to head upstairs?"

Fleur looked back at her customer, who had already found another girl. "Doesn't look like it."

Tess hesitated for another moment, gazing deeply into Fleur's eyes. She knew that Fleur was very discreet. Unlike some of the other girls who gossiped whenever they thought Tess wasn't listening, Fleur never talked about what she did upstairs or about the secrets her customers might have let slip in the heat of passion. She was kind enough not to laugh at Luke and experienced enough not to run from the room screaming. And Luke would surely appreciate her soft beauty and feminine curves. In some respects, her friend was not so different from the man she pretended to be. "I have a customer I want you to take care of. The fee is already covered. He's a friend of mine, so please treat him well."

Fleur tilted her head. "Are you sure you don't want to entertain him yourself?"

"I would, but I have to entertain a town official tonight." Tess exchanged a meaningful glance with Fleur. The local authorities were willing to turn their heads in exchange for a few favors. For the most part, Tess as the madam of the brothel could pick her customers and saw only a few special guests, but she had no choice tonight. She had to ensure that town officials continued to turn a blind eye to her establishment.

"And the one you want me to take care of? Is he a regular?" Fleur asked.

Tess shook her head. "No. But he's special, so I don't trust any of the other girls to take care of him."

Fleur turned to look in the same direction Tess did. "The dark-haired, slender one standing alone at the bar? He doesn't look like one of your special customers."

A smile played around Tess's lips. "Oh, he is special, trust me." She turned toward Fleur and looked her in the eyes, her smile now gone. "You still remember the first rule I taught you?"

"Don't steal your silverware?" Fleur said with the mischievous grin she still hadn't lost completely after three years.

Tess suppressed a smile of her own. "Discretion."

A russet eyebrow rose, but Fleur didn't ask what it was about this customer that required her absolute discretion. After a few seconds, she asked, "Is there anything I should be careful about?" A glimmer of fearful caution shone in her green eyes.

"No." Tess shook her head. "You've got nothing to fear from him. He's a real gentleman."

One corner of Fleur's lips lifted into a humorless half-smile. "That would be a first. But all right. I'll take care of him." She turned and made her way toward the bar.

"I hope I did the right thing," Tess whispered as she watched her go.

Nora eyed her potential customer warily as she walked toward him.

He had nothing in common with the men who usually made arrangements for Tess's time. The battered, wide-brimmed hat under his arm and the worn flannel shirt made it unlikely that he had a lot of money to spend on whiskey and women. His blue pants with the yellow stripe running down the leg seam had clearly been part of a uniform—he was a simple ex-soldier, not one of the rich, powerful men who shared Tess's bed from time to time.

Even his posture was different. She saw the tension in his lean frame from across the room. While all around him the other men were laughing, chucking down whiskey, and trying to get their hands on the girls, he stood quietly sipping his drink. His gaze was alert, roving over anyone who ventured too close.

Nora grimaced. She didn't like that type of customer. If they finally lost their rigid self-control, all hell might break loose.

She straightened her shoulders and sent a glance downward to ensure that her bodice still showed enough to arouse interest, but not enough to satisfy it. With a deep breath, she stopped next to him but didn't attempt to touch him in any way. The remoteness emanating from him discouraged any attempts at familiarity. "Hello," she said, giving her voice a seductive timbre.

The man set his glass on the bar and turned around. He was not at all what Nora had expected. Most of her customers had shaggy hair, matted beards, tobacco-stained teeth, and filthy clothes, reeking of stale drink, smoke, and sweat. This man kept his dark hair short, the ends just brushing against the collar of his faded shirt. His clothes were a bit worn, but clean, and his pants still maintained a razor-sharp military crease. There was no hint of beard stubble on the tan face—either he had shaved immaculately just before his brothel visit, or he was even younger than he appeared to be.

Nora took a half-step toward him, pleasantly surprised to smell only leather, soap, and a hint of horse on him. Maybe this customer really was a gentleman. *And he's young and probably inexperienced enough for me to pull off my virgin act.* Maybe that was why Tess had assigned her to this customer.

Whenever a visitor entered the brothel who seemed to be sufficiently naïve, usually a very young man or a soldier with his pay in his pocket, he was offered a night with a virgin at double the cost. Because virgins were not readily available in their line of work, almost every brothel had a girl still looking sweet and innocent enough to pull off the act—and Nora was the official "virgin" of Tess's establishment.

"My name is Fleur," Nora said. Nearly all girls used pseudonyms or nicknames, so there were a lot of Roses, Marys, and Daisys residing in houses of ill repute.

The customer said nothing. Not that Nora had expected or wanted him to tell her his name. Even if he had, she wouldn't remember it in a few days. He was just one of many customers.

"You look a little lonely standing here all by yourself." Nora used her big, green eyes for good measure, playing the friendly, naïve young girl she had once been. "I thought maybe I could keep you company for a while."

The young man looked at her without answering. His gaze made Nora shudder even though it was neither cruel nor leering. Something about him irritated her finely honed instincts, but she ignored it. She couldn't afford not to work tonight. She smiled sweetly at him and tucked her hand into the bend of his arm as if she were a lady and he the beau courting her.

The muscles under her fingers clenched. "I don't have the money for...this."

"Hush, don't worry about that. It's already taken care of." Nora stroked the arm her fingers rested on. "Shall we retreat to my room, where it's a little quieter, and talk for a bit?"

He shook his head. "No, thank you. I just want to finish my drink, and then I'll be on my way."

Nora worked hard not to stare. No man she knew had ever entered a brothel only to enjoy a quiet drink, and she didn't believe that he had either. "Then why not enjoy the whiskey I have upstairs? It's a much better brand than this one."

"No, thank you," the young man said. "I'm tired, and I should—"

"Tired?" Nora smiled and tugged on his arm, trying to get him to move closer to the staircase. "It just so happens that I have a nice, soft bed upstairs." Nothing about that bed was nice. Not for Nora. She hated it and what she had to do in it night after night, but since she had no particular skills, no family, and no husband who cared for her, it was that or starving. And she would rather head upstairs with this strange, but polite young man than with one of the wild, drunken men leering at her from across the room.

"Hey, Lieutenant, you still down here?" A bearded soldier leaned against the bar next to Nora and her potential customer. He eyed Nora as if she were a piece of cattle. "What's the matter? The girl not to your liking?"

Nora pressed her lips together, trying not to show her humiliation. Was that the reason for the young man's refusal to head upstairs with her? Would he prefer one of the other girls?

But he slowly shook his head. "No. I like her just fine. But—"

"Then go and enjoy yourself." The bearded soldier reached around Nora to clap the younger man roughly on the shoulder. "You don't want to insult me by refusing my good-bye gift, do you?"

"No." It sounded almost like a sigh of resignation.

Nora used the opportunity to tug him toward the stairs and led him to her room on the upper floor. She opened the door and watched him take in the gaudy rug, the paintings of nude women on the wall, and the big brass bed in the middle of the room. She closed the door behind them and listened to the muted sounds of the piano and coarse laughter from downstairs for a second before she took a deep breath and turned toward him. "If you want, I could bring up hot water and you could take a bath," Nora said. Maybe it was the best strategy to get the probably inexperienced young man to undress first.

He fixed his gaze on her. "That's not necessary. I'm already clean."

Nora bowed her head in a gesture of deference. She had to take care not to arouse his anger in any way. "Yes, of course, I didn't mean to suggest otherwise. I just wanted—"

"It's all right," he said.

Encouraged by his kindness, Nora stepped closer. Maybe she had to give up the virgin act and take the first step. "Do you want to undress me?"

"No."

All right. This is not going well. Not about to give up, Nora started to undress herself.

He grabbed her hand that was just about to loosen the thin straps holding up her tight silk dress. "Don't."

Nora's confusion grew. What did he expect of her? Whatever she did, it didn't seem to be what he wanted her to do. Her other customers had always found her beautiful, and most couldn't get her naked fast enough. What was it that made her so unattractive to him?

Maybe he's just a bit shy. She leaned forward, encouraging him to get a good look at her cleavage, but his gaze remained stubbornly fixed on her face. She threw back her head, baring the soft, fair skin of her throat and causing her red hair to tumble over her bare shoulders.

The movement attracted his attention. Nora felt his gaze following the path of her freckles from her shoulders to where they disappeared into the low-cut bodice of her dress. There, his gaze snapped back to rest again on her face, but the fleeting glance had been enough to assure Nora of his interest.

"You don't need to be afraid," she said. "I'm not. Not with you. I know you'll be gentle. I'm really glad that my first time—"

"You don't have to do this," he said.

"Do what?"

"You don't have to pretend with me. I know this business, so don't bother."

Nora eyed him with new interest. *So he's not as naïve and innocent as I thought.* She cocked her head and gave him a smile that was flirtatious and at the same time conveyed the innocent curiosity of the virgin she pretended to be. "So, you've been with other women?"

The young man didn't answer; he just looked at her, his gray eyes cool and sharp like steel. "I know you're not a virgin."

Nora struggled to maintain her smile. Even the men who saw through her virgin act usually played along to fulfill a fantasy of theirs. Not this man.

"And I know that you don't desire me," he said. "You don't want to go to bed with me."

No. Not naïve at all. Nora bit her lip. *Want?* She suppressed a bitter laugh. *I have to.* She had to earn money to survive, and this man was making it impossible. A look into his eyes made her give up all pretenses. "I need to make a living, and you look like a decent enough man, so…" She gestured to the bed.

He turned away from her. His clothes rustled.

With grim satisfaction, Nora began to loosen her bodice. She didn't want to waste any more time now that he was finally undressing.

But when he turned back around, he hadn't removed a single garment. He wordlessly handed her ten dollars.

Nora made no move to accept the money. "What's this?"

"You said you needed to earn money, so..." He again extended his hand with the money.

"No." Nora stepped aside. "I don't need your pity. I'll take the money I earn for my services, but not a cent more." She knew that pride was something a prostitute couldn't afford, but she was too angry, afraid, and confused to think clearly. It worried her to have this young man refuse her advances and appear entirely unimpressed by her attempts at seduction. He had obviously shared Tess's bed more than once, so it was not a dislike for prostitutes in general—he just didn't like her. Her very life depended on her ability to enchant men. Was she losing her skills?

"All right." He pocketed his money and strode to the door.

The printed sign that hung in the parlor flashed through Nora's mind: *Satisfaction guaranteed or money refunded.* If he left now, there would be no money for her, maybe none at all tonight, because judging from the sounds filtering in through the thin walls, most of the customers had already headed upstairs with other girls. "Please." She didn't know what else to say.

He looked back at her over his shoulder, and for a second, she saw something in his eyes that looked almost like regret. Then he shoved his hat onto his head, and with another step, he was gone. The door closing behind him echoed loudly in Nora's ears.

Independence, Missouri, April 29th, 1851

Luke urged her spotted Appaloosa mare to a faster gait, eager to reach the relative safety and tranquility of the livery stable where she had boarded her horse. Independence's main street was pure chaos.

All around her, men bartered at the top of their lungs for their provisions while others shouted and cursed their ox or mule teams that they couldn't yet handle. Mules brayed as two wagons bumped into each other. Even louder was the incessant clanging and hammering coming from various blacksmiths' shops, where the prospective emigrants had their covered wagons repaired and their horses and oxen shod.

Having been stationed in the nearby Fort Leavenworth, Luke could hardly believe that this was the same sleepy town she had visited on paydays. Every spring, Independence woke from its sleep. Emigrants began to arrive by steamboats or in covered wagons, and by the end of April, thousands of people were camped in and around Independence, giving it the look of a besieged town. Tents and hastily erected shacks dotted the hills between the town and the muddy banks of the Missouri River, three miles to the north. Saloons, gambling dens, and red-curtained whorehouses seemed to pop up overnight.

By early May, the prairie grass was finally long enough to provide enough feed for the livestock, and emigrants left Independence in haste, trying to complete the two-thousand-mile journey before snow fell on the high mountain passes. After the wagon trains left, Independence would once again become a sleepy town, but this time, Luke wouldn't be there to witness it.

The day after tomorrow, she would join a wagon train heading west and begin a new life. The shabby barracks of various forts had been her home for over a decade, but now she longed for a place of her own, where she had to answer to no one but herself. *You still have more than two thousand miles to go.* This wasn't the time to daydream about the horse farm she hoped to build in Oregon.

First, she'd have to survive living in close quarters with the other members of the wagon train for six months. On the trail, there was even less privacy than in the fort's barracks, so she had to be constantly on her guard. Civilian life was more unpredictable than the daily routine as a cavalryman. She was convinced that no one would suspect her true identity from observing the way she moved or spoke. Luke had lived as a man for so long that it wasn't an act any longer. In her own mind, she was former Lieutenant Luke Hamilton, not a woman. But actions and thoughts were one thing; the reality of her body was another. Bathing or relieving herself would be a real problem. The good camp sites were usually crowded, and she would be in constant danger of being discovered.

When she reached the livery stable, Luke shoved her worries back into the recesses of her mind. In front of the building, flames danced on the blacksmith's forge as he worked the bellows. Luke dismounted and led her horse toward the stable doors.

The stable owner appeared from somewhere inside and wordlessly reached for the reins.

Just then, a small figure shot around the corner and barreled into Luke.

The spooked mare threw back her head and tried to break free of the stable owner's grip on the reins, almost kicking him in the process.

Automatically, Luke caught the small body that had hit her and stared down at the child holding on to her leg for balance. Had it been a horse or even an attacking dog bumping into her, Luke would have known what to do, but children were completely out of the range of her experience. She had lived a solitary life, and children had never been a part of it.

The small girl stared up at her with wide eyes, a ragged doll clutched protectively to her chest.

Before Luke could think of something to say or do, the stable owner started to yell and roughly grabbed the girl's arm.

A knock on the door woke Nora. She groggily rolled over and blinked at the sun peeking in through the window. She hadn't been asleep for very long and was tempted to just close her eyes and go back to sleep, but the knock came again. "Fleur? Fleur?"

She promptly reacted to the name that by now was as familiar to her as the one her parents had given her and threw back the covers. After opening the door a few inches, she peeked into the hallway. When she saw that it was just Sally, she opened the door wider. "What's going on?"

Sally had once been a prostitute herself, but at forty, she was long past the prime years for the trade. No other woman her age lived in the brothel, many of them killed by violence, addictions, disease, or suicide long before they had earned enough money to leave. When Tess had taken over the brothel, she had offered Sally a position as a cook for the girls. Sally also looked after Amy while Nora worked or slept.

"Amy ain't with you?" Sally asked, peeking past Nora into the room.

Nora stared at her. "I thought she's with you." *Lord, what has that daughter of mine gotten into now?*

Sally shook her head. "I was just kneadin' the dough, and when I looked again, the young'un was gone. I thought maybe she came up here for a nap."

"No. I haven't seen her all morning." With trembling hands, Nora reached for the long skirt and high-necked blouse that she wore whenever she left the brothel. Out on the streets, she had to dress more respectably, or she risked being run out of town by the proper ladies of the neighborhood.

Sally watched her dress—both of them had long since lost any shyness concerning their bodies—and then followed her downstairs.

"When did you last see her?" Nora asked while she checked the kitchen and the pantry. No sign of Amy, though.

"Musta been a while ago," Sally said. "She came and asked for an apple. Didn't see her since."

Without losing another second, Nora gathered her skirts and ran. There was no doubt in her mind where Amy had gone. If she had asked for an apple, she probably intended to visit the horses of the nearby livery stable. Amy loved horses, and they'd often been there together, but it wasn't safe for the girl to visit alone. One of the big horses might hurt the child. The rough stable owner was just as dangerous. He hated children and had a reputation for scaring or even beating them if they ventured too close to one of his horses. Just last week, he had thrown a neighborhood boy into the manure pit, and Nora didn't want to even imagine what he might do if he discovered the bastard child of a prostitute alone on his premises.

She weaved between riders and wagons on the busy main street, almost falling when her heel caught on her skirt because she wasn't accustomed to its length. She stumbled but never slowed down. Gasping for breath, she rounded the last corner, just in time to see her daughter colliding with a man who was standing next to the stable owner.

Oh no. Nora squeezed her eyes shut for a second. It was the aloof stranger who had refused her services two nights ago. She clenched her hands into fists, sure that the unapproachable man would react none too kindly to being run over by a child. Her eyes snapped open.

The stable owner grabbed Amy's arm. He lifted his hand to slap her.

"No!" Nora rushed forward, determined to protect her child even if it meant being hit herself.

∝𝒪

Luke caught the stable owner's wrist before he could hit the girl.

When he whirled around to face Luke, the child ran away. Her sobs echoed across the yard.

Cursing, the stable owner turned to follow her.

"Hey, Mister, wait a minute." Luke held him back. "My horse could use a good rubdown." She handed him a quarter dollar and held his gaze. *Come on, you greedy bastard. Take the money and forget about the girl.*

The stable owner glanced from the girl to the coin in Luke's hand. Finally, he took the quarter dollar and led Luke's mare away.

Luke turned and looked for the girl.

The child stood with her face buried in the skirt of a woman. Her shoulders heaved as she sobbed.

After hesitating for a second, Luke bent to pick up the apple the girl had dropped. Slowly, she approached what she guessed to be mother and daughter. "Ma'am," she tipped the brim of her hat, "I think your daughter lost something." She extended her hand with the apple.

Her hands still resting protectively on the girl's shoulders, the woman looked up.

Luke blinked, for a few seconds unsure if her imagination was playing tricks on her. She had often thought about the prostitute she had left standing in the middle of her room. Somehow, the young woman with the wary, forest green eyes had made a lasting impression. "You…you have a child?" There was no doubt that the small girl with the mop of reddish curls was Fleur's daughter.

Fleur pulled the girl closer, away from Luke. "Yes." She stared at Luke with a hint of defiance.

Luke studied her closely. The young woman wore no rouge today—and she didn't need any to make her attractive, even though there were dark circles under her eyes. Since she worked nights and cared for a child during the day, she probably wasn't getting enough sleep.

Luke glanced over her shoulder. The stable owner lurked in the doorway, piercing Fleur and her child with hostile glances. "How about I accompany you back home?" *If you can call where she lives a home.*

Fleur looked down at the politely offered arm, then at the packed street and the boardwalk, where a few elegant ladies had gathered to stare at them. "It would be better if you aren't seen with me. People will talk."

Luke laughed, but it wasn't a happy sound. "I don't care what they say. I accompanied you to your room two days ago, so it would be pretty hypocritical if I refused to accompany you now, wouldn't it?"

Both of them were silent for a few seconds, then Fleur slowly shook her head. "You're a strange man."

Normally adept at hiding her emotions, Luke had to work to keep a neutral expression. *I'm an even stranger 'man' than you think.* But, of course, Fleur had no idea. Or did she? Fear stabbed Luke's heart. Fleur was familiar with a variety of men. Would she recognize Luke's strangeness for what it was?

But then Fleur slid her hand into the curve of Luke's arm, and the confident Luke Hamilton was back.

Very much aware of the warm fingers on her arm, Luke set them off toward the brothel.

Independence, Missouri, April 29th, 1851

"You will do as I say, bitch!" The customer grabbed Nora and jerked her against his hard body.

Nora struggled to break free but succeeded only in ripping her bodice. She opened her mouth to call for help.

He used the opportunity to force his tongue past her lips.

Nora gagged. In desperation, she bit down on his tongue.

He grabbed a fistful of her hair and yanked her head back while his other fist hit her in the face almost casually.

Pain exploded in Nora's cheekbone. She cried out and wrapped her arms around herself to protect her middle.

He spat in her general direction, spraying her with spittle and blood. "Little whore! You've got quite the temper." He laughed and ripped her dress off one shoulder.

Her struggles only seemed to excite him more, so Nora let her body go limp and decided to let him do whatever he wanted while she busied her mind with other things—mainly worrying about how much it might cost to replace her ruined dress and how much rouge it would take to cover the bruises on her face.

INDEPENDENCE, MISSOURI,
APRIL 30TH, 1851

"Fleur?" Sally's voice came through the closed door.

Nora forced her aching body up from the edge of the bed and opened the door a few inches. "Hush, Sally," she whispered. "I've just gotten Amy to settle down for a nap."

Sally lowered her voice, but the teasing grin never left her lips. "My, my, girl, seems I didn't give you enough credit for your services. You musta been spectacular. That customer of yours is back and quite adamant that he see you right now."

Knots formed in Nora's stomach. She had to swallow against the lump in her throat before she could ask, "The one from last night?"

"Oh, no, girl, don't worry. It's not him," Sally said.

Nora shook her head. If it wasn't him, why had Sally interrupted her private time with her daughter? She had promised Amy that she'd be there when she woke up, and she intended to keep that promise. "Whoever it is, send him away, Sally. You know that I never see customers in the middle of the day."

The creaking of the stairs made Nora look up.

The young man who had rescued Amy from the stable owner's wrath just yesterday stood on the top step, hesitating with one hand on the banister.

Her furrowed brow stretched the skin over Nora's bruised cheek. He had been polite when he had escorted her and Amy home, but their first encounter hadn't ended well. What did this strange man want from her now? Had he changed his mind about not wanting to share her bed?

"Don't worry," he said as if reading her thoughts. "I'm not here for... I'm not here as a customer. I only want to talk to you for a moment."

The last three years had taught her to be cautious. Last night's beating had once again shown her how dangerous her job was and that no customer could be trusted. The lack of facial hair might have made him appear young and harmless, but Nora had an inkling that appearances were deceiving in his case. His slender frame was all sinews and muscles, and his eyes held a wary look.

"It will only take a minute," the man said when she hesitated.

"All right," Nora said. "One minute. What do you want?"

"Uh." He glanced at Sally. "Can we maybe talk inside?" He nodded at the half-open door but didn't move toward her, calmly waiting for her decision. "I promise that you'll be perfectly safe, and if you say no to my offer, I'll pay for your time."

Finally, Nora nodded. She couldn't afford to turn down easily earned money, so she would hear him out. If he had wanted her body, he could have taken it three days ago. With one last glance to Sally to make sure that she would keep an eye and ear on her room, she opened the door to let him in. "But please speak quietly," she said over her shoulder. "My daughter is asleep."

"Oh. Of course," he whispered. With his hat in his hands, he followed her.

She watched him closely as he took in the clean, lovingly decorated room with the personal nick-knacks and toys lying around.

"This is not the same room as…" He paused and cleared his throat.

It wasn't. The other room was cold and businesslike, catering only to the desires of her customers. Here, she had tried to create a safe haven, a home for her daughter. "You may think it's a waste of money, but I pay Tess extra for this room. I won't have my daughter grow up in the room where I…" Nora shook her head, interrupting herself. She positioned herself between her visitor and the sleeping child in the bed and raised her chin. "Anyway, what do you want?"

He took a step toward her, keeping his movements slow and nonthreatening. His intense gaze rested on her face.

Nora studied him in the soft light of the afternoon sun. For the first time, she detected the faint lines at the corner of his eyes and the slight bump on the bridge of his nose, attesting to an old break. He was probably older than she had first thought.

"I'm here because I wanted to ask you…" He looked away, hesitating, then back into her face. "I wish to marry you."

Silence.

Nora blinked once, twice. Then she snorted. "Which of your stupid friends put you up to this?"

"What? No, this—"

"If you think it's funny to make fun of me like—"

"I'm not trying to make fun of you," he said. "I'm trying to marry you."

Nora stared at him. First he refused to lie with her, and now he wanted to marry her? She laughed incredulously. "You want to marry me?"

"I do," he answered as if they were already standing in front of the altar.

"This is ridiculous. I don't even know your name." She never asked customers for their name and never offered hers.

He smiled calmly. "I don't know yours either—unless it's really Fleur, which I doubt."

This man knew more about life in a brothel than she had expected. Nora continued to stare at him but didn't offer her real name. She hadn't trusted any man enough to do that for the last three years, and she saw no reason to start now.

It seemed he didn't trust easily either, because it took a minute before he offered his hand. "Luke Hamilton."

Nora hesitated for another moment, then reached out her own hand. His palm was rough against her softer one and a bit clammy, indicating that he was not as calm as he appeared. "Now, if you would please explain what gave you the ridiculous idea to propose to me, Mister Hamilton?"

"I'm about to join a wagon train heading west," Luke Hamilton said. "Most other settlers are married or traveling with family, and so I thought it best to take a wife with me."

At least he didn't try to impress her with a charming answer, and that secretly pleased Nora. She harbored no romantic illusions about marriage or love. She had long ago given up on waiting for the handsome hero to ride into her life and sweep her off her feet. "I understand why you'd want to take a wife, but why me? I'm not the type of woman a man would make his wife. You're handsome, I guess, and if you can afford to join a wagon train, you probably have enough money to provide for a family. You would have no trouble finding a wife who's not…soiled." She knew very well that as much as men might enjoy her company in the bedroom, most preferred an untouched bride.

"I have no use for one of those high-society girls who'll do nothing but whine and complain every step of the two thousand miles to Oregon." He looked her right in the eye. "I figure you've had enough hardship in your life not to give up at the first sign of trouble."

Nora still wasn't satisfied with the answer. "Why me?" she asked again. She gestured toward the door, indicating the hallway that lay beyond. "You could knock on any door up here on the second floor, and I suspect you'd get an immediate 'yes' from each and every one of the girls. So why did you knock on my door? Why burden yourself with a prostitute you don't desire and a child that's not your own?" Her eyes widened. "You're not expecting me to leave Amy behind, are you?"

"Of course not. I could provide for your daughter and give her my name."

Now Nora understood even less why he'd chosen her. When they first met, he'd clearly signaled her that he didn't want to lie with her. *What else do I have to offer a man like him? I don't even have a large dowry. What is it that he wants from me?* Experience had taught her that most things in life came with a price. Surely men like him didn't go around marrying fallen women for selfless reasons. "Why me?" she repeated. "Don't tell me that you've suddenly become infatuated with me."

"No," he said. "This has nothing to do with love. We'll be like business partners. I want to start a new life in Oregon, and I think you and your daughter could use the chance to do the same."

His words seemed honest, and for the first time, Nora allowed herself to think about it. Every spring, when the emigrants left Independence, she had secretly wished she could travel with them. Rumor had it that people were less strict in the West. In the newly developing country of homesteads, cattle ranches, and mines, people didn't ask prying questions about other people's pasts. Most wagon trains refused to let single women join them, though, and even if they took her in, she didn't have the means to afford the journey or to survive in the West. So she stayed because she had nowhere else to go even though she had long since grown tired of suffering daily humiliation at the hands of strangers. *But is it better to be subject to the whims and desires of one man than to those of many? You could jump out of the frying pan and into the fire here, girl.*

"I won't tell you that it'll be an easy trip, and I won't pretend to know anything about being a good…husband and father, but I can guarantee you that no one's gonna hurt you again." He took a step closer, for the first time coming into touching distance, and gently brushed her bruised cheek with a single finger.

Nora flinched. Not because his touch was hurting her—it wasn't—but because he had seen through her carefully arranged rouge and the façade of normalcy too easily. She was so tired of constantly hiding her bruises, the occasional split lip, and the reality of her job from her daughter. The older Amy got, the harder it became to hide what she was really doing for a living. If she married this man, she could be a respectable woman and her daughter would have the future she deserved.

This might be your chance. What if you really won't be able to work anymore in a few months? What will you do then? Tess was her friend, yes, but as the madam of the brothel she couldn't afford the luxury to keep on a woman who wasn't able to work. Even if Tess didn't throw her out to fend for herself, Nora wouldn't be able to pay for a separate room to make a home for Amy anymore.

"So? What do you say?" He waited for her answer as if it didn't matter to him one way or the other.

Nora knew that she didn't really have a choice. "Are you sure that you're not going to regret this?"

"No. Not sure at all."

The honesty of his answer surprised Nora, and once again she thought what a strange man he was.

"I admit it's one of the craziest things I've ever done," he said.

One of the craziest? He's done things crazier than this? I'd really like to know what that was. She felt his gaze on her, knowing that he was still waiting for her answer. "Yes," she simply said.

A dark eyebrow rose. "Yes, this is crazy? Or yes, you'll marry me?"

"Both."

"All right." He nodded as if he had just closed a business deal. "Can you be ready in an hour?"

Now it was Nora's turn to lift an eyebrow. "One hour?" How could her life change so dramatically in one short hour?

He shrugged. "There's not much time. My wagon train pulls out tomorrow morning at seven. I'm leaving then—with or without you."

Nora gave a nod. *With me,* she silently decided. She would grab this chance to change her life and hold on to it with both hands.

"All right. Then you better start packing," he said.

"Not much to pack."

He looked about the room as if counting her few belongings, then strode to the door. "I'll be back in an hour with the judge and the ring."

Nora nodded numbly. The thought that she was going to be a married woman in an hour was still unreal.

At the door, he paused and turned back around to look at her. "So, will you tell me your name, or should I just call you 'darling'?"

Nora had to smile. At least her future husband had a sense of humor. She hesitated for another second, then decided that she had to trust him, if only a little bit. "Nora will be fine," she answered. "Nora Macauley."

"Nora Hamilton," he said over his shoulder and closed the door behind him.

"Luke? Luke, is that you?"

Tess's voice stopped Luke before she reached the stairs. She turned around with a sigh, not looking forward to explaining to her old friend what she was doing in the room of one of her girls in bright daylight. "Hello, Tess," she said, trying for nonchalance.

Tess folded her arms across her ample chest. "You know that I don't allow male visitors upstairs in the middle of the day." A hint of a smile played around her lips at the mention of male visitors, but Tess didn't relax her threatening posture. Outside of the bedroom, she had never treated Luke any different from male customers she had befriended—and Luke didn't want it any other way.

"I…" Luke cleared her throat. "I know. I just wanted to speak to her for a minute, nothing else."

Tess looked at her for another moment, then finally relaxed and grinned. "So you liked speaking to her, huh?" She winked at Luke. "I'd hoped that I didn't make a mistake in introducing you to Fleur."

So Fleur…Nora didn't tell her that I refused to share her bed. It was good to know her future wife knew the meaning of the word "discretion." *Just in case.* "It's not like that."

"Of course not." Tess was still grinning. "You visited her room in the middle of the day because you didn't find her appealing at all, uh-huh."

With a sigh, Luke gave up her attempts to explain. A quick glance at her battered pocket watch told her that she had to hurry if she wanted to catch the judge before he left his office for the day. Another thought made her pause. Would the judge require a witness to the marriage ceremony? She had been expected to take part in one or two military weddings, and as far as she could remember, there had always been a best man and a matron of honor. Taking a deep breath, she turned back around to face Tess. "I asked her to marry me. Would you do us the honor and stand up for us when the judge arrives?" she asked as fast as she could.

Tess stared at her. "You are going to marry?"

"Yes." Luke could hardly believe it herself.

"A woman?"

Luke nodded. Marrying a man had never been an option for her.

Tess's eyes widened, and her gaze strayed to the room Luke had just left. "You want to marry Fleur?"

Luke straightened her shoulders. "Nora, not Fleur," she said. Among many other reasons for her proposal, she had wanted to give Nora the chance to leave behind her old pseudonym and the life that came with it.

"She told you her real name?" Tess asked.

Luke nodded. "She agreed to becoming my wife, so of course I had to know her name."

For a moment, Tess didn't say anything. Then she sighed. "Luke, I'm not sure this is a good idea. I know in the heat of passion, everything seems—"

"There was no heat of passion," Luke said. "I never shared a bed with her. She doesn't even… She doesn't know about…me."

"Are you insane?" Tess posed the question Luke had already asked herself a hundred times today. "You asked her to marry you even though she has no idea that you're not—"

"Tess!" Luke looked left and right, making sure that no one could overhear their conversation.

Tess lowered her voice. "She doesn't know that you're not exactly what one would expect in a husband?" She laughed roughly. "I'm sure Nora thinks that after working in a brothel for three years, there's nothing left that could surprise her on her wedding night, but, Lord, the body under that male attire…" Tess shook her head. "You can't hide that from her."

"Yes, I can," Luke said. "There's no reason why she should know. I won't share her bed on the wedding night—or on any other night. We both agreed that this marriage is gonna be a business arrangement, nothing else."

"A business arrangement?" Tess's brows rose. "And in what way do you profit from this arrangement?"

Luke shrugged. "Well, for one thing, it certainly won't hurt my reputation to be married to a beautiful woman. If people think I'm married and even fathered a child, no one will suspect my true nature."

They stared at each other for a few moments, then Tess sighed. "I still think you should tell Nora and let her decide if she still wants to marry you."

That was not an option in Luke's mind. No woman who knew who she really was would ever want to share her life with her, not even a desperate prostitute. "So, will you be the matron of honor at the wedding?" she asked instead of answering.

"I should really tell you no. You're intending to steal my best girl." Tess shook her index finger at Luke.

Best girl? Luke swallowed and tried not to think about her future wife's talents. "You'll be there?"

Tess sighed. "I'll be there."

INDEPENDENCE, MISSOURI, APRIL 30TH, 1851

"It's not exactly the kind of wedding we all dreamed of when we were growing up, but it'll do," Tess said as she pinned orange blossoms to Nora's hair.

No, it sure isn't. Nora glanced down at herself. Instead of a white wedding dress, she wore her best respectable blue dress. A few years ago, when she had still dreamed of marrying Raphael Jamison, she had pictured a large ceremony in a flower-decorated church and Boston's wealthiest families dancing at her wedding. Now an impatient judge and a handful of parlor house girls waited for her. "It doesn't matter. I don't have the money or the time for anything else."

Tess adjusted one of the orange blossoms. She looked into Nora's eyes. "Fleur...Nora, are you really sure you—?"

"Auntie Tess." Amy tugged on Tess's skirt. "Can I have pwetty flowers too?"

"I don't know, sweetie. Only the bride gets to wear orange blossoms at weddings." Tess looked from Amy to Nora. "What do you think?"

"This isn't exactly a traditional wedding, so I think we can make an exception." Nora smiled at her daughter. Growing up in a brothel, Amy had few joys in her life, so Nora tried to show her how special she was whenever she could. She plucked two of the blossoms from her hair and weaved them through Amy's locks.

Amy held her head up high as if she were a queen receiving the crown. Then she skipped away to show off her flower-crowned head to Sally and the other women.

"All right." Nora straightened her shoulders. "Let's—"

"Wait a minute." Tess held on to her elbow. "Did you really think this through?"

Nora shrugged. "What's there to think about?"

"You're marrying a total stranger. You don't know anything about Luke."

She was right, of course, and Nora secretly admitted to herself that she was worried, but what other options did she have? If she wanted to start a new life, she needed to take a chance. "I know my life here, and I don't want to live like this any longer." Nora paused when she realized how that sounded. She touched Tess's hand. "I mean, compared to the girls in other parlor houses, we have a good life. I'll always be grateful to you for taking me in and helping me care for Amy. But this is no place for a child, and Amy's getting older. If we stay, she'll find out what I'm doing for a living."

Tess squeezed Nora's hand. "I'm not blaming you for wanting to leave. But are you sure this, marrying Luke, is the best alternative?"

Nora tilted her head and studied Tess, trying to read her expression. "Is there something you're not telling me? You said Mr. Hamilton is a friend of yours, so why don't you want me to marry him?" She furrowed her brow. "Is he a drunkard?"

"No. I never saw him have more than one drink."

"Then he's a gambler?"

Tess shook her head.

"Is he... I mean, has he ever hit you?"

Tess's eyes widened. "What? No, no, Luke would never hit a woman. He's got a good heart, but..."

"But what?"

Averting her gaze, Tess hesitated.

"There's something wrong with him, isn't there?" Nora tapped her knuckles against her thigh. "I should've known. What man in his right mind refuses to share a prostitute's bed if he doesn't even have to pay for it?"

Tess's face remained calm. If she was surprised that Luke Hamilton hadn't shared Nora's bed, she hid it well. "There's nothing wrong with him. Not the way you think. He's just... He's not like other men."

Nora gripped both of Tess's elbows and stared into her eyes. "You'd tell me if I put Amy and myself in danger by marrying him, wouldn't you?"

"Of course I would. Nora, you're much more to me than just an employee. You're a friend. I would never let you marry Luke if I thought it would put you in danger."

"Good." Nora let go of her. "Then let's go before he changes his mind."

Now it was Tess's turn to grip Nora's arm. "If you're determined to go through with this, at least promise me one thing."

Nora smiled. "Naming our first-born after you?"

Tess blinked, then burst out laughing. "Tempting, but no, that's not what I mean. I taught you how important discretion is. Promise me you'll stand by Luke and never give away any of the things he might tell you."

What kinds of secrets does he have? Men who kept secrets were nothing new for Nora. A lot of her customers crept into her room in the middle of the night, when their families were sleeping. They hid their marital status, their money, and their preferences in bed. Surely whatever Luke Hamilton had to hide couldn't be that much different. But a nagging worry remained. *What isn't she telling me?*

"Miss Swenson," the judge called from across the room. "If you'd bring the bride over here. I want to get started."

Tess didn't look away from Nora. "Promise you'll stand by Luke, no matter what?"

A frisson of unease trickled down Nora's spine. "And here I thought I was supposed to say my marriage vows in front of the judge, not in front of you."

"Promise."

Nora sighed. "All right, all right."

"Thank you."

They hurried across the room and joined Luke and the judge.

The judge opened his worn Bible. "We are gathered here today in the face of this company," he looked up and grimaced at the prostitutes who were the only guests, "to join together this man and this woman in matrimony, which is an honorable and solemn estate and should therefore not be entered into unadvisedly or lightly. If there is anyone here who has just reason why these two must not be lawfully joined together, let that person speak now or forever hold their peace."

Tess cleared her throat, and for a moment, Nora thought she might object, but then Tess only sighed.

"Do you, Lucas Hamilton, take this woman to be your lawfully wedded wife? Will you love, honor, and cherish her, forsaking all others, for as long as you both shall live?" The judge turned to a serious-looking Luke.

Luke shuffled his newly polished boots and looked at Nora for an endless second. "I do." His voice was a bit scratchy.

"And do you, Nora Macauley, take this man to be your lawfully wedded husband? Will you love, honor, and cherish him, forsaking all others, for as long as you both shall live?"

Now it was Nora's turn to answer. She pressed a hand to her belly, calming the butterflies there. "I do." *No way back now.* She let out a shuddering breath.

"The ring," the judge said.

Nora looked down at the hand that took hold of hers. Luke's calluses rasped against Nora's soft skin. *Hardworking. Strong. Steadfast.* As Luke slipped the simple gold band on her finger, Nora hoped that his hands told her the truth about the man. The ring was a bit too tight, and Nora reached down to help Luke work it over her knuckle.

"By the powers given me by the state of Missouri, I hereby pronounce you husband and wife." The judge snapped his Bible closed. The sound echoed through the room, giving his words an air of finality. "You may kiss the bride."

Nora lifted her face to Luke's. For a second, she met his startled gaze before he lowered his head and brushed his lips over her cheek.

He's strange. Where any other man would have tried to establish his dominance and claim his wife with a passionate kiss, he settled for a quick peck on the cheek.

When he stepped back, Nora tried to look into his eyes, but he busied himself with signing the marriage certificate.

Tess walked up to Nora and enclosed her in a sisterly embrace. "I suppose congratulations are in order, Mrs. Hamilton."

For a few moments, Nora didn't react to the unfamiliar name. Then she shook her head at herself. *You're somebody's wife now. Mrs. Lucas Hamilton. A respectable woman.*

"So, you're leaving in the morning, huh?" Tess nodded at Nora's packed-up bags.

Nora shrugged. She pointed at Luke, who was paying the judge. "You know how it is: Whither thou goest I will go, whither thou lodgest I will lodge."

"I'll miss you, but I'm glad to see you go and start a new life."

"Me too." Over the years, she had bickered and argued with the other girls and had competed with them over the most generous customers, but they had become the only family she had, and she would miss them, especially Tess.

When Tess's gaze strayed to the side, Nora realized that Luke stood next to her.

Tess leaned forward and embraced him. "Congratulations." She brushed her lips against his in an affectionate gesture that should have probably made Nora jealous but mainly left her wondering how close her new husband and Tess really were.

Luke turned to Nora with a businesslike demeanor. "Can you be ready tomorrow morning at six?"

Nora nodded. "I'll be ready."

"All right." He carefully tucked the marriage license behind his belt. "I'll see you then."

"You won't stay here tonight?" She had assumed that he would want to spend their wedding night in the comfort of her room.

Luke shook his head. "I have to stay with the oxen and check the provisions."

"Should I come with you?"

"No." Another shake of his head. "You stay here and enjoy your last night sleeping in a real bed. I'll come for you tomorrow morning." He strode away without another word to his new wife.

"Oh, young love," Tess said wryly.

Luke felt as if every man and woman in the parlor was watching her as she climbed the stairs to Tess's room. Did they think it strange that she was here, visiting the brothel's madam, on her wedding night? *Nonsense. The men don't know you, and if anything, the girls think you're here to spend the night with your new wife.*

But she walked past Nora's room and stopped in front of the door to Tess's private rooms. She paused with her fist already lifted. *What if Tess is entertaining tonight?*

Someone walked by behind Luke.

Not wanting to linger in the hallway, Luke knocked on the door.

Seconds later, the door was opened a few inches. Tess peeked out. She smiled and opened the door wider. "I hoped you'd come by."

"I would never leave without saying good-bye."

Tess pulled her inside. She turned down the wick on the kerosene lamp, dimming the light, before she directed Luke toward the large bed. "Sit."

Luke sat on the edge of the bed. "Remember the first time I was here?" It seemed like a million years ago. Luke hardly felt like the same person anymore.

"Yes." Tess chuckled. "I practically had to force you to sit down." She stepped closer and stood between Luke's legs. Slowly, she reached out and touched Luke's cheek with one fingertip. Tess's blue eyes were brimming with emotions. "Will I ever see you again?"

"I hope so," Luke said. As much as she wanted to, she couldn't promise. Tess's life was in Independence, and two thousand miles was a long way just to visit an old friend.

Still standing, Tess cupped Luke's face and bent down. Their lips met gently.

Luke sank into the kiss, enjoying the warmth and the softness of it.

Then Tess pushed her back to lie on the bed and moved to straddle her.

"Stop." Luke planted both feet on the floor and held on to Tess's shoulders.

Tess blinked and straightened her skirts. "Are you all right?"

"I'm fine. I just don't think we should…you know."

"Why?" A line formed between Tess's blond brows. "I thought we'd say a proper good-bye, just like I promised you when you told me you're leaving."

Luke sighed. "That was before I got married."

Tess looked down at her as if she didn't know whether to laugh or to cry. "But you're not in love with Nora, and you'll never even consummate the marriage."

"That doesn't matter." Just hours ago, Luke had promised in front of a judge to forsake all other women, so that was what she was going to do.

After continuing to stare for a few seconds more, Tess smiled. She leaned down to kiss Luke's cheek. "You're one of a kind, Luke Hamilton. It's such a pity that you hide who you really are. You so deserve to be loved."

Luke pulled her down to sit next to her on the bed and returned the kiss to Tess's cheek. "So do you."

Tess wrapped her arms around Luke and buried her face against Luke's neck. "Stay the night?" she whispered against Luke's skin.

For a moment, Luke was tempted to forget about her loneliness and the dangers of the trail ahead of her by spending a few hours in Tess's arms, but then she shook her head. "I told you I can't."

"Not like that. Just hold me. That's all I'm asking."

Instead of an answer, Luke let herself sink back and pulled Tess with her.

Independence, Missouri, May 1st, 1851

The sun hadn't even risen when Nora dragged the trunk Tess had given her and her travel bag out of her room. She turned and stared at the door she had just closed behind her. This was it. She had just closed this chapter of her life. But before she could start a new chapter, she needed to find someone who could help her with her baggage.

The doors to her left and right were closed. Daisy and Laura were still asleep or with customers, as were all the other girls.

Amy yawned next to her.

Nora knelt and regarded her daughter. "Can you be a good girl and wait here with Rosie?" She nodded down at the doll that never left Amy's side. "I need to find someone to help us carry the trunk downstairs."

Clutching Rosie to her chest, Amy nodded.

Nora hurried down the stairs.

Sally was bent over the cast-iron stove, trying to get the fire going.

"Morning, Sally," Nora said. "Would you mind helping me bring my baggage down?"

Sally turned and wiped her hands on her apron. "Oh, I thought you already left. I saw your new husband tiptoeing downstairs an hour ago."

Tiptoeing downstairs? What was he doing upstairs? Nora frowned.

Grinning, Sally nudged her. "You don't need to play innocent, girl. This ain't a convent, and it was your wedding night after all."

If Luke had shared anyone's bed on their wedding night, it hadn't been hers. Had he shared the bed of another girl? Or maybe Tess's?

Nora thought about it for another moment, then shook her head. *It doesn't matter.* If Luke had paid someone else to share his bed, then at least she didn't have to. That way, she'd been able to spend her last night in Independence relaxing with Amy.

"I guess he—"

A knock on the front door interrupted Nora.

Sally went to open the door and returned with Luke.

He took off his hat. "Good morning. Are you ready to go?"

"Yes. I just need some help carrying my trunk."

Luke nodded. He took the stairs two at a time while Nora followed more carefully. At the top of the stairs, he stopped, stared at Amy, and then approached more slowly. He hefted the trunk on his shoulder and immediately started down the stairs. "We have to hurry," he called over his shoulder.

Five minutes later, Nora waded through the mud on Main Street, half carrying, half dragging her overloaded travel bag while she desperately tried to rescue the hem of her dress from the red mud. She had traded her elegant silks and fine slippers for a plain calico dress and sturdy boots, but she didn't want them ruined before the journey started.

All around them, chaos broke out while emigrants prepared for the departure. The Courthouse Square with the red brick courthouse building in its center was jammed with wagons. Liberty and Lexington Streets were crowded by braying mules and slow-moving oxen. Men cursed and shouted as they fiddled with their oxen's yokes while women tried to find a place for some family heirlooms in the already overloaded wagons. Children darted in and out of the wagons, treating the dangerous journey like one big game.

Nora reached out to clutch Amy's hand in hers, wanting to pull her away from the throng of people and nervous animals. The next step almost made her stumble over the hem of her dress as she let it go and it sagged to the ground. *I need a third hand.* "Mister… Luke," she called out to her new husband, who hadn't noticed that they had fallen behind.

He stopped and looked at her.

"Could you…?" He was already carrying her trunk on one shoulder, so she couldn't very well ask him to take the heavy bag too. Nora nodded down at her daughter. "Could you please take her by the hand? I don't want her to get lost in this chaos."

He looked at her as if she had asked him to offer his hand to a rattlesnake. His gaze darted to Amy. He swallowed, and then, after a few seconds, he slowly extended his hand to the child.

"Amy." Nora gently nudged her daughter, but Amy didn't budge. She clutched Nora's skirts with one hand and her doll with the other and refused to even look at Luke.

Luke shifted and looked back over his shoulder to the town square, where a wagon train was beginning to form. "We need to hurry."

When Nora leaned down to encourage her daughter, Amy whispered, "Mama?"

"What is it, sweetie?" Amy was clearly scared, but Nora wasn't sure of what.

"Who is dat man?" Amy peeked around Nora's skirt, pointing to Luke with the doll in her hand.

Nora swallowed. For a moment, she didn't know what to say. Since she had agreed to marry Luke Hamilton, she had allowed herself to think about only the positive consequences it would have on Amy's future. Never again would Amy be ridiculed by other children for not having a father, never again would the general store's owner refuse to sell her candy because her mother was a prostitute, and never again would people on the street call her a bastard. Nora had thought only about what Amy having a father would mean to other people, not how Amy would deal with it.

Amy had never met the man who had fathered her, nor had she had any other male role model in her life. Life in the brothel and in a neighborhood where everyone knew that her mother was a prostitute had taught Amy to be wary of men. So how could Nora explain what role Luke would play in her life from now on? *I don't even know what role he wants to play. He agreed to take Amy with us, but that doesn't mean that he's willing to play daddy to a prostitute's child.*

"That is…" She looked at Luke, hoping he would finish the sentence for her. She didn't dare to give him a title or role he might not want.

Luke stood frozen, not kneeling down to be at a level with Amy as Nora had hoped he would. He was clearly not used to dealing with children. "Luke," he finally said.

"He's our friend," Nora added. "He's going to take us for a ride in his wagon. Do you want to see it?"

Reluctantly, Amy nodded but still didn't step toward Luke.

Nora tucked the hem of her skirt behind the ties of her apron, clutched Amy's fingers in one hand and the bag in the other, and hurried after Luke.

Finally, they reached the wagon train.

"This one is mine…ours," Luke said, pointing to one of the wagons. "It'll be your home for the next six months."

Well, one thing's for sure: He won't have to carry me over the threshold of this home. Nora looked the covered wagon over. A ten by four feet wagon box, covered by a still white canvas bonnet, held all their belongings. She leaned over the wagon's tongue and lifted the flap to peer inside.

The wagon was packed with neatly stored boxes and bundles. Even the canvas cover was lined with storage pockets. Pots and pans hung from the wooden bows. Hens clucked in the coop that was tied to the end of the wagon. On the outside, tools and water barrels were fastened to the wagon.

I wonder where we will sleep.

Luke stepped onto the wagon tongue and reached into the wagon. He moved a sack of flour and a keg of pickles to find a place for Nora's belongings. "Have you ever driven an ox team?" he asked when he turned back around.

Nora looked at the six oxen hitched to the front of the wagon. The huge beasts returned her stare without much interest. She swallowed. "Me?" She had assumed that Luke would handle the oxen.

He seemed to guess her thoughts. "I need you to drive the oxen some of the time while I earn some extra dollars helping the captain out with his cattle."

"But what about my daughter?" Amy was only three, so she couldn't leave her unsupervised.

"She'll be fine in the wagon or walking along," Luke said. "The oxen move real slow. You just have to keep an eye on the child so she doesn't get crushed by the oxen's hooves."

Nora tried not to let her emotions show as she stared down at the oxen's heavy feet. Growing up as the only daughter of a wealthy family back east, she had never needed to do physical labor in her life, and she had certainly never driven an ox team, but she was not afraid to try. Anything would be better than working in a brothel. She straightened and nodded. "Where are the reins?"

Luke shook his head. "Oxen aren't driven by reins. They don't wear bits in their mouths." He pointed to the wooden yokes around the oxen's necks. "You walk alongside, shout commands, and crack your whip to keep them moving."

Nora's fingers closed numbly around the whip Luke handed her.

At the front of the wagon train, a bearded man on a large black horse lifted his arm in the air, and his yell "to Oregon" was repeated down the line of wagons. The wagon in front of them began to move forward, falling into line with the rest of the wagon train.

"Your turn." Luke gave her a nod. "Let's get these boys movin'."

After watching the teamsters in front of her for another moment, Nora lifted her arm and tried to imitate the elegant flick of the whip.

Luke's hat sailed through the air and landed in the mud.

"Whoa!" Luke ducked. "Your aim's a tiny bit off, dear wife."

Nora squinted and again sent her whip through the air.

The oxen didn't budge.

"Hey, Hamilton," the man perched on the seat of the mule-drawn wagon behind them shouted. "Need help with the oxen or the woman?" He laughed.

Luke sent him a cold glance but didn't bother with an answer. He bent and picked up his hat. Nora had expected him to take the whip from her and show her how it was done, but he didn't. "Try again," he said.

"Move!" Nora yelled and prodded the lead ox with the whip's handle.

With an indignant "moo," the oxen took a step forward, and Nora flicked the whip in their direction to keep them moving.

"Think you can handle it?" Luke asked, looking down into her face.

Nora wiped a bit of sweat from her forehead. "Of course." She was determined to prove that she would be a hardworking wife and useful partner for this man.

"All right, then I'll leave you to your new friends." He walked to the back of the wagon, untied his horse, smoothly swung into the saddle, and rode away.

The wagon train rumbled along the muddy main street.

When they reached the edge of town, Nora looked back over her shoulder. Her gaze found the two-story building that had been her home for three years. Weeping members of someone's family stood waving along the streets, but no one was there to say good-bye to Nora and her family. Nora's friends and colleagues were still sleeping after a long work night, and Luke... *Does he have any family or friends?* Nora didn't know. *I don't know a thing about my husband.*

Her thoughts were interrupted when the oxen, left unattended for a few moments, began to slow down.

Nora quickly cracked her whip through the air. She wasn't sure whether she would be able to get them moving again if they stopped.

"Mama!" Amy shook her doll at her. "Don't hurt the cows!"

Nora suppressed a groan. "They're not cows, sweetie. They're boy cows, and you call them 'oxen.' And I'm not hurting them. I promise. I'm just telling them where they have to go."

"Where do we go, Mama?"

"We're going to a place called Oregon." Nora realized that she didn't know their exact destination, and even if she had known the name of the town Luke planned to settle in, she would have been none the wiser. She had never been west of Independence and knew nothing of these faraway places.

Amy looked up at her with her innocent green eyes. "Is it pwetty?"

Nora was spared from telling her daughter a possible lie about Oregon's prettiness by a horde of children that ran by their wagon.

Amy's gaze followed them. "Mama, can I go play with them?"

Nora hesitated. Amy had never had a lot of friends because their neighbors hadn't allowed their children to play with the illegitimate bastard of a prostitute. She wanted Amy to build friendships, but would she be safe running around in this chaos of wagons, mules, oxen, and horses?

"It's all right." A dark-haired woman maybe fifteen years her senior walked over and smiled at Nora. "My Hannah will look after her. She'll be fine."

Slowly, Nora let go of her daughter's hand. "Don't go too close to the animals." She watched Amy run off with a girl of about eight.

"She's your only child, huh?" the dark-haired woman asked.

Nora nodded, still looking in the direction the children had gone.

"Not for long, I'll bet."

Nora whirled around. She stared at the woman.

The woman chuckled. "I've seen your husband," she said with a wink.

Nora relaxed a bit. Yes, her husband was a young, healthy man, and on this journey with no single women, it wouldn't be long until he wanted to share her bed.

"Bernice Garfield." The older woman extended her hand.

Transferring the whip to her left hand, Nora greeted her new neighbor. "Nora M... Hamilton."

Luke had a lot of time to think while she coaxed along the small herd of milk cows, spare horses, and extra oxen that plodded behind the wagons. Time to think and to curse herself. "What the hell are you doin'?"

She had never imagined starting this journey as a married "father." From the day when she had begun to disguise herself as a man, she had known that she was destined to live a solitary life. Over the years, she had sometimes longed for companionship and a place to belong, but she always knew that she would never have love or a family. *And you still haven't. She's your wife in name only.*

"What on earth gave you the idea that you could get away with this?" Luke muttered, shaking her head at herself. She had acted on instinct, completely impulsive, when she had met the young prostitute. Something about Nora and her daughter just made her want to change their lives for the better. But would she really be able to play the husband and father without anyone discovering what she really was?

Being around Nora made her uncomfortable. She couldn't relax in her presence, because she was afraid to give herself away or at least sound and act like a clumsy fool who had never been around women. *You haven't,* she mocked herself. Luke had lived most of her life in a world without women. The only females she had any experience with had been prostitutes—and Nora wasn't a prostitute any longer.

"Hello, Lucas." Abner McLoughlin, the wagon train's captain, stopped his horse next to Luke's mare and looked down at Luke from his large gelding.

Luke's mare was not a tall horse, but she was hardy and well-trained, and Luke hoped that she would be part of a successful breeding program one day.

"Luke," she said. "No one's called me Lucas since I was eight and broke my mother's prized china plates." No one had ever called her Lucas, and her mother had never owned china plates, but the captain didn't know that.

McLoughlin nodded and pointed to the last wagon in the line. "Isn't that your daughter?"

Luke blinked. Hearing someone refer to the girl as her daughter was going to take some getting used to. Her saddle creaked as she shifted forward and stood in the stirrups to get a better look at the girl the captain had pointed out.

A small girl with a mop of red hair ran after the last wagon.

Luke hadn't paid all that much attention to Nora's daughter and how she looked, but she was probably the only redheaded child in the wagon train, so Luke nodded.

"Then you better go and take her away from there. She's gettin' mighty close to Potter's cow," McLoughlin said.

The red-haired girl was running and playing with an older girl and didn't pay much attention to her surroundings, not noticing that she was getting closer and closer to the nervous cow that was tethered to the rear of the last wagon.

Luke opened her mouth to shout out a warning but then closed it with a curse when she discovered that she didn't even know the girl's name. *For God's sake! You're supposed to be her father, and you act like you don't even know the child.*

The girl was dangerously close to the cow's hind legs now.

With a loud yell, Luke spurred her horse forward and, leaning sideways in the saddle, snatched the girl up, out of harm's way.

The girl's eyes widened, and for a second, she just stared at Luke. Then, realizing she was in a stranger's arms, she began to cry and struggle against Luke's secure grip.

Now it was Luke's turn to stare wide-eyed. Even as a child, she had never been around children much, so she didn't have the slightest idea how to comfort one. "Don't cry. Please." The girl continued to cry, and Luke looked around nervously, afraid that someone would think she was hurting the child. "If you don't stop struggling, you'll fall off the horse."

The girl sniffed and looked down with watery eyes, noticing for the first time that she was on a horse. Instantly, she stopped struggling. "Amy rides horsie!"

Amy. Yeah, that's her name. Luke watched as the girl reached out a small hand and patted the mare. *Great. She can't stand me, but she loves my horse.*

Amy leaned down to press her wet cheek against the mare's neck. A sloppy kiss landed on the Appaloosa's mane, and the girl giggled as the brown and white strands tickled her chin. "What is his name?" she asked, looking up at Luke with big eyes.

"It's a she, and she doesn't have a name." Luke had been calling her mare "girl" but didn't allow herself the sentimentality of naming the animal. She didn't want her comrades to think she was soft in any way.

"No name?" Amy eyed her incredulously.

Luke shrugged. "Well, maybe you can find one for her."

The girl smiled for the first time, her tears now forgotten. "I know! Daisy! Dat is pwetty."

Daisy? Luke tried hard not to grimace. *That would ruin my reputation.* "I think there already is a Daisy in the herd, and we wouldn't want her to have to share her name, would we?"

Amy nodded and hung her head. Her lower lip trembled.

"You're a clever girl. I bet you know another pretty name," Luke said before the crying could start again.

The girl looked up again. A shy smile dimpled her chubby cheeks.

I bet she didn't have much praise and compliments from men in her life.

Amy thought for a while and then mumbled, "Mea'les."

"What?"

"Mea'les," the child said again.

"You mean 'Miles'?"

The little girl shook her head. "Mea'les."

Luke scratched her head. Were they speaking the same language? She didn't understand what the girl was saying. "And what is Meales?"

"I haved dat when I was vewwy sick. Look." With a grave expression, Amy pulled the neck of her dress down a bit and pointed to a small, round scar just above her collarbone.

Luke looked down at the white spots dotted over the mare's hindquarters and had to laugh. Amy's logic was impeccable. "Measles!"

"Yes." Amy grazed the clueless adult with a that's-what-I-said gaze.

My prized mare is gonna be named after a contagious disease? Maybe Daisy isn't so bad after all. But Luke didn't have the heart to reject another of Amy's suggested names. "Measles," she said. "That's very…um…unique. No other horse has such a clever name."

"Mea'les don't need to share." Amy clapped her hands.

"No, she doesn't," Luke said, suppressing a sigh. "She has that name all for herself." *Lucky horse.* She directed the newly named mare along the line of wagons until she reached her own wagon.

"Mama!" Amy squealed when she spotted her mother, who was still walking beside the oxen. "Mama, look! I ride Mea'les!"

Nora whirled around. Her eyes widened, and her hand flew to her mouth when she saw her daughter in Luke's awkward grip.

She doesn't seriously think that I'd hurt the kid, does she? Luke wondered as she watched Nora rush toward them. *Children make me nervous as hell, but I'd never hurt them.*

"Amy! What happened? Is she all right?"

Luke watched as the girl happily jumped into her mother's arms. *Who would have thought…a prostitute who is a caring mother.* "She's just fine," she said. "My horse may be a bit traumatized, but otherwise, everything's fine."

Nora kissed her daughter's cheek and eyed the mare. "What's wrong with the horse?"

"Her name." Luke grimaced.

"Mea'les!" Amy squealed.

"She named her Measles," Luke said, pointing at the mare. "Because of the spots, I suppose."

Nora threw her head back and laughed.

Luke felt her lips form an unfamiliar smile. She wheeled Measles around and rode back to the rear of the train.

Nora's feet ached and burned, and she struggled with the weight of her sleeping daughter in her arms, but she was determined to keep up with the others. She had walked fifteen miles today, but it felt more like fifty. When Luke had taken over the driving of the oxen, she had climbed into the wagon to travel more easily for a while but had soon given up on that idea.

With supplies and tools piled high, there was hardly any place to sit. The springless wagon bounced and swayed along the rutted road. The inside of the wagon was stuffy and smelled of the various foods stored there, adding to the queasy feeling that the constant jostling caused.

Like most of the other women in the train, Nora had preferred to walk for the rest of the day. For the first few hours, she had talked with Bernice Garfield and Emeline Larson, the shy young woman from the wagon behind them. After years of being on the outside, Nora loved to be included and to be asked for her opinion by respectable women. But as the afternoon and the miles dragged on, the easy chatter had ceased. Now only the creaking of the wagons, the shouts of the drivers, and the clanking of chains filled the air. Sometimes, when a wagon hit a rock or a hole in the muddy trail, the pots and pans hanging inside the wagon clanged against each other, and the chickens in their coop raised a ruckus.

In the distance, Nora detected three large brick buildings, and she sighed with relief. That had to be the Shawnee Methodist Mission the captain had told them about when they'd stopped for an hour of rest at noon. Here, they would set up camp for their first night out of Independence.

The sun dropped over the horizon just as they reached the mission. The captain called a halt and swung his arm in a great circle.

Nora watched as the wagons formed a circle and the oxen were unyoked. The tongue of each wagon extended under the rear wheels of the next one. The men laced the wagons together with chains until only one opening remained.

Nora turned to Luke, who was checking their oxen for sores. "Is that really necessary?" She pointed to the circled wagons. "I'd have thought the Indians wouldn't be hostile here at the mission." She had heard the whispers about ferocious Indian attacks and what they might do to captured women, but she tried not to think about that.

She watched Luke's hands trailing along the oxen's backs. He was surprisingly gentle with the animals, and she hoped he'd be gentle with her too.

Luke turned around. "I know a lot of people spread rumors that'll tell you otherwise, but I think Indians will be the least of our problems on this trip. With most tribes, bargaining skills will be more important than marksmanship."

"Then why do we circle the wagons?"

"Not to ward off any Indian attacks," Luke said, his gaze steady and reassuring. "The circle provides a corral for the animals. That's all." Without another word, he led the oxen through the gap between the circled wagons to a nearby creek.

Nora stayed behind and looked around. She had never lived the life of a pioneer woman. She had never been expected to cook, build a fire, or milk a cow. For a few seconds, she stood helplessly, not knowing where to start and what to do. Then she observed what her neighbors did. "Come on, Amy, let's gather some wood for a fire."

Fifteen minutes later, they returned to the camp with armfuls of wood. Most of it was damp, though, so Nora struggled to get a fire started. All around her, the women were already heading for the nearby stream with dented pots or preparing their family's dinner. Her stomach rumbled when Mrs. Garfield ladled out a delicious smelling stew to her brood of children. Nora's tired hands struck flint and steel together again but didn't produce more than smoke.

"Mama," a sleepy voice said next to her, "I'm hungwy."

Nora bit her lip. "Soon, Amy, soon." A shadow fell over her, blocking out the last light of the setting sun, and Nora looked up.

Luke, having returned from tending the animals, stood there and looked down at her.

Oh, no. A shiver raced through Nora. The other men were already enjoying their evening meal and coffee next to a warming fire while she had accomplished nothing. She had heard Mister Larson yell at his shy wife when she hadn't worked as fast as he'd have liked. Would Luke get angry too? He had married her to have someone who cooked, washed, and provided a comfortable home for him—and now it turned out that she couldn't even get a fire started.

She felt him kneel next to her and held out the flint and steel to him.

He shook his head. "No. If I do it, you won't learn. Strike it again."

Nora did and produced a spark, which Luke caught with a patch of dried grass, patiently coaxing a small flame to life.

When the flames licked at the wood and the branches finally caught fire, he sat back on his heels and looked at her. "You didn't grow up on a farm, huh?" he said with a sigh, but there was no anger in his voice.

Nora stared into the flames. "It's painfully obvious, isn't it?"

"You'll either learn or give up and turn back around." Luke moved to the back of the wagon and pulled off the tailgate to lift down the box of cooking utensils. He drove two forked sticks into the ground on both sides of the fire and swung the heavy water kettle up onto the pole between them.

Hastily, Nora began to grind coffee beans.

"Mama," Amy said around the thumb in her mouth, "we go home now, please?"

Tears burned in Nora's eyes, and she didn't know what to say. They didn't have a home anymore. "Sweetie…"

"Why don't I take her to say good night to Measles before we eat," Luke said.

Amy smiled for the first time in hours. She looked back and forth between Nora and Luke.

Nora hesitated. She had never trusted anyone but Tess and Sally alone with her daughter, and she had certainly never sent her off with a man she hardly knew. She looked into the gray eyes of the stranger who was her husband and finally nodded.

Luke looked down at his hand, hesitating before he extended it.

Amy slipped her small hand into his larger one and walked off with him.

When someone cleared her throat behind Nora, she looked away from Amy and Luke and turned.

Bernice Garfield stood there, holding a steaming pot in both hands. "Would you like to have some stew for yourself and your family?"

"Oh, no, thank you. I can make my own." At least Nora hoped she could. Since she'd left her parents' home, she had always been self-reliant and had never taken anything from anyone when she knew she couldn't pay for it one way or another. She took a certain pride in making it on her own.

"I'd consider it a favor," Mrs. Garfield said with a smile. "I made too much, and we can't possibly eat it all, so if you don't take it, it'll go to waste."

Nora bit her lip. She knew that wasn't true. Each family had to make their food last until they reached Oregon. Any leftovers would make a good breakfast for tomorrow.

"I couldn't help noticing that you don't seem to have much experience cooking on an open fire," Mrs. Garfield said.

Nora's cheeks heated. Now even strangers noticed her lack of skills. How embarrassing. She opened her mouth to defend herself.

Mrs. Garfield shook her head. "That's not an accusation. I guess you just come from a wealthy family, so you never had to learn."

Of course, it was more complicated than that, but Nora nodded and left it at that.

"You'll learn," Mrs. Garfield said, "but until then, I'm here to help you out."

Pride wouldn't fill her daughter's stomach. Finally, Nora nodded. "Thank you," she said quietly and took the pot of stew.

Nora looked toward the Garfields' fire, where most of the men had gathered with their pipes and a well-thumbed pack of cards to play Pinochle. *It must be nice to be a man and get to sit down for a while.* While the men relaxed after dinner, the women's work was never done. With a little advice from Mrs. Garfield, Nora had milked and fed the two cows, scrubbed their tin plates clean, and used the embers of the fire to cook a kettle of beans for their noon meal the next day. Finally, she took their provisions out to air them and prevent mildew and made up a bed in the wagon box for the tired Amy. She pushed the boxes and trunks in the bottom of the wagon bed together, then laid a straw tick and a quilt on top. After kissing Amy good night, she sat down to mend a few burn holes in the hem of her skirt.

Fiddles and a banjo began a lively tune. Men with mouth organs joined in. Soon the younger couples were dancing around the fires.

Nora set her needlework down and looked at Luke, who knelt by the fire and stirred the embers to keep it alive. All evening, he had kept himself apart from the other emigrants. He was clearly not a man of many words, but Nora saw his booted foot move to the music's rhythm. Did he expect to dance with his new wife?

She heaved her protesting body up and walked over to him. "Do you want to join the other dancers?"

"I don't dance." His eyes were dark and mysterious in the light of the fire. "And you should save the energy and go to bed."

No longer in the mood to dance or socialize, Nora turned away and forced her heavy limbs to climb into the wagon. She stared through the half-open flap and spent a few minutes trying to count the numerous campfires from other wagon trains all around them before she turned and watched her peacefully sleeping daughter.

The creaking of the wagon alerted her that someone else was climbing inside. The flap opened, and Luke peeked inside. He said nothing and just watched her.

Her stomach roiled a bit, but the sack of grain and other provisions prevented her from moving back. *He's your husband, and this is his wagon. He has every right to be in here.*

"Take off your dress," he said and climbed into the wagon, ducking so he wouldn't hit his head.

Nora wasn't surprised. She had known this would come, but the time and the place were a little astonishing nonetheless. *Yesterday, when he could have had me in the privacy of my clean room, in my soft, comfortable bed, he refused. And now that I'm sweaty and smelly and can hardly move a limb, he wants to lie with me.* She suppressed a sigh. *Come on, you don't need to move much for this. He's your husband, and this is the price you're gonna have to pay. It won't be that bad.* She slipped into the familiar role of Fleur. "Why don't you do it?" She gave her voice a seductive timbre.

"Nora." His voice held a silent warning.

He wants to take the lead. All right. With a groan, Nora lifted her arms and tried to slip off her bodice. Every inch of her body hurt, and her muscles, stiff from walking and swinging the whip all day, protested every movement. She would probably be in acute pain tomorrow, but she was determined that Luke would hear no complaint from her. She bared her fair shoulders as seductively as her aching muscles would allow, but when she looked up, Luke stared at the wagon cover.

"Lie down." He pushed back the sack of grain to make room for her.

Nora sighed. *He doesn't want seduction. Right down to business it is.* "Let me ask Mrs. Garfield if she would take Amy for tonight."

"What?" He lifted his gaze and stared at her but still didn't look down at her half-naked body. "Why?"

"I don't want her to wake up and see."

"See what?" His brows drew together.

Nora stared at him. "Well, us."

"Oh! Oh, no, no, no." Luke took a step back and almost fell out of the wagon in the process. "That's not what I...I don't expect that of you. Ever. All right?"

Nora didn't understand it, and she didn't believe it.

"That's not why I had you undress," Luke said. "I just wanted to rub your back."

Nora gave an incredulous laugh. *He wants to rub my back?* She squinted and tried to read his expression in the almost darkness of the wagon. *What's this, some kind of fetish?*

"I know what you're probably thinking, but this is not about...that," Luke said. "I'm doing this for strictly practical reasons. If I don't loosen your muscles now, you won't be able to move tomorrow, and I'll need you to drive the oxen again."

Stunned, Nora continued to undress.

Luke bent down and rummaged through one of the bags. When he straightened up, his arm brushed her bare shoulder in the cramped space of the wagon. "Sorry." He lowered his head, but for a moment, Nora thought she had seen a blush on his face. "Lie down."

With one last look up at him, Nora settled her sore body onto her bedding, crammed between a hoe, the butter churn, and a sack of corn meal.

"Scoot over." Luke knelt next to her, and she heard him open a tin. A moment later, his calloused palm slid over her skin, spreading soothing ointment over her back.

Nora shivered, not really sure if it was because of the cool salve or the strange, unfamiliar gentleness of his rough hands. She moaned as his fingers began to loosen her tight muscles.

From a nearby wagon came an answering moan as one of the other couples made love.

Luke's hands disappeared from her back. He cleared his throat.

So, he's not as unaffected as he wants me to believe. As a prostitute, Nora had learned to read her customers' needs and wants—and she was good at it. She took no pride in that, but it had helped her and Amy survive when she had no other skills. She couldn't make a fire; she couldn't milk a cow; she wasn't a good cook, and she'd never be able to give him the devotion and love a man deserved from his wife, but one thing she could give him. One thing she was good at.

Nora rolled onto her back, took Luke's hand, and pressed it against her bare breast.

His fingers twitched against her skin, and for a moment, he stared down at her. Then he drew back with a growl. "I told you that I don't expect you to share my bed." Heat emanated from his body.

Why is he holding back? "If you're worried about getting me with child while we are out here on the trail…" She had heard some of the other women worrying about giving birth on the trail, so far from their families and medical help. She shivered at the thought but struggled to keep a seductive smile on her face. "You don't have to worry about that. In my line of work, we know means of preventing pregnancy other than practicing abstinence." She tried to draw him down again, but still he resisted.

"It's not that."

"What is it, then?" Nora didn't understand. She didn't understand this man at all. In the last few years, her interactions with men hadn't been pleasant, but at least they had been simple, easy to understand. It had always been clear what they wanted from her. With Luke, nothing was clear or simple. She didn't know what he expected of her, what he got out of their marriage. If he had married her to have a cheap cook and maid, he would have been more upset at her lack of skills in that department. And he clearly hadn't married her for the conversation, because since becoming husband and wife, they hadn't exchanged much more than a few polite words at mealtime. *What does he want from this marriage? I don't have anything else to offer him.*

Why did he find her lacking? Why did he seem immune to her attempts of seduction? A sudden thought occurred to her. "Is it that you prefer the company of men?"

Luke's eyes widened.

Another man might have struck her across the face for suggesting such a thing, but even if she didn't know much about her husband, her instincts told her that he was not a violent man.

His chuckle made her look up. "No," he said with a mysterious grin. "I do enjoy the company of women."

"Just not mine." Nora hung her head.

Luke stood and moved to the front of the wagon. "Go to sleep now. Good night." Without answering her comment, he slipped outside and vanished into the darkness.

Luke pulled off her boots and lay down on her bedroll that she had unrolled beneath the wagon. She was tired, but still sleep wouldn't come. She lay awake for a long time, listening to the sounds around her. In the wagon next to theirs, someone snored loudly, crickets chirped down by the gurgling stream, and in the distance, a lone coyote called to its mate.

The sounds were familiar; they weren't the reason why she couldn't sleep and neither was the coarse blanket that did little to cushion her body against the hard ground. Luke lay with her arms folded back and tucked under her head and stared up at the boards of the wagon above her.

The tar that rendered the wagon watertight made it impossible for her to see Nora, but she could hear her tossing and turning and sometimes groan when she tried to stretch her aching muscles.

Am I really helping her? Or did I only manage to make her life harder instead of better? When Nora had undressed, Luke had tried to act like a gentleman, but still she felt guilty because Nora's beauty hadn't left her unaffected. Luke had promised herself long ago not to take advantage of a woman who was forced to sell her body. As much as her body wanted her to, she wouldn't break that promise now. Nora didn't really want her, and she would want her even less if she knew who Luke Hamilton really was.

With a sigh, Luke rolled onto her side and closed her eyes.

SHAWNEE METHODIST MISSION,
MAY 2ND, 1851

Nora jerked awake. She looked around bewildered until she remembered. *The wagon train. I'm on my way to Oregon.* Groaning, she lifted a hand and rubbed tired eyes. She wasn't used to getting up early and felt as if she'd just gone to sleep. Every muscle in her body screamed at her when she turned around to look at Amy.

The place at the rear of the wagon was empty.

"Amy?"

"She's with the Garfields," Luke said from right outside the wagon. "And you better get up if you want breakfast before we hit the trail."

Nora forced her tired body out from under the blankets, tugged on her boots, and opened the flap to peer outside.

The sun had already risen, streaking the sky with pink, and the camp was teeming with activity. The men brought in the oxen and mules and drove them to the wagons for yoking and hitching. The women had already milked the cows, gathered the eggs, and prepared breakfast and were now busy stowing away their cooking utensils and reloading the wagons.

"We're pulling out at seven," Luke said without looking up from the running gear he was checking.

Nora didn't know what to say to him. After last night, the silence between them was awkward.

She was glad when Mrs. Garfield wandered over with Amy. "He let you sleep in today, huh?" She helped Nora stow the blankets in the wagon. Judging from her smile, she had heard the moans coming from their wagon last night—and had mistaken the groans of pain for sounds of passion.

There was no privacy in a wagon train. Whereas the girls in the brothel would have teased her without mercy, Nora knew that as a "respectable lady" she wasn't expected to comment on anything that might have gone on in her marriage bed. *Which is a good thing, seeing how I don't have anything to comment on.*

Luke had let her sleep in. From the looks of it, he had even prepared a quick breakfast of beans and bacon and milked the cows, tasks that most other married men would have refused to do. But Nora knew it was not the romantic gesture of an enamored husband. He had simply wanted to avoid having to interact with her because he felt as uncomfortable around her as she did around him.

With a sigh, Nora sat down for a hasty breakfast.

Luke leaned against the wagon, hidden in its shadow, and stared out into the darkness. The fires had finally burned down, and the camp was quiet. This was her chance. Everyone was asleep, exhausted from the twenty miles they had made that day.

Luke was tired, too, but she couldn't go to sleep until she had taken care of an urgent business. The monthly reminder that she was not the man she pretended to be had once again set in.

The latrine, a hastily dug hole, wasn't far away from the circled wagons, but Luke couldn't use it to relieve herself and remove her soiled undergarments because anyone who was answering nature's call at this time of the night might stumble upon her and discover her secret. The landscape around the camp had no trees for cover, even the lone elm the campground had been named for had fallen victim to the axe of emigrants searching for firewood years ago.

So, Luke had waited until after dark.

When the howl of a lone wolf came from the right, the guard who had taken up position outside the wagon circle looked in that direction.

Luke quietly slipped away from camp.

The grass, growing tall as a man's waist here at Lone Elm Campground, provided sufficient cover. Luke hastily took care of business and was soon on her way back to camp. She crawled forward on her knees and elbows, then paused when she noticed that the guard wasn't where he had been before. Had he fallen asleep?

She parted the grass in front of her, trying to get a glimpse of his position.

A gunshot shattered the silence.

Fire burned across her skin, and Luke sank back into the grass with a groan.

"Mrs. Hamilton? Mrs. Hamilton? Wake up, Mrs. Hamilton."

Nora shot up into a sitting position. "W-what?" She stared bleary-eyed into Captain McLoughlin's bearded face.

From the tent's opening, the captain looked down at her with a grave expression. "Your husband."

Nora squinted in the light of the captain's oil lantern and looked around the tent that another emigrant had abandoned along the trail. Amy was sleeping nearby, but Luke had once again preferred to bed down elsewhere. "He's not here," she said.

McLoughlin nodded grimly. "He was shot."

"What?" Nora, now wide-awake, scrambled out from under her blanket. "What happened? Was there an attack? Did he…? Is he…?"

The tent's flap opened, and Luke ducked into the tent. "I'm fine," he said. "You didn't have to wake her, Captain."

Even in the dim light, Nora could see that his face was pale under its tan. His expression was grim, but Nora wasn't sure whether he was trying to hide pain, anger, or both. "What happened?" she asked again.

"Some goddamned overzealous greenhorn wanna-be-guard shot at me because he thought I was an attacking Indian. That's what happened." Luke grunted. "Can you imagine all the letters home? Former lieutenant and war hero Luke Hamilton shot while following the call of nature."

Nora had to giggle in sudden relief. She lifted her hand to hide it.

Luke's head snapped up. His dark gaze seemed to pierce her. "You think that's funny?"

Captain McLoughlin stepped back. "I don't think I'm needed here." He hastily retreated from the tent.

Nora crawled out of her bedroll and got up. The tent was high enough so she could stand upright in the middle, but Luke needed to duck his head a little. Silently, Nora looked at him until he stopped scowling at her. "Are you hurt?"

Luke rummaged through his saddlebags. "My pride, more than anything else," he said without looking up.

Nora had to hide another smile. "Well, I can't help you with that, but I can tend any other wound that you might have."

"That's not necessary." With bandages and a small bottle in hand, Luke turned toward the tent's opening.

Nora quickly held on to his elbow. "I'm your wife. Let me help you."

"It's nothing," Luke said and shook off her hand. "The bullet just grazed me." He pointed to his left upper arm, where blood dotted his white shirtsleeve.

Nora hadn't been a squeamish girl in a long time, but now her stomach threatened to revolt at the sight of Luke's blood. A few inches to the side and… "It's not nothing," she shouted. With a glance at Amy, who slept rolled up against the tent's canvas wall, she lowered her voice. "You could have died."

Luke just stood and stared at her.

"You could have died," Nora repeated, this time in a whisper. "And what would have become of Amy and me then? A woman and a child alone on the trail for two thousand miles? Even if we made it to Oregon, we could never build a cabin and survive the winter on our own."

Luke swallowed.

He hasn't thought about it. Luke had married her, yes, but he hadn't thought about the responsibilities that came with being a husband and father.

"Mama," Amy's small voice came from the darkness.

Nora knelt down next to her. "Everything's all right, sweetie. Go back to sleep."

But Amy was wide-awake now and stared up at her with wide eyes. "Why are you yellin'?"

"I'm not yelling. I'm just talking to Luke," Nora said, caressing her daughter's reddish locks.

"Luk'." Amy looked around in search of her stepfather and smiled when he crouched on his heels next to her.

In the last two days, Nora had watched her daughter go from fear and distrust toward Luke to shy hero worship. Amy was still cautious, but something about this new person in her life seemed to fascinate her, and it wasn't just his horse as Luke had repeatedly commented.

"Hello, little one," Luke said. He kept his left side with the bloody sleeve away from Amy, something Nora was thankful for. "Do as your mother says and go back to sleep."

"We go and say Mea'les good night," the girl said.

Luke shook his head. "She's already asleep."

"Oh." Amy's lower lip quivered.

Luke cleared his throat. He looked as helpless as a newborn calf. "But she told me you could come visit her tomorrow if you are a good girl and go to sleep right now."

Obediently, Amy clutched Rosie, her doll, to her chest and closed her eyes. A few moments later, she was fast asleep again.

"Now let me look at that wound," Nora said.

"It's just a scratch. I can dress it myself."

Nora raised one eyebrow. *Why do men have to be so darned stubborn?* "With one hand? Let me do this." She took the bandages from the still protesting Luke and pressed him down to sit on her blankets. "Take off the shirt," she said when he just sat there without moving.

Luke started to roll up his left sleeve.

"No." Nora shook her head. "I can't reach the wound that way. Take it off."

He fiddled with the top button of his shirt but didn't open it.

Nora suppressed the urge to tap her foot. She was tired and just wanted to slip back under her blanket. "Excuse me if I have to be blunt for a second. It's not like I've never seen a man in his altogether before. I won't faint if I see your bare chest."

The corner of Luke's mouth twitched. He mumbled something that almost sounded like "I'm not so sure about that," but then he finally pulled his suspenders down, undid the buttons, and slid the shirt off his left shoulder. Under the shirt, he wore a sleeveless undershirt. "This doesn't have sleeves," he said. "You can reach the wound."

Nora pulled his arm toward her. How smooth it was. She was used to the hairy, beefy limbs of her customers, and Luke's slender muscles were surprisingly appealing. *He's bleeding, so stop ogling and start helping him.*

She took a clean piece of cloth out of her carpetbag and gently wiped away the blood around the wound. The bullet had just grazed him, but it had left a deep cut across his upper arm. "I think it would be better if I stitch it up." She searched in the carpetbag for needle and thread.

Luke's eyebrows rose. "Do you know how to do that?"

"You mean am I as bad at it as I am with most other tasks around here?" Nora said with a smile.

Luke grinned. "Are you?"

"You're gonna find out. Do you want some whiskey?" Alcohol was forbidden in the wagon train, but each family had packed some for medical emergencies.

Luke shook his head.

Nora had already noticed in the brothel that he didn't care much for whiskey, and after meeting far too many violent drunkards, she was glad about it. She kept her eyes on his face as she poured herbal tincture from a small bottle onto the wound to clean it. She knew from experience that the liquid stung, but Luke's expression remained calm. Nora threaded her smallest needle and tried to pretend that it was a ripped shirt she was piercing with the needle and not Luke's flesh. She had done this a few times before, but it never got any easier. By the time she was tying off the thread and put a light bandage over the stitches, she felt lightheaded and queasy. Swallowing heavily, she looked up into his face. "You all right?"

"Yeah, but you look a little pale." He shrugged his shirt back on while he studied her.

Nora put away needle and thread. "It's nothing."

"That's exactly what I said, but you didn't believe me either."

Without really wanting to, Nora answered his smile with one of her own. "It is nothing," she said and rubbed her palm over her nervous stomach. "I wasn't the one who got shot."

Luke buttoned the cuff of his shirt. "You should be thankful for that because I'm not half as good as you are with needle and thread."

"Don't you want me to stitch up the shirt?" Nora asked.

"No, it's fine. I have another one in my saddle bags. Thank you," Luke said, nodding down at his arm. He strode toward the tent's opening.

"You're not going back out to sleep under the wagon, are you?" Nora asked.

"Yes, I am," he answered without stopping.

Now that they had a perfectly good tent, Nora saw no reason why he should sleep under the wagon any longer. She had no real desire to share his bed, but if he continued to sleep apart from her, people would start to talk. After three years on the edge of society, she didn't want to be the woman everyone talked about again. "People will talk, you know."

Luke had already lifted the tent's canvas flap, but now he stopped and turned back around. "Are you afraid of what people might say about us?"

"Afraid?" Nora listened to the sound of that word. "No. But it is nice not to be looked down upon for a change."

Luke shook his head. "No one's gonna look down upon you just because I prefer to sleep outside instead of in a stuffy tent."

Is he really that naïve about human nature? Of course there's gonna be talk. "I'm your wife. Of course they'll judge me by how happy I make you."

He didn't even try to tell her that she did make him happy. With a sigh, he stared through the half-open flap into the darkness outside. "If it makes you happy, I'll sleep inside tonight."

Happy? Nora had long ago given up on waiting for another person to make her happy. *That's one thing we have in common at least.* She didn't even strive for personal happiness anymore but would be content with a quiet life and a good future for her daughter. She couldn't tell him that, so she hid her somber mood behind a smile. "Well, if you stay inside, at least you won't get shot again."

"That sense of humor is gonna get you into trouble one day," Luke said as he reached for a blanket and lay down at the far edge of the tent.

Nora blew out the lantern, hiding her smile in the darkness.

BLUE MOUND,
MAY 4TH, 1851

Why did it have to be Oregon? Nora sent her husband, who was riding just ahead of her, a resentful glare. *Why not settle down in a nice place in Missouri? A nice, dry place.* Nora had been tired, wet, and miserable for hours. Her daughter slept in the wagon, but she didn't want to add to the weight of the already overloaded wagon the oxen had to pull. The animals appeared to be as miserable as she was.

A steady drizzle had been falling since they broke camp that morning. The rain turned every rut in the trail into a muddy obstacle that each passing wagon carved deeper and deeper into the earth.

Nora sighed as the wagons in front of theirs stopped again because one of the wagons had gotten stuck in the clinging mud.

Cursing, the men began to dig and push the wagon free.

Nora adjusted her soaked-through bonnet and looked down at herself with another sigh.

She had never been a vain woman, but the way her physical appearance had changed in the last few days was disconcerting nonetheless. For the last three years, her looks had been a means to attract men and make money, and it worried her that those skills might slowly fade away. Her once fair porcelain skin was now sunburned and dusted with freckles; her formerly soft hands were blistered and rough; mud splatters and burn holes covered her skirt, and the once elegant red tresses hung down in sodden strands. *Just what I need when Luke didn't find me all that appealing to start with.*

When the wagons began to roll again, Nora looked up from the calluses on her hands. She sent her whip cracking through the air, and the six oxen strained heads-down against the rattling chains. "Come on, Cinderella! Pull, Snow White!"

Next to her, Luke grimaced at the names Amy had given to the oxen.

Nora's lips formed a tired smile. "What can I say? Amy likes the old German fairy tales." She pointed ahead, where a tree-covered hill was rising from the flat grassland surrounding it. "What's this?"

"Blue Mound," Luke answered.

Nora waited for further explanations, but none were forthcoming. "Can we climb it to get a look at what lies ahead?" She was eager for anything that might interrupt the monotony of traveling over endless prairie.

Luke shook his head. "We don't have the time. If we don't reach the Wakarusa River soon, we won't be able to cross it for days."

"I thought you said the Wakarusa is a narrow river with a gentle current?"

"Normally, it is, but after all this rain..." He shrugged and looked down at her. "We better hurry. Do you want to ride for a while?"

Nora eyed the mare. Measles was well-trained and went smoothly under her experienced rider, but Nora had never ridden a horse before—it hadn't been considered ladylike in her family. "No, thanks."

"You know, pride is a ballast we can't afford on this journey."

Oh, now he lectures me when he was the one who was too proud to let me tend his wound? Nora secretly rolled her eyes. "It's not pride." With a deep breath, she swallowed her pride and said, "I don't know how to ride."

Luke stared at her; then he moved forward in the saddle and pulled his foot from the left stirrup. "Why don't you ride with me, then?"

Her feet hurt, and she was too exhausted to argue. She gripped his offered hand and placed her foot in the stirrup. When he pulled, Nora gave a hop and swung up behind him.

"All right?" Luke turned his head to look at her.

Nora glanced at the ground. The horse had looked much smaller from down there. She exhaled. "Yeah."

Luke nudged the mare forward, and Nora wrapped her arms around him, afraid to fall off if she didn't.

The body under her hands stiffened, but he didn't say anything.

Had she pressed against his still healing arm? Quickly, Nora backed away. "I'm sorry. Your arm. Did I...?"

"No. No, you didn't. It's healing fine. It's just..." Luke cleared his throat. "I don't like being hugged."

She stared at her hands that rested on muscled hips. "This is not a hug," she said. "I'm just holding on so I don't fall off the horse." She wasn't particularly fond of hugs and physical closeness either, at least not with men. Being physically close to men had always gone hand in hand with having to endure their unwanted attentions, but to her surprise, she found that she didn't find Luke's closeness repulsive at all.

The oxen next to them fell into a faster trot.

Luke looked up. "There's the river."

Nora looked down the steep, muddy banks to the river that wound through limestone rocks. As Luke had predicted, the once sluggish river was swollen by the rain. "Is it already too deep to ford?"

"Yeah, looks like it."

"Then how will we get across?" There was no ferry that Nora could see, and they couldn't afford to wait for the river to go down because with every day they lost, they risked getting caught by a snowstorm in the Rockies.

Luke dismounted and helped Nora down. "I guess we'll build a raft and float everything across."

Nora helped to unload the wagons while she watched as the men cut trees and built a raft. They took the wheels off the wagons and lowered the wagon beds down the steep banks by ropes. The best swimmers of the train swam across with the end of a rope that was attached to the raft. They slid the first wagon bed onto the raft, and then the men on the other side pulled it across. Men with poles balanced on the raft, helping to push it in the right direction.

It was a slow process, and darkness was beginning to fall when it was finally Nora's turn to step onto the raft. She directed Amy toward a place in the middle of the raft, so she wouldn't be in any danger to fall over board, and took the place closer to the edge.

Next to her, Luke and a few other men began the backbreaking work of poling the raft across.

"Mama!" Amy pointed at Rosie, her beloved doll, which was sliding toward the raft's edge. She stood and took one step toward the doll.

"No, Amy." Nora pulled her back. "You stay there. I'll get it." She let go of her safe hold and stretched out her arm to reach the doll.

They had almost made it across when something crashed into the raft.

The raft swayed and threatened to tip over.

Nora made a desperate grab for the doll.

The raft swerved again.

With flailing arms, Nora tumbled over the side.

Cold water crashed over her, pulling her down and choking her. The raging current shoved her downstream, and the weight of her soaked clothes pulled her down.

Panic rose. Her lungs burned. Nora kicked and thrashed.

Finally, she broke through the surface. *Air!* She gasped for breath, swallowed water, and almost went under again.

She glanced around wildly, searching for something to hold on to.

Nothing.

"Nora!" Luke leaned over the edge of the raft and extended the pole as far as he could in her direction.

Since she didn't know how to swim, Nora couldn't reach him.

The current swept her away.

Items that had gotten loose from other wagons and were now carried downstream slammed into Nora. She struggled to keep her head above water.

Something broke through the water's surface right next to her.

She cried out, thinking it was another object that would crash into her.

Luke looked at her through sodden bangs.

"Luke!" Nora threw her arms around his neck and clung to him with a stranglehold.

They both went under. Luke fought to pry her fingers from his neck. Gasping and coughing, they resurfaced.

"Let go," he yelled at her over the roar of the water. "Let go, or we're both going to drown."

Nora fought down her panic. Slowly, she loosened her frantic hold on him.

He grasped her under her arms. With powerful kicks of his legs and a one-armed sidestroke, he towed her toward the riverbank. Finally, after what seemed like hours to Nora, they reached the other side.

Coughing and spewing water, Nora crawled up the muddy bank. "Amy." She gasped.

Luke plopped into the mud next to her. "She's fine," he said, slicking his hair back. "I told McLoughlin to stay with her. They should have made it safely across by now."

Nora stared upstream, where she could barely make out the wagons.

"How long did you live in Independence?"

"What?"

"How long did you live in Independence?" Luke asked again.

He's asking me about my sordid past now of all times? "A little over three years," she said, her teeth chattering from the cold water and the shock.

"You lived right next to the Missouri for more than three years, and you never learned how to swim?" he asked.

Nora looked at her soaked boots. "I didn't exactly spend my time there taking swimming lessons."

For a few seconds, Luke was silent. Then he cleared his throat. "Why didn't you tell me that you don't know how to swim?"

"I didn't think it was important," Nora said.

"Not important?"

Nora shrugged and felt her wet bodice cling to her skin. "I didn't plan on swimming across."

Luke sighed. "Come on." He helped her up. "We have to get back to the wagons. You need to get into some dry clothes before you catch your death."

Captain McLoughlin met them halfway, some blankets and a crying Amy in tow.

"I'm fine, sweetie." Nora wrapped her sobbing daughter into her arms. She absentmindedly nodded her thanks at Luke as he draped a blanket around her shoulders.

By the time they reached the wagon train, all wagons had made it safely across, and Nora went in search of their wagon to change into some dry clothes.

Luke made no move to follow her.

With Amy still clinging to her, she turned toward him. "Luke? Aren't you coming? You've got to get out of those wet clothes too."

He tugged his wet shirt and vest away from his skin with two fingers but shook his head. "I have to go back and help swim the cattle across. There's no sense in changing now because I'll be wet again by the time I finish." He kept his gaze fixed on her face.

Nora drew the blanket a little closer around her shoulders, aware of the way her wet clothes clung to her.

"Mama," Amy mumbled against her shoulder. "Rosie falled in the water." She looked up at Nora with watery eyes.

"I know, sweetie." Nora caressed Amy's locks. "We're going to get you another doll as soon as possible, all right?" Out here on the trail, it would be nearly impossible, though, and she couldn't afford the overpriced toys in one of the forts along the way. Sighing, she climbed into their wagon.

The smell of gunpowder, sweat, and blood burned in Luke's nose. She squeezed the trigger of her Walker Colt again and again, but the Mexicans just kept coming. With a click, the hammer fell onto an empty chamber. Cursing wildly, Luke grabbed the Hall carbine from the scabbard at the side of her saddle. As she swung up the barrel, the smoke of the artillery and rifles lifted for a moment, and she caught a glimpse of her friend Nate, fighting right next to her.

A Mexican soldier behind Nate pointed his revolver at him.

"Watch out! Behind you," she yelled, but Nate didn't seem to hear her. "Duck, Nate! Duck!"

A shot rang out.

"No!" Luke sat up, breathing heavily. She wiped her sweaty brow and listened in the darkness. There were no voices bellowing out commands, no whinnying horses, and no screams of terror, only the sound of the steady rain that pelted the canvas of the tent.

Luke sank back onto her blanket. *God.* It had been a long time since she had last dreamed of the war. *Maybe it's that damp hardtack you had for dinner.*

The rain had made a fire impossible, so their dinner had consisted of cold beans and hardtack, a salty cracker that had been army food since the Mexican War.

Of course, Luke knew that the nightmare had nothing to do with the food. Having to watch someone she felt responsible for nearly die had brought back the memories of Nate's death. She clenched her hands into fists as she remembered the helplessness she had felt when she had seen Nora being swept away by the swift waters.

She turned onto her side, facing the back of the tent, where Nora slept, intent on letting her quiet breathing lull her back to sleep. But Nora wasn't breathing quietly. Luke heard her teeth chattering from across the tent.

Luke took the blanket that had served as her pillow, ducked her head, and tiptoed through the tent. As she settled the blanket over Nora, she noticed that the sleeping woman was already covered by three blankets. Still, she was noticeably shivering under her pile of blankets.

"Nora?" she whispered.

Nora's eyes opened. She stared up at Luke through the almost darkness, but Luke still wasn't sure if Nora was really awake.

"Everything all right?" Luke asked quietly.

"C-can't g-get w-w-warm."

Luke looked down at her. "You have four blankets."

"S-still c-cold."

I hope she's not gonna suggest we share body heat to warm her up. "It's just the shock," Luke said. She had been in battle, so she knew how terrifying it was to come this close to dying.

Nora didn't answer, but her teeth continued to rattle against each other.

I've never been good at that whole giving-comfort thing. With a sigh, Luke lifted her hand to fleetingly brush it over Nora's cheek. "Jesus!" She pulled back. "You're burning up."

"A-Amy?" Nora asked.

Luke glanced to Amy's side of the tent.

Amy's blanket lifted and fell beneath her steady breaths. Her teeth weren't chattering.

"She's fine. I'm gonna make you some tea," Luke said, though she had no idea how she'd manage to do that in the rain. She didn't know what else to do, so she stumbled outside in search of some half-dry wood to build a fire.

"Luke? Is that you?" Jacob Garfield stood from the place where he'd settled down for guard duty.

"Yes, it's me." Luke looked up at the sky. Rain drops pelted her face, and a sudden idea came to her. "Your wife wouldn't happen to own an umbrella, would she?"

Jacob stared at her. "An umbrella?"

"It's not for me," Luke said. She didn't want him to think she had any personal interest in ladies' accessories. "Nora is sick, and I want to make her some tea, but I can't get a fire going in this rain."

Half an hour later, Luke returned to the tent, her arms piled high with every medicine she could think of. She knelt next to a still shivering Nora and pressed a tin cup of hot tea into her cold hands. "Here. It's willow bark tea. That should help with your fever."

Nora stared at the cup. "N-no," she croaked and tried to hand back the tea. "I...I can't drink that."

Luke glanced at the brownish liquid. "Why not?"

"Because it...it upsets my stomach."

"All right. Then put this around your neck." Luke held out the poultice of fried onions that Mrs. Garfield had given her.

Nora didn't move.

Luke sighed but hesitated to touch her. *Oh, come on, Luke Hamilton. This is not about having relations, this is about helping her.* Reluctantly, she pulled the long, red hair away from Nora's neck and stared down at the fair skin for a second before she put the poultice in place. She took the cup from Nora and helped her lie back down.

When Luke lifted the blankets away from her feet, Nora shivered. "C-cold."

"Just for a second," Luke said. She had wrapped hot stones from the fire into an old shirt to help warm Nora's feet, but as she set them down, she noticed that Nora's stockings were damp from the rain. Hot stones wouldn't help her any if Nora slept with damp feet. "Is it all right if I take off your stockings? They're wet." She didn't want to remove any article of Nora's clothing without her permission.

Nora nodded weakly.

After pulling back Nora's skirts a bit, Luke rolled down the black cotton stockings. She allowed herself just a second of admiring the subtle curve and soft skin of Nora's calves, then reached down to dry off her feet. When she got a good look at Nora's feet, she stopped. Blisters covered the soles of her feet. Some had broken already, leaving her feet raw. *Oww, that must hurt.*

She looked up into Nora's pale face. Despite the pain she must have felt, despite the hardships on the trail, she had never complained or asked for help. She was clearly used to taking care of herself, but now Luke yearned to be there for her.

She reached for the ointment in her saddle bag and applied a thick coat of salve to Nora's feet before she replaced the stockings with dry ones from Nora's bag and covered her with the blankets again.

Nora finally stopped shivering and lay still when the hot stones warmed up her feet.

"Better? Do you think you can sleep now?" Luke knew that sleep would be the best medicine now.

Nora nodded and closed her eyes.

Luke watched her sleep for quite some time, making sure Nora's breathing was deep and even, before she returned to her own blanket.

WAKARUSA RIVER,
MAY 5TH, 1851

Nora's head began to pound as she sat up. She wrapped her arms around her belly and waited until her vision had cleared. Looking around the tent, she saw that Luke had already risen. "All right," she said. "Get up. There's work to do."

Every single bone in her body ached, but she clenched her teeth and forced herself upright. She ignored the burning in her feet as she slipped into her boots.

Just as she was about to leave the tent, Amy crawled out from under her blanket. "Mama? Me go too!"

Nora didn't feel up to dealing with the energetic child and her endless questions, but she nodded nonetheless and knelt down to help Amy dress. She grabbed the dented pot they used for fetching water. Even in its empty state, it seemed much heavier than usual, and Nora had to struggle not to drag it through camp.

Finally, she reached the river and bent down. She filled the pot with water, but when she tried to lift it, she almost fell into the river as the heavy weight pulled her down. Gasping for breath, she half-emptied the pot and tried to lift it again. Her head pounded. Sweat broke out along her back.

Another hand grabbed the pot. It was too big to be Amy's.

Nora flinched away from the unexpected touch. Her unsteady feet slipped on the muddy bank. She flailed her arms as she began to pitch forward.

Strong arms grabbed her around the waist and pulled her back against a warm body. "What the hell are you doing?" Luke's voice rumbled through her.

Nora broke his grip and moved away from him. If he was going to touch her, she wanted it to be on her terms—in a short, businesslike encounter with clear roles, not in this half-angry, half-worried embrace. "Getting water for breakfast," she answered with a hint of defiance.

Luke snorted. "You can hardly stay on your feet, much less carry that pot or cook breakfast. You'll stay in the wagon today."

Nora would have liked nothing more than to crawl back between the covers and stay there for the rest of the day, but she knew that she couldn't. She had to gather eggs, milk the cows, and prepare breakfast, then wash and repack the dishes. She needed to set some dough to rise, or she would have no bread to bake this evening. "I'm fine, just a little bit off-kilter," she said, but her voice ended in a croak.

"Nonsense. You're anything but fine," Luke said. "Go and lie down in the wagon. It's only going to get worse if you don't."

She hesitated. He was right, of course, but that didn't change the fact that she had a lot of things to do before she could allow herself to rest.

"I managed not to starve before I met you," Luke said as if guessing her thoughts. "I'll take over your chores for today."

"But…" Nora swallowed against her sore throat. She looked down at Amy, who listened with wide eyes. "What about Amy? I can't lie in bed all day. Someone has to take care of her, and I can't impose on Mrs. Garfield again."

Luke cleared his throat and stared down at the child. For a moment, he looked helpless, then he shrugged. "Um. I suppose I can do that too."

"You suppose?" Nora arched an eyebrow. "Luke, either you look after her or you don't. There is no supposin' about it." She would take no halfhearted promises when it came to the well-being of her daughter.

"I will look after her," Luke said. "I have absolutely no experience with children, but I've trained stubborn mules, wild horses, and hundreds of recruits, so I guess we should be all right."

Nora opened her mouth to object, but a sneeze shook her body, and she shivered. She had never before let anyone but her closest female friends take care of Amy and had never trusted a man enough to leave Amy in his care. But now, she had no choice. She had to trust this man who was her husband. "Just for a few hours," she said, sniffling. She relinquished the pot to Luke and shuffled back to the wagon.

"I don't need no naps no more."

Luke forked her fingers through her hair. "Amy…"

"No!" The girl stomped her foot and stuck out a pouting lip.

Lord, give me the most stubborn mule, the wildest horse, and a dozen recruits on their first day. Anything but this. After half an hour of fruitless discussion, Luke was at her wit's end.

The girl had started rubbing her eyes and yawning at noon break but had stubbornly refused to follow Luke's suggestion that she lie down in the wagon with her mother. An hour later, Luke had tried again, this time ordering Amy to take a nap.

Once again, Amy had refused, and Luke didn't know how to react to that blatant insubordination. She had been a soldier for most of her life and was used to the clear military hierarchy. Giving and following orders was the most normal thing in the world for her.

But Amy was a three-year-old, not a soldier, and ordering her around obviously didn't work. The girl didn't need a drill sergeant; she needed someone to comfort her. *You're her father…or her second mother or whatever, not her commanding officer.* That was the problem. Luke knew how to be a soldier and an officer, but she had no idea what being a parent meant. *It's not like I had great role models.* She pinched the bridge of her nose. *You're a woman, remember? You're supposed to have these maternal instincts, so use 'em.*

She took a deep breath, listening to whatever her instincts might tell her. Her first panicked thought was to just take the kid and stuff her into the wagon with her mother, but that probably wasn't a good idea. She had promised to take care of Amy while Nora was sick. *She's your responsibility now. When you said "I do," you agreed to be there for her too.*

Luke exhaled sharply. *Obviously, I didn't think this through.* She had thought about the fact that others would see her as a father and therefore as someone who was unquestionably male, but she had never imagined having to take over the day-to-day caring for a child.

She scratched her head when whatever innate sense of how to interact with the girl remained utterly silent. *All right. Think. What would Nora do or Mrs. Garfield? They're both so good with children. How do they do it?* A mental image of Nora cuddling her crying daughter popped into her mind, but this was not her way of interacting with people. In order to hide her true gender, she had to keep people at a distance—not only physically, but also emotionally. In her effort to blend in and appear totally male, she had forgotten what it meant to be a woman, how to reveal her emotions and show affection. She had been so afraid of being thought effeminate and weak that she had buried her softer side deep inside. After acting tough and "manly" for so long, she now found it hard to be affectionate and soft-spoken with the child and her sick mother.

Luke eyed the teary-eyed, still pouting girl. *What does she need from me?* She tried to think back to her own childhood, but that wasn't much help either. Her mother had never been the caring type. *All right. Try to put yourself in her shoes. She's a little girl who has been taken away from the only home she has ever known and from the people who were her friends. She had to watch her mother almost drown, and now she's sick, and that leaves you, a total stranger, to take care of her. She's not rebellious. She's just scared.*

"Amy?"

The girl turned away, refusing to even look at Luke.

Luke sighed. *All right. Last resort—good, old bribery.* "Do you want to go for a ride with Measles?" She managed to say the name without wincing.

Slowly, Amy turned back around and studied her.

Luke sent her a smile of encouragement. "Come on, she's waiting for us." She left Wayne, the oldest Garfield boy, in charge of the ox team and bent down to pick up Amy.

Small arms wrapped around her neck, and she was eye to eye with the three-year-old.

"You can even hold the reins this time," Luke said, uncomfortable with the girl's silent stare.

A delighted grin broke out on Amy's face. She threw herself forward against Luke's body and pressed a wet kiss on her cheek.

Luke's hands clutched reflexively at the girl's dress, then she forced herself to relax and returned the embrace. She lifted one hand to caress the silky red locks and stood just inhaling their scent for a few seconds.

"Mea'les?"

"Right." Luke shook herself out of her almost trance. She unhitched the horse from the back of the wagon and lifted Amy up before she swung into the saddle behind her.

The girl bounced in the saddle and squealed in delight as Luke urged the mare into a fast trot. Soon, she slowed the horse to a walk. The slow, rhythmic gait and Luke's warm arms around her made Amy sleepy. It didn't take long until her small hands loosened their grip on the reins, and with a sleepy sigh, she slumped back against Luke. "Rosie?"

"Huh?" *Rosie? Was that a friend of hers? One of the girls in Tess's establishment, maybe?*

"Rosie." Only half-opened, sad green eyes looked up at Luke. "She falled in the water."

Luke squinted and then remembered that Rosie was Amy's doll. "We'll look for a new toy later. Now sleep."

Amy snuggled her head against Luke's shoulder and did just that.

Uniontown,
May 7th, 1851

The creaking of the wagon alerted Nora to another person who was climbing inside. She blinked open her still heavy eyelids.

"Hi." Luke's face appeared in her line of sight. He looked down at her. "How are you?"

"Better," Nora croaked. It was a lie. Even after spending the last two days in bed, she felt weak and feverish. Her violent shivering made her head ache.

Luke settled down next to her. "Here. You should eat a little."

Nora didn't even look at the tin plate he held out to her. "I'm not hungry." The swaying of the wagon made her so queasy that her stomach roiled at the mere thought of eating.

"But this'll be good for you," he said.

Groaning, Nora lifted her head and looked. "What's that?"

"Raw onions with cucumbers in vinegar on bread and butter. Mrs. Garfield says it'll help with your cold. Come on." He invitingly lifted the bread to her mouth.

Nora stared up at him. *He's surprisingly good at playing nursemaid for his sick wife.* She wasn't sure whether he really cared about her well-being or was just eagerly awaiting the moment she could take over caring for Amy again. Reluctantly, she opened her mouth and took a small bite. Swallowing hurt, and she sank back after only that small crumb. "Did we stop for the night?"

"No. We reached the Uniontown ferry across the Kansas River and are still waiting our turn to cross."

"Uniontown?"

Luke nodded. "It's not much more than a trading post, but it's the only town for many miles."

Nora looked up. "Could we go to town and buy a new doll for Amy?" This might be a chance to make her daughter smile again.

"I don't think so. The town's just being reestablished. I doubt that they have anything but the bare essentials to buy."

Nora's thoughts seemed much slower than usual. "Reestablished?"

Luke nodded. "The town was burned down after cholera broke out last year."

Cholera. Nora grimaced. "How long do you think it will be until I'm back on my feet?"

"I don't know."

Nora's head started to pound as she raised an eyebrow. Her heart echoed the frantic beat. It was the first time Luke hadn't known the answer to a question. He seemed to have a vast knowledge about everything that might occur along the trail. *Does he really not know, or does he want to spare me from the truth?* Nora wasn't stupid. Like many of the train's other women, she had counted the hastily dug graves alongside the trail. They constantly reminded her how fragile life was, especially on the Oregon Trail. In some years, only one-third of the people that had started out from Independence reached their final destination. Many succumbed to cholera, influenza, infections, and other diseases, or they died in accidents or shootings. "I will eventually get better, won't I?"

"Of course you will," Luke said.

His reassurance didn't make her feel better. Even if she did survive this sickness, whatever it was, there was no guarantee that she wouldn't succumb to any of the other dangers on the trip. Already, she had nearly died when she had fallen into the Wakarusa River without knowing how to swim. Panic gripped her. She was all Amy had. *What would become of Amy if something happened to me?* Luke might be a somewhat acceptable stand-in for a few days, but Nora couldn't see him raising Amy on his own.

Luke bent down to look into her face. "Are you in pain?"

"I'm..." Nora hesitated. After three years as a prostitute, she had learned to hide her emotions, but she didn't want to lie to the man who was doing his best to take care of her daughter. "I'm afraid."

"Afraid?" Luke repeated as if that emotion was completely foreign to him. His eyes widened, and he moved back from her. "I would never harm you in any—"

"Oh, no, that's not what I meant." Nora closed her eyes for a second. For such a confident man, he was surprisingly unsure of himself when it came to human interactions. "I'm not afraid of you. It's just... It suddenly occurred to me how dangerous this whole journey will be."

Luke studied her through narrowed eyes. "You're afraid to die."

It was hard to hold his gaze. "I'm not afraid for myself, just for Amy. She would be all alone if something happened to me," she whispered as if saying it out loud would somehow make it happen.

Luke rubbed his nose, playing with the little bump. "She would have me," he said in an equally low voice.

What was she supposed to say to that? She didn't dare to reject his offer to take responsibility for Amy, but she also didn't dare to accept it. He might be her husband, but she still didn't know and trust him enough to let him raise her daughter.

When she just stared at him without answering, Luke looked away. "Do you want to turn around? It's been less than a week. I could take you back to Independence."

Nora's gaze snapped back to him. *Take you back.* He was clearly not intending to stay in Independence too. *He would leave us behind without a second thought. This farce of a marriage obviously doesn't mean much to him. So much for "Till death do us part."* "No." She slowly shook her pounding head. "There's nothing there to return to."

"All right." Luke stood. "Sleep now. I'll wake you when it's our turn to cross."

Nora closed her eyes, but sleep wouldn't come.

Rock Creek Crossing,
May 11th, 1851

Nora sank onto the wagon tongue and stretched out her sore feet for a moment. While she had recovered from her sickness, she still felt exhausted. Was it just her imagination or were the hardships on the trail especially hard for her? Nora tried to tell herself that it was just because she wasn't used to living off the land, with no stores to provide for her. But secretly, she was afraid that her constant state of exhaustion was a symptom of something else. *Don't think about it now. You're just making yourself crazy.*

She looked across the long grass, sprinkled with wildflowers, that was gently undulating in the May breeze. They had followed the Little Blue River northwest, traveling over rolling prairie where water, wood, and grass were always available. For the most part, it was an easy way to start the trip and get used to handling the oxen, but thunderstorms and downpours had flooded creeks and rivers and made them difficult to cross.

Fording Rock Creek the day before had been difficult for another reason. Here, the country became hilly, with an abrupt descent into the valley and an equally steep, rocky bank on the other side. The oxen had pulled the wagons halfway up the bank, but when they stopped exhausted, the wagon began to slip back. The men had to grip the spokes and help push the wagon forward until the narrow path widened farther up the bank.

For the first time, Captain McLoughlin decided to stop traveling and remain in camp this Sunday. The week before, after long discussions, they had pushed on, afraid that losing a day per week on the trail might mean getting caught in snowstorms on the western end of the journey.

While most men set off to hunt—more for sport than food—the women started on the laundry. The banks of Rock Creek were lined with fires, kettles, and piles of unwashed clothes.

Mrs. Garfield came over and sat next to Nora on the wagon tongue while they both waited for their water to heat up over the fire.

Nora studied her new friend and sometimes-mentor. The older woman looked tired too, but her friendly smile never wavered. Bernice Garfield stretched out her feet and dried her hands on the white apron that was tied around her ample waist. Nora looked down at her hands—they were as rough and reddened as her own. The hot water, the sun, and the harsh lye soap were hard on their bare skin.

Doing laundry—pounding clothes against washboards or stones, then lugging the heavy, sodden laundry to the line strung between wagons—was backbreaking work.

Emeline Larson, the young woman from the wagon behind Nora's, hesitantly wandered over and stood staring into the fire.

Mrs. Garfield looked up. "Lord, Emmy! What happened to your eye?"

Emeline fingered her black, swollen eye. "I stumbled with the kettle and bumped into our wagon," she said without looking at them.

Nora didn't even need to look to know that she was lying. She had been beaten enough times by moody or drunk customers to recognize the signs. *He's her husband. It's none of your business how he chooses to treat her.*

"You should put some ointment on it," Mrs. Garfield said.

Emeline just nodded and continued to look at anything but the two other women. "Your husband," she whispered, peeking up at Nora, "is a real sweetheart."

"Yes," Mrs. Garfield said, "you were lucky to land such a good husband."

Nora turned her head to look in the same direction.

Luke was sitting on a rock at the edge of the river, carefully balancing Amy on his lap. They were both holding on to a fishing pole, and Nora had to admire his patience with the small hands that hindered more than they helped. *Well, yes, I suppose I've been lucky in some regards.*

Unlike Emeline's husband, Luke didn't drink, smoke, or chew tobacco. She had never seen him engage in fist fights, lose his temper, or raise his voice. He was always polite and respectful toward women. He even helped her with chores that no other man would do, and he praised her cooking skills even if there sometimes were mosquitoes in the bread dough or the meat had an ashen crust. It was a strange experience for Nora. In all her life, no man had ever shown appreciation for anything she did—except maybe for her skills in the bedroom. Luke was still reluctant to show too much affection, but he never made her feel unimportant or inadequate as her father and brothers often had.

And the most important thing, Nora thought, smiling when she watched Amy fall asleep on Luke's lap, *he's trying hard to be there for Amy even if it doesn't come naturally to him.*

Even in her sleep, Amy clutched the wooden horse that Luke had carved for her, complete with little dots that resembled those of Measles. Amy's head fell limply back against Luke's shoulder, and she began to drool on his jacket.

Nora giggled. The look on Luke's face was priceless.

Even Emeline Larson had to smile. "I think you better give that jacket a good scrubbing too."

ALCOVE SPRINGS,
MAY 14TH, 1851

"We should start crossing right now," Jacob Garfield said, pointing in the direction of the large, deep Big Blue River.

"What's the hurry?" Bill Larson asked. "This is the best campsite we've had since we started. I say we stay here until at least tomorrow."

Luke looked around. Alcove Springs really was the most idyllic campsite. Lush grass and wildflowers grew everywhere. A spring of clear, cold water cascaded over bluffs and splashed into a rocky pool twelve feet below. The boulders around the spring had the names and dates of emigrants from past years carved into them. Luke could understand that many of her fellow travelers wanted to stay and enjoy this place.

Many of the wagon trains around them had already set camp, and most would stay for several days before they continued west. The roads from St. Joseph and Ft. Leavenworth joined the main trail just north of Alcove Springs, making it a favorite campsite. Last year, Luke had led a military expedition to the Rocky Mountains, and she had seen thousands of emigrants encamped at Alcove Springs. This year, word of the cholera epidemic of 1850 had spread and had discouraged many prospective emigrants. The trail was less crowded this year, and Luke was thankful for it.

"The Blue rises fast," Jacob said. "If a rainstorm breaks, we'll be stuck on this side for a long time until the water goes down again."

Larson rolled his eyes. "You old croaker. Someone said there's a ferry somewhere, so we won't have to ford the river."

Jacob snorted. "Yeah, if you want to pay through your nose. Five dollars per wagon. There are many rivers, toll bridges, and ferries ahead. We don't have the money to pay for each and every one of them."

Other men began to voice their opinion, and soon a loud argument began.

Luke leaned back against a rock and said nothing.

Disputes were all too common in the wagon train. Men seemed to argue about every decision they had to make along the trail: how fast or how slow to move, when and where to camp, whether to take a shortcut, how many guards to post at night.

Luke had an opinion about these things too, but fistfights and shouting matches were not her thing. Part of her successful disguise was never to draw attention to herself. She avoided making enemies—and, for the most part, making friends too—so that no one had a reason to take a closer look at her.

When the hotheaded Bill Larson took a swing at one of his opponents, Luke stood and wandered off in search of a quieter spot. She walked along the rocky basin where several emigrants were splashing and playing. One of the Garfield boys called out for Luke to join them, but she just waved and walked on by. After two weeks on the trail, she would have loved a bath, but it had to wait. Maybe she could take a quick dip after darkness had fallen. With that appealing thought in mind, Luke went to scout out a more secluded spring.

She left the busy camp behind and wandered until she came to a place where the valley was more heavily timbered with cedar, oak, and ash trees. Through the trees, she heard the gentle gurgling of another spring and parted a few branches to get a glance at her possible "bathing tub."

Instead, she got an eyeful of something else—or rather someone else.

There, in the middle of a small, natural basin, stood a stark naked Nora, scrubbing the scalp of her giggling daughter.

Luke had upheld the image of a gentleman for many years, but now she couldn't help staring. Only a few times in her life had she seen a naked woman, and never one so beautiful. Nora had none of the worn, excessively made-up looks of a typical parlor house girl. Luke's gaze flickered up Nora's shapely legs, opaque beneath the water of the pool, and paused on a gently rounded stomach to admire the creamy skin there before it wandered up to the flaming red curls that loosely tumbled down over full breasts.

Her fingers let go of the branches she still held parted, and one smacked her in the chin, finally making her look away from the unsuspecting woman. *Stop staring. You're not a fifteen-year-old boy.* The thought that the woman in the pool was her wife made her head spin and her heart pound.

When Nora and Amy waded to the edge of the pool where their clothes lay, Luke hastily backed away and hurried back to camp.

THE NARROWS,
MAY 21ST, 1851

Nora paused next to the oxen as the trail in front of them narrowed. The Little Blue River, which they had followed for days, flowed on one side of the trail. Rugged bluffs rose high above them on the other side.

Whenever possible, the wagons had spread out to avoid the dust that the wagons in front of them had thrown up, but in this bottleneck the trail became so narrow that the wagons had to proceed single file and the pace slowed to a crawl.

Nora watched as Luke directed his mare toward her. Unlike her, he looked like a born horseman. The reins rested loosely in his hand, and he seemed to steer the horse mainly with little movements of his slender body. When he dismounted and glanced at her, Nora quickly looked away.

"Do you want to take over?" she asked as he fell into step next to her. She moved to hand him the whip. Behind them, Bill Larson had long ago taken the whip from his wife to guide their team safely through the bottleneck.

But Luke made no move to take the whip from her. "Nah," he said. "You've gotten really good with them. I think they like you better than me."

Nora's head jerked around, and she stared at him. Was he making fun of her?

But he just looked at her calmly. There was no hidden agenda. He really believed in her skills.

Stunned, Nora flicked the whip again. She noticed that Luke no longer had to duck or risk having his ear taken off. Maybe she really had become good at this.

Amy started to fidget on the wagon seat.

Nora whirled around. "Amy! Sit still, or you're gonna—"

Amy toppled forward.

Nora threw away the whip and tried to break Amy's fall.

Before she could reach Amy, Luke snatched her up. "Christ, Amy! You almost fell. Your mother told you to sit still."

Nora let a shuddering breath escape. Just last week, one of the Mason children had fallen out of the wagon and had been run over by the heavy wheels. The little boy had died within an hour. Nora shuddered to think that it could have happened to her daughter too.

Amy started to cry and reached out her arms to Nora.

Nora took her from Luke, who was still berating the girl. "Stop. You're scaring her."

Luke stiffened and took a step back. "I'm sorry. It's just... The Mason boy..."

"I know," Nora said and touched his arm for a second. She set down Amy and crouched next to her. "Amy," she said seriously but didn't raise her voice, "look at me." She waited until teary green eyes looked into her own. "Falling off the wagon is a really, really, really bad thing. You could get hurt. You have to sit very still up there on the wagon seat, and if you want down, you just tell me and don't try to climb down yourself. All right?"

Amy held her gaze for a second, then she nodded and looked away.

"Good. Now, why don't you go and play with Hannah?" She pointed at the eight-year-old Garfield girl.

Amy looked from her to Luke and then ran off.

Nora turned to Luke and repeated his words from earlier, "You've gotten really good with her."

Luke squinted at her. He laughed, a sound bare of any humor. "I just scared her to death."

"It wasn't that bad. And you probably saved her life—again." She wanted to lean forward and kiss his cheek, thanking him for saving the most precious thing in her life, but his stiff posture told her that he wasn't ready to accept her thankfulness.

"Well, that seems only fair, seeing as to how I'm the one who's responsible for her starting on this dangerous trip," Luke said and turned away.

Before Nora could think of a response, he started to run. Nora stared after him, but then her eyes widened when she caught sight of Amy bending down to pick up something that she probably thought was a stick. "Amy! No!" she yelled and ran after Luke.

The Narrows was a haven for rattlesnakes. One of the poisonous rattlers had slithered out of its hiding place and clattered menacingly, warning the curious child to back away.

Luke reached Amy just as the snake was about to strike. There was no stone or stick to find in the vicinity, and his weapons were back in the wagon. Never slowing down, Luke careened into the rattlesnake and tried to crush it beneath his boot.

The snake slithered around and sank its fangs into Luke's leg before his other boot came down on its head.

Cursing, Luke scanned the sandy ground for other snakes. When he found none, he sat down and pulled off his boot.

Nora wrapped a crying Amy into her arms. "Did it bite you?" she asked over Amy's red locks.

"Yeah." Luke pulled up his pant leg, revealing two small puncture marks right above where the edge of his boot had been. He unwrapped the bandanna from around his neck, tied it around his upper calf, and grunted as he pulled it tight. "Close your eyes, Amy."

Amy hid her face against Nora.

Without hesitation, Luke moved his knife across the bite marks in an x-pattern.

Nora groaned. Bile rose in her throat as he squeezed with both hands and blood squirted out. She swallowed heavily. "Is it bad?"

"Not if I get all the poison out right away," Luke murmured without looking up. He bent as if trying to get a better look at the wound.

"What are you doing?"

"I have to suck the poison out." Luke grunted while he tried to reach the back of his calf.

Nora stared. "I don't see how you're going to do that, unless you're a contortionist."

"A what?"

Nora didn't answer. "You can't reach the wound. Let me do that."

"No." He wrapped his hands protectively around the leg, holding it out of Nora's reach.

"We don't have the time for childish discussions." Nora knelt down and pulled his hands away. She gently laid her hand against his calf. It was already hot to the touch and starting to swell. Nora bent her head, absentmindedly noticing the fine black hairs that dotted the soft skin of his leg.

Luke shuddered as her lips met his skin. His breath came fast and hard. Sweat glistened on his forehead.

This poison works fast. It's already in his system. Nora knew that time was of essence, so she took a deep breath and started to suck.

The taste of blood and the bitterness of the venom made her head spin. Her stomach started to rebel, and she wrenched her mouth away, spitting out blood and poison.

Luke moaned.

"Oooh, you like that, huh?" She winked at him, trying to lighten the mood and hide that she was nauseated and scared to death.

"That was not a moan of pleasure," Luke said. "I'm in pain here."

Nora lowered her lips to the wound again.

Amy tried to crawl around her to see what she was doing, but Bernice Garfield came over and pulled her away. "Mama kiss the owie. Make it good," Amy said.

Nora nearly spat blood all over her clothes. Her tattered nerves almost made her break out in wild laughter.

Jacob Garfield handed her a small flask of whiskey and a bandage, clearly expecting Nora to handle her husband's injury.

Her hands trembled as she opened the flask and poured some whiskey onto the incision. Luke groaned but held still.

"I'm sorry," Nora whispered.

Luke looked up. His normally silver-gray eyes were now a darker color, like the sky seconds before a thunderstorm broke loose. "It's all right. It just burns a little."

"That's not what I'm talking about," Nora said, nodding down at the flask in her hand. "You got hurt while you rescued Amy—for the second time today."

Luke cleared his throat. "Well, better me than her. I don't think she would have liked it if I cut her leg with a knife."

Nora shuddered and wrapped her arms around herself. Her stomach roiled again, and her tongue was starting to go numb from the poison. Her body was going into shock. Only her responsibility for her daughter kept her from breaking down completely.

"Come on. Let's get him into the wagon," Mrs. Garfield said. "And you, li'l one, better keep your father company before something happens again."

Nora followed them numbly.

BETWEEN THE LITTLE BLUE AND THE PLATTE RIVER, MAY 22ND, 1851

Luke leaned back against her saddle and stared out into the darkness with her carbine on her knees.

Soft footfalls approached.

She swung the barrel around.

Nora stepped into the circle of the firelight.

Luke lowered the weapon. "You shouldn't sneak up on me when I'm standing guard. What are you doing up?"

"I brought you something to eat." Nora held out a tin plate like a peace offering. "You hardly touched your dinner."

Luke had been too exhausted to eat. Soon after leaving the Narrows with its serpent inhabitants behind, they had said farewell to the Little Blue, the river they had followed for days, and trudged over low sand hills—a strenuous twenty-mile trek without creeks, water, or trees for shade to rest in. After a sleepless night, sweating with the remnants of a fever, Luke hadn't had any appetite. And she, like every other emigrant, had long since gotten tired of beans and salt pork, day after day.

But when Nora set the plate down next to Luke, it wasn't leftover dinner.

"What's this?" Luke mumbled around the first forkful. Sweetness exploded on her tongue, and she hummed as she swallowed.

"Fried dried apples with cinnamon," Nora said with a proud smile.

Though Luke would never admit it, she had a sweet tooth, and she made short work of the dessert. Finally, she offered Nora the empty plate. "Thank you. After that steady diet of beans and pork, it was a real treat."

Nora took the plate but didn't stand and walk away as Luke had expected. Instead, she settled down next to Luke.

What does she want? She peeked at Nora from beneath the brim of her hat.

A spray of sparks popped up from the fire, and they both watched them float back to earth.

"How's the leg?" Nora finally broke the silence.

"Fine," Luke answered.

Nora looked at her, clearly expecting more of an answer.

"The swelling has finally gone down," Luke said.

"Do you already feel good enough to stand guard?" Nora peered at her more closely than Luke would have liked.

Luke was not used to someone worrying about her. She wasn't sure whether she should be annoyed or thankful. "I told you. I'm fine. I can't very well advise the captain to double the guard and then refuse to take a turn."

"Bill Larson did," Nora said.

Luke held herself back from spitting into the fire. She was coming to detest Larson. He was always starting fights, avoiding the most hated male chores like chasing lost stock and standing guard at night, and if Luke wasn't mistaken, he was beating his wife. "I wouldn't want to do the same things that Larson does."

Nora's gaze met her own.

So she knows about the beatings. Nora had never said anything about it. *She probably thinks it's his right as her husband to treat her however he sees fit.* Many people in the wagon train thought like that, so they looked the other way.

A loud howl interrupted the awkward silence.

Nora stared into the darkness as if trying to pinpoint the source of the howling. "Wolves?"

While traveling along the Little Blue River, the emigrants had grown used to the company of wolves at night. But this time, Luke wasn't so sure. "That or Pawnees."

"Pawnees?" Nora pulled her knees to her chest and wrapped her arms around her legs. She shivered. "You mean Indians made that noise?"

Luke shrugged. "It's possible. This is Pawnee country, and in this area, between the Little Blue and the Platte, they like to do most of their thieving."

"They're thieves?"

So far, they had mainly encountered the so-called civilized tribes, the Shawnee and the Potawatomi. These tribes spoke English, had learned the white man's customs, and had become farmers.

"It's a sport for their young braves," Luke said. "They don't attack outright. They're clever and silent, so you don't notice that your horses are gone until the next morning. It's said that they can almost steal a horse from under its rider."

"Why the howling, then?"

She's a clever one. "They make all that noise to hide their advance. You'll never hear rustling grass or the snap of a dry branch when wolves are howling all around you."

Nora turned her head and looked at her, making Luke want to squirm under the intensity of her gaze. "How do you know so much about all the things along the Oregon Trail?"

Luke shrugged. "Ah, I've been around."

"You don't like to talk about yourself, do you?"

It wasn't really a question, so Luke didn't bother with an answer.

"Do you mind if I ask a question anyway?"

Luke sighed but had to suppress a smile nonetheless. On the surface, Nora was as submissive and as eager to please as Luke had expected from a woman who had worked in a brothel. But if you looked a little closer, you got glimpses of a courageous and caring woman. "I mind, but you can ask anyway."

"What made you give up your military career and want to leave the States? I mean, what are you gonna do in Oregon?"

Luke was not used to explaining her decisions. As an officer, she had never had to justify her orders. Before she'd joined the dragoons, her decisions had affected only her and no one else. *It's not only you anymore. She's your wife.* The word still sounded strange. *She's got a right to know why you're dragging her across the country.* "I felt like the dragoons didn't have anything to offer me anymore." She had joined the military because she wanted order, structure, and stability in her life, but as she grew older and more secure in herself, that need began to fade. Now she wanted to make it on her own. "I saw Oregon when I led an expedition after the Cayuse Wars, and it's good land with fertile soil in the Willamette Valley."

Nora frowned. "You're a farmer?"

Luke shook her head. She couldn't imagine spending her life farming. Many of their fellow travelers were farmers, but not Luke. "No. I want to raise horses, not crops. I plan on building a horse farm."

Nora lowered her head, dragging a branch through the ashes of the fire. "Horses, huh?"

"Yeah."

Nora snapped the stick apart and hurled the pieces into the fire. "You couldn't have picked a worse wife for a horse rancher than me."

It was true. Nora had no experience with horses; that much was obvious. She couldn't even ride, but that didn't bother Luke. She had never thought further than reaching Oregon. A wife had never been part of her plans. In her mind, she would be alone when she was going to build a log house, when she dug a well, and when the first foal was born. She couldn't imagine sharing her life with someone when she couldn't share who she really was. But she also couldn't just leave Nora and Amy upon reaching Oregon. An inexperienced woman and a child alone wouldn't make it through the first winter.

Maybe she'll find someone who'll care for her. There are a lot of bachelors in Oregon who would give their right hand for a beautiful wife like her. "You'll learn whatever you have to in order to survive," she said.

Nora turned her head to look at her. Her green eyes appeared almost black in the light of the slowly dying fire. "Like I always have."

Luke cleared her throat, uncomfortable with Nora's allusion to her job as a prostitute. It was clear that Nora still thought her and Amy's survival depended solely on herself. Part of Luke wanted to tell Nora she could depend on her, but she couldn't make such promises— not when she knew Nora would go her own way if she ever discovered Luke's secret.

Another howl came out of the darkness. Nora shivered. "I think I'll turn in now."

Luke watched her walk away until she disappeared into the night.

PLATTE RIVER,
MAY 25TH, 1851

Nora's wagon topped a rise. She halted the oxen next to the other wagons and looked down across the prairie. In the distance, she could make out a line of white shapes that marked another wagon train, and beyond that, a broad, muddy river formed lazy S's.

After miles and miles of only level prairie and the dust of the sand hills, the Platte River was a welcome sight. The oxen seemed to sense the water, and they quickened their steps.

As they neared the river, Nora studied the valley of the Platte that would provide the path they would follow westward for more than a month.

"Good thing we don't have to cross the river," Jacob Garfield said. "Looks as broad as the Missouri."

The captain reined in his gelding next to them. "Yeah, they say the Platte is a mile wide and an inch deep."

Nora couldn't tell the river's depth just by looking at it. Its color resembled more that of coffee than that of clear water.

Grass covered the plains on either side of the river, ensuring that their livestock would find enough to eat. Nora detected no trees along the banks of the Platte, though. How would they build a fire tonight?

Then she flicked the whip again and grinned as something occurred to her. Only a few short weeks ago, she would have naïvely enjoyed the sight of the river without wondering about such practical things like feed for the animals or wood for a fire.

"Mama, look!" Amy peeked out of the wagon and pointed forward. "Dat's where the piwats live."

Nora looked into the direction her daughter indicated. The river flowed around a long island, bigger than any of the others. It went on for miles and was covered with grass and dense timber. *Ah, there's wood on the islands.*

She nearly forgot about Amy's comment until Luke directed his mare around the wagon and asked, "Piwats? Is that a native tribe I'm not aware of?"

Nora grinned. "I think she means pirates. I've read her a bedtime story yesterday where a bunch of pirates lived on an island."

"There are no pirates on Grand Island, I'm afraid, but there's a fort at the western end of it." Luke winked at the girl in the wagon.

Bernice Garfield strode over, her skirts rustling loudly, while Emeline Larson followed more meekly behind her. "Have you heard?" Bernice grinned from ear to ear. "We'll reach the fort by this evening. We can visit together and see what their stores have to offer. Maybe they have fresh apples, so we could bake a pie."

Nora smiled at her older friend's enthusiasm. She glanced at Luke, knowing that she was expected to get his permission.

Luke nodded without hesitation.

"Great!" Bernice clapped her hands. "We're going."

Nora looked at Emeline, who was hanging her head. "Don't worry if you don't have any money to spend. We're all just looking at things for the most part. We don't have much to spend either."

Emeline didn't meet her eyes. "It's not the money. Bill doesn't want me to go. He says I'm to stay here and keep an eye on the wagon."

"What?" Bernice crossed her arms over her ample chest. "But no one stays here except for a few guards, the sick, and the old."

"He doesn't want me to go," Emeline said in a whisper.

Bernice still couldn't let it go. "But why?"

Emeline picked a piece of lint from her apron. "I don't know. He didn't say."

I bet I know why he doesn't want her to visit the fort. Nora pressed her lips together. *He wants complete control over her.* Her father had been the same, and she had encountered a lot of men like Bill Larson since she had left her parents' home.

"I could talk to your husband," Luke said. "If he doesn't think it's safe for you to go alone, I could accompany you ladies to the fort."

Nora looked at him. She studied his face, noticing the fine lines that touched the outer corners of his eyes. *That's sweet. Sweet, but clueless.* "That's not a good idea, Luke."

He blinked. "Why not?"

Nora sighed. How could she explain that to an honorable man who would never beat his wife or control every aspect of her life? She knew that any attempt to intervene on behalf of Emeline would result in even more complications for the shy woman. Bill Larson would take his anger about them butting into his business out on his wife. *Luke is a man. He has never thought about what power a man holds over his wife, because he just takes it for granted. Bill Larson is Emmy's husband, and he has the right to decide. There's nothing we can do about it.*

"Please, don't," Emeline said. She clutched Luke's sleeve, then let go as if only now becoming aware of it and backed away. "It's all right. I don't feel up to going anyway. I think I might be with child." She forced a smile onto her lips.

With child? Nora stared at her. It should have been a joyful occasion, but Nora couldn't help worrying. She couldn't imagine Bill Larson as a loving father. Would he beat the child as he beat Emeline? But even if he did, what other options did Emeline have than to stay with him?

"Well," Bernice said after an awkward pause, "then we'll bring you back some nice fabric for baby clothes from the fort."

Bernice Garfield nearly skipped across Fort Keary's parade ground, behaving like a girl when a circus came to town and she got to see an elephant for the first time.

Nora trudged after her, still thinking about Emeline. *Having a baby in the wilderness, with no doctor nearby, and then tending to a baby during the first winter in Oregon...* She smoothed her hands over her apron. *Not a good idea, especially if you have a husband like Bill Larson.* But Emeline didn't have a choice. She was at her husband's mercy. *Just like me.*

The fort was not as impressive as she had imagined and couldn't distract her from her glum thoughts. Instead of a walled fortification, Fort Kearny was a collection of rugged sod huts, a few adobe buildings, a store, a small post office, a blacksmith, and a crude hospital. Most soldiers were unshaven and wore patched-up uniforms, and many of them were not much more than homesick young boys.

Prices were too high for Nora and most others to buy anything, but they planned on visiting other wagon trains later and trade their excess supplies for things they needed.

"Well, at least there's a post office," Bernice said. "We can send off our letters and tell our families that we made it safely so far."

Unlike most of their fellow emigrants, Nora had no family anxiously awaiting news from her, but she had already penned a letter to Tess and the other girls. She turned to Luke. While almost every other man and woman on the train had been writing letters last night, he had busied himself with carving another wooden animal for Amy. "Is there no family you want to write to?"

"No."

"What about friends? I know that Tess would love to hear from you." Nora didn't understand why he tried to constantly hold himself apart from other people.

Luke sent her a dark gaze. "I don't have time for such sentimentalities."

Only weeks ago, Nora would have flinched back from his anger and apologized, but since leaving Independence, she had gotten glimpses of his gentle nature, and she was no longer afraid of him. Most often, his gruffness served to hide any insecurities on his part.

He shoved his hands into the pockets of his pants and lengthened his strides to walk away from her.

"Wait!" Nora lifted her skirt a bit and hurried to keep pace with his long strides.

He slowed down but didn't look at her.

"You can't write, can you?" she said.

"I can write just fine."

Nora had been born into a wealthy family and had a good education. She was very aware that he must feel like a stupid fool in comparison to her. "I know that you can sign your name," she said, thinking back to their wedding day when he had signed the certificate, "and for most people, that's all they ever need to be able to do." Growing up, Nora had dreamed of becoming a teacher. Her father wouldn't hear of it, though. He had sternly insisted that no Macauley woman had ever needed to work and that he would provide anything she needed until she married and then her husband would take over that role. Her mother had taken his side. After all, men didn't like women who were more intelligent than they were. They didn't marry a woman for her intelligence; they married for beauty, docility, and house-holding skills. Her father had often yelled at her whenever he caught her with a book in her hands, accusing her of daydreaming. For the last three years, her parents' advice had proven true. The brothel's customers paid well for beauty and submissiveness, but most didn't care about having a well-read, intelligent conversationalist.

She didn't know why, but something about Luke made her hope that he was different from all the other men. He hadn't married her to have a beautiful bed partner or a skilled housewife, so maybe he would come to appreciate her other talents. Hesitantly, Nora peeked up at Luke. "If you want to, I could teach you to write and to read."

"We'll see," Luke said. "I doubt that we'll have time for that."

Nora didn't say anything else, not daring to pressure him.

When they reached the post office, Luke muttered something about having to see the blacksmith and hurried off.

Nora threw a glance back, making sure that Amy was following her with Hannah, and entered behind Bernice.

A long line had already formed in front of the counter. Nora looked around, trying to distract herself from her aching feet. On the whitewashed adobe wall in front of them hung a poster, and Nora began to read while they waited. The poster informed her that the Donation Land Claim Act, which had become law just last fall, granted a hundred and sixty acres of land in the Oregon Territory to every single white man who staked out his land and filed a claim. A married man could claim another hundred and sixty acres for his wife. Nora stared at the poster, forgetting about the letter in her hand. *A man can claim twice the amount of land if he's married?* Nora hadn't known about that law, as she knew very little about life in Oregon. *Is that why Luke married me? To get more land for his horse farm?*

Finally, it all made sense to Nora. Why else would a man marry a woman without an even passing interest in sharing her bed? He had married her for strictly practical, egoistic reasons. Nora had assumed that from the start, refusing to believe that he harbored any romantic feelings toward her, but now that she knew for sure that her gentle, kind husband had only used her like every other man, it felt like a punch to her stomach. *Why did you allow yourself to think that he might be any different from the rest of 'em? You should know better.*

A frightening thought occurred to her. *Will he try to divorce and abandon me once he owns that extra quarter section of land?* Then another thought came, and she clutched at the wall to keep her balance. *He doesn't even have to get a divorce. He can have an annulment because we never consummated the marriage. That's why he refused to lie with me. Does he plan on just leaving me and Amy to our own devices once we've reached Oregon?*

Every bit of excitement about sending off her letter had vanished as she worried about her future and began to frantically think of ways to prevent Luke from filing for an annulment.

PLATTE RIVER,
MAY 26TH, 1851

Luke left her mare behind and tiptoed through the grass, listening intently. The wind howled, but she was far away enough from the wagon train not to hear anything else.

After leaving Fort Kearny, they had traveled uphill along the sandy left side of the Platte. Now it was almost dark. Only campfires glowed on both sides of the river in the distance. Sweat and sand clung to Luke's skin and made her itch. Her clothes smelled of smoke and buffalo chips, the dried dung they used to build fires in the absence of wood. Clouds of mosquitoes made her even more miserable.

When they had encamped near Twenty Islands, two dozen islands of varying size, for the night, Luke had decided to risk a quick bath in the river tonight. This might be her last chance for many miles because the treeless country ahead would provide no cover for her.

After glancing left and right to make sure she was alone, she pulled off her boots and pants and waded into the yellowish water of the Platte. She rounded a small island, hiding behind its trees and shrubbery. When she was sure that no one had followed her, she continued to undress. She slipped off her shirt and hung her clothes on the branches of a tree to prevent them from getting wet. After pausing to listen into the darkness once again, she lifted her hands to the bindings around her chest. Slowly, she unwrapped them.

Goose bumps formed on her chest. She looked down at herself and smoothed her hands over the lines that the broad strips of fabric had carved into her skin. She splashed water onto her chest and watched as drops ran down her small breasts.

Sometimes she went for days without consciously thinking about the fact that she was not a man until moments like this reminded her of what she was—and what she was not.

The last month on the road had shown her that she was not really "one of the boys." She had kept herself at a distance from the men on the train, especially those who secretly indulged in drinking and gambling whenever the captain looked the other way. She was not a man, but she didn't want to live the life of a woman either. She felt as if she was stuck somewhere in the middle, not really a part of either world. Nora and Amy had eased her loneliness a bit, but she still couldn't relax around them, and she saw no chance that this would ever change. As long as she had to hide a major part of her identity, no true emotional intimacy could develop, and she didn't plan on revealing her secret to Nora or anyone else.

Measles nickered softly.

Luke's head jerked up. Her heart hammered. Hastily, she wrapped the bindings back around her chest and pulled them tight. When she heard footfalls come closer, she ducked behind the shrubbery. Luke had lived with horses long enough to know who had found them out here. Horses generally had little to say to humans, so Measles's nickering probably meant that the mare hoped for some delicious treat from a person she knew.

Nora. For a woman without any experience with horses, Nora sure had a soft spot for the gentle beasts. Luke snatched her shirt from the tree and quickly slipped it on.

Water splashed, and then Nora's voice reached her through the darkness. "Luke? Are you out there?"

Luke hesitated for a second, but she didn't want to scare Nora by not answering. "Yes, I'm here." She waded back through the shallow water and joined Nora on the river's bank. Nora's gaze seemed to burn her skin as she quickly pulled up her pants and closed the top button on her shirt.

"What were you doing out here on your own?" Nora tucked her hand into the bend of Luke's arm as if they were out on a stroll along the river.

"That's the question I should ask you," Luke said with a stern tone. She didn't like to stress her domination and make Nora feel inferior, but at times like this, being thought of as a man came in handy. It gave her the freedom to do whatever she wanted, whenever she wanted. Nora had to answer to her husband, but not the other way around.

Nora's warm hand wandered up her arm. "I've been searching for you. I missed you."

Luke narrowed her eyes. She had seen that act often enough to know that Nora was once again falling back into her role as a prostitute. *What the hell is she doing? I thought we got that over and done with.* "I just needed a bath," she said.

"It seems I found you just in time to help." Nora's fingers skimmed over Luke's shoulder and reopened the first button of her shirt.

Luke tried to pull away. "I already had my bath."

Nora didn't listen. She leaned forward and pressed soft lips against the skin that the opened button revealed.

Heat shot up and down from that place just below Luke's collarbones. "Nora!" she got out, partly a warning, partly a groan.

Ignoring the warning part, Nora pressed closer until Luke felt the warmth of her body against her own.

Luke's eyes threatened to close. Her rational mind fought against her bodily instincts that were telling her to wrap her arms around Nora and pull her even closer. In a haze, she felt Nora undo another button.

The soft lips wandered lower, caressing the skin of Luke's upper chest.

Luke swayed.

Nora's teasing tongue created a blazing path downward.

Luke moaned, knowing that she had to stop this, but not really wanting to.

Nora scraped her fingernails lightly over Luke's neck and traced the rim of a sensitive ear before following the path of her lips.

With a groan, Luke pulled back from the gentle touch. "Wait!" One more button and Nora would encounter the bindings and become suspicious.

"Why? It's just you and me out here. Amy is asleep and with the Garfields." Nora stepped forward into Luke's space and reached for the buttons of her shirt again.

Luke sidestepped her and captured her wrists, careful not to hurt her in the process of trying to escape her seduction. "Stop it, Nora. I mean it."

Nora bit her lip and hung her head like a rejected child. For a moment, Luke thought she would just turn around and slink away, but then Nora looked up, and a hint of defiance shone through the tears in her eyes. "Why? I'm your lawfully wedded wife, Lucas Hamilton. Tell me one good reason why we shouldn't do this."

No, you're not Lucas's wife, and I doubt that anything about this marriage is really lawful. Luke's thoughts raced. What should she say? She couldn't very well tell Nora the actual reasons for refusing to sleep with her. "Nora…"

"Is it because…? Did you get hurt in the war?" Nora asked.

The question caught Luke off guard. *What does the war have to do with this? And how does she even know I fought in the war? Did Tess tell her? And what else did she tell her about me?* Knots formed in her stomach. "How do you know that I fought in Mexico?" She eyed Nora.

Nora looked down and tugged at her skirt. "Well, when the guard shot you, you said something about 'war hero Luke Hamilton.' And sometimes you're crying out and talking in your sleep."

Luke froze. *I'm talking in my sleep? That's not good, not good at all.* What if she accidentally gave away her secret while she slept? She took a deep breath and forced the panic down, concentrating on Nora's words instead. "And you think I got hurt in the war?"

"Yes, um…" Nora gestured down Luke's body, nodding toward the padding that Luke wore in her pants. "Did you maybe suffer an injury of certain…important body parts? Because if that's the case, there are other ways to make love to a woman, you know? And

I'm an excellent teacher if I do say so myself." She gave Luke the rakish grin that Luke had seen hundreds of times on the faces of various prostitutes when she was growing up.

For a few seconds, Luke just stared at her. Nora was so much blunter than the officers' wives and daughters in Fort Leavenworth. Luke wasn't sure whether this was a good or a bad thing. At the moment, it was mainly embarrassing. "No," she choked out. "No important body part of mine suffered any lasting injury in the war."

"All right." Nora nodded. She studied Luke intently. "What is it, then?"

Luke suppressed a groan. *Damn. I should have told her that I had a disabling injury and left it at that. But no, that damn pseudo male pride wouldn't allow that, huh?* She didn't know how to answer Nora's question without revealing her true identity, so she used her husbandly dominance as a last resort. "I don't want to. That's all you need to know. End of discussion."

"I think I know the reason," Nora whispered, facing the ground.

Luke swallowed against the lump that had developed in her throat. She doubted that Nora knew the true reason, but her heart began to thump anyway, pounding in her ears until she almost missed what Nora said next.

"You want to have our marriage annulled once we reach Oregon. I saw the poster."

"Poster?" Luke was too stunned to do much more than repeat the last word of Nora's revelation. She shook her head to clear it. "You saw a poster that said I want to get an annulment in Oregon?"

Nora dug the tip of her boot into the muddy riverbank. "It said that as a married man, you're entitled to twice the amount of land that you could claim as a bachelor."

She must have read a poster about the Donation Land Claim Act and immediately assumed that it was the reason why I married her. Luke couldn't fault Nora for thinking that. *She must have figured it all out in her mind: As soon as I claimed the land in her name, I'd abandon her and the child and keep the land for myself.*

So far, getting an annulment hadn't occurred to Luke, because she hadn't really thought about what would happen once they reached Oregon. Whenever she thought about the future, she had never pictured herself living with someone, sharing bed and table, even if that was what was traditionally expected of husband and wife. "Those hundred and sixty acres would be in your name," Luke said. "So even if we separate, the land is yours. Maybe getting an annulment would be for the best."

Nora's eyes widened. "But what would happen to Amy and me? We can't survive in a strange, wild land all on our own."

"No. That's not what I meant. I won't just leave you while you still need me." Luke stopped as she realized what she had just said. *They need me.*

"While we still need you?" Nora echoed. "We will always need you. The West is no place for a woman and a child living on their own."

Luke knew that better than anyone else. If anyone suspected her true gender, she would never have the chance to build a new life for herself out west. A single woman would have to find a husband or work as a schoolteacher or a seamstress to survive, but no one would employ an unmarried woman who had a child out of wedlock. Without a husband, Nora would soon be working as a prostitute again. "If we annul the marriage, you're free to find yourself another husband," Luke said. "With your good looks and the number of unmarried men in Oregon, you could have another husband in a matter of days if not hours." *Someone who can really make you happy. Someone who can share your bed and give you children. Someone who doesn't have to keep secrets from you.*

Nora shook her head. "Why would I want to take another husband? I'm already married to you, and marrying another man wouldn't improve my situation."

Luke almost had to smile at Nora's practical mind. Nora didn't associate marriage with love. All she really wanted was someone who would take care of her and be kind to her daughter. *From Nora's point of view, I must be the perfect husband. She doesn't want to take the risk of marrying another man who might be abusive.* This discussion would get them nowhere. With a sigh, she took Measles's reins. "We should get back before I get shot by our own guard again."

She looked back over her shoulder and saw Nora follow silently behind her. She knew that Nora would try to seduce her again. Seduction had been her primary means of survival for so long that she knew no other way to convince Luke of her worth as a woman and wife. The journey to Oregon would be a long one indeed.

SOUTH PLATTE CROSSING, JUNE 10TH, 1851

Nora chuckled as she watched her daughter make a game out of gathering buffalo chips. Since traveling along the Platte, the scarcity of wood had forced them to resort to using dry buffalo dung for building fires. After leaving Fort Kearny, the landscape had changed. Long, green grass had given way to short, brown grass, and the road was very sandy. Sagebrush and thin-bladed yucca plants had taken the place of the cottonwoods.

Amy and the other girls raced around their camp, trying to see who could fill the sack hanging from the side of their wagons the fastest. Nora had gathered chips all day while she walked because she knew that they would burn so rapidly that she would need three whole baskets to cook their dinner.

She grinned to herself. Just a few weeks ago, she would have refused to touch the dried buffalo droppings with her smooth hands that were a requirement for her former profession. Now her hands were covered in calluses, and she picked up the buffalo chips without hesitation.

She winked at Bernice as she carried another basket back to the camp. "More wood of the cow."

Bernice laughed. "Gives the food its own special touch, doesn't it?"

"Oh, yes." *If Mother could see me now, she would be horrified.* But then again, her mother would have been horrified about a lot of things Nora had done in the last three years. Nora directed her thoughts back to the task at hand. She dug a trench to prevent the wind from blowing away the burning chips, then lit a fire with a skillful stroke of flint and steel. What a difference to her first pitiful attempt at building a fire.

Under Luke's patient guidance and with Bernice's help, she had learned a lot about living on the trail. Since her last failed attempt to seduce her husband, she had even tripled her efforts to learn. She wanted to be the best wife he could wish for and make herself indispensable for him until he no longer thought about annulling their marriage.

While Bill Larson in the wagon behind them constantly complained that eating his wife's food was like chewing shoe leather, Luke had repeatedly praised Nora's pancakes, and he always took a second helping of her stew.

Learning to cook over the campfire was even more challenging than Nora had thought. Her first attempts at baking bread had resulted in a lump that was burned on the outside and still doughy on the inside, but now she was finally beginning to master it.

Nora ignored the shouting that once again came from the Larsons' wagon while she chopped up bits of antelope meat and added it to the boiling pot of beans. Finally, she seasoned the meal with wild onions that she had found while she walked.

She spread freshly churned butter on a slice of bread and handed it to Amy.

Buttered bread in hand, Amy ran toward the riverbank. Nora tensed when she saw her running toward the river's edge until she noticed that Luke was standing there, talking with some of the other men. Luke's initially nonexistent protective instincts had gotten much better in the last few weeks. Nora blew out a breath as he caught Amy before she could slip in the mud near the water. He swung her up into his arms and playfully took a bite from her bread before he sent her back to the wagons.

Sometimes, he still seemed a little clumsy and uncomfortable when dealing with a child, but he treated Amy with a patience and gentleness that she had never witnessed from a man toward a child that was not his own. He might act tough and aloof, but Nora sensed his sensitivity and compassion.

She didn't love him—and had never expected to—but she was convinced that she would never find a better husband, and she was determined to wear him down until he gave in. If her job in Tess's brothel had taught her one thing, it was to be perceptive about the wants and desires of the men she had serviced. That night at the river, she had sensed that he was not as indifferent toward her feminine charms as he pretended to be.

When she saw the men walk back toward the camp, she began to ladle the stew onto tin plates.

Jacob Garfield and three of the other men took their own plates from their wives but then walked over to the Hamilton fire. "That's one crossing that shouldn't be too difficult," one of the men said. "What do you think, Luke?"

The three men stopped eating and looked up from their plates, waiting for Luke's answer.

Luke scooped a large forkful of beans into his mouth and chewed thoroughly as if stalling for an answer.

Nora had often watched how he kept himself apart from his fellow travelers, never taking part in any of the social gatherings. She didn't understand his tendency to keep people at a distance. After being shunned by the citizens of Independence and the forced seclusion of her life in the brothel, she enjoyed being part of a community.

On the trail, the importance of status and the veneer of respectability faded while they shared their struggle to survive. As Luke's wife, she even enjoyed a certain standing in the wagon train. Despite his attempts to separate himself from the rest of them, the others came to him for advice. He seemed to know even more than the captain about the Oregon Trail and all the things they encountered on their journey. With every mile, he became more and more of a natural leader for them.

Nora studied him while he sat with the other men. Most of the men were taller, but Luke had a powerful, if unassuming presence to him. He was a man of few words, but when he spoke, everyone listened. Nora took a certain pride in belonging to a husband like that.

"Don't underestimate the South Platte," Luke said.

"Hamilton, you yellowbelly!" Bill Larson strutted over to their fire and looked down at Luke as if Luke were a handful of buffalo dung. "You are not afraid of that little river, are you? It's shallow, with gentle banks, and not moving too fast. But, of course, if you're scared, I could take your wagon and your wife over for you."

The other men around the fire tensed, but Luke never even looked up. He kept eating as if Larson had never spoken.

A part of Nora was glad that her husband was too levelheaded to engage in fistfights. In the brothel, she had seen so many brawls that she didn't find them heroic anymore. But another part of her couldn't understand that he would sit quietly while Larson insulted him. He hadn't even reacted to Larson's thinly veiled threat to take Nora away from him.

Nora shuddered, and her stomach flipped at the mere thought of that.

"All I'm saying is that we should be careful," Luke said without raising his voice or looking at Bill Larson. "The river bottom is partly quicksand, and if a wagon gets mired down in it…"

Nora looked at the deceivingly harmless river. She had learned to trust Luke's assessment, and that made her dread the river crossing. Still, they had no choice but to cross the river. The Platte River divided into a north and a south branch at this point, and they had to cross the South Platte to gain access to the north branch of the river, which would lead them west.

After the midday meal, they raised the beds of the wagons a few inches by putting blocks under them. Nora hoped that it would be enough to keep their belongings and the food that was stored in the wagon dry.

Bill Larson's wagon was the first in line to cross. They double-teamed, so that now six yoke of oxen were pulling the wagon across the river. Walking next to the wagon, Larson forced the oxen through the murky water with an iron hand.

As they had learned to do, the wagon crossed at an angle, first going downstream, then upstream so that they would land across the river from where they had started. When Larson reached the middle of the river, he turned the oxen upstream to finish the crossing. He paused for a moment, throwing a triumphant glance back at Luke, who was watching from the bank.

"Keep them moving, or you'll get stuck," Luke shouted.

Larson flicked his whip. The oxen strained against the harness but didn't succeed in moving the wagon forward. The wagon wheels only sank deeper into the quicksand of the riverbed. The more Larson yelled and the more the oxen struggled to free themselves, the more the sand held and sucked them deeper. Water smashed against the wagon, nearly upsetting it. The oxen bellowed.

"He's mired," Luke shouted and waved at his neighbors. "Jacob, Tom, Gus. I need some help here." Without hesitation, he waded into the river.

The three other men followed him.

The water rose on Luke's chest as he struggled against the current to reach the mired wagon.

Nora watched with growing concern. She clutched Amy's hand when Luke and the other men finally had to swim.

"Mama." Amy looked up at her with wide eyes.

"It's all right, sweetie." Nora gently stroked the red curls. "Luke will be back soon. He'll be fine." She prayed that fate wouldn't make her a liar.

The current nearly swept Luke past the wagon. At the last moment, he grabbed hold of the wagon box. He straightened and shook himself.

The three other men reached the wagon and clung to it too.

"Grab the wheels, boys," Luke shouted. "Bill, move the oxen!"

They put their shoulders to the wheels.

For a moment, nothing happened. Then the wagon shot forward.

Tom Buchanan lost his hold on the wheel and splashed into the river. He reappeared a few yards downstream and managed to make his way back to shore.

Nora breathed a sigh of relief when Luke swam back and finally emerged from the river, stumbling up the bank in sodden clothes. With Amy at her side, she ran to meet him halfway. She had planned on offering him dry clothes, but instead she found herself saying something else. "Why did you risk your life for him?" She jerked her head in the direction of Bill Larson, who had safely reached the other side by now. "Just an hour ago, he called you a coward in front of the entire wagon train, and now you…" Nora trailed off, feeling as if she didn't understand her husband one iota better than on the day she had met him.

He certainly didn't understand how afraid she was that something would happen to him, leaving her and Amy without a protector and provider.

He looked up, pushing wet strands of hair from his face with a weary hand. "I didn't," he said as he fell into step next to her.

Nora shot him an incredulous glance.

"I didn't do it for Larson," Luke said. "I did it for his wife."

Nora stopped walking for a second, then hastened to catch up with him. "You wouldn't have swum out to rescue him if Emeline hadn't been in the wagon?"

Luke didn't answer.

He didn't need to, as far as Nora was concerned. She was certain that she already knew. *He would have waded out to save Larson's life. He's just that kind of man.* She wasn't sure whether that was a good or a bad thing. "You should change into some dry clothes," she said as they reached their wagon.

Luke shook his head. "No sense in that. I have to wade right back in, 'cause we're the next to cross the river." He glanced inside the wagon. "We should leave a few things behind to make the wagon lighter. Every extra ounce could cause us to get stuck."

Nora swallowed. The abandoned items that littered the side of the trail had become an everyday occurrence. She had seen stoves, trunks, anvils, china plates, and even food left behind to lighten the load of the weary oxen, but this would be the first time that she had to leave something behind.

She turned back the flap and looked into the wagon, studying each item. Unlike most other emigrants, Luke had packed wisely and without overloading the wagon, so now she was at a complete loss as to what she should discard.

She didn't dare to leave any of the sacks or kegs of food behind. The cooking utensils, Luke's weapons, their bedding, and some extra clothing were also indispensable, and they would need the tools once they reached Oregon.

With a sigh, Nora lifted the fine linens that Tess had given her as a wedding gift as well as the heavy trunk that came with them and set both down on the sandy ground. After a second's hesitation, she put her leather-bound diary down on top of it. Quickly, she turned around before she could change her mind.

Her heart pounding in her throat, Nora perched on the wagon seat with Amy behind her in the wagon. She stared down as their wagon reached the river's edge and began to travel through the moving mass of sand that was the river bottom. The water became deeper and deeper as they traversed the river diagonally down with the current. She glanced longingly at the other side, more than three-quarters of a mile away.

A few times, she felt sand give way beneath the wheels, jarring the wagon, but Luke kept the oxen moving. If they stopped for even a moment, the wheels would bog down.

Amy squeaked when a flood of water soaked her feet, but then they were finally past the halfway point, and Luke turned the oxen, making them struggle back up against the current. After forty endless minutes, they reached the opposite bank.

By the time all wagons were safely on the other side of the river, the oxen and mules were exhausted. Each animal had been double-teamed and used repeatedly to haul the wagons across. As soon as the last wagon struggled up the bank, Captain McLoughlin gave the go-ahead to make camp for the rest of the day.

Luke disappeared into the wagon while Nora was busy building a fire. When she put on a pot of coffee to brew, Emeline Larson's surprised gasp came from the wagon. "Oh, I…I'm sorry. I didn't know. I just wanted to…"

Nora turned to see what was going on.

Luke emerged from the wagon, quickly closing the top button on his shirt and slipping into the vest, while Emeline Larson looked away.

Nora grinned when she saw both of them blush. *Have I ever been that innocent?*

"I just came over to tell you…to thank you," Emeline stammered, still not raising her gaze to Luke's face. "You saved our wagon today…and probably our lives."

Luke nearly crumpled his hat between his hands and studied the tips of his boots. "You don't need to thank me, ma'am." He seemed almost embarrassed at Emeline's thankfulness, and if Nora hadn't known how confident he could be, she would have thought he was shy. Once again, she wondered just how much experience with women he had. Had he ever lain with a woman besides Tess?

"Here," Luke said, pressing something into Nora's hands as he shouldered past her on his way to take care of the oxen.

When Nora looked down, she discovered that she was holding her leather-bound diary that she had left behind on the other side of the river. Smoothing her hands over the leather, she looked up at Luke with a question in her eyes.

Luke seemed to feel her gaze on him. He shrugged and said back over his shoulder, "I threw out two cans of peaches instead."

Canned peaches. Nora pressed the diary against her chest. *He can't read, so the diary holds no importance to him, yet he traded it for the canned peaches.* She knew it was quite a sacrifice for the man with the sweet tooth.

"He's a good man," Emeline Larson whispered next to her.

Nora saw the longing and the sadness in her eyes. She just nodded. *Better than yours, you mean.* With a sigh, she went back to work.

California Hill,
June 11th, 1851

Nora gasped for breath, struggling to keep up with Bernice as they trudged up a long, steep grade. After crossing the South Platte, the scenery had changed from flat, open prairie to steep hills with deep ruts. Nora was so exhausted that she sometimes nodded off while sitting down for a bowl of beans and pork at noon. *This is the first hilly terrain since Blue Mound. You just have to get used to it again.*

She had attempted to ride in the wagon for a while, but the constant jolting motion of the wagon had made her queasy, so she had climbed back down. Wiping a damp strand of hair away from her overheated face, she looked back over her shoulder and gave Luke a small nod. She was glad that he had offered to carry Amy because if she was honest with herself, she wouldn't have been able to carry the extra weight up the hill.

After what seemed like hours to Nora, the terrain finally stretched out into a high, flat tableland. She gratefully accepted the canteen that Bernice offered her. "Thanks." She took a large swallow. The tepid water made her gag, so she handed the canteen back.

"You can take a little more," Bernice said.

"No, it's all right." Nora wiped her mouth, hoping that her nervous stomach would finally settle down. "Luke said that we won't find fresh water until we reach the North Platte tonight. We have to make do with what we have."

Bernice gripped her elbow and turned her around to face her. "Are you all right?" She lightly cupped her cheek, and for a moment, Nora allowed herself to lean into the motherly touch. "I noticed you barely touched your breakfast this morning."

Nora swallowed. Her stomach roiled at the mere thought of food. "I'm fine."

The older woman squinted at her. "Do you have a stomach ache?"

With a sigh, Nora nodded. "It's not too bad. Probably just all these beans we're eating."

"Vomiting?" Bernice asked.

Nora hesitated. *Anyone would have vomited after traveling in that stuffy, bumpy wagon, right?*

"Convulsions?"

"Excuse me?"

"Diarrhea?" Bernice asked.

Nora shook her head. Whatever might have been going on with her, she hadn't experienced that. "What are you getting at?"

"Well, you know what they've told us about cholera."

Nora's head jerked around, and she swayed for a moment as a wave of dizziness hit her. "You think I have cholera?"

"Are you sure that's not it?" Bernice's brow knitted as she studied her.

"Very sure," Nora said. She hadn't felt quite right for some time, and cholera victims usually were in intense pain within minutes and often dead within hours.

Bernice blew out a breath. "Well, what is it, then?"

Nora had a long, internal battle with herself while they continued to travel over the high plateau. Biting her lip, she turned to see where Luke and Amy were, only to find that Luke had dropped back a bit and was no longer within earshot. He had probably done it on purpose, giving the women some privacy for whatever they might have to discuss. Nora had never encountered a man with that much sensitivity regarding the needs of women.

With a frown, Bernice followed her gaze in Luke's direction. "I don't want to intrude, but is everything all right between you and your husband?"

Nora knew how much courage the simple question must have required. Things between a man and his wife were generally thought to be no one's business but the husband's—even if Nora happened to be miserable in her marriage. She squeezed Bernice's hand while they walked. The older woman had become the first friend she had made for herself on the train. "Everything is fine," she said, praying that this wouldn't change if her suspicion proved to be true. "This has nothing to do with my marriage." She didn't want Bernice to think that Luke was the kind of husband that Bill Larson was.

The expression of concern didn't leave Bernice's face. "What is it, then? There is something wrong with you, no matter what you say."

Nora couldn't deny that any longer even if she had tried to deny it to herself. "I'm not sure." She didn't want to voice her suspicion, maybe because that would lend an air of finality, of reality to it.

Bernice gave her an encouraging nod. "Tell me."

"I'm not sure, but..." Nora looked over her shoulder, making sure that neither Luke nor any other emigrant was within earshot. "Well, I'm not sure, but maybe... There's a possibility that I...I might be pregnant."

"A baby!" Bernice squealed.

"Shhhh!" Nora ducked her head and waved at Bernice to lower her voice.

"A baby," Bernice repeated more quietly. "That's wonderful. Congratulations."

Nora suppressed a grimace. *It might have been if the baby had been my husband's.* She had missed her monthly cycle repeatedly, had been constantly tired, and had experienced bouts of nausea and dizzy spells since before she had left Independence, but she had blamed it on the beating at the hands of a customer and then the strains of the journey. But in the last few weeks, she had also gained weight, and the poor quality of their food sure couldn't explain that, so Nora finally had to face the fact that she was pregnant again.

"Oh, come on, girl." Bernice hugged her, still beaming from ear to ear. "You have every reason to celebrate. Why that long face?"

Nora licked her lips. How could she explain that to the warmhearted older woman without revealing her past? She turned to glance at Luke again.

Bernice followed her gaze. "What did he say? I bet he's—"

"I didn't tell him." Nora had only recently accepted the fact that she was pregnant. She had no idea how to tell Luke. Her life had just begun to go in the right direction, and she didn't want it to change.

Bernice blinked. "What? Why not?" She gave her a disbelieving stare. "Surely you don't believe that he wouldn't want a second child? He clearly adores his daughter. Just think how happy he would be having a son."

Nora pinched the bridge of her nose. It just wasn't that easy. *Nothing in my life ever seems to be. Maybe I'm just not destined for a quiet, happy life.* Yes, Luke had married her, even knowing that she already had a daughter, but another child that was not his own hadn't been part of the equation when he had proposed to her. She still wasn't sure what made him refuse to share her bed even though he wasn't totally indifferent toward her female charms. Her most plausible hypothesis was that he wanted to avoid binding himself to a wife and a child for the long term. If a baby was added to the mix, he would surely attempt to buck that more constant responsibility. She stared at the horizon. "It's complicated."

"Complicated?" Bernice raised thick brows. "What's so complicated about being pregnant?"

"That's hard to explain."

"But you will tell him, right? You can't hide this from your husband."

Nora sighed. She knew that she couldn't go on like this for much longer. Soon, her pregnancy would be obvious even to an unsuspecting man who didn't have Bernice's keen eye for female problems. She had to tell him, but she lacked the courage to do it.

She was still searching for the right words that might magically make Luke not want to run away as soon as she revealed her secret when they reached the edge of the high tableland hours later.

The wagons halted on the edge of the steep slope where the tableland dropped toward the North Platte River below.

Nora gazed down Windlass Hill. She swallowed as she took in the splintered wood and torn canvas that littered the trail down. Could they really make it safely down that steep grade?

Her gaze searched for Luke, automatically looking to him for assurance and practical advice. When he turned toward her, she pinched her cheeks to give them some color. She didn't want him to know how queasy she once again felt.

Luke stepped next to her and lifted a protesting Amy down from his shoulders. "Are you all right?"

Nora had to fight down her rising panic. *It's a harmless question. He doesn't suspect anything.* But how much longer could she hide her pregnancy from him? At times, Luke was surprisingly observant. "I'm fine," she said. "I just wonder how we're ever going to make it down this hill. Bernice said it's called Windlass Hill. Do we really need a windlass?"

"No," Luke said with a small smile. "We're gonna lock the wheels and slowly skid the wagons down by ropes."

Nora watched as the men did exactly that. Captain McLoughlin set the brakes of his wagon, while Luke and Jacob Garfield chained the hind wheels to the wagon box. They tied long ropes to the first wagon, and every available man took up a position behind the wagon, tightly clutching the rope in gloved fists.

Then they urged the oxen forward.

The men holding on to the ropes were dragged down the steep hill. Luke dug in his heels. His arms trembled as he tried to resist the downward pull and slow the wagon's descent. Sometimes, he and the other men had to lift the wheels to ease them over solid rocks. It seemed to take forever before the bumping wagon finally reached the bottom of the canyon.

The men unfastened the chains and ropes and trudged back up the hill to use them on the next wagon.

Wagon after wagon was slowly skidded down the steep slope. After watching them master the difficult journey down the hill, Nora relaxed a little.

Another wagon had almost made it safely down when one of the men slipped on the rocky, trampled ground and lost his grip on the rope.

The wagon jerked forward. The other men on the ropes were pulled down the hill.

Men yelled; women screamed, and the oxen being dragged down the hill roared. Rising dust and the wagon cover that had come loose obstructed Nora's view. She craned her neck.

Finally, she caught a glimpse of Luke.

He took a desperate leap and raced after the wagon, refusing to give up his grip on the rope.

But then one after another of the men fell or had to let go of the rope to avoid getting dragged down the hill at a break-neck speed.

Luke fell and disappeared in a cloud of dust.

Nora froze. Helplessly clutching Amy's hand in her own, she watched as the wagon tumbled down the hill and crashed at the bottom in a shower of splinters.

Pained moans came from somewhere within the cloud of dust.

Nora's stomach flipped.

After a few seconds, Jacob Garfield emerged and limped down the hill. The dust settled a little, and Nora discovered another man sitting on the ground, spitting and cursing.

It wasn't Luke.

"Mama?" Amy's worried voice drifted up to her.

"Luke's fine, sweetie," Nora said, praying that she was right. "He's just…resting a bit." She stepped closer to the edge of the plateau, but she still couldn't see Luke. Bile rose in her throat. Darkness threatened at the edge of her vision. A dull roar filled her ears, and she realized numbly that she was going to faint.

"Nora!" A secure grip on her elbow brought her back to reality.

Luke! Bonelessly, Nora slumped against his dust-covered form. "Oh, God, Luke!" She clutched at his back, holding on as if for dear life. His body was reassuringly solid against her own trembling form.

"What? What is it?" Luke finally managed to loosen her grip on him and stepped back to take in her expression.

Nora stared at him. "I thought you…you…" She gestured down the hill, where men and women tried to salvage what they could from the Bennetts' destroyed wagon.

"You weren't really worried about me, were you?" His lips curled into a disbelieving smile.

Nora wasn't sure whether she should kiss him or slap him. He still had no idea how important his survival was for her and Amy—not for sentimental reasons, but because they needed a provider and protector. Her stomach roiled again. She abruptly turned away from him.

"Nora?" Luke bent down and looked into her face. "Are you all right? You're kind of green."

Nora tried to straighten, but another wave of nausea overtook her, and she lost what little she had eaten at noon. When she was finally just dry-heaving and holding her stomach, she became aware of a comforting touch at her back. She turned around, swaying a little, and looked into Luke's worried gray eyes.

Amy pressed herself against Nora's legs, clutching her skirt. "Are you sick, Mama?" The girl stared up at her with wide eyes.

Nora rested a soothing hand on her daughter's head while her other hand remained on her roiling stomach. "Just a little tummy ache. It'll soon go away." She knew it wouldn't, but she didn't want to worry Amy, and she was very aware of Luke's presence next to her.

"Why didn't you tell me that you're sick?" He wrapped his arm around her, supporting her.

Where Nora had usually recoiled from men's touches outside the context of her work, she found herself leaning on him. "I'm not," she said, almost wishing she were sick. "I'm fine, just an upset stomach. That's all."

Luke studied her.

Under his skeptical gaze, Nora began to fidget. He had seen through her considerable acting skills right from the start.

Finally, a small smile replaced his serious expression. "Maybe you should leave that strong, silent routine to us men."

"Oh, yes, because you're so much better at it than I," she said, nodding down at his hands.

The taut rope had ripped through his gloves. Blisters and raw skin peeked through the rips in the material.

"Let me patch them up," Nora said.

Luke shook his head. "There's no time for that. It's our turn to go down the hill. We can lick our respective wounds when we're down there. Will you be able to make it?"

Nora straightened and squared her shoulders. She was determined to prove that she was no shrinking violet, but a hardy pioneer woman. "Of course."

Luke's intense gaze rested on her for another second, then he nodded. "All right. Then let's tie everything in the wagon down." He climbed into the wagon and fumbled with his stiff fingers.

Nora followed him. The stuffy air inside the wagon made her gag again, but she suppressed it. "Why don't you let me finish this while you check on the oxen?"

She half-expected him to decline due to male pride, but he nodded without hesitation. "Thanks," he said and jumped from the wagon.

Nora opened the flap to let in some fresh air and started to tie down every loose item in the wagon.

Minutes later, Luke urged the oxen forward over the edge of the plateau and down the steep hill.

Nora clutched her apron as the wagon bumped over rocks, barely held back from tumbling down the hill by the men holding the ropes.

Bernice joined her, and they started down the hill.

Nora kept an eye on Amy, who ran along with Bernice's children. "How's Jacob?" Nora asked. "I saw him fall when they tried to stop the Bennetts' wagon."

"He hurt his leg, but otherwise he's fine. What about Luke?"

Nora watched her slender husband grip the brake handle. "His hands are badly scraped and blistered."

"Did you tell him about…you know?" Grinning, Bernice gestured at Nora's belly.

The mere thought of telling Luke threw Nora into a state of panic, but of course she couldn't admit that. She looked left and right, making sure that Amy was still running around with Bernice's youngest daughter and wouldn't overhear their conversation. She didn't want her to repeat anything of what was said to Luke. "No, I'm…I'm still waiting for the right moment."

"Ah." Bernice laughed. "You want it to be romantic, huh?"

"Something like that," Nora said.

"I'm so happy for you and Luke." Bernice beamed like a proud grandmother-to-be. "You're such a nice couple."

Nora forced a smile. She loved Amy, and she loved children, and under different circumstances, she would have been happy to find herself pregnant again. *Everything would have been perfect if this was Luke's baby.* But since Luke had never shared her bed, that wasn't possible—and Luke would know it too. They would never be the happy little family that Nora wished for.

She breathed a sigh of relief when their wagon finally reached the bottom of the valley.

They camped in Ash Hollow, a wooded canyon named for its ash trees. After their strenuous, dusty trek down Windlass Hill, the place seemed like an oasis with its cool springs, tall trees, and bushes with sweet berries. A carpet of colorful wildflowers dotted the lush grass. Nora deeply inhaled the fragrance of roses and jasmine that permeated the air.

"Well, looks like this is the romantic place you've been searching for." Bernice winked at her. "Do you want some time alone with your husband? I could take Amy tonight."

Nora grimaced. Romantic place or not, she didn't intend to tell Luke anytime soon. She wasn't ready to have her new life end so soon. "No, thank you. I think I'll wait a few weeks until I tell Luke. You never know what could go wrong, and I don't want him to worry."

She busied herself with wandering through the meadow and picking berries with Amy. When she walked over to the clear pond in the middle of the meadow to wash Amy's berry-smeared face, she found Luke next to the spring, trying to clean his hands.

"Good berries?" Luke asked. He smiled as Amy climbed onto his lap.

"Vewy good. Mama make a pie."

"I'm planning on baking a gooseberry pie," Nora said. "Don't smear your face on Luke's shirt, honey." She took her protesting daughter away from him and started to clean her face. "Now you." She turned to Luke.

Luke's smile made his clean-shaven, normally stoic face appear years younger. "I didn't eat any berries."

"I'm talking about your hands. Let me clean them for you." Nora held out her hand and waited until Luke laid his own into her palm. She stripped off the remnants of the gloves and looked down, studying his hands. They were slender, but strong, equally capable of handling a dozen oxen or shoeing a horse and rocking her daughter to sleep. Nora gently dabbed at the blisters and scrapes and then, without really thinking about it, bent down and pressed a kiss to the calloused palm.

Luke's hand jerked in her grip. "What are you doing?" he asked, his voice rough.

Nora looked up. His half-tempted, half-angry expression told her that he thought that this was another one of her attempts of seduction. It wasn't. She hadn't planned on kissing his hand. Even if she had wanted to, she was too scared that Luke would discover her pregnancy should she share his bed now. It had simply been a gesture of relief, sympathy, gratitude, and reluctant affection. To her astonishment, she felt herself blush under his gaze. When was the last time that had happened? "Sorry, I didn't think. It's just what I do when Amy hurts herself."

He drew his hand back and flexed it. "Well, I'm healed, then. Thank you." A quick nod and he strode away.

ASH HOLLOW,
JUNE 12TH, 1851

Luke stared through the darkness toward the gurgling Ash Creek. Everyone else had already bedded down for the night, except for Luke, who had volunteered for guard duty tonight. She leaned back against her saddle, deliberately staying out of the circle of firelight. This way, she would make no target for any enemy that might lurk in the darkness.

She knew from experience that Sioux often camped near Ash Hollow, and she was determined to take no risks. As a soldier, her life had been a constant alternation of boring routine and life-threatening danger. She had fought in wars and skirmishes, but she had never been afraid to die. Her only fear had been to get injured so badly that her true identity would be discovered by the army doctors or her comrades.

But now, with each mile that they got farther away from Independence, the possibility of her own death took on another meaning for her. Nora's reactions whenever Luke's life was in danger had been far from indifferent. Luke wasn't naïve enough to believe that it was selfless love for the "man" she had married just six weeks ago. Nora's concern was for her own future and for that of her daughter.

At first, Luke had seen her marriage as a business transaction between strangers, but now she realized that her life was inescapably entwined with those of the two Macauley females. *At least until we reach Oregon. I'll think of something by then.* Even had she wanted to, she couldn't spend the rest of her life with Nora. She had come to appreciate the courageous woman, who had managed to hold on to her warmth and friendliness despite her former occupation. Nora was also a lot more intelligent and cultured than the average prostitute, and that was one of the reasons why Luke was afraid to spend more time than necessary with her. Sooner or later, Nora would discover her secret. Out here on the trail, she could always sleep apart from Nora and Amy, and she could take a quick bath at some out-of-the-way corner of a creek. If they lived under the same roof, Nora would expect her to share her bed and bathe in the tub she prepared for her "husband." There would be no hiding for very long.

Footsteps made Luke lift her head. She snapped out of her gloomy thoughts.

Jacob stepped into the circle of firelight.

She lowered her carbine.

He sank down next to Luke and looked at her with an eerie smile.

Normally not one for idle conversation, Luke felt the need to break the silence. His grin made her nervous. "How's the leg?"

"Suppose it's gonna give me trouble for a few more days, but it could have been a lot worse." He reached into the pocket of his jacket and offered her a small flask of whiskey.

Luke shook her head. "I'm still on guard duty."

"Oh, come on, young man." He gave her a friendly slap on the back. "You can make an exception this once. You have a very good reason to celebrate, after all."

Luke shrugged. The antelope she had shot this afternoon wasn't a big reason for celebration, but it provided a nice change in their steady diet of salt pork and beans.

Jacob took a healthy swig. "Let's just hope it's a boy this time, huh?"

A boy? He isn't talking about the antelope, is he? Luke put another thick branch onto the fire and stared at Jacob. "I'm not sure I know what you're talking about."

"Oh, no false modesty now. My wife can't keep a secret to save her life, so I know that congratulations are definitely in order." Jacob offered her the flask again.

Luke made no move to take it. "Congratulations?" she repeated, hoping to catch up with his weird thought process. "For what?"

Jacob laughed. "Don't tell me you don't know that your wife is with child?"

"What? W-what do you mean…with child?"

"With child. In a family way. In a delicate condition. Pregnant," Jacob said, his grin widening with every word.

He was definitely enjoying this a bit too much for Luke's comfort, but by now she knew him well enough to know that he wasn't joking. "Nora…she's pregnant?"

Jacob nodded, still grinning.

The fire blurred before Luke's eyes. "B-but…how?"

"The usual way, I'd imagine." Jacob laughed heartily. "Come on, boy, take it like a man."

Luke grimaced. *I'm not a man,* she wanted to shout. *And this is not my child.* But of course she said nothing while questions, doubts, and assumptions somersaulted through her mind. *Who is the father of this child? A customer? A beau back in Independence? Someone from the wagon train? Did she cuckold me?* Luke gazed toward the wagons, trying to picture Nora's interactions with the men on the train. Nora had always been friendly toward everyone, but Luke had never noticed her behaving inappropriately toward one of the mostly married men.

Was she already pregnant when she agreed to marry me? Was that the reason she accepted my proposal so readily? Was that why she tried to get me to share her bed? Did she want to make me believe that she was expecting my child? Luke snorted at the irony of the situation. Her hat nearly sailed into the fire when she buried her fingers in her hair. *What am I gonna do now?* She felt trapped in a situation that she had never counted on happening. She had planned on finding a way to end her sham of a marriage, not take on even more responsibilities.

"Well? What are you waiting for? Get going." Jacob gave her a good-natured slap on the back, pointing toward the tent that Nora was sleeping in.

With a great deal of effort, Luke held herself back from glaring at him. He couldn't know that she wasn't the overjoyed, proud father that he expected her to be. "I'm still on guard duty," she mumbled.

"I'm taking the rest of your watch," Jacob said. "You can go and be with your wife."

Luke wanted to refuse. Being in the tent with Nora was the last thing she wanted to do, but the close-knit community of the wagon train would soon become suspicious if she kept away from the woman who was supposedly expecting her child. "All right." She bent down and picked up her saddle, taking her time because she wasn't in any hurry to reach the tent and the woman it housed.

She slowly raised the tent's flap and tiptoed inside. Everything was quiet, and Luke exhaled a long breath. A sleeping Nora meant that she wouldn't have to face the reality of this new situation just yet.

Quietly, she settled down in her bedroll, even knowing she wouldn't be able to sleep tonight.

Nora's blankets rustled.

Luke slammed her eyes shut and pretended to be asleep.

From under lowered lids, she watched as Nora abruptly threw back her blankets and hurried past her to the flap. She had barely made it outside when Luke heard her gag and retch.

Luke pinched the bridge of her nose and stared at the flap. She wanted to pull the blanket up over her ears and ignore the pitiful sounds and what they meant, but as the minutes went by and Nora didn't return to the tent, she sat up and listened into the darkness.

There were no more sounds. No vomiting, no retching, no footsteps.

Was Nora all right? Had she passed out? The thought made her jump up and rush out of the tent. "Nora?"

"Uh." Nora cleared her throat. "I'm…I'm here."

Luke's eyes adjusted to the darkness, and she could make out Nora, who was huddled on the ground, her arms wrapped around herself. "Are you all right?" The question sounded stupid in her own ears, but the thousand other questions in her mind were much more complicated. She wasn't ready to ask them yet.

Nora wiped her mouth. "I'm fine. I just couldn't sleep and came out here for a breath of fresh air."

Looks like we're evenly matched. She's as good at lying as I am. Luke couldn't stand the many lies that made up her life any longer. "I don't think a breath of fresh air will cure what ails you," she said.

With a half-suppressed groan, Nora straightened and looked up at Luke. Her face was pale in the moonlight. She stared at Luke with wide eyes.

"Is there by any chance something that you wanted to tell me?" Luke found herself holding her breath. She wanted to hear it from Nora, half hoping that Jacob was wrong.

Nora swallowed audibly. Her gaze darted away from Luke's. "You...you know, don't you?"

Luke closed her eyes for a second. *It is true.* She nodded.

"How?" Nora whispered.

Luke snorted. "That's exactly what I want to know. How can you be with child when we both know..." She snapped her mouth shut. Nora didn't know just how impossible the thought of her fathering a child was.

Nora hung her head. "It's not yours," she whispered.

"That much is obvious. Whose child is it, then?" Luke asked. An unexpected wave of jealousy swept over her.

"I...I don't know."

"Who...?" Luke began to ask again but then stopped herself when she realized that Nora wasn't protecting the identity of the father—she really didn't know it. "A customer."

Nora raised her head for the first time and pleadingly looked into Luke's eyes. "I haven't been with anyone else since I agreed to marry you. I know that you probably won't believe the word of a prostitute, but I swear to you that I haven't—"

"I believe you," Luke said.

Nora still looked at her warily, as if she was waiting for the other shoe to drop.

Luke took a deep breath. "When did you first learn that you were with child? Before or after you agreed to marry me?"

"I wasn't sure for a long time. I thought I might be exhausted and queasy because of the strain of the journey."

"Look at me." Luke waited until Nora made eye contact. "This isn't something that you discovered just now. You probably began to worry the moment you missed your monthly courses." Luke knew too much about life in a brothel to believe otherwise. Children had no place in a prostitute's life; they meant only a loss of money. "How far along are you?"

"I'm not sure, but I'd guess five months." Nora quickly looked down again.

Luke eyed the still mostly slender woman. "Five months? That's impossible."

Nora bit her lip. "I assure you, it is possible. You haven't seen me naked, and these skirts and the apron are hiding my little bulge quite well. It was the same when I was pregnant with Amy—I could hide it until I was six months along."

She had to hide that pregnancy as well? Why? Was Amy's father a customer too? She stopped herself. She had other problems at the moment. "You agreed to marry me and travel two thousand miles through mountains, wastelands, and flooded rivers, knowing that you're with child? What the hell were you thinking?"

"Thinking?" Nora's head snapped up. She met Luke's gaze without submissiveness for the first time. "I wasn't thinking at all—I was just trying to survive."

"By trying to pass off a customer's bastard as my child? Was that the reason why you were so hell-bent on going to bed with me?" Heat shot up Luke's body as she glared at the pregnant woman.

Nora blinked. The glimmer of anger that had started in her eyes died. She hunched her shoulders. "I'm... I don't know. I really don't. I didn't want to lie to you, but..."

"Then why did you? Why didn't you tell me from the start?" Luke asked. *Oh, you're one to talk about trust and telling the truth, Luke Hamilton.*

Nora wrapped her arms around her middle. "Would you have married me if you knew?"

"No," Luke said. "But not for the reasons you're thinking." Not wanting to be responsible for a pregnant woman and a baby that wasn't her own was only one of the reasons. "If I had known, I wouldn't have risked exposing you to all the dangers along the trail." She shuddered when she thought about all the stories about miscarriages and death in childbirth she had heard along the trail.

"I understand," Nora said. "But it's my decision to make, and that's why I didn't tell you."

They stared at each other.

"What is going to happen now?" Nora finally asked in a small voice.

"We're going back inside, and we'll make you some ginger tea," Luke answered. "That should help with the nausea."

Nora raked her teeth over her bottom lip. "No, I mean, what's going to happen with me, with this baby?" She gently touched her rounded stomach. "With us?" Now she pointed at Luke and herself.

Luke shook her head. "I don't know, and I don't want to think about it now." She rubbed her temples, where a dull throbbing had started. "Give me some time, all right?" Without waiting for an answer, she headed back inside and started searching for some ginger root.

COURTHOUSE ROCK,
JUNE 15TH, 1851

Nora groggily lifted her head from the pillow and blinked her eyes open. The first pale light of predawn was filtering in through the canvas. She could make out Luke's blanket-wrapped body on the other side of the tent, his back to her. His position illustrated the distance that had sprung up between them. Not that they had been overly close before, but in the five hundred and fifty miles since Independence, an easy camaraderie and mutual respect had developed between them. Nora had cherished that wary friendship because she had never thought that she would ever have that kind of relationship with a man. But now…

It had been three days since he had learned of her pregnancy, and still they hadn't spoken about the future. His silence became more frightening with every hour that went by. She pressed both palms to her middle, hoping to calm her unborn child. She had started to feel its movements two days earlier, but the joy of the moment had been overshadowed by constant fears and worries about her uncertain future.

After passing Ash Hollow, the trail had begun a slight, but constant uphill climb, and the nights grew colder with the rising altitude. Far off on the horizon, she sometimes caught glimpses of the snow-patched Laramie Mountains. They were well past the point where Luke could just send her back to Independence—not on her own, at least. But every time they met a family or a group of disillusioned gold seekers traveling back east, fear shot through her when she saw Luke talking to them. Each time, she was afraid that he was arranging for her to go back with them, but it hadn't happened yet.

Luke had been distanced, but not unfriendly with her. He hadn't yelled when she didn't have breakfast ready when he rose, because the smell of the food made her nauseated. He had calmly taken over the task of frying the bacon and sent her back to the wagon to rest.

As far as Nora knew, he hadn't even told anyone that it wasn't his child she was expecting. Whenever someone from the wagon train congratulated him on the baby, he pressed his lips together but accepted the congratulations with a shrug. So far, no one suspected that he was not the baby's father. Everyone was still treating Nora with respect, but she lived in the fear that this would change very soon, and she would be on her own once again.

With a sigh, she rose to begin her chores.

When she turned to the place right next to her, where Amy always slept, she froze. The blankets were empty. Amy was gone.

Nora stumbled to the tent's flap but stopped when she passed Luke's blanket.

Her daughter slept peacefully next to Luke. Her red curls peeked out from under the blanket that he must have covered her with. She had cuddled up to Luke, clutching him like an oversized doll.

Nora stared at the two of them. If Luke left them, it would break Amy's heart. Nora had taken care to protect her own heart by hiding it away behind a protective shield, but her daughter didn't have that kind of protection. For the first time in her life, Amy had given her trust to a man, and Nora didn't want to see that trust trampled on. She knew exactly how much that hurt.

She watched as Amy moved in her sleep, snuggling closer into the fabric of Luke's shirt.

A strong hand came out from under the blanket they shared and spread protectively across Amy's small back, keeping her warm and safe.

Nora bit her lip. She had never thought that she would trust any man with the welfare of her daughter, but now she found that she did trust Luke. Despite Luke's inexperience with children and Amy's distrust of men, they had bonded during the last few weeks on the trail.

Everything in her life had been perfect for once, but Nora had been afraid to let herself be truly happy, afraid that something would destroy her happiness. *And now it did.*

With one last glance at the two sleeping forms, Nora slipped from the tent. She shivered in the cool morning air and hastily stoked the fire. When she bent down to pick up the dented kettle, she heard footsteps behind her.

"Morning," came Luke's sleep-roughened voice.

Nora turned and took her yawning daughter from him. "Good morning. I didn't wake you, did I?" She was still tiptoeing around as if on eggshells around him.

"No," Luke answered. "Let me do this." He took the kettle from her and started toward the river.

Amy began to struggle in her arms, demanding to be put down. "Amy go too!"

Nora looked down. Dew clung to the grass and would soak Amy in seconds. "No, Amy, you stay with me. You'll only get wet in the grass."

Amy bent down to look at the dew too. Her lower lip quivered.

"How about you help me make your favorite breakfast?" Nora said before tears could start to fall.

Amy stopped struggling. "Apple pancakes?"

"I don't have any apples, but pancakes, yes." Nora was fairly sure that her stomach could handle making pancakes. She set Amy down and showed her how to stir the flour and the milk for the pancake batter.

All around them, campfires came to life as the other women started breakfast.

Nora pressed her lips together, trying to ignore the various smells of bacon, beans, bread, and onions that wafted over. Bile rose in her throat. She turned away from Amy and the pancakes for a second to take a deep breath.

When she turned back around, Amy had set the pancake batter down and was running through the grass toward the river. "Amy! Amy Hamilton! Stop and come back here right this second."

But Amy had almost reached Luke now, who was returning with the water kettle. "Papa!" she shouted across the distance between them.

Nora froze in midstep.

The kettle almost slipped from Luke's grip. He had stopped too and stared at Amy with an expression that almost made Nora laugh despite the grimness of her situation.

"Amy!" She hastily caught up with her daughter. "Don't call Luke that, sweetheart." Calling him by that title meant forcing him to adopt the role of a father when he was neither Amy's nor the unborn baby's. She didn't want him to think that she had told Amy to call him "Papa." Clearly, he wasn't ready to accept that role in their lives.

Amy stopped hopping through the grass toward Luke. She turned and stared up at Nora with an expression of utter confusion. Her lower lip trembled—a clear sign that she was fighting to hold back tears. "Sowwy."

Nora bit her lip. Amy didn't even know why she was apologizing. She was afraid that she had done something wrong, but it was clear to Nora that her daughter had no idea why it would be so wrong to call Luke "Papa." From the day of her birth, Amy had been the child of a prostitute, and she had been treated as such. Amy had often been yelled at and disapproved of by "respectable" townspeople. Even now that she was around people who treated her like any other child born in wedlock, she was oversensitive toward disapproval.

With a sigh, Nora knelt down next to her daughter. "You didn't do anything wrong, sweetheart. You didn't know." She lifted her head and looked into Luke's eyes, hoping he would understand. "She must have heard the other children on the train calling their fathers by that name, and she probably thought... Amy, sweetie, Luke is n—"

"No." Luke held up a hand, stopping her midword. "It's..." He cleared his throat. "It's all right."

Nora stared at him. "It's all right?" What did that mean? It was all right as long as Amy never referred to him like that again?

"Your children need a father, and I'm willing to fulfill that role for as long as it takes you to find a better man," Luke said.

A better man? Nora felt like laughing and crying at the same time. *Then you're gonna be their father for as long as you live, because the longer I know you, the surer I am that you are the best man I could ever wish for.* Slowly, she stood and rested her hand on Amy's shoulder. "You really mean that? You would accept Amy and the baby as your own?" She couldn't hide the hope that shone in her eyes.

Luke shrugged as if it was no big deal. "As long as you're my wife, your children will be mine too."

Nora blinked and dazedly shook her head. *His wife, his children... Is it really that easy for him?* She couldn't imagine that any other man would have reacted like that. Some might have tolerated that stepsisters or stepbrothers were growing up along with his own children, but she had never seen a proud man like Luke Hamilton just accept another man's child as his own.

Doubts immediately began to grow in her. Pessimistic thoughts and worries crept back into her mind, but then she watched Luke pick Amy up, out of the dewy grass. The wet hem of her dress soaked his shirt. He shivered in the cool morning air, but he didn't set Amy back down.

Maybe... Nora allowed a timid hope to grow in her chest as she followed them back to the fire.

Chimney Rock,
June 15th, 1851

A shout from the end of the wagon train made Luke look back over her shoulder. The Buchanans' wagon slowed and then stopped.

She raised her arm and shouted out a warning to Jacob Garfield in the wagon in front of hers, who repeated it until the message had reached the front of the train. The command to halt was repeated back the same way until every wagon had stopped almost level with the slender stone column that jutted nearly five hundred feet into the sky.

Chimney Rock was one of the rock formations that rose from the plains along the banks of the North Platte River. The landmark had loomed on the horizon for days and always appeared to be much closer than it really was.

Some of the emigrants had walked three or four miles out of their way to climb the cone or etch their names into the sandstone, but their halt had other reasons.

Mrs. Buchanan had been too sick to walk when they had set out this morning. By noon, the captain had sent riders out to other wagon trains in search of a doctor.

Luke looked at Nora to make sure she was all right, something she found herself doing regularly since she had found out that Nora was pregnant.

Nora sat down on the wagon tongue while they waited for word from the Buchanans' wagon, stretching her swollen feet out before her.

Now that Luke knew, she could detect a slight bulge where the baby grew. She was still alternating between horror and awe at the thought that she would soon be the "father" of a newborn baby.

Mr. Buchanan emerged from his wagon with a shovel and began to dig a hole right in front of his wagon.

Luke pressed her lips together and silently grabbed her own shovel to help him. She didn't need to ask to know that Mrs. Buchanan had just died. When the doctor from a nearby wagon train had told them it was cholera, she had known this was the most likely outcome.

Cholera had killed more emigrants than anything else. She had seen people in good health start out cheerfully whistling in the morning. By noon, they writhed in agony with horrible cramps, vomiting, and diarrhea, and they were dead before evening.

Luke dug shoulder to shoulder with Jacob Garfield and Tom Buchanan.

Bill Larson, the neighbor from the wagon behind Luke's, didn't come out of his wagon. "Stupid fools," Larson shouted from behind the wagon cover. "You'll all die if you don't stay away!"

Luke ignored him and kept digging. She didn't believe that cholera was contagious. Last year, when she had seen a lot of people die along the Platte, she had gotten the impression that cholera had to do with the low quality of the drinking water from the shallow river. She couldn't prove it, but Bill Larson's superstitious assumption was not enough to make her abandon her neighbor when he needed help. Digging a grave in the packed ground of the trail was hard work, but Luke knew it was the only way now that they'd come this far west.

Chimney Rock marked the end of their travel over flat plains and the start of the mountain portion of the journey. The scenery changed from lush green to dry, brown grass. There was no wood in the area, and that meant they couldn't build a coffin for Mrs. Buchanan.

Tom Buchanan wrapped his wife's body in a quilt and lowered her into the shallow grave that they had dug into the ruts of the trail. They hoped that the constant passing of wagons over the grave would wipe away the scent and disguise the location of the grave so that the body would be safe from Indians, grave-robbers, and scavenging animals in the packed earth.

Finally, the emigrants stood together in a loose semi-circle around the fresh grave.

When the captain started to read from his Bible, Nora stepped next to Luke.

Out of the corner of her eye, Luke watched Nora sniffle and wipe her eyes as she helped Amy join her hands in prayer.

Luke wasn't familiar with the Lord's Prayer that the others were mumbling in chorus, so she just moved her lips and watched the others.

Mr. Buchanan stood with his head hanging while those of his children that were old enough to understand the irrevocability of death wept openly.

A picture of Nora and Amy weeping at her grave shot through Luke's mind. She gritted her teeth as she realized the grimness of Nora's situation if something happened to her. If Luke died or were too sick to continue, if her identity was exposed in the process, Nora and Amy wouldn't even have the support of the usually close-knit community of the wagon train. No one would have much sympathy for a woman who had married such a freak of nature. No one would believe that she hadn't known, that she had never shared Luke's bed.

Luke looked at the assembled emigrants. She had no doubt that Nora would stand alone at her grave if it ever came to that. *That is, if she'll stand at my grave for longer than it takes to spit on it.* If anyone attended the funeral at all, they would whisper and talk behind Nora's back, just as they had talked behind Luke's back during her childhood.

Luke had long since gotten used to it. She had learned to distance herself from others. Luke hadn't cared about anyone, and no one had cared about her or what happened to her. She had only ever been responsible for herself.

Now all that had changed. The sudden impulse to take Nora's hand scared her. It was something a husband, a lover would have done, and she was Nora's spouse in name only. She curled her hand into a fist. No sense in letting Nora—or herself—hope for something that could never be.

When the prayer ended, she strode away and readied the oxen.

"Are you all right?" Nora's voice came from behind her.

Luke didn't turn around. "Sure." She shrugged as casually as possible. "I didn't even know Mrs. Buchanan all that well."

Nora stepped next to her and idly rubbed the lead ox's flank. "She was a really nice woman. In the beginning, when I couldn't bake bread to save my life, she shared hers with me more than once."

Luke shuffled her feet as she watched Nora wipe at her tears. While she had taken care to hold herself separate from the rest of the emigrants, Nora had become a part of the community. She didn't know what to say.

"I'm sorry," Nora mumbled. "I don't want to make you uncomfortable with such a display of emotions. I think it's all that…" She gestured at her growing belly. "It's making me a bit emotional."

Luke just nodded. For the last few days, she had avoided discussing the pregnancy with Nora, preferring to just ignore it for the time being. Avoiding the topic once again, she looked away from Nora and detected Amy laying a small bouquet of hand-picked wildflowers next to the grave. "You're a good mother."

Nora blinked up at her, and her hands came to rest on her stomach. "Do you really think so?" Hope and doubt mixed in her voice.

"I do." Luke had never thought that she would say that about a woman who had once been a prostitute, but there was no doubt in her mind that Nora loved her daughter and tried everything she could to do right by her.

The last of Nora's tears disappeared, and she smiled up at Luke. Golden highlights twinkled in her green eyes, and the charming smattering of freckles across her nose and cheeks seemed to dance as dimples formed.

Dancing freckles? Oh, come on. What are you, a fifteen-year-old smitten boy? Luke shook her head at herself. Nora's looks didn't matter. She turned away and urged the oxen forward.

Near Chimney Rock,
June 15th, 1851

Nora licked dry lips that had cracked during a long day's travel over a sandy road. Clouds of dust had hung in the air all day like fog. A thin layer of dirt had coated her skin, and it had been a relief to dip into the small creek where they had set up camp. Even Luke had returned from one of his solitary walks with his hair still damp from a bath.

Finally, after their evening meal, rain began to fall, settling down the clouds of dust and turning them into mud, which forced them to retreat into their tents.

Her tongue flicked over her cracked lip as she concentrated on threading her needle in the dim light inside the tent. When she had finally managed the task, she slipped the bodice of her dress over her head and looked down at the frayed cuff.

She pierced the needle through the fabric. When she pulled the thread through, her gaze fell on Luke.

He quickly turned away, making it obvious for Nora that he had been watching her.

Nora looked down at her thin chemise and smiled to herself. Moments like this were a healing balm to her battered self-confidence because they proved that she could still entice her husband with her female charms—at least a little bit.

The other men on the train were already engaged in more than just looking at their wives. Judging from some of the sounds that came from nearby tents, some of the other couples took advantage of their forced retreat from the rain to make love behind the canvas walls. Nora had worked in a brothel during wartime, so she understood that they were basically celebrating life, reassuring themselves and each other that they were alive and well.

"You know, I don't mind," she said.

Luke barely looked up. "You don't mind what?" He sounded gruff, but Nora had learned that this was his way to avoid showing his emotions.

"I don't mind you looking at me," Nora said. "At my body. You are my husband. You are allowed to look."

Luke glanced up but didn't answer.

"You're allowed to do more than just look," Nora said. She moved over to him and took his hand. His fingers jerked in her grip, but she held on and gently pressed his hand against her belly. She felt his calluses through the thin fabric of her chemise, the slight trembling of his fingers an astonishing contrast. That sign of vulnerability in the normally self-assured man affected Nora. She felt none of the revulsion that usually accompanied a man's touch.

He tried to pull away, but then his fingers fluttered over her growing belly as if trying to communicate with the unborn child.

To her own surprise, Nora felt herself relax into the gentle touch. She had endured men's touches hundreds of times in the last three years, but somehow this was very different. Leaning even closer, she deeply breathed in the unobtrusive scent of leather, horse, and something that was just Luke. There was no hesitation on her part as she slowly led his hand upward and pressed it to her half-covered breast.

Luke froze. His gaze flickered over to Amy.

"Don't worry," Nora whispered. "She's fast asleep. She won't wake up."

"Yeah." Luke's voice was raspy. "Because we won't give her any reason to. I told you before that I have no intention of sharing your bed." He slid his hand out from under hers.

Nora had expected him to refuse her again, but she still found herself a bit disappointed. Every time she thought she had finally established any sort of intimacy between them, he distanced himself from her again. "But why? There's no risk now. I can't get pregnant twice after all." She forced a grin.

Luke clenched his hands into fists. "This arrangement would be much easier on both of us if you finally stopped trying to seduce me."

"Arrangement?" The word left a bitter taste in Nora's mouth. "The business relationships that I had with my customers were arrangements. What we have is a marriage, Luke."

Still keeping his gaze fixed on his knees, Luke folded his arms across his chest. "I gave you and Amy my name and a chance to start a new life. I do my best to provide for you and protect you, and I agreed to be a father for your children until you find someone else. Isn't that exactly what you wanted from our marriage? What more do you want from me?"

Nora swallowed heavily. Having a protector and provider was exactly what she had hoped for when she had agreed to marry him. If she was honest with herself, she had to admit that Luke had already surpassed all expectations. He treated her with a kindness and respect that had been missing from her life, and he showed more interest and patience toward Amy than her own father had ever had for Nora. So what more could she expect of him? What more did she want from him?

Shouts from outside their tent interrupted Nora's thoughts. The flap was thrown back, and Captain McLoughlin appeared in the tent's opening. Thick droplets of rain splashed from his graying hair and beard. "Strike the tent," he shouted over the pouring rain outside. "We have to get away from here right now."

Then he was gone. In the shocked silence, Nora heard him repeat his shouted message in the next tent.

She blinked and looked at Luke.

As she had expected him to, he immediately took charge of the situation. "You wake Amy and pack up the bedding. I'll take care of the tent. We'll meet at the wagon."

"Amy! Amy, wake up!" She frantically shook her daughter.

Amy's eyes opened, and she blinked sleepily. With a groan of protest, she tried to turn around and go back to sleep.

"No, Amy, you have to wake up. We have to leave." While her daughter sat up and struggled halfheartedly out of her sleep-warmed blanket, Nora rolled up her own bedding and Luke's.

Clutching Amy's hand in her left hand and the bedrolls under her other arm, she ran outside. Raindrops pelted her face. She bowed her head as she fought against wind and rain. The fire had long since gone out, so the camp lay in darkness. Nora could hardly make out the contours of the wagons. Which one was theirs?

Mud clung to her boots. Every step was harder than the one before.

Chaos prevailed all around her. Everyone was shouting, hurrying through the rain with crying children and a few belongings clutched to their chest.

Nora stumbled. She stopped for a second and turned back around, peering through the rain. She couldn't make out their tent and hoped that meant Luke had already struck it. *Maybe it would be better to wait for him?* He always seemed to know a way out of the troubles they found themselves in, and Nora realized that she felt safe with him. *No. I have to make it on my own. Luke can't deal with helping me and taking care of the tent at the same time.*

She leaned forward to protect Amy's body from the rain with her own and then hastened onward.

A bolt of lightning zigzagged across the sky and gave her a brief glimpse of the wagons. *This one!* She veered to the right and breathed a sigh of relief when she finally reached their wagon. She lifted Amy inside and climbed after her to stow away the now wet bedrolls.

Another lightning lit the sky, revealing the small creek where they had set up camp this evening. *Small creek?* Nora stared for the second the lightning lasted. It wasn't a gentle stream any longer. Right next to the circle of wagons a raging river burst over its banks and threatened to overturn the wagons if they stayed any longer.

"Nora?" Luke's voice was almost drowned by the booming thunder.

Nora stuck her head through the flap. "Here! We're here!"

With her voice guiding him, he reached the wagon and lost no time strapping the tent poles on the sides of the wagon. "Stay here. I have to bring in the oxen," he said when he handed her the folded tent cover.

Nora could only imagine how frightened the animals must be by lightning and thunder. From what she had experienced on their journey so far, she knew that a stampede could break out any second. "Luke," she shouted against rain and thunder.

He turned back around. In the glaring light of another lightning, she saw that his soaked-through shirt was plastered to his skin, and for a second, she thought she saw something like a bandage under the half-transparent fabric. Then the surrounding of the wagon was once again thrown into darkness.

I must have been mistaken. Surely he would have told me if he'd been hurt.

"What is it?" Luke asked.

"It's just…" Nora swallowed. "Take care, all right?"

"I will." He disappeared into the night.

Nora forced herself to move away from the flap. She bundled Amy into a halfway dry blanket and pulled the strings to draw shut the covers at Amy's end of the wagon. "Amy," she said as calmly as she could, "I have to go outside and help Luke. You stay here. Don't climb out of the wagon by yourself. I'll be back soon, all right?"

She waited until Amy nodded, then climbed back out. The rain was still falling hard, but she ignored it. She readied the wooden yokes and unchained the wagon from the others that it had been bound to overnight.

When Luke returned with the nervous oxen, the wagon was ready to go.

They worked together in silence, yoking the oxen and urging them forward, away from the dangerous river. Theirs was the first wagon to pull out, but Nora could see others following behind them. With a firm grip on the lead ox's yoke, Luke led them through the night.

Nora concentrated on putting one foot in front of the other, trying not to stumble or get stuck in the ankle-deep mud. Their trek through the darkness seemed to last forever. When Luke brought the wagon to a halt, Nora almost fell.

"Careful!" Luke caught her but pulled back when she had secured her footing. "I think this is far away enough from the river," he shouted toward Captain McLoughlin's wagon behind them. "We should camp here for the rest of the night. It's not safe traveling in the dark."

The captain agreed, and the soaked-through emigrants settled down for the night in their wagons.

Between trunks, sacks of flour and beans, and a keg of pickles, there wasn't much space for them in the wagon bed. Nora settled down between a feeding bag and her butter churn, curling herself around Amy's body for added warmth. She closed her eyes but couldn't sleep.

The wagon covers had been rubbed down with linseed oil to make them waterproof, but the night's downpour had been too much for them, and now they leaked anyway. A steady succession of drops hit her shoulder, and she moved a little to the right to avoid them. She closed her eyes again, but now another leak had built at her feet.

She had just resigned herself to a sleepless night when she felt another blanket being settled over her and Amy, followed by the rainproof tent cover.

Without a word, Luke returned to his place at the end of the wagon, staring out into the rain with his back resting against a sack of flour.

"Thank you," Nora whispered. She tried to make out his face in the dark but couldn't. "Do you want to join us in our little nest?" She lifted the edge of the covers in invitation.

"There's no room," he answered.

Careful not to wake Amy, Nora stood and balanced the butter churn on top of the keg of pickles, then shoved the feeding bag as far to the side as it would go. "There's room now." She lay back down and again lifted the covers for him to join them.

"No, it's all right," Luke said. "I have to go out in an hour anyway to ride guard over the herd."

Nora was determined not to give up this time. Luke had taken care of everybody tonight, and now she would take care of him. "Then you should rest for that hour, not sit up and be miserable. Come on, it's getting cold in here." She again lifted the blankets.

Slowly, Luke edged toward them. He lay down with his back pressed against the keg of pickles, careful to keep as much space between them as possible.

"You have to move a little closer, or the blanket won't cover you," Nora said.

He hesitated but then inched closer.

Amy turned around in her sleep, probably feeling his heat, and snuggled up to him.

This close, Nora could make out his expression and stifled a laugh as she saw him blush. She settled the blanket over him, leaving them in a warm cocoon of shared heat. *Now he is sharing my bed.* She giggled.

"What?" Luke asked.

Nora pressed a hand against her lips. "Oh, nothing."

"We have to break up camp in the middle of the night or risk getting drowned. Our wagon is leaking. A stampede could break out any second. I don't even want to imagine tomorrow's travel through knee-deep mud, and you're giggling over nothing? Uh-huh." He gently poked her in the shoulder, making Nora giggle again. "Tell me." He raised his finger in mock threat.

If any other man had raised his hand and used a tone this threatening with her, Nora would have been scared to death, but this time, with Luke, her finely honed instincts told her that she had nothing to worry about. "Well, it just occurred to me that you're finally sharing my bed." Not giggling now, she stared into his face and held her breath while she waited for his reaction.

Luke snorted. "This is not exactly what you had in mind, huh?"

Isn't it? Nora wasn't so sure what she had or hadn't wanted anymore. She had never really enjoyed going to bed with men, and after three years in a brothel, she certainly wasn't eager to have relations with one of them again. Yes, she had wanted Luke to share her bed, but not for carnal reasons. She had wanted to get closer to her husband and share an intimacy that would ensure that he wouldn't leave her.

"Nora? You asleep?" he whispered when her answer didn't come.

"No, just thinking."

This close, his gray eyes were like silver mirrors in the light of the moon that peeked out from behind heavy clouds. "About what?" he asked after a minute of silence.

Nora hesitated. She had been taught from a very early age that women should never speak their mind. Life in the brothel had only enforced that. Her first instinct was to keep her thoughts to herself and tell him that she had been thinking about what condition the trail might be in tomorrow. Then she shook her head. She wanted to start a new life, be a new, respectable woman. She didn't have to keep up her old habits. "I was thinking about what I want from you."

Luke sucked in a breath. He was quiet for so long that Nora began to fear that she had annoyed him. When she opened her mouth to try soothing his ruffled feathers, he asked, "And what is it that you want?"

That was the point where Nora's ruminations had stopped. She didn't have a clear picture about what she wanted from him; she just knew it wasn't only his protection. "I…I want to…be closer to you." She closed her eyes for a moment, realizing the truth of her words as she spoke them. "I feel like I don't really know the most important person in my life. Adult person," she said, briefly looking down at her sleeping daughter. "I don't know anything about you."

Luke's formerly relaxed expression became guarded again. "You know everything you have to. Why would you want to know more?"

"Because I—"

"Hamilton?" A shout from outside interrupted Nora. "Hamilton, are you in there? We need your help with the animals."

Nora recognized the voice. *Bill Larson. One more reason to hate him.*

Luke scrambled out from under the blankets.

Larson had spoiled her one chance to talk to Luke. She knew that he would avoid discussing this topic again. With a sigh, she settled back down and pressed a kiss into Amy's red curls. "Sleep tight, sweetie." *At least one of us should.*

Scotts Bluff,
June 17th, 1851

From under the brim of her hat, Luke glanced up to the high cliffs that loomed like a bastion above the plains. An hour ago, she had glimpsed a band of Indians watching the wagon train from the pine-covered top of the massive bluff.

This was Sioux territory, so as far as Luke was concerned, the natives had every right to be there. She kept a watchful eye on them, but otherwise didn't pay them much attention. She didn't have the time to, because unlike Chimney Rock, Scotts Bluff was an obstacle for the wagon train.

Ravines and eroded wastelands stretched from the bluffs to the river, making it impossible to continue on their usual trail along the North Platte River. Luke and two other scouts had been sent out to look for a pass through the bluffs.

From the distance, the bluffs seemed to be an impenetrable barrier, but Luke knew from her military expeditions that there was a lower, less rocky area several miles to the south.

Larson and some of the other men grumbled about the detour, but in the end, the captain had agreed to use Robidoux Pass instead of the shorter, but steeper and more dangerous Mitchell Pass.

Luke wiped the sweat from her brow. After the downpour two days before, the weather had turned oppressively hot. Humans and animals suffered alike under the blazing sun and the clouds of mosquitoes. Fortunately, the ascent was a gradual one until the last half mile before the summit, where they had to double-team the oxen to navigate the hundred-foot rise.

They stopped at the crest of the pass to rest in the shadow provided by nearby cedar trees and to renew their water supplies.

Luke gratefully took the ladle of cool, clear water that Nora handed her and swallowed slowly while she looked around.

In the distance, the faint blue shadow of the Black Hills loomed on the horizon to the west. The snow-capped Laramie Peak seemed to reach into the clouds. Luke watched Nora stare west with as much anxiety as awe.

Luke couldn't blame her. Laramie Peak signaled the beginning of their ascent into the mountains. Ahead of them lay difficult terrain. Firewood, water, and even buffalo chips would become scarce. They would have to leave more of their possessions behind to lighten the load of the weary oxen as they tried to cross the Rocky Mountains.

Luke dipped the ladle into the water barrel again. When she lifted it, she caught a glimpse of half a dozen Sioux cresting the rise.

"Indians!" Bill Larson reached around his faint-looking wife for his rifle.

"No!" Luke sprang forward and grabbed the barrel of Larson's rifle before he could aim at the Sioux.

Larson refused to let go. A tug-of-war ensued. "Let go, you fool, or we're all gonna die." Larson tried to kick Luke from his elevated position on the wagon seat.

Luke used his forward momentum to pull Larson down from the wagon. She never let go of the rifle because she knew how it would end. The Lakota, as the Sioux called themselves, hadn't attacked emigrants so far, but they started to eye the streams of white men passing through their land and leaving behind herds of slaughtered buffalo with distrust. They were a powerful and proud tribe, and when pushed by trigger-happy settlers, they would respond with hostility.

"Stop it! Both of you." Captain McLoughlin stepped between them. "We have to show strength in front of the Indians. Fighting among ourselves doesn't help with that."

Slowly, Luke let go of Larson's rifle. The captain was right. She straightened and watched as the six braves slowly led their horses toward the wagon train.

"Keep on your guard," Abe McLoughlin said over his shoulder, "but nobody lifts a weapon without me ordering it." He stepped out of the shadow of Larson's wagon and greeted the Lakota in their own language. From time to time, he turned back around to translate for the other emigrants.

Luke didn't need the translation. In her eight years with the dragoons, she hadn't made a lot of friends and had kept to herself a lot, particularly after Nate's death. She had spent a lot of time with the other outsiders of the company, including the native and half-blood scouts. As a result, she understood at least some words of half a dozen native languages. She caught that they wanted to trade before McLoughlin translated it for them.

"They want to trade?" Bill Larson roared with sarcastic laughter. "I don't need no stinking Indian blankets. Tell them no."

"Abe," Luke said before the captain could turn back around to translate Larson's refusal, "if we refuse to trade with them, they'll follow us for days and try to steal our stock at night. Let's trade with them, give them some clothes or coffee. That's all they want."

The captain nodded. He turned and asked the barrel-chested leader what they had to offer.

The tall Lakota pointed to the only female in his group, then at Measles.

Luke blinked and then wildly shook her head. She wouldn't trade her horse and certainly not for an Indian wife.

When the captain translated the offer, Bill Larson laughed and slapped his thighs. "Hamilton can't even handle one wife. What would he want with two?"

Luke ignored him. "That's a very generous offer," she said slowly, in the Lakota's language, "but I already have a wife."

The tall Lakota fixed the gaze of his intense black eyes on Nora, who was inching closer to Luke. He looked at her for much longer than Luke was comfortable with.

Luke half-turned toward Nora, trying to understand what had captured the Lakota's attention. Now that Nora was no longer hiding it, her pregnancy was quite obvious, but to Luke's continuing surprise, that was only adding to her beauty. Officers that she had served with had often extolled the glowing beauty of their pregnant wives, but Luke had always taken it for the sentimental talk of love-sick fools. Now she had to reconsider that opinion.

Nora didn't have the perfect porcelain complexion that she had started out with in Independence any longer, but still she was much more fair-skinned than anyone else on the wagon train. The constant sun had tanned her skin to a creamy, golden complexion. She had taken off her bonnet while they rested in the shadow, and her flaming red hair contrasted nicely with her green eyes.

The Lakota slid from his horse and offered Luke the braided leather reins.

"That's the ugliest pony I've ever seen." Bill Larson smirked. "You still want to trade, Hamilton?"

The horses of the native tribes were much smaller than that of the white settlers. Compared to the captain's large black gelding the chief's gray mare looked downright tiny. But Luke knew better than to think the small horse inferior. She let her gaze pass over the mare's flank, shoulder, legs, and chest. She knew without a doubt that the horse was hardy, fast, a good climber, and able to live on vegetation that wouldn't sustain McLoughlin's pampered gelding. "What do you want for the mare?"

The Lakota didn't hesitate. He pointed at Nora.

A wave of possessiveness swept over Luke, making her ears burn. She felt Nora press against her back. Trembling fingers closed around her own, and she gave them a reassuring squeeze. She had to unclench her jaw before she could speak. "No." She looked the chief right in the eye, leaving no doubt about the finality of her decision.

But the Lakota didn't give up. He now offered three horses for "Red Hair."

Luke understood: The Lakota were fascinated with Nora's flaming red hair. She shook her head again. "She is my wife. I won't trade her."

The Lakota chief shoved the young Indian girl in her direction. "Three of my best horses and her. You'll still have a wife to care for you," he said in his language.

"No," Luke said. "I already have the wife I want. I won't trade her for anything you offer."

The Lakota frowned and turned to his braves. One of them fiddled with his bow, and another one rested his hand on the butt of an old smoothbore musket.

The emigrants began to reach for their weapons too.

"Maybe we should just turn her over," Bill Larson said.

Before Luke could turn toward him, the Lakota chief stepped forward. "If you don't want to give away the red-haired woman, give us the child." He pointed at something behind Luke.

Luke turned.

Amy peeked out from under the wagon cover's flap, her flaming red hair glowing in the sun.

Cursing under her breath, Luke faced the Lakota. She knew that she had to do something before the situation escalated. Briefly, she thought about offering Measles, but then she had another idea. "The woman is not a good worker." Even though Nora couldn't understand her words, Luke squeezed her hand in silent apology. "And the child is weak and sickly. I have something better that I can offer you."

The Lakota stood waiting, his face expressionless.

With slow movements, careful to keep her hands half-raised so that no one could misinterpret it as an attack, Luke turned toward the wagon and opened one of the trunks. She unfolded her navy-blue uniform coat. Suppressing a sigh, she turned back around and presented the jacket to the braves. She pointed out the row of the carefully polished brass buttons and the shoulder boards with embroidered gold bars.

The Lakota chief stepped closer and extended a hand to finger a gleaming button with almost childlike curiosity. He seemed interested, but then he lifted his head to look at Nora.

Before he could decide that the red-haired woman would be a better deal than an old military jacket, Luke reached into the trunk again and pulled out her saber. She showed him how to unsheathe it, then handed the weapon over to the chief.

The chief tested the blade's sharpness and grinned as he lifted a bloody thumb in the air.

"Luke," Nora whispered, gripping the back of her shirt. "Do you really want to give up your uniform?"

"It's all right," Luke whispered so only Nora could hear her. "I promised to take care of you and Amy until you find another husband. You don't want to marry him, do you?" She nodded at the chief.

The grip on Luke's shirt tightened. "No."

"You're supplying the Indians with weapons?" Bill Larson's brows lowered until they formed one thick, black line. "Do you want to encourage them to slaughter us all?"

Luke didn't even turn toward him. She kept her gaze on the chief, who was still weighing the saber in his hand. "A saber is a dangerous weapon in the hands of a trained dragoon officer, but it won't do much harm in the hands of a Lakota brave fighting against white men armed with revolvers and rifles." It was the truth. She had seen how much trouble the volunteers in the Mexican War had learning how to handle a saber. In the early months of the war, there had been a lot of lop-eared horses in their remuda.

She took a step forward, extending the saber's sheath in the chief's direction. "Do you want to trade for it?"

The Lakota took one final glance at Nora, then nodded and handed Luke the reins of his mare. Without another word, he took the saber and the uniform jacket and mounted one of the other horses he had initially offered Luke.

Within a minute, the emigrants were alone on the crest.

FORT LARAMIE,
JUNE 20TH, 1851

A collective sigh of relief went through the emigrants when the fifteen-foot adobe walls of Fort Laramie, topped with a wooden palisade, came into view.

"The captain said it's the halfway mark on the way to Oregon," Nora said.

Closer to the one-third mark, Luke thought but didn't say anything. She didn't want to discourage Nora.

After crossing the deep Laramie River, the captain had decided to set up camp two miles from the fort. They would remain there for a couple of days because their mules and oxen needed to regain their strength before continuing their way to the Rockies.

After taking care of the animals, most emigrants had decided to visit the fort.

Situated in the foothills of the Rockies, near the conjunction of the Laramie and North Platte Rivers, Fort Laramie was a much more impressive sight than Fort Kearny. Towerlike bastions in the form of blockhouses had been erected at two of the corners and over the main gate.

As they neared the main entrance, Luke saw a group of Lakota selling beaded moccasins and leather leggings outside the fort. Some were reclining on the low roofs of the buildings, looking down at them.

Luke felt Nora tense next to her. After passing through the Robidoux Pass, they had sometimes caught glimpses of the band of Lakota braves that had followed them for two days as if hoping that Luke would reconsider and offer them the scarlet-haired woman or the child. Nora had stayed in the wagon, suffering the constant jolting and jostling in silence.

"Don't worry," Luke said, gently pulling Nora a little closer. "This is not the same group, and your hair is barely visible beneath your sunbonnet. You'll be fine."

Nora settled her hand into the crook of Luke's elbow but didn't answer.

Then they passed through the gate, and Nora was instantly distracted. Luke smiled as she watched her take in the two-story frame houses with white porches, the blacksmith building, the wagon maker's shop, the sutler's store, three bakeries, and the garden that belonged to the fort.

"It's like a town," Nora said. She clapped her hands like a little girl.

"Do they have candy?" Amy asked.

Luke laughed. "Come on, we'll go look for some peppermint candy sticks while your mother sends off her letters."

Without hesitation, the girl grabbed two of her fingers and swung their joined hands back and forth as she dragged Luke across the parade ground.

Like every other item in the store, the candy was outrageously expensive. Luke gritted her teeth but handed over the coin. On the trail, Amy had to do without any of the luxuries that the children in towns back east enjoyed. She didn't have much entertainment, and neither Nora nor Luke had much time for her while the wagons were rolling. They hadn't had the opportunity or the money to replace Amy's doll yet. Now she wanted the girl to have something extra.

After a moment of hesitation, she counted out another dollar for a pound of tea. Nora preferred tea over coffee, but she had run out of it days ago and none of their neighbors had any left to trade either. When they left the store, Luke's gaze fell on the wooden sign posted outside of a small building. She couldn't decipher much more than that whatever was offered in the building cost a dollar.

One of the two doors opened, and a man emerged.

Amy took a nervous step back, hiding behind Luke's leg.

The stranger stopped and looked down at her with a smile. "Don't be afraid, li'l one. I'm not a monster, just an old man. I even took a bath."

Luke rested a protective hand on Amy's shoulder. She studied the stranger but couldn't detect anything threatening about him. He was tall and slender, his black hair neatly cut and damp from a recent bath. He looked down at Amy with twinkling gray eyes.

"A bath?" Luke looked at the wooden sign that she couldn't read. "Is that what they offer in there?"

"Yeah." The stranger rubbed a clean-shaven chin that was noticeably paler than the upper half of his face. "The only bathhouse within a few hundred miles."

A bathhouse. Privacy. Not having to hurry for fear of someone seeing me. It sounded like heaven to Luke. Her gaze wandered down to Amy, who was still holding on to Luke's leg with one hand while she nibbled on her candy. *Damn. That bath is gonna have to wait.* She had assumed responsibility for the girl, so she couldn't just send her off in search of her mother. As they walked toward the post office, she looked back over her shoulder. *Later,* she promised herself.

Fiddling with the letter in her hand, Nora waited for her turn to step up to the counter in the post office. Last night, it had taken her hours to decide what she should write. Tess had been much more than her employer; she had been the only true friend that Nora had ever had. There had never been many secrets between them. Tess even knew what circumstances had driven Nora to work in a brothel.

But now... Nora had delayed writing about the most important topic. She had started out the letter with some descriptions of the ever changing country they had traveled through, and she had written about the Lakota's attempt to trade her for three horses, laughing it off for Tess's sake. Then she had paused with her ink pen over the paper, hesitating for a long time. In the end, she had carefully penned the words. *I'm with child again.*

What she hadn't added was the fact that it was not her husband's. She would rather forget about that herself. While she wasn't ashamed of it, she wasn't proud of it either; she just tried not to lose any sleep about the things she had done to survive. But Luke was a friend of Tess's, and somehow being pregnant with another man's child while she was married to Luke felt like a betrayal. So, worrying that Tess would also think that, she had written only two sentences about being pregnant before folding up the letter.

Still thinking about the letter she had just mailed east, Nora stepped back outside. She wandered over the parade ground, looking for Luke and Amy.

Instead, another voice stopped her. "Hello."

She was long since used to that suggestive tone of voice. Nora forced a smile onto her face. Then she remembered: She was no longer a lady of the evening. She didn't have to grin and bear it any longer. Straightening her shoulders, she slowly turned around.

A tall, clean-shaven man leered down at her. "Don't I know you from somewhere?"

"I'm sure you confuse me with someone else," Nora said with as much dignity as she could muster.

His gaze seemed to drill into her. "I don't know. You sure look—"

"No," Nora said. "You don't know me. I don't think we've met." She eyed the stranger, trying to remember if they had met before. Whenever someone had approached her like this in Independence, he'd been a customer or at least someone who had seen her in the brothel, but now she wasn't sure. In the course of more than three years, there had simply been too many customers, and she had tried to forget them as fast as possible.

She breathed a sigh of relief when Amy came running to proudly show her a bag of candy sticks. Feeling Luke's comforting presence at her side, she relaxed further. "This is Lucas Hamilton—my husband," she said. This was one of the reasons why she had agreed to marry Luke. Surely the stranger wouldn't dare to bother her anymore. Maybe he would even think he really had her confused with some prostitute back east, now that he knew she was a married, respectable woman.

"We already met," Luke said, readily offering his hand to the other man.

"Brody Cowen."

Nora frowned as she watched them converse. Was it just her imagination or was Luke much more friendly toward the stranger than usual? Under normal circumstances, Luke was not exactly a social person. While the other emigrants sat together every evening, playing cards, dancing, or telling stories, he mainly watched the others from afar. Now he was having a lively conversation about their journey and what lay ahead. *With a former customer of all people.*

"I'm about to head west myself," Cowen said. "Do you think I could join your wagon train? It's safer not to travel alone."

Nora stopped breathing and clenched her fists behind her back. *God, no. Not that, please. Not now, when I have just built a new life. If he remembers where he knows me from, he'll destroy everything. Is this never gonna end?*

"I can't see why not." Luke craned his neck. "Let's talk to our captain, Abe McLoughlin. I just saw him heading into the post office."

When McLoughlin left the post office, Luke waved him over.

The roaring in Nora's ears drowned out the men's words. She watched their lips move as if from far away. Then the sound returned.

"Of course I'll have to ask the other members of the train," the captain said. "But if no one objects, you can join us." He glanced from Luke to Nora.

Nora's jaw tightened. She wanted to shout out her objection, but what was she supposed to say? That Brody Cowen shouldn't be allowed to join the train because he had probably paid to share her bed? She couldn't tell them that.

As Nora watched McLoughlin and Cowen shake hands, she started to tremble inside.

With a wry grin, Luke stepped through the door marked "men." The bathhouse cabin was partitioned into two sections, strictly separating the men from the women.

She locked the door and tested it, making sure that no one could walk in on her. Only then did she take the time to look around. The small room was pleasantly warm and smelled of soap and smoke. Stacks of towels and jars of bath salts lined the shelf against one wall. Steam rose from the tin tub in the middle of the room. She noted with satisfaction that the room had no windows.

Intent on enjoying every single minute that she had paid for, she tested the door once more and then stepped toward the tub. She dipped a finger into the water. *Mmmm.* She grinned. *Just the right temperature.*

Quickly, she pulled off her boots and socks. Her hat and her bandanna landed on top of a small stool; then she slipped the suspenders from her shoulders and shucked her pants. Standing in the middle of the room, she paused and glanced down at herself. The shirttails hung down her thighs, covering them, so all she could see were her lower legs. They were muscular and covered with fine, dark hairs. *Not much different from a man's.*

She lifted her hands to her shirt and released the buttons one by one. Finally, she parted the cotton and slid it down her arms. With movements that she had practiced a thousand times, she unwrapped the bindings around her chest and let them fall to the ground. Her gaze followed the path of the fabric downward. *Now that is very different.*

The tight bindings had left a criss-cross pattern of red welts across her skin, and Luke smoothed her hands over them. The touch of her callused palms on her breasts brought the image of a lover, a woman, touching her there. She had dreamed of such touches, especially since meeting Nora, but in reality, she had never allowed anyone to touch her without restraint, not even Tess.

She shook her head, trying to shake off the fantasies. *Stop daydreaming and get into the tub. The clock is tickin'.*

Carefully, she stepped into the tub and slid down until the water covered her shoulders. She leaned back and shivered pleasantly as the hot water engulfed her. The water got into her ears, muffling every sound as if it came from a distance. Luke closed her eyes and allowed herself to relax for the first time in weeks or even months. The world, her complicated life, seemed far away for the moment.

Some time later, she jerked awake, sputtering and spitting out water. Her neck hurt from resting on the rim of the tin tub, but the rest of her body felt limp and relaxed. Noticing that the water had begun to cool, she sat up and fished for the small bar of lavender soap next to the tub.

She scrubbed her hair and behind her ears, then smoothed the soap bar over her arms, enjoying the creamy bubbles on her skin. She rubbed her hands together and slid soapy palms over her breasts, down her stomach, and to the curls between her legs.

The sensations made her whole body tingle, and still, it felt as if what she was touching wasn't really her body, but that of a stranger. She didn't hate her body; she'd just never had the opportunity to get to know and like it.

And this is not the place or time to make up for it. Her time was almost up, and a lot of work was waiting back in camp. Reluctantly, she stepped out of the tub and dried herself off. One last stroke with the towel over the fair skin of her chest, then the wrappings covered it again.

Lucas Hamilton was back.

WARM SPRINGS,
JUNE 22ND, 1851

Nora swallowed the last mouthful of the cold meal of beans and buffalo meat that she had prepared that morning. The ever-present dust made her feel as if she were swallowing wood shavings.

Since leaving Fort Laramie, they had traveled uphill over sandy, rough roads. They were still following their constant companion, the North Platte River, but it was wider and clearer now and flowed much faster, slowly assuming the character of a mountain stream. At the same time, the landscape was becoming more barren. The wagons bumped over rocks and stones, jostling up and down steep ravines. No longer could they spread out to avoid choking on the dust generated by the wagons in front of them.

Nora's lips were cracking, her skin itched, and her eyes stung. With a groan, she got to her swollen feet. The morning sickness had all but disappeared in the last few weeks, and she finally felt better, but her growing stomach didn't let her forget about her delicate condition. *Your stomach's not all that's getting bigger.* She looked down at her bosom with a half-grin. *Not that Luke would ever notice or appreciate it.*

"You all right?" Luke asked while he put away the last of the washed dishes and readied the wagon.

"Uh, yeah, of course." Nora quickly straightened, a bit embarrassed to have been caught ogling herself. "My eyes are bothering me. That's all."

Luke took something from the back of the wagon. After a second's hesitation, he stepped close to Nora. "Hold still," he said.

Nora did. She held her breath as his fingertips gently touched her face. What was he doing? It took a second for her to understand that he was spreading zinc sulfate ointment over the irritated skin around her eyes.

"Better?" The gentleness in his eyes belied the matter-of-fact tone of his voice.

Nora had to swallow. It was just because of the dust, she told herself. "Yes, thank you."

"Me too! Me too!" Amy hopped up and down next to the wagon.

Luke crouched so that he was at eye level with Amy. A smile played around his lips as he applied the ointment to Amy's eyes. "There you go." He tried to straighten, but Amy had grabbed an edge of his shirt and held fast.

"Papa need too."

The new title still made him blush. He held still while Amy's clumsy hands spread ointment over the majority of his face. "Uh, thank you." He waited until Amy ran off to search for her friends, then hastily wiped at his face, trying to get the excess of ointment off.

"Here, let me help." Nora lifted her hand to his face.

Luke shook his head and tried to move away from her. "No, it's all right. I have it."

Of course he hadn't. Streaks of white still remained across his forehead and his left cheekbone.

Nora smiled up at him. "You're gonna scare the oxen," she said and again lifted her hand. She touched the skin of his face, wiping away the ointment with her thumbs. For a second, she admired the smoothness of his skin, but then Jacob's yell broke the silence, and the wagon in front of theirs started to roll again.

Luke turned away from her. His whip cracked through the air with more vigor than necessary.

Sighing, Nora fell into step next to him.

Just a few minutes later, Bernice hurried over from her wagon. She nodded at a point to the right of the road and grinned at Nora. "Do you feel like a hot bath?"

"Lord, yes." Nora longed to get the sweat and dust off her skin. Every muscle in her body screamed at her. "But I don't think that's gonna happen for some time—or do you have a tub full of hot water in the back of your wagon?" She flashed a regretful smile at Bernice.

"You won't need one. Jacob says there's a hot spring ahead, and we're gonna camp there for the night."

Nora's eyes closed as she imagined sinking into clean, pleasantly warm water. "Mm-hm. That's my kind of campsite."

When they set up camp, Nora did her chores as fast as she could while she waited for her turn to use the natural tub.

Finally, her half-hour to use the thermal springs had arrived. Quickly, she grabbed her precious bar of soap and reached for Amy's hand. Then she stopped in midstep and looked back over her shoulder at Luke. "Do you want to go first?"

"No, no, you go ahead." He waved her away.

"You could come with us."

Again, Luke shook his head. "I already had a bath in Fort Laramie. Go on, don't waste your time. The Larsons are already waiting for their turn."

For a man who always smells good, he sure is shying away from every opportunity to bathe. With one last glance at Luke, Nora led her daughter toward the hot spring.

Amy squealed as she saw the steam rising up from the rocky tub.

As the wagon train approached the Rockies, the air grew colder in the evenings, and the bubbling hot water filled the air with steam.

Nora helped Amy, who could barely hold still, with her clothes and held her hand while she carefully tiptoed over the rocks. When Amy was safely settled in the tub, she stripped off her own clothes and slipped into the water. "Oh, this is nice."

Amy splashed water at her.

Nora swallowed some of the water and spat it back out. *Ugh.* The spring's water was unpalatable. *Sitting in it is much nicer than drinking it.* She made a face.

Amy giggled.

"Oh, you want to start a water fight, little lady? You can have that." She shoved a wave of water at her squealing daughter, who began to splash with her hands and feet, drenching Nora to the very last hair on her head.

"My, my, look at that. The whore and her daughter, the picture of domesticity."

Nora almost slipped on the slippery rocks as her head jerked around.

There, right in front of her, stood Broderick Cowen, the man who had probably once been one of her customers. So far, she had managed to stay away from him, but apparently, he didn't plan on staying away from her. He leered at her, letting his gaze wander over her naked body with a grin.

She crossed her arms in front of her chest and tried not to let him see how scared she was. She knew it would only encourage a man like him. "Leave us alone. You shouldn't be here," she said, trying to keep her voice steady.

"I shouldn't, huh? Who's gonna stop me?" Cowen took a step closer.

Nora moved her own body in front of Amy's. She didn't want her to have anything to do with Cowen or any of her other former customers. "My husband—"

"Oh, yes, I almost forgot." Cowen laughed. "You got yourself a gullible little husband, huh? Does he know that you used to open your legs for any man who had a piece of silver in his hand?"

Nora's teeth ground against each other. His insulting words made her cheeks burn, but this was not the time or place for pride. In the last three years, she had trained herself never to show any of the pain or humiliation she might be feeling.

Cowen took another step forward. He was right at the edge of the rocky pool now, and Nora scrambled back as far as she could, wrapping a protective arm around her trembling daughter. She eyed her surroundings, but there was no help, no chance to hide or flee. "Please."

"Does he know that the bun you've got warming in the oven is not his?" Cowen asked. "Hell, for all I know, it might be mine."

Every muscle in Nora's body stiffened. The metallic taste of fear coated her tongue, and for a moment, even breathing was difficult. She rested her free hand protectively on her belly. *God, don't let him spread that around.* The worst thing was that she couldn't even rule out the possibility that he had fathered her baby. She hadn't kept a record on her customers, had always tried to forget about them as soon as possible, so there was no way for her to know if and when Cowen had shared her bed. "It isn't. This baby is my husband's," she said with as much determination as she could muster.

"Mrs. Hamilton?" Bill Larson shouted from some distance away. "Your time's up."

Nora had never thought that she would be glad about Larson's presence in the train.

With one last smirk, Broderick Cowen turned around and was gone.

Her knees shaking, Nora stood and lifted an equally trembling Amy from the rocky tub. She dried them off and dressed quickly. Afraid to be caught alone by Cowen again, she headed straight for the wagon and Luke.

"That was quick," Luke said from his place by the fire. He didn't look up from the frying pan that he was watching over.

"There was a bad man," Amy said as soon as they reached Luke.

Amy, no, Nora wanted to shout, but it was too late.

Luke was already taking the frying pan from the fire and turning around. He knelt down to be at eye level with Amy. "A bad man?"

Amy's head bobbed up and down as she nodded. "Vewwy bad. He scared Mama and me."

Still kneeling, Luke fixed his gaze on Nora. "What happened? Who frightened you?"

"Nobody," Nora said. She didn't want Luke to know what had happened because it would give him one more reason to send her away. She could tell that one of the reasons why he had married her had been to fit in with the other emigrants of the wagon train. Every other settler was taking his family with him and had someone to care for him. Even with a wife and a child, Luke was already the outsider of the wagon train, and Nora felt that she was somehow a link to the others for Luke. To be able to do that, she had to keep up appearances.

"Nobody?" Luke raised both brows. "Then why do you both look scared to death?"

"It's just... Mr. Cowen just scared her a bit." Nora shrugged as casually as possible. "He came upon us bathing. It took us by surprise. That's all."

"If you're sure that's all."

"It is," Nora said.

With a nod, Luke returned to his frying pan.

Nora let a trembling breath escape. For once, Luke's blind spot where Broderick Cowen was concerned came in handy. For some reason, Luke seemed impressed with Cowen and would never think him capable of tormenting a woman and her child. Luckily, Amy was quiet now, and Nora prayed that she would forget the incident soon. *And that it's gonna stop with this one incident.*

AYERS BRIDGE,
JUNE 26TH, 1851

"There." Brody Cowen reined in his horse on a hill and pointed.

Luke stopped Measles next to him.

A herd of antelopes grazed below them.

Brody hummed. "Finally, we'll get some antelope steaks for dinner." He lifted his rifle and aimed.

Before he could squeeze the trigger, one antelope raised its head. Its tail flicked, and then the antelope ran, followed by the rest of the herd. They stopped just outside of gun range.

Luke groaned. "Let's leave the horses here and try our luck down at the creek." She settled her rifle in the crook of her elbow and led the way. "Want to see something amazing? There's a special place not far from the watering hole."

Brody shrugged. "Why not. So you traveled through here before?"

"I led a few expeditions during the Cayuse Wars," Luke said.

"You were a dragoon?"

Luke nodded.

"Me too," Brody said. "Nearly lost a leg—and my soul—in the Mexican War."

He left it at that, and Luke didn't ask questions.

They walked along the creek in silence. Many of the emigrants Luke had met along the way told stories around the campfire about how they had single-handedly won the war. Luke suppressed a snort. Most of them had probably never even been in Mexico. Only people who had never experienced war seemed to think it a heroic adventure.

Brady didn't brag about his wartime experiences. Maybe that was why Luke had taken a liking to him.

Oh, come on, Hamilton. Have you gotten so used to lying to the world that you're starting to lie to yourself? You know exactly where that sympathy is coming from.

Growing up, she had often asked herself—and her mother—who her father might be. Was he a good man? Was he tall? Were his eyes gray like her own? Did he like horses? Her mother had soon grown tired of the questions and had forbidden her from ever asking about her father again. But the questions in her mind had never stopped. During her years as a cowhand, then as she worked herself up through the ranks of the dragoons and fought in Mexico, whenever she had met an older man who resembled her, she had wondered, *Could this be my father?*

Brody's black hair and gray eyes had started these questions again. As a child, she had often dreamed that her father would come and take her with him, but then she had realized that, even if he ever learned of her existence, he probably wouldn't care. Still, those old daydreams were hard to extinguish.

"So, where is that wonder of yours?" Brody asked.

"There." Luke stopped and pointed.

Ahead of them, in a hidden red canyon, a natural bridge of solid rock arched across the little stream.

"Nice." Brody gave a surprised whistle.

They walked closer, fighting through thickets and undergrowth, balancing from rock to rock and over the pebbles in the low-level creek. Wading into ankle-deep water, they stood right under the stone arch that spanned thirty feet high over the water. The singing of the birds swooping into their nests echoed around them.

"Idyllic, huh?" Luke lowered her voice so she wouldn't disturb the peaceful atmosphere in the little canyon.

"Not bad, yeah, but I think we better hunt down our dinner and rejoin the others before they're too far ahead."

He's not one to stop and smell the flowers, huh? With a suppressed sigh, Luke started up the bank and through the thicket.

They circled back around until they reached the waterhole.

"Look at that." Brody pointed with the barrel of his rifle. He flashed a grin. "I think your little wife is gonna make some buffalo stew tonight."

Little wife? Luke's hackles rose, but she said nothing. She didn't want to start a fight with the older man. Instead, she looked in the direction he indicated.

A lone buffalo stood at the edge of the creek, his muzzle in the water, drinking heavily.

A few years ago, when Luke had first started riding expeditions along the Platte River, big herds of the shaggy beasts had roamed the prairie. Sometimes, the soldiers had to stop and wait for hours until a herd had passed.

On this trip, there hadn't been moving masses as far as the eye could see. Instead, the valley of the Platte had been dotted with buffalo skulls. Whenever they had encountered a small group of buffalos, most of the men had abandoned the wagons and rushed off to shoot a buffalo, not for food, but for sport. Luke had never done that. There was no point in killing more than you could eat.

She laid a hand along the raised barrel of Brody's rifle. "It's an old bull—very tough meat. We should wait for an antelope."

Brody shook his head. "That could be a very long wait. I say we seize the moment. I don't want to return empty-handed." He looked pointedly at her hand that still rested on his rifle.

Reluctantly, Luke lifted her hand.

Careful to stay downwind of his prey, Brody swung up the barrel and took aim. He didn't aim at the head—the skull was too hard to penetrate—but set his sights on the spot right behind the shoulder. Brody exhaled, then pulled the trigger.

The shot echoed through the canyon.

The bull threw his head up and started to run. After the second step, his legs collapsed, and he went down. Sand and pebbles scattered in all directions as his massive weight came crashing down.

Finally, the bull lay still.

NORTH PLATTE CROSSING,
JUNE 29TH, 1851

"I could do this for you, you know?" Nora said again. She watched as Luke mended his torn pant leg. This was something that she could do for him, offer him in return for his name and his protection.

He didn't look up from his task. "No, thank you. I've done this for years. No need to change things now."

The grass along the trail had given way to sage and thorny greasewood, and Nora knew the roads would only get worse, so there was still hope that she would get an opportunity to mend his torn pants another time.

Today, they had encountered a bend in the North Platte. The river swung sharply away to the south, blocking their way, so they'd had to cross it. The North Platte with its swift current and deep waters was notorious, leaving them no choice but to pay the overpriced toll of the ferry that the Mormons had established.

The captain had warned them that the next fresh water was twenty miles away, so they had decided to start out for Willow Spring before dawn the next day and camp here for the rest of the day.

While Amy spent the afternoon under the watchful eyes of the older Garfield children, Nora was determined not to stray away from Luke even for a second. Since Broderick Cowen had joined the wagon train, he pestered her the moment Luke's back was turned, but he was never anything but polite when Luke was around. That made sure that Luke's odd hero worship for the man wouldn't stop anytime soon, but at least Nora had some moments of peace while she stayed close to her husband.

So Nora sat back and busied herself with sewing baby clothes while she watched him ladle hot water from the kettle over the fire into a washbasin. *What's this? Is he going to wash up right in front of me? Now, that would be something new.* She continued to watch from under half-lowered lids.

He set the washbasin down on the wagon tongue, but instead of unbuttoning his shirt, he took his razor blade and ran it over a broad strap of leather. With nimble fingers, he lathered his brush with shaving soap and spread the thick foam over his cheeks and chin.

"Why do you shave every day?" Nora asked. "Why not just grow a beard like every other man on the trail?" *Not that I'm complaining, mind you.* She didn't care for the straggled hair and matted beards of many other men.

Luke paused with the razor blade raised halfway to his cheek. "I don't like feeling like an unkempt drunkard."

"You wouldn't look unkempt even if you didn't shave every day. For a man with black hair, your beard is very light." When she'd first met him, the soft downy hairs on Luke's cheeks had made her think he was young and inexperienced.

Luke's expression darkened. Obviously, he didn't like to be reminded of his boyish looks. "Every man in my family had light facial hair. It's nothing unusual."

"Of course not," Nora said. *Ouch. I think I've hit a tender spot.* She watched in silence as he moved the razor blade over his face, carefully removing the lather and whatever facial hair there might be.

When he wiped away the rest of the shaving soap, Nora let her gaze wander over his face. "You could use a haircut."

Luke lifted a hand and self-consciously touched the hair in the back of his neck.

"Why don't I cut it for you?" *Yes!* Finally she had found something that she could do for him. *He certainly can't cut his own hair without risking an ear or looking like a herd of buffalo munched on his head.*

"All right."

His answer came with hesitation, so Nora knew she had to move quickly or he would change his mind. She gently pressed him down to sit on the trunk that held their cooking utensils and grabbed the scissors he had used for mending his pants. She stepped closer until she could rest one hand on his shoulder for balance. Experimentally, she let her fingers glide through his hair, surprised by the silkiness of it. "How do you want it?"

"W-what?"

Nora rolled her eyes and hid a grin. She had often asked that question in a very different context, and Luke seemed to be well aware of that. "Your hair. How do you want it cut?"

"Short."

Stepping even closer, Nora lowered the scissors to his neck. "Relax," she said right into his ear. She wanted to run her hands soothingly over stiff shoulders and down rigid back muscles, but she knew it would only chase him away, so she concentrated on her task instead. She fingered a strand of hair, enjoying the way the sunlight danced over it, making it shine like the fur of the panther whose picture she had once seen in a book.

Luke turned his head to see what she was doing. "Are you gonna use those scissors or not?"

Nora gently turned his head back around. "Hold still." She started with the dark waves that fell onto the collar of his shirt. When she had it all at the same length, she leaned forward to work on the hair around his ears. Her rounded belly pressed against his shoulder, and both of them froze for a second.

"Is that…?" Luke turned and stared up at her with wide eyes.

The childlike awe on the usually stoic face robbed Nora of speech for a moment. "Yeah. He's really active today, moving around a lot."

"He?" Luke repeated. "You know that it's gonna be a boy?"

Nora laughed. For a mature man, he was quite naïve about some things, and to her surprise, she found it endearing. "There's no way to be sure. I can't look inside, you know?" She grinned at his embarrassed expression. "But I figure it's a fifty-fifty chance, and I know most men wish for a boy. A son." She spoke the last words cautiously, watching his reaction. Would he really accept the baby as his own, now that its existence was no longer just an abstract concept but became more real each day?

"Not me," Luke said after long seconds of silence.

Swallowing heavily, Nora blinked to fight down threatening tears. She started to turn away, but Luke's next words stopped her.

"I like girls, you know?" He looked back over his shoulder and winked at her.

The wave of relief swept away the last remains of her composure. She swung around and hit him in the shoulder, laughing while she felt hot tears run down her face.

"Careful." He caught her as she threatened to fall.

Nora burrowed her face against his neck, deeply breathing in the scent of him and his shaving soap.

"What is it?" he asked. "I was only joking. I would care for a boy as much as I would for a girl. It doesn't matter to me. I'll take care of you all until you've remarried."

Nora drew back and sniffled. She didn't know what to say now that he had seen her blatant display of emotions.

"Do you think you can finish that haircut now?" He fingered the hairs above his right ear. "It's gonna look a little uneven like this."

With a smile, Nora went back to work.

SALERATUS LAKE,
JULY 2ND, 1851

"Eek! Papa, that smells bad." Amy wrinkled her nose.

Luke smiled down at the child sitting in the saddle in front of her. *Lord, I never thought I would grow used to having someone call me "Papa."* "Yes, Amy, it smells very bad, and it tastes even worse. It's very important that you never drink that water."

Since leaving behind the Platte River, they had encountered the worst section of the trail so far. They had to struggle up steep hills and through barren land with almost no grass for their animals. All around them, clouds of mosquitoes swarmed.

"Lord Almighty!" Jacob waved his arm to chase away the mosquitoes. "They're so big that you could mistake them for turkeys."

Even worse were the foul-smelling alkaline swamps they now traveled through. The soil and the water in this area were heavily impregnated with salt, alkali, and sulphur, making what little water there was undrinkable.

Luke was riding circles around the herd of spare oxen, cows, and horses, trying to keep the thirsty animals away from the poisonous water. The bleached bones of animals around the alkali ponds told them what would happen if their livestock drank from this water.

"Take care. There's another one," Jacob said from the back of his gelding. He pointed to the left of the road.

Luke turned in the saddle, careful to keep an arm wrapped around Amy. Another small lake lay in front of them, ringed with a yellowish crust around its shore. "Oh, at last. That's Saleratus Lake. Now it won't be long until we reach Sweetwater River."

"Saleratus Lake?" Jacob asked.

"Yeah. See that alkaline crust on the shore?" Luke pointed. "That's saleratus. Tell your wife to gather some of it. It makes a good substitute for baking powder." She shifted in the saddle to face the wagon train. Her gaze immediately found her wagon.

Nora walked next to it, urging the tired oxen onward with a practiced crack of her whip. The oxen plodded through the sandy ground, their heads bobbing with weariness.

Finally, a large valley opened in front of them. The glittering band of the Sweetwater River, clear and a hundred feet wide, ran through the valley.

The oxen fell into a clumsy trot.

They stopped to water the animals but then traveled on. An hour later, they reached the large granite mound that had loomed in the distance for days. It rose a hundred and thirty feet from the Sweetwater Valley, looking like a giant turtle.

The river ran by the foot of the giant boulder, and there was enough grass to last their animals for days. Captain McLoughlin decided that they would stay here for two days, celebrating Independence Day around the rock with the same name, as many other emigrants had done before them.

They circled the wagons and erected the tents under tall cedars and pines next to the river. As soon as they had tended to the animals, most of the emigrants set out to climb Independence Rock. Wayne, the oldest Garfield boy, started the climb with two young girls of the train, promising to carve their names on top of the rock.

Luke had climbed Independence Rock before. She knew it was covered with thousands of names from emigrants, trappers, and explorers, earning it the nickname "Great Desert Register."

"Mama, I want to go too." Amy tugged on Nora's apron.

"I'm sorry, sweetie." Nora stroked the red curls with one hand while the other rested on her belly. "I'm too tired to climb that rock, and you're not old enough to go on your own."

"I'm vewwy old." The girl straightened to her full thirty-five inches.

Nora sighed. "Amy."

"It's all right," Luke said. "I can take her." When she saw Nora's concerned gaze, she added in her most reassuring voice, "It's an easy climb, and I promise to take good care of her."

"I go with Papa." Amy hopped up and down, her big eyes begging Nora to allow it.

"All right," Nora finally said.

Amy skipped toward Luke and grabbed her hand.

"I'll stay down here," Nora said. "You two go and enjoy yourselves. But please be careful."

"Good," Luke said. "I mean, it really is an easy climb, and I would love for you to enjoy the sight from up there too, but…" Since she had learned of Nora's pregnancy, every slight risk the young woman took tended to make Luke nervous as hell.

"I know what you mean." Nora waved them away. "Go."

Holding on to Amy's hand, Luke headed toward Independence Rock. After a few steps, she looked back over her shoulder.

Nora stood watching them walk away, an expression almost like fear or maybe sadness on her face.

Is she sad that she can't go too? "Just a second," Luke said to Amy and turned back around. "How do you write 'Nora'?"

"What? Why?"

"Since you can't make it, I thought I would carve your name into the rock for you," Luke said.

Nora's smile was oddly shy for a woman who had once been a prostitute. "I'd like that. Thank you." She picked up a stick and drew the letters into the sandy soil.

"And Amy? How do you write that?"

Nora scratched three letters into the dust. "Can you remember that?"

Luke flashed a smile. "Well, you'll never know if I get the letters mixed up, and Amy won't tell, will you?"

"Nooo." The girl giggled and shook her head even though it was clear that she didn't know what the adults were talking about.

"All right, let's go." Luke held firmly on to the girl's hand as they slowly made their way to the top of the rock. From the summit, she saw the Sweetwater meandering through the surrounding prairie until it tumbled through Devil's Gate, the next landmark on their journey west.

"Look, Papa. Little, little wagons."

Luke knelt and wrapped an arm around Amy's shoulder, making sure that the girl didn't step too close to the edge. Only then did she take the time to look down. From on top of Independence Rock, other wagon trains approaching the Sweetwater looked tiny, like children's toys. "I see them, Amy." Truthfully, she barely noticed the landscape around them. She focused on keeping Amy safe and marveling at how Amy had tucked her small hand into Luke's bigger one, trusting her completely.

Amy finally grew tired of watching the wagons below. She turned to study the host of names, dates, and initials that were chiseled into the rock or painted on with axle grease. "There no more place," she said, waving her arm.

"Oh, yes, there is." Luke smiled. "Amy is a really short name, and so is Nora. There's plenty of space for your names." In her mind, she repeated the letters that Nora had drawn into the dust, hoping that she had memorized them correctly.

Amy gazed up at her. "Is 'Papa' a short name too?"

Papa Hamilton, huh? Luke suppressed a grin. "Yes, it is. There's enough place for all of them." After directing Amy another step away from the edge, she drew her knife and started to carve the first letter of Nora's name into the rock.

Compared with carving names into the softer sandstone of Register Cliff, another natural register of emigrants to the east, this was much harder work. She broke out in a sweat but continued to work, determined to leave the girl's name and that of her mother on top of the rock. Finally, she stepped back. "There."

Carved into the gray stone, side by side, were three names: Nora, Amy, and Luke Hamilton.

Carved in stone. Luke stared at the names with a sudden, frightening realization. She had never planned on being linked to a woman and a child for eternity, but now she was. She rolled her eyes at herself. *It's just a dumb rock, not a divination of your life.*

"Papa?"

"Yeah?" She turned toward the child, but half of her attention was still on the names in the rock's surface.

Amy wrapped her arms around Luke's legs in an affectionate embrace. "I love you."

Luke's breath caught. *It's just the thin air up here.* She dragged the back of her hand over her eyes. *Damn, that stingin' dust is everywhere.* With burning eyes, she stared at the girl, who expectantly gazed back. She wanted to remain silent or change the topic of conversation, anything to avoid making promises that she couldn't keep, but she still remembered the many rejections during her own childhood and how much they had hurt.

Amy still stared at her without even blinking. As the seconds went by without a word from Luke, the hope in her eyes began to dim. Her smile faded, and her bottom lip started to tremble.

"I…" Luke cleared her dry throat. "Amy…" She searched for words, but then she realized that there could only be one answer to Amy's declaration of daughterly love. She took a deep breath. "I love you too, sweetie."

A big smile spread over Amy's face.

Luke reached out a hand and tussled the girl's locks, trying to relieve the emotions of the moment. "All right. Let's get back down that rock before your mother starts to worry."

"It's green," Nora said, holding up the freshly baked loaf of bread.

Bernice looked up from her own bread dough. "Green as Irish clover," she said and grinned.

"Mine too." Emeline Larson gazed at her loaf of bread with a horrified expression.

"Oh, don't look so glum," Bernice said. "You used a bit too much saleratus. That's all. It'll taste slightly bitter, but it's still eatable."

Nora nodded. Greenish bread wouldn't impress Luke, but it certainly wouldn't kill him either.

"I c-can't let Bill see this."

"Oh, come on," Bernice said. "He's no better than the rest of us. We all had to eat things that we wouldn't have touched back home. He's gonna have to eat it or go hungry."

Nora knew it wasn't that easy for Emeline. Bernice's husband was good-natured and quiet, but Emeline's wasn't. The green bread would give Larson a reason to beat his wife again—not that he needed a reason. Just the way she was breathing seemed to enrage him sometimes.

Nora shuddered. *I could have ended up being married to that kind of man.* She had been lucky, but she never forgot that she could have easily been in Emeline's place. "You know what? I'm gonna help you bake a new one, and this time, we'll use less saleratus. Bill won't have to know."

"Oh, thank you, thank you. That's so kind of you."

"No need to thank me." Nora stood and moved toward her wagon. *I better give her a bit from our supply of flour. Larson controls every aspect of her life. I'm sure he knows exactly how much flour was in their sack.* She rounded the wagon and collided with the person leaning against their wagon's back.

Broderick Cowen. For a few seconds, she stood paralyzed, trying to get enough air through the lump in her throat. "What…?" She wanted to take a proud stance and demand to know what he was doing by their wagon, but she didn't dare to. She couldn't even look him in the eyes.

"Ah, look at that." He grinned down at her, but his smile was void of humor. They were cold as steel. "Nora Hamilton. Or should I say Fleur, the whore?"

Nora gasped. She hadn't been called by that name in more than two months. When she had married Luke, she had thought that she'd left that part of her life behind, but with Broderick Cowen, her past had caught up with her.

"What? You thought I wouldn't remember you?" Cowen laughed. "We had an unforgettable night back in Independence, so how could I forget you? Imagine my delight in meeting you here, just when I thought that I wouldn't have a woman until we arrive in Oregon."

Thoughts and emotions somersaulted through Nora's head. "I-I'm married now," was all she could get out.

Cowen snorted. "You don't fool me. You're no respectable woman, married or not. Once a whore, always a whore." He grabbed her by the arms, pulled her against his body, and roughly covered her mouth with his.

His body pressed against her rounded belly. The stubbles on his face scratched over her cheek, making her stomach roil. Panic shot through Nora, but then old instincts took over. *Stop struggling and hold still. If you're lucky, it'll be over soon.* No one in the wagon train would need to know, so no one would question her past. *Maybe he's right. Once a whore, always a whore.*

"Nora? Do you think you could maybe lend me some flour?" Emeline Larson's voice came from the other side of the wagon, just a few steps away. "Nora?"

Cowen pushed her back and walked away.

Nora stumbled and almost fell. At the last second, she grabbed the edge of the wagon, preventing a fall, but scraping her hands in the process. With trembling fingers, she wiped her mouth and tried to put her hair into some semblance of order. Still holding on to the wagon, she stepped toward Emeline. "Yes, of course you can have some flour," she answered, hoping that her voice wasn't trembling.

Emeline came around the wagon. "Was that Brody Cowen? What did he want?"

Me. Nora pressed both hands against her stomach, feeling the nervous fluttering as the baby moved. "He... I...I think he wanted to talk to Luke."

"About what?" Luke's voice came from behind her.

Nora almost fell for the second time in less than a minute. *No. Why does he have to return now of all times?* She was not ready to face him.

"Mama, Mama, I goed all the way up the big rock. All on my own. Papa only helped a little." Her cheerful daughter was a welcome distraction.

"That's great, sweetie. I'm proud of you. Did you carve our names into the stone?" Nora tried to lose herself in the normalcy of the conversation and forget about her unpleasant encounter with Broderick Cowen. Up until two months ago, that was what she had been doing on a daily basis.

While Amy started to chatter away, Nora felt Luke's gaze on her.

"Are you all right?" he asked.

Nora bit her lip. Had she gotten so bad at hiding her feelings in such a short time? Or had he become so good at reading her? "I'm fine," she said.

"Your hands are bleeding." Luke's gray eyes gazed at her with concern, so unlike Brody Cowen's, even if they were the same color.

Nora looked at her hands. They were still resting on her belly, so the scratches were on open display. "Just a scratch. I stumbled and caught my clumsy self. That's all."

Emeline stared at her with wide eyes.

Nora imagined that she was all too familiar with "being clumsy." She shook her head at the young woman, begging her to say nothing.

"You stumbled? I thought those dizzy spells were finally over?" Luke pointed at her stomach.

"They are. My heel just caught on a stone." Being a good liar and actor had been a part of her former work, and she hoped that she was still good at it.

"Maybe you should rest for a bit," Luke said.

The sincere concern in his voice began to thaw Nora's heart that had been frozen with fear. "I will, as soon as we've finished baking bread."

Luke nodded. "Good. Then I'm off to see what Brody wanted."

Nora almost bit through her lip. The bitter tang of copper stung her tongue. *No. Stay away from him.* But she didn't know what to say, and before she could think of something, Luke was gone.

Something was going on with Nora. Luke sensed it, but she didn't have the slightest idea as to what it was. *Maybe it's the baby.* She had never been around pregnant women for any length of time, so she wasn't sure what to expect as the pregnancy progressed. *Maybe pregnant women do become clumsy when their bellies grow.*

She shook herself out of her thoughts when she detected Brody sitting by his fire, smoking a pipe.

He smiled as she took a place next to him and offered her the pipe.

Luke didn't care for tobacco, but this was part of the price that she paid for living in disguise. Smoking and drinking were part of male camaraderie, and if she wanted to be regarded as a man, she couldn't reject these offers. With an inward sigh, she took the pipe and inhaled as shallowly as she could get away with.

"So," Brody said, taking back his pipe, "how was Independence Rock?"

Luke shrugged. "Big." She had learned that most men didn't lose a lot of words describing the scenery, so she acted accordingly.

"Not too big for that young'un of yours?"

A mental picture of Amy bravely marching up the rock appeared before her mind's eye. An affectionate smile formed on her lips. "No, she was fine. She's a feisty one."

"So is her mother, huh?" Brody looked at her through a veil of smoke.

Luke frowned. Feisty wasn't the first word that came to mind when she thought about Nora. If she had to use just one word to describe the woman she had married, it would have been "survivor." Nora was good at adjusting and doing anything necessary to ensure the well-being of her daughter. Luke knew that the men who visited brothels liked their women to be submissive, so Nora had learned to hide her feistiness, a quick wit, and a keen intelligence. Luke tried every day to show Nora that she wanted a wife who thought for herself and was not afraid to offer her opinion, and she was beginning to see glimpses of how Nora had been before she had become Fleur. But from what she had seen, Nora didn't feel comfortable with Brody. She eyed Luke's new friend with distrust and tended to keep her distance, so what was Brody referring to?

"Feisty?" she asked, trying to discern Brody's expression through the smoke of his pipe. Brody shrugged but didn't explain why he thought Nora feisty. "How did you meet her?"

Luke blinked. No one had ever asked her about their marriage, so she hadn't worked out what to tell people about their imaginary first meeting or courtship. "Oh, you know, the usual."

"And what's that? I've never been married, so you better explain," Brody said with a grin.

"We kinda ran into each other in front of the livery stable, and I offered to escort her home." Luke didn't want to lie to her new friend, and this was at least partly true.

Brody blew rings of smoke into the air. "Did her family own that stable?"

Why is he asking all these questions? In Luke's experience, men seldom asked a lot of questions about relationships, but for some reason, Brody seemed to have taken a special interest in Nora. "No, she had an employment nearby. She was a seamstress," she said before he could ask.

"Seamstress? Is that what she told you?"

A piece of wood cracked under Luke's feet as she straightened and turned more toward Brody to stare at him. Despite the cautious friendship she had formed with him, she felt her hackles rise. "What are you implying?"

Brody knocked out his pipe against the felled trunk he was sitting on. "I'm not sure I should tell you. I don't want to cause trouble between you and your wife."

"You won't." Whatever Brody might tell her about Nora, it probably wouldn't surprise her. "Tell me." If she found out what Brody knew about Nora's past, she could take measures to protect her from becoming the object of gossip.

Brody leaned forward, fixing an intense gaze on Luke. "Well, this will come as a shock to you, but I have reason to believe that your wife is a prostitute."

Luke felt the blood rush to her face, coloring her cheeks—not with embarrassment, but with anger. She forced herself to remain sitting and unclenched her hands before she answered, "She is nothing of the kind. She's my wife, a good mother, and a decent person."

"I understand that you don't want to believe—"

"I know what she's been, but that's the past. It doesn't matter now," Luke said. Brody probably meant well and thought he was doing Luke a favor by enlightening her about Nora's past, but she didn't want it spread around camp.

"You know that she worked as—?"

"Yes."

Brody shook his head. "And still you think it doesn't matter? It doesn't matter to you that she shared her bed with hundreds of men before you? It doesn't matter that you're probably not the father of the bastard that she's trying to pin on you?"

Every muscle in Luke's body stiffened. She felt protective instincts rise that she hadn't even known she possessed. "The baby is not a bastard, and Nora is not trying to pin anything on me." Other emigrants looked over from their campfires, so Luke lowered her voice. "I know you mean well, but you're not doing me any favors by bringing up Nora's past. I'm asking you to keep quiet about it. Please." It had been a long time since she had asked a favor of someone, but protecting Nora was more important than pride.

"You're running headlong into disaster, son." Brody pointed the mouthpiece of his pipe at Luke. "What spell has she put you under? I know she's an enticing woman, but—"

"Stop." Luke had waited all her life for someone to call her son—or *daughter*—and show her some fatherly concern, but right now it was only annoying her. It was a bittersweet experience. "I know of her past, and if it doesn't matter to me, it shouldn't matter to anyone else. So please keep quiet about it."

"If that's what you want." Brody put away his pipe and stood. "But you're gonna change your mind when that naïve infatuation has worn off." Not waiting for an answer, he walked away.

Independence Rock,
July 4th, 1851

Nora leaned back against the wagon wheel, slowly nibbling on the tender meat of a quail to make it last while she listened to the lively music.

All around her, her fellow travelers were laughing, singing, and dancing to celebrate Independence Day. Wayne Garfield swung around one girl after another, and even Bill Larson stiffly led his wife across the improvised dance floor.

Bernice leaned over to offer her a piece of freshly baked bread. "Why don't you join the others? You're still young, so why not enjoy a dance with your husband?"

Nora stole a glance at Luke. He was sitting back, watching the activities around him. After the harsh rebuff at the hoedown the day after they had left Independence, she didn't dare to ask him to dance again. "I'm pregnant and tired and my feet are swollen enough as it is," Nora said.

"Oh, nonsense." Bernice gave her an encouraging shove toward the other dancers. "None of my pregnancies kept me from dancing. I had to be dragged off the dance floor the night I gave birth to Wayne."

"I don't remember it quite that way," Jacob Garfield said.

Bernice shushed him. "You two should lead out the next waltz."

As the three-man orchestra struck up the strains of a waltz, Jacob tapped Luke on the shoulder.

Dragging his feet, Luke tried to escape the inevitable, but when the captain joined Jacob in his efforts, he finally approached Nora. "May I have this dance?" He awkwardly offered her his hand.

Nora closed her fingers around his. Luke's palm was a bit clammy, despite the coldness of the night air. She suspected that he hadn't danced with too many women. *I'm not sure if he's done anything with too many women.* "Do you know how to dance?" she asked. Maybe that was the reason why he refused to dance with her.

One corner of Luke's mouth curled upward. "Are you afraid for your toes?"

Nora felt herself returning the smile. "Do they have anything to fear?"

"I've been an officer," Luke said with false indignation.

"You're stallin', Lucas Hamilton," Bernice said from behind them. "Dance with your wife."

Hesitantly, Luke took a step toward her and rested his hand on her waist in a touch so light that she could hardly feel it. He kept a respectable distance as he led her in the dance.

Nora's fingers came to rest in the curve of his shoulder. She felt his muscles flex under the linen of his shirt. The gentle pressure of his hand on the small of her back guided her without force, and she followed his movements in the swirling steps of the dance.

The fingers that held hers twitched, and his gaze often slid away from hers.

Unlike Luke, Nora didn't feel uncomfortable at all. In fact, she couldn't remember when she had felt so comfortable with any man. Not even in the presence of her father or her brothers had she felt so relaxed, as if she could truly be herself.

She had often danced with the customers of the brothel, but it had been nothing like dancing with Luke. Her customers had tried to press her against their bodies, had trailed their hands down her back and grabbed her bottom, or had taken advantage of their closeness to ogle down her cleavage. Luke did none of these things. Even when her protruded belly rubbed against his lap, he didn't try to pull her closer. The only reaction was the blush that crawled up his neck.

Tess was right. He's truly unlike any man I've ever known. She sighed. *He's also the only man who's ever resisted my charms.*

"Are you all right?" Luke asked. "I didn't hurt your toes, did I?"

Nora shook off her thoughts and looked up from where her belly touched his body. "No. No, they're fine."

Luke nodded and pulled her a bit closer as if he was trying to ward off anything that could hurt her or make her sad.

Another couple danced too close to them, almost causing a collision. Nora felt herself swung around in a tight circle and would have lost her balance if not for Luke holding her safely. She stared up into his eyes. Something flickered in the silvery irises, and it wasn't just the fire's reflection.

Nora wasn't sure how it had happened or who had started it, but suddenly, she found herself kissing him. His lips were softer than she had expected, and they moved against hers in a movement as gentle as a whisper. She clutched his shoulders, not aware and not caring whether they were still dancing.

With a gasp, Luke pulled back and held her at arm's length. His face looked flushed in the firelight. "I…I can't."

A wave of dizziness swept over Nora.

Once again, Luke caught her before she could fall.

She closed her eyes for a second, enjoying the warmth of his body against hers that warded off the cool air. "I told Bernice that it wasn't a good idea to waltz while pregnant," she mumbled into the fabric of his shirt. The pregnancy had nothing to do with her wobbly legs, though.

"Come on," he said. "I'll take you home...to the tent, I mean."

Home. The tent and the wagon weren't exactly comfortable homes, but they had become places that she belonged to.

They quietly slipped into the tent, where Amy was already sleeping.

While Nora undressed, Luke turned away and covered Amy with another blanket.

"Luke?" she said into the darkness.

He didn't turn around. "Yeah?"

"Why...?" She faltered, not knowing how to continue. There were so many whys, so many unasked questions between them that she didn't know where to start.

Luke's sigh reverberated through the cramped space in the tent. "It's complicated."

That was the one thing she was sure of. From their very first meeting, nothing between them had ever been easy and uncomplicated. "Then please try to explain because, frankly, I don't understand you at all—and I want to." She moved closer, trying to make out his face in the darkness. "You enjoyed that kiss." *As much as I did,* she silently added but didn't voice the thought. Her mother had taught her that a good woman was not supposed to react in any way to her husband's sexual attentions; she only endured her husband's desires for the sole purpose of bearing children.

Luke was silent for a long time. When his answer came, it was barely audible. "Yes, but—"

"Then why did you stop?"

"It's just not right."

"Not right?" Nora repeated. What on God's green earth was he talking about? "We're married, Luke, what could be wrong with—"

A shadow against the tent cover showed Luke tearing at his hair. "You don't understand the situation."

"No," Nora said. "I clearly don't."

"Nora, I—"

"Mama?" Amy sat up under her blankets.

Nora didn't know whether she should be angry or glad at the interruption. Too upset to speak, she knelt down next to her daughter.

Amy immediately reached for her. "Mama."

"I'm here, sweetie." She settled the girl against her, careful not to press her too hard against her growing belly. "Did you have a bad dream?"

Amy nodded, snuggling against her with a relieved sigh. "Mama?" she asked after a moment, her small fingers tentatively feeling Nora's belly. "Is there a baby growing in your belly?"

Nora stroked the reddish locks. "Yes, sweetie. You'll have a sister or a brother soon." *Not soon enough for me, but soon.*

"How did it get in there?" Amy patted her belly, testing its solidity.

"Uh." Nora had been afraid of that innocent question for some time. She had heard another expecting mother explain her pregnancy to her children: When a man and a woman love each other very much and they get married... But her husband wasn't the baby's father, and it certainly hadn't been conceived in love.

Behind her, Luke cleared his throat.

"Papa." Amy let go of Nora, crawled onto his lap, and promptly fell back asleep.

"Uff!" Luke looked down at the sleeping girl. "Saved by the sandman, huh?"

"She'll ask again," Nora said.

Luke stood and gently settled Amy back down under her blankets. "Then you'll have to handle that. I don't have any idea what to tell her."

"You think I do?"

Luke shrugged. "You're her mother."

"And you think just because I'm her mother, I have an answer to all her questions? Well, I don't. I don't know how to explain this to her." Nora pressed her hands to her belly. "She's much too young to understand my former line of work—and I pray that she'll never have to know."

"She won't," Luke said. It sounded like a promise.

With men like Broderick Cowen in the train, Nora wasn't so sure, but she said nothing.

DEVIL'S GATE,
JULY 5TH, 1851

"Devil's gate," Brody Cowen said. "Damn, that sounds inviting."

Luke turned in the saddle to look back at him. "It's not that bad. We're not going through it. We have to go around."

Right in front of them, still in sight of Independence Rock, was Devil's Gate, a huge, narrow cleft that the Sweetwater River had carved through the high granite rocks on either side. The cleft was only thirty feet wide at the base, where the Sweetwater shot through the crack, much too narrow for the wagons to pass through, so they had detoured to the south.

Some emigrants had left the wagon train to climb to the top and peer over the edge or wade the river through Devil's Gate.

As much as Luke had wanted to join them, to escape from the wagon train and Nora's intense gaze that she felt on her throughout the day, she kept a watchful eye on the gathering clouds and preferred to stay with the wagons and the herd. From time to time, she relieved Nora from steering the wagon, but she couldn't look her in the eye after last night's kiss. *You're an idiot. What did you think you were doing?* Guilt and confusion had kept her awake half of the night. She told herself again and again how wrong it was to kiss Nora even if it had felt so very right. Nora didn't know who she really was. Had she known, she would have never even thought about kissing Luke. *By kissing her without her knowing, you're taking her choice away. You're no better than her customers.*

The heavy bank of clouds above them was as dark as her mood, blocking out the sun and throwing shadows over the rolling prairie. The wind had picked up and brought with it a damp smell that promised rain. The sky got darker by the minute until Luke could hardly see Split Rock anymore, the cleft in the top of the Rattlesnake Range that aimed them at South Pass like a gun-sight notch.

From the front of the wagon train came the sign to make camp.

Luke anchored their wagon by driving stakes into the ground and fastening the wheels to them with heavy chains. The Garfields' oldest boy hurried over to help her set up their tent.

Before they could even think about making a fire, the first rain drops mingled with the wind, and within seconds, a pelting shower was falling from the sky.

Luke turned in a circle, searching for Nora, and found her wading through the mud and lifting down a box from the wagon. "Stay in the tent with Amy," Luke shouted over the sounds of chaos in camp. She didn't want to risk Nora slipping in the mud. "I'm gonna take care of this."

"But—"

"Go!"

Without further protest, Nora took Amy's hand and hurried over to the tent.

Luke tucked the bedrolls under her arm, picked up the box with their tin plates, and hurried through the rain. When she finally ducked into the tent, she was soaked to the bone. She set down the box, took off her hat, and shook her head.

Amy giggled as droplets of rain sprayed to all sides. "Eeww! Like a dog."

"Here." Nora took a towel and rubbed down Luke's hair.

"I can do it." Luke tried to take the towel from her, but Nora didn't let go.

She continued down Luke's neck, dabbed her face with the towel, and took care to dry her ears. When the gentle touch made Luke shiver, Nora said, "Take off these sopping clothes."

Despite the wet clothes, heat shot up Luke's body. She gazed around wildly, looking for a way out, any excuse to leave the tent.

Finally abandoning the towel, Nora bent down and searched in one of the bags for a dry shirt. "Aah." She froze in midmovement and clutched her belly with both hands.

Luke leaped forward. In one big step, she was at Nora's side and touched her to make sure she was all right. "What is it? Is it the baby?"

Nora was still bent over, but she had let go of the shirt. Her face was paler than the linen as she stared up at Luke with wide eyes. "It hurts." She groaned.

"Mama!" Amy rushed forward and reached out her hands to clutch her mother's skirts.

"No!" Luke stopped her, enfolding the girl in her own arms instead. "Don't touch your mama, little one. She has a bellyache." She felt Amy tremble in her embrace, and for a second, she was completely overwhelmed, not knowing what to do. Then she took a deep breath. *No time for panic now. They're depending on you.* "Maybe you should lie down?"

One palm still pressed against her belly, Nora reached out a trembling hand.

Gently gripping her elbow, Luke helped to ease her down. "Amy," she said as calmly as she could, "I have a very important task for you. Run over to the Garfields' tent and tell Bernice to come. Can you do that?"

With tears running down her face, the girl nodded.

"Good. I'm proud of you." Luke gently directed the girl to the tent's flap, away from her whimpering mother. "Stay with Jacob, all right?"

As soon as the crying Amy had slipped from the tent, Luke knelt down next to Nora. "Nora." She gently touched the clammy face and stroked damp red strands. "What can I do?"

"I-I don't know. I don't know what this is." Tension radiated off Nora's body. "It's almost like… It feels like it did when I gave birth to Amy. It's too soon, Luke, it's… God, that hurts!"

Luke stared down at her. Fear gripped her, more intense than anything she had experienced since fighting for her life against the Mexicans. Hot tears burned her eyes at the terrifying thought that Nora might lose the baby. She slid down until she was sitting on the damp ground, covered her wet pants with one of the bedrolls, and pulled Nora up so that she was resting across her lap.

"If I… The baby…"

Luke laid a finger across Nora's lips. "Hush, you're gonna be fine. Both of you. It will be all right. Rest now. Relax. I'm here with you." She pressed her lips against the crown of Nora's head that rested just under her chin. She concentrated on the almost translucent skin, on the tendrils of hair hanging damply into Nora's face. Suddenly, everything about Nora seemed fragile and precious.

"Luke…"

"It's all right. It's all right," Luke said, willing it to be so. She felt Nora tremble in her arms and tightened her hold on her. Luke hadn't prayed for a lot of years, preferring to take her fate into her own hands, but now, as they waited in terrified silence, she found her lips moving in silent prayer.

"That box." Sobs shook Nora's body. "I shouldn't have lifted it down from the wagon. If the baby—"

Luke shushed her once again. "You're only making yourself more upset. You didn't do anything wrong." She stroked Nora's face with her fingertips, trailed her palms down Nora's arms, and then laid her hand on Nora's belly, silently telling the unborn child to stay put.

Nora rested both of her hands over Luke's, clutching her fingers in a death grip.

They waited while heavy raindrops pelted the tent cover. Thunder boomed from time to time, sounding closer and closer. The tent started to leak, and pools built. Rainwater saturated the soil. Water soaked through Luke's pants, but she ignored it and pulled Nora higher on her lap, concentrating on keeping her warm and dry.

Their own little universe that consisted just of the two of them and their shared fear was interrupted as the tent flap lifted. "What happened?" Bernice entered, shedding her wet coat.

"I don't know. I bent down, and suddenly, there was this sharp pain, and now I have cramps. I think it's the baby." Nora's fingers bore into Luke's forearms, but Luke suffered the pain in silence as if she could somehow take away Nora's pain by bearing it herself.

Bernice knelt down.

Glad that help had finally arrived, Luke tried to move back to give Bernice room to work, but Nora didn't let go of her. "Please, stay."

Bernice gave her a silent nod and continued her examination around her.

Anxiously watching the older woman, Nora pressed her cheek against Luke's shoulder while they waited for Bernice to say something.

"Just a second," Bernice said and hurried out. She returned a minute later, carrying a cup. "Drink this."

"What is it?" Luke asked while she helped Nora hold the cup steady and bring it to her lips.

"A mixture of herbs," Bernice answered. "It should help with the cramps."

Nora grimaced but swallowed bravely. She emptied the cup and let her head sink back against Luke's shoulder.

They waited with bated breath.

"Luke?" Brody Cowen stuck his head through the flap. "The captain needs you."

Luke glanced at the waiting Brody, then back down at Nora, who was looking up at her with pain in her eyes. After a lifetime of following orders and respecting authority, Luke didn't even hesitate. "Not now."

"But—"

"Whatever it is, it has to wait," Luke said. "I won't leave my wife now."

"You can go. I'll be fine," Nora said, but the grip of her fingers on Luke's sent another message.

Luke didn't move from her place, holding Nora. "Get someone else to help you, Brody. I won't come right now."

With a grunt, Brody turned and disappeared.

Nora's fingers tightened around Luke's, and then they slowly relaxed as the herbs did their job and the cramps started to ease.

"How are you? Better now?" Luke realized she was whispering, almost afraid to talk too loudly.

Nora's head bobbed against her shoulder as she nodded. "Tired."

"That's the herbs," Bernice said. "They will help her relax, stop the cramps, and make her sleepy." She picked up the empty cup and stood.

Luke realized that Bernice was about to return to her own family and would leave her alone with Nora. A lump formed in her throat. "Bernice," she said, looking down at the drowsy woman on her lap, "is she gonna be all right?"

"Yeah, I think so. She needs some rest now."

"And the baby? Is it...?" Luke couldn't finish the sentence, too afraid to voice her worries.

Bernice lifted her hands in a helpless gesture. "We won't know for sure until it's born. But for now, it should be all right. The contractions stopped. Let's just hope that everything stays quiet tonight and we don't have to break up camp in the middle of the night again. It wouldn't be good for Nora."

Luke nodded and watched her walk toward the flap. "Bernice?" She waited until the older woman had turned around to look at her. "Thank you for coming over to help us."

"You're welcome," Bernice said. "Amy can stay with us tonight if you want her to."

Looking at Nora, who was already half asleep, Luke started to nod. She would have enough on her hands just caring for Nora. But then she thought about how Amy would feel if they left her with the Garfields. She remembered the many times when she'd had to stay with other people as a child, staring at the wall all night and wondering how her mother was doing. "No, thank you. I think it would be better if she stays with us. She has to see for herself that her mother is well."

Bernice nodded. "You're right. I'll bring her over."

As Bernice left, Luke helped Nora settle down on her bedroll and spread a dry blanket over her.

"You should finally change out of that shirt," Nora said, looking up at her.

Luke fingered her sleeve. The fabric had dried in the meantime. "It's dry now, but we should get you into your nightwear." She searched in Nora's bag until she found a nightshirt that hadn't gotten wet in the rain. Then she looked down at Nora, waiting for her to undress, but Nora lay without moving, her eyes half-closed. Biting her lip, Luke began to unbutton her bodice.

Nora didn't react, but her gaze followed Luke's fingers as they moved from button to button and finally stripped off bodice and skirt.

For a second, Luke touched her fingertips to Nora's bulging belly.

Their gazes met.

"I was so scared," Nora whispered.

Luke took her hand and squeezed it. "Yeah, me too."

"Really?"

Luke just nodded. She didn't know how to explain what she had felt during those terrifying minutes.

"Mama?" Amy's voice came from outside.

Quickly, Luke helped Nora sit up a bit, eased the nightshirt over her head, and pulled it down just as Bernice lifted the tent's flap so Amy could enter.

Nora held out her arms. A sobbing Amy sank into her mother's embrace.

Luke settled one arm around each of them and nodded her thanks at Bernice over their heads.

After nodding in return, Bernice turned and disappeared into the darkness.

"Will you lie with us?" Nora asked, turning her head to look into Luke's eyes.

Luke rubbed the bump on the bridge of her nose. She should probably head out and help the captain with whatever task he needed her to do, but she couldn't bring herself to leave Nora just yet. Awkwardly, she slid down until she rested along the edge of Nora's bedroll.

Amy immediately snuggled down between them, and with a content sigh, she fell asleep.

Knowing she would not sleep tonight, Luke kept her eyes open and gazed over Amy's small body at Nora.

Nora's eyelids drooped, but she fought against sleep, returning Luke's gaze.

"Sleep now," Luke said.

"Luke?" the captain's deep voice came from the tent's opening. "You there?"

With a regretful gaze to Nora, Luke turned. "I'm here." She stood and stepped toward him, not wanting him to enter and disturb the peace in the tent.

Abe McLoughlin stood in the pouring rain, his beard dripping and his eyes wild. "Luke, we need you. The herd is nervous as hell in this weather, and I don't trust those deadbeats and greenhorns with 'em. One wrong move and they'll stampede for sure."

Sighing, Luke looked back over her shoulder.

Nora met her gaze and nodded.

"All right," Luke said. "I'm coming." Under the pretense of collecting her hat, she turned and knelt down next to Nora. "Will you be all right on your own?"

Nora felt for her hand and squeezed it. "I'll be fine. Take care of yourself, please."

With a grim nod, Luke settled the hat on her head, turned, and walked out into the rain.

Luke directed Measles along the edge of the herd, circling them in some distance. One lightning bolt after another flashed across the sky, showing her the restlessly milling oxen, mules, and horses. One of the dairy cows lifted her head, the white of her eyes gleaming, and gave a panicked moo.

I don't like this. We should have kept them within the circle of wagons tonight. The best grass grew farther down the river, though, so they had driven the herd away from camp and left some men to stand guard.

On the other side of the herd, barely visible through the curtain of rain, Wayne Garfield ventured a little too close to the nervous animals.

Gripping the reins more tightly, Luke tried to give him a sign to back away, but Wayne didn't look in her direction. She wanted to shout a warning, but every yell, every unexpected sound could cause a stampede, so she just watched with growing concern.

Another flash of lightning zigzagged across the sky, bathing the prairie in white light for a second. Then thunder boomed right above them.

The herd bolted into the darkness, not caring what stood in their way.

Oh, shit. They were heading straight for her! The black drove looked like one big, impenetrable wall as they came closer and closer. Luke ducked over Measles's crest and let the mare surge forward. They raced just ahead of the stampeding herd.

One quick glance over her shoulder showed her that she was gaining a lead on them. She breathed a sigh of relief—until she remembered in which direction they were running. They were heading straight for the corralled wagons and tents less than a mile away. *Nora! Amy!*

Luke could make out the lanterns in some of the tents, but nothing moved. She couldn't even see a guard watching over the camp. Everyone who wasn't out with the herd was probably asleep or resting unsuspectingly in one of the tents. *They probably think that roar in the air is caused by thunder, not a stampeding herd.*

There was no time, no place for letting the herd run themselves out. If they didn't change direction, they would trample right over the tents and the sleeping emigrants. Even if someone noticed the herd before it reached them and the emigrants hastily fled from their tents, Nora might lose the baby if she didn't get some rest tonight.

Instead of breaking off to the left, away from the herd behind her, Luke galloped straight ahead. With one hand, she lifted her Walker Colt and fired shot after shot into the air, hoping it would frighten the animals behind her away from the camp.

Another bolt of lightning illuminated the sky, giving her a glimpse of the roiling mass bearing down on her. They hadn't changed their direction. The sounds of her shots had mingled with the roar of thunder and hooves and had done nothing to slow the herd.

Damn. Gritting her teeth, Luke drew her rifle from its scabbard and turned around in the saddle. She was holding on just with her legs now. She lifted the rifle and sighted down the barrel.

In the darkness, it was almost impossible to make out individual animals in the black mass. Then a bolt of lightning momentarily shattered the darkness.

There was no time for hesitation. Luke pulled the trigger.

McLoughlin's big lead steer fell. The confused cattle that followed behind him veered slightly to one side.

Not enough.

They had almost reached the camp now.

Luke squeezed the trigger again.

The ox that had taken the lead stumbled, then fell, making the others veer even more to the side.

Then Wayne and Brody were there. Luke slowed her mare, and the three of them forced the cattle in the front even farther to the side. With the first tents just ten yards to the right, they thundered past the camp.

The riders forced the cattle to the left until they ran themselves out in a wide circle.

Coughing and gasping, Wayne Garfield slid from his horse. He trembled as he looked up at Luke. "I'm sorry, I…"

Luke was too shaken to talk. The thought of how close she had come to losing Nora and Amy was the only thing on her mind. She just nodded at the young man and directed her mare toward the tents without a word.

"Luke?" Nora blinked up at her when she slipped into the tent. "Is it still raining? I thought I heard…"

"Yeah, just raining," Luke said and knelt down next to Nora. "But I think it'll be quieter now."

Nora freed one hand from the blanket and touched Luke's shoulder. "Your shirt is wet again."

Luke gazed down. Not only was her shirt dripping wet, it was covered in sweat, mud, and grass. Knowing that neither she nor Nora had the energy for another fight about changing clothes, Luke turned around and, in the darkness of the tent, slipped the wet shirt off and a new one on. She hoped Nora wouldn't notice that she had left the damp undershirt in place.

"Doesn't the captain need you anymore?"

"No." The herd was all run out now, too tired for another stampede. "He doesn't."

"Good," Nora whispered, "because I do."

Luke wanted to step out into the rain and run in blind panic, as the herd had. Something had changed between them tonight, but she wasn't sure what. Staying aloof and objective was no longer an option. She searched for words but found none. Taking care to keep Amy between them, she lay down next to Nora. She closed her eyes and concentrated on her aching muscles, anything to keep her thoughts away from the woman next to her and what could have happened to her tonight. She still hadn't succeeded when she felt Nora's hand grasping her own.

"Do you mind? I don't think I can sleep without…"

Luke smoothed her thumb over Nora's palm. "It's all right." In the dim light in the tent, she studied the slender fingers, the work-roughened palms, and the delicate curve of her wrist. "What's this?" She gently rubbed over a greenish, almost faded spot on the inside of Nora's wrist, easily visible because the skin was paler there.

Nora turned her hand, hiding the bruise. "It's nothing. One of the oxen got a bit overzealous when I fed them. That's all."

"Even naming one of them Snow White didn't make them more cautious about food, huh?" Luke smiled at her, then closed her eyes. For the first time in her life, she fell asleep holding someone's hand.

THREE CROSSINGS,
JULY 6TH, 1851

"I could really learn to hate this river." Bernice looked up from the noon meal she was preparing and sent resentful glances toward the gentle Sweetwater River. "This must be the hundredth time we had to cross it."

Nora smiled tiredly. It wasn't the hundredth time, but it felt pretty close to it. The Sweetwater was notorious for twisting back on itself. Unlike the river, the emigrants had somewhere to be and weren't content to meander across the landscape, so they were forced to cross the river time after time. "Didn't someone mention that we could avoid three crossings if we take the Deep Sand Route?"

"Yeah, we could," Bernice said, "but after last night, the oxen are too exhausted to pull the wagons through the deep sand."

After last night? Nora furrowed her brow, but Bernice's oldest daughter distracted her from asking about it.

Sixteen-year-old Mary sat down next to Nora and rested her chin on her folded hands, intently gazing at Luke, who was using the noon break to grease the wagon's axle. "Oh my, he's marvelous." She sighed.

Nora gave her a tolerant smile. She hadn't been much older than the girl when she had gotten pregnant with Amy, but she could barely remember ever being so naïve and innocent. *But I have to admit, if I had to spend my time gazing adoringly at someone, it would probably be Luke.*

"He's a true hero," Mary said. "Wayne told me how he led the stampeding herd away from camp, risking his own life."

Nora's frying pan almost slipped into the fire. "Stampeding herd? Risking his own life? What are you talking about?"

Mary finally looked away from Luke. "You haven't heard?"

Now Nora was the one staring at Luke. "No, obviously I haven't. What happened?"

"The herd stampeded last night and raced right toward the camp, with only Luke between them and us. He was so close that he could have touched them. They had almost reached us when he shot the lead steer and forced the herd to veer to the side." Mary's eyes sparkled as if it were all just one big, fun adventure.

Nora, however, wasn't excited at all to hear that Luke had risked his life without even telling her about it.

"It was a very foolish thing to do," Bill Larson said from his place at the fire.

Nora looked at him through narrowed eyes. She knew that her levelheaded husband wouldn't have risked his life if there had been another way, but it wasn't her place to openly contradict a male member of the wagon train.

"He should have just ridden ahead and warned us, instead of shooting our best steer," Larson said.

"There wouldn't have been enough time to break up camp," Bernice said.

Nora froze. *Breaking up camp?* Again, she heard Bernice's words from the night before: *Let's just hope that everything stays quiet tonight and we don't have to break up camp in the middle of the night again. It wouldn't be good for Nora.* She stared at Luke, who was just crawling out from under the wagon. *Is that why he risked his life to direct the herd away from camp? For me?*

Last night had certainly changed the way she saw her husband. Seeing his reaction to the almost miscarriage, the fear in his eyes told her more than any declarations that he would accept the baby as his own. She remembered his gentle hands soothing her as cramps had racked her body.

Never before had she felt so safe, so comforted in the presence of a man. Some of her customers had been kind and gentle; a few had even professed feelings of love for her, but Nora had never felt close to any of them. Being in Luke's company felt different from being with any other man. She tried to pinpoint what it was that made Luke so different, but she couldn't put her finger on it.

"I think your beans are done," Bernice said, interrupting her thoughts.

Quickly, Nora stood to take the big kettle off its hook over the fire.

"Ah, ah, ah. Hold on. Let me do this." Luke stepped around her and lifted the pot down. "There's no need for you to lift these heavy things when I'm around."

After years of having to fend for herself, Nora found it hard to depend on someone for everything. "But it's not fair that you have to do all the work," she said. At the very beginning of their journey, she had promised herself that she would prove herself a worthy pioneer woman, not a pampered city wife.

"You're doing the most important work," Luke said, pointing at her belly.

Nora's hands wandered to her belly. She pressed her lips together as she felt the lack of movement that continued since last night.

"Besides, if you want to do some work, you could take your daughter to the river and clean her up," Luke said with a grin.

"I helped Papa," a grease-smeared Amy said.

Nora had to laugh. "I can see that. Come on. Let's go clean up." As she led Amy to the riverbank, she felt Luke's gaze on her. Luke had stayed close to her all day, which was a relief for more than one reason. On top of her worries about the baby, she didn't feel up to dealing with Brody Cowen, and whenever Luke was close, Cowen stayed away.

As she knelt down at the river's edge, a healthy kick almost made her topple into the water. With flailing arms, she fought for balance.

"Nora!" Luke leaped over the fire and skidded down the bank. "What is it?"

"The baby." Hot tears slid down Nora's cheeks.

Luke paled. He started to wave for Bernice.

"No. It's kicking! I felt it move for the first time since last night." Nora laughed, giddy with relief. She grabbed Luke's hand and pressed it against her belly. Right at that moment, the baby gave a second kick, then a third.

Luke looked as if he might collapse from sheer relief. "Oh, thank God."

They came together in a spontaneous embrace, his hand still between them, resting on Nora's belly.

Nora tightened her arms around his neck, breathing in his comforting scent.

"Mama, I want to feel the baby too," Amy shouted next to them.

Luke instantly let go and rubbed his flushed face.

Amy took his place, eagerly touching Nora's belly with her small hands.

As she held still, Nora swore that she would never again complain about the baby's kicks keeping her awake at night.

Ice Slough,
July 7th, 1851

Luke drew back her aching arm and flicked her whip again to keep the sluggish oxen moving. The big animals strained heads-down against the rattling chains. They were moving even slower than usual in the stifling heat. Their pace was too slow to escape the cloud of dust, so it had settled over their clothing and coated the flanks of oxen and horses.

Even Nora's reddish eyebrows were almost white under a layer of dust. Nora sneezed and licked her chapped lips.

"Bless you," Luke said. She squinted against the bright sun and gazed ahead, hoping to find a resting spot for Nora and the others. Behind them lay miles of shadeless trail, but ahead she saw a shallow basin covered with a variety of marsh grasses and green-brown tufts. The water glittered silvery in the sun. "Hold back the oxen," Luke shouted back to the other wagons. "The water's alkaline."

Nora gazed longingly at the water, then, after Luke's warning, marched on with a sigh.

"How would the two of you like a glass of cool lemonade with ice?" Luke asked, grinning down at Nora and her daughter.

"You're being mean, Lucas Hamilton," Nora said. "To tease us with something that you can never deliver is pure torture."

Luke lifted her arm, giving the signal to stop. "Come on, let's see how mean I am." She shouldered a spade and took Nora's arm, not wanting her to stumble on the swampy ground.

Nora held out her other hand for Amy to take, and they cautiously wandered through the small valley.

After a while, Luke stopped and dug with the spade, cutting away the swamp grass. Then she rammed the spade down a few times. Grinning, she lifted a small block of ice to the surface. "Voilà, madame. Your ice, as promised."

With an enthusiastic squeak, Amy grabbed a bit of ice and put it into her mouth.

"Don't worry," Luke said at Nora's alarmed gaze. "The ice is pure, no alkali in it at all."

Nora cautiously lifted a sliver of ice and touched it to her chapped lips. "Where is it coming from, right in the middle of this barren land during a very hot July?"

"The water freezes in the winter," Luke said. "The marsh grasses and sedges act as an insulating layer and keep the ice frozen until summer." She liked pampering Nora and Amy a bit even if it was just with a glass of ice-cold lemonade.

While Nora and Bernice prepared the promised lemonade, Luke and the men dug up large chunks of ice and stored it in their water barrels so that they would have cool water for the journey ahead.

After half an hour of rest, they traveled on. Luke relinquished her place next to the ox team to Nora and rode ahead to scout for a spot where they could camp for the night. She continued west along the banks of the Sweetwater, sometimes dozing in the saddle under the blazing sun.

The surface gave way beneath them. Measles snorted in terror as she sank belly-deep into the sand.

Luke lost her grip on the reins as her world tilted and she was catapulted over the mare's head. She tried to twist in midair to cushion the fall, but the ground was already too close.

The air was knocked from her lungs. An edgy rock ripped along her forearm as she skidded across the ground. Then, finally, she lay still. Cautiously, she moved an arm, then a leg. Everything seemed to be in working order.

Groaning, Luke stood and beat the dust out of her clothing. When she turned to look for Measles, her heart began to race.

The horse was thrashing helplessly, fighting in vain against the quicksand sucking her in. She was already submerged to the belly, and her struggles caused her to sink in deeper.

Luke rushed toward her, taking care not to get mired down herself. She grabbed the reins, then as she noticed how useless it would be to pull on the reins, she tried to help the mare by pushing from behind.

Still, the mare was stuck. The sand climbed even higher on her flanks.

Luke raced around and pulled on her neck instead, but that was equally useless. Her gaze darted around for anything she could use to pull Measles out.

The first wagon crested the hill above them.

Luke nearly sank to her knees. "Jacob! Tom! I need some help over here."

The men abandoned the wagons and rushed over. Jacob Garfield threw a rope around the mare's neck and pulled with his sons while Tom Buchanan, Brody, and even Bill Larson pushed from behind.

Nora hurried forward to join their efforts.

"No." Luke took one hand from the saddle horn to hold her back. "Not you. Stay back. I've got enough help now." She wouldn't risk causing a miscarriage even if it might mean losing Measles.

Nora blinked.

For a second, Luke could make out the hurt expression on her face before she hid it away behind a mask. Luke regretted her sharp tone but had no time to reassure Nora. Digging in her heels, she pulled with all her might.

From somewhere, a second rope was fastened to the saddle horn, and with their combined efforts, the terrified mare was pulled from the treacherous ground, inch by inch. Finally, Measles stood by the water's edge, her flanks heaving and her long limbs trembling.

Luke trembled too. Measles was a key element to her plans of building a horse ranch, but she meant more than that to her. The mare had been her companion for many years, faithfully carrying her through long expeditions and a dozen battles. Now she had come close to losing that trusted friend. Much too close.

If not for her fellow travelers, the mare would have died. *Maybe being part of a community is not so bad.*

On wobbly legs, she walked over to Nora, who held a crying Amy in her arms. "I'm sorry for yelling at you," Luke said. "I just don't want anything to happen to you or the baby. I didn't want to save Measles at the cost of losing you."

Nora stood frozen for a few seconds. She stared at Luke over Amy's head, probably not used to hearing apologizes. In the past, people had hurt her feelings without noticing or caring. "I...I didn't think. I just saw Measles and—"

"It's all right," Luke said. "No one got hurt, not you and not Measles. That's all that counts."

Nora let out a trembling breath. Without answering, she led Amy over to lavish kisses on Measles.

SOUTH PASS,
JULY 12TH, 1851

"Where's Amy?" Bernice asked as she wandered over with Hannah, her youngest daughter.

Nora pointed to the horizon. "Off with Luke and Measles."

"That girl sure loves her papa." Bernice smiled affectionately.

Nora sighed. "Yeah, she does." She stared off into the distance, where snow-covered peaks loomed, their white-and-brown flanks looking like chocolate cakes dusted with powdered sugar.

"So tell me, what do you think about Sarah?"

Sarah? Nora had missed whatever Bernice might have said before that. "Which Sarah?" There were three women with that name in the wagon train.

Bernice rolled her eyes but kept smiling. "I'm talking about names in general. For your baby, you know? Didn't you already think of some names?"

Actually, Nora hadn't. The birth wasn't that far off, but still, she was just getting used to the thought that she would soon have another child. Only since Luke had promised to treat the baby as his own had she started to look forward to having another baby. "I'm not really sure yet," she answered.

"Any nice names in Luke's part of the family tree?" Bernice asked.

Nora swallowed, once again reminded of how little she knew about her husband. "I'll have to ask him if he has any favorites." Searching for a way to distract Bernice, she pointed to two twin hills ahead of them. "Is this South Pass?"

"I don't think so. I would imagine a pass over the Rocky Mountains to be a bit steeper."

"Then your imagination is much too vivid, dear Mrs. Garfield," a male voice said from behind them.

Nora didn't have to turn to identify the speaker. Brody Cowen had sneaked around her wagon since Luke had ridden off with Amy.

"It might look more like a meadow than a mountain pass, but this is South Pass." Brody pointed at the wind-swept, sage-covered slope ahead of them, but his gaze remained fixed on Nora. "If you ride ahead, you can be the first to reach the other side of the Rockies and to enter Oregon Territory."

"Please, Mama." Hannah Garfield tugged on her mother's hand. "Let's go. I want to be the first on the other side."

With a sigh and a shrug to Nora, Bernice let herself be dragged to her wagon, where a saddle horse was trailing behind.

Nora shivered, but it had nothing to do with the cooler air in the mountains. She watched in dreadful silence as the Garfields rode off.

"Alone at last." Cowen grinned crookedly, his eyes devoid of any humor or kindness.

"Leave me alone," Nora said. To her surprise, she found that her voice was barely more than a shaky whisper.

Cowen reached for her. "Where would be the fun in that? But don't worry, I'll even pay and leave you a nice tip. It won't be your loss."

Nora didn't want his money. She wanted nothing from him, but she couldn't find her voice to tell him that. For too long, she hadn't been allowed to say no or to voice her wishes at all. "Mr. Cowen…"

"You can call me Brody," he said.

"No, I—"

"You think you're too good for me now, huh?" He grabbed her wrists, shackling her hands with his broader paws. With a rough jerk, he pulled her against his body. "Let's see if you still think so when I'm through with you. It'll be good. You just wait and see."

Nora struggled, but she was as powerless against his strong grip as Measles had been against the suction of the quicksand.

"Brody? Nora?" Luke's voice interrupted Cowen's plans. "What's going on?"

"Nothing," Cowen answered, letting go of Nora. "Just talking, right?" He laid an arm around Nora's shoulders, but she recoiled, flinching back from his touch.

Luke's gaze darted back and forth between her and Cowen. "Nora? Is that true?"

For the first time, someone asked her, apparently ready to believe her word above that of a man. *Tell him,* a voice in her head urged, but another one cautioned, *Cowen will only take revenge if you do. He'll claim to be innocent, and if Luke believes the man he admires, where does that leave you?*

"Nora?" Luke asked again. "Tell me what's going on, please."

Nora stepped away from Cowen, searching out Luke's comforting presence. Her fear eased a bit as she looked into the familiar gray eyes of the man she had married. Then her gaze fell onto Amy, who was sitting in the saddle in front of Luke. Her entire front was covered in vomit. "Amy! Sweetie, what happened?" Nora forgot about her own situation as she rushed forward and pulled her groggy daughter into her arms.

"She vomited," Luke explained the obvious. "We weren't going all that fast, really. It must have been something she ate."

Nora led Amy to the wagon, with Luke following.

Brody Cowen hurried away as she began to tend to her daughter.

"Nora?" Luke peeked over her shoulder at the now blanket-covered girl.

"It's not your fault," Nora said. "It has happened before. Sometimes, children just get sick to their stomach. Nothing a little rest won't cure."

"Nora?" Luke's voice came again.

With a sigh, Nora turned. She stared at the collar of his shirt, not wanting to look him in the eyes.

"Nora, look at me. Please."

She lifted her head.

His eyes weren't judging, just waiting. "What happened with Brody?"

Nothing that hasn't happened a hundred times before. And I'm sure it'll happen again, wherever I go. Nora hesitated. A part of her wanted to break her silence and tell Luke the truth. But in the past, complaining and voicing the injustices she had suffered had never helped her. Suffering in silence had become her philosophy.

Luke stepped closer. He touched a single finger to her chin, keeping her gaze level with his. "Are you afraid of him?"

Sometimes, Luke was much too perceptive. "He..." Nora pulled in a breath. "He touched me. He tried to fondle me and kiss me."

Under his tan, Luke paled visibly.

Nora clenched her teeth. Would he believe her, or would he think that his friend would never molest a woman? For some reason, he seemed to have a blind spot for that man's character flaws.

"He touched you?" Luke's color went from pale to red. "Why didn't you fight him off? Or at least call for help?"

Nora shrugged. At least, he believed her, but she didn't know how to explain.

"Why did you just stand there, letting him touch you?" Anger crept into Luke's voice.

"I...I don't know," Nora stammered. "I didn't know what to do."

Luke closed his eyes. He took a deep breath. When he reopened his eyes, they were calm again. "It's not your fault. I know you weren't allowed to fight back in the past. But that part of your life is over now. You're allowed to fight back if someone touches you without permission."

Allowed to fight back. These words were pure theory for Nora even if she was glad to hear them from Luke. Fighting against a tall, strong man like Brody Cowen was useless. "I don't know how to fight back," she said, looking away from him.

"Then you come to me and tell me. I'll try to protect you, whatever happens," Luke said. He gazed at her in earnest.

"But you can't always be around. He's clever. He waits until you're gone before he goes anywhere near me."

Luke's expression darkened. "He's done this before?"

Nora hung her head.

Luke took it for the affirmation that it was. "You could have told me, you know."

Nora nodded, still not looking at him. "Yeah, I know."

"Then why didn't you?"

"I wasn't sure if you'd believe me over Brody Cowen." When Luke opened his mouth as if to protest, Nora added, "And I didn't want to put you in an awkward situation."

"The situation seems quite straightforward to me. You're my wife and—"

"And he's like a father figure to you. At least you'd like him to be," Nora said. She had watched Luke's behavior toward Brody Cowen, had seen him act with natural respect toward the older man. He tended to defer to Cowen's opinion and didn't question his advice, seeming to expect only good things from him. He must have had a happier childhood with a better father than she had. Her own father had never paid her much attention; only his business and his three sons were important to him. When his ambitious plans to marry her off to his business partner failed, he no longer had any use for her and left her to fend for herself.

Luke gazed down at the fading bruises on Nora's wrist. "Not if he molests my wife."

Nora had to swallow as she looked into his eyes. Even though he had repeatedly told her that he wanted her to find a "better man" in Oregon, there was something possessive in his gaze. "What if he refuses to stop?" Nora asked.

For a few moments, Luke said nothing.

Nora knew that he had always tried to lead a quiet life. Since leaving Independence, almost every man on the train had gotten into at least one fistfight and a dozen shouting matches. Not Luke. No matter how much others provoked him and tried to get him involved in a confrontation, he quietly walked away. He wasn't a coward, but still, Nora wasn't sure whether he would get into a fight with Brody for her. She wasn't sure whether she wanted him to.

The muscles in Luke's jaw bunched. "Then I'll make him stop."

An image of Brody shooting Luke flashed through Nora's mind. She squeezed her eyes shut. "No," she said. "That's not worth the trouble. I'm sure he'll stop."

"What if he doesn't?" Luke shook his head. "I'm not taking that chance. I'll go confront him right away."

Nora clutched his sleeve. "No. No, please, don't. If you do that, the others will ask what's going on. Brody will tell them that I was a whore. Everyone will know. I don't want that. Please."

Luke hesitated. "Then how am I supposed to protect you? Like you said, I can't always be around." He tapped the butt of his revolver and chewed on his lip. "I should at least teach you to defend yourself."

Little old me, learning how to fight? Nora had her doubts, but on the other hand, learning how to defend herself and Amy could only be of value, no matter where and with whom she ended up in life. "You would do that?"

Luke nodded.

Another thing he's doing for me. "I could teach you how to read and write in return," she said. He had repeatedly rejected other "services" from her, but this was something she could do for him.

He shrugged. "We'll see. Your lessons are more urgent. So, tonight, after Amy is asleep?"

"All right." It was the oddest rendezvous she had ever made.

PACIFIC SPRINGS,
JULY 12TH, 1851

Luke leaned against the wagon and breathed into her hands to warm them. This afternoon, they had crossed the backbone of the Rocky Mountains, the ascent and descent through South Pass so gradual that they hadn't believed that they had crossed the Continental Divide until they had reached Pacific Spring, a green oasis in the harsh eastern region of the Oregon country.

The animals were grazing contently, and the other emigrants were busy celebrating their arrival in Oregon Territory. No one would miss them, and Bernice had promised to look in on Amy while they were out on their "romantic stroll" along the creek.

She tilted her head and listened to the story that Nora read Amy inside the wagon. Listening to Nora's stories had been one of the guilty pleasures that she allowed herself every evening. Her own mother had never told her any of these fairy tales, adventures, and legends.

Finally, Nora came to the "happily ever after" part of the story, and then everything went silent as Nora probably kissed her daughter good night. A few seconds later, she slipped from the wagon. She froze and stared in Luke's direction.

"It's only me." Luke stepped into the circle of light from the oil lantern hanging from the wagon.

Nora visibly relaxed and smiled as if she hadn't been afraid at all.

Luke knew better. She promised herself that this would change. Nora shouldn't have to live in fear any longer.

Silently, they left the circle of wagons and wandered up the creek until they were far enough away from camp not to be seen or heard.

Luke stopped and rolled up her sleeves.

"I'm not sure this is a good idea," Nora said.

Luke looked up from her cuffs, meeting Nora's gaze in a silent question.

"I can't win against Cowen. He's much taller and stronger than I."

"You don't have to win," Luke said. "All you have to do is fight him off long enough to call for help or run away. Do you think you can do that?"

Nora straightened her shoulders. "Show me how."

"All right. I'm playing Brody, and you…you're yourself. So, what does he usually do?"

"He…he grabs me."

A vivid picture flashed before Luke's mind's eye. Anger boiled up in her, heating her cheeks. She took a deep breath. "How?"

"He grabs my wrists." Nora demonstrated, closing her fingers around her other arm.

Luke took hold of Nora's wrists. "Like this?"

"No, he…he holds my wrists with just one of his hands, leaving his other hand free to grope me," Nora said. "And he holds on more roughly."

Nodding, Luke laid both of Nora's wrists against each other and encircled them with her left hand. It was hard to get a secure grip like this, not only because her hands were not as big as Brody's, but also because she didn't want to hurt Nora in the process. "And then? What does he do now?"

"He pulls me against his body, as close as possible, so that I can feel him press against me, his breath on my face." Nora shuddered.

Luke looked down at her. "We don't have to do this."

"Yes. Yes, I have to. I want to learn how to stop him."

Luke gazed down into Nora's eyes. For once, Nora held her gaze. Luke had never thought that she would one day admire a former prostitute, but Nora had earned her respect. "All right." Now it was her turn to hesitate. Slowly, she pulled Nora closer.

"Closer," Nora whispered. "He holds me so close that I can't move."

She moved Nora another inch closer. Then another. Nora's belly pressed against her hip, and her breath brushed over Luke's neck. Luke forced her thoughts back to what they were doing. "What do you do when he holds you like this?"

"I try to break free, but it only makes him hold on tighter." Nora demonstrated her struggles, pressing their bodies even closer together.

Good God. Luke's eyes threatened to close. "And then?" Her voice was rough.

"Then he usually tries to kiss me." Nora stopped her struggles and looked up at her.

Reenacting this was not a good idea. Luke couldn't look away from Nora's lips. Her free hand lifted without conscious thought and touched a smooth cheek.

Nora didn't pull back. She held her place, still gazing up at Luke.

Their lips touched, and Luke lost her grip on Nora's wrists and on reality. Heat rushed through her. She felt Nora's fingers slide up her neck and into her hair, holding her in place as Nora deepened the kiss.

Nora's tongue teased her bottom lip, asking for entrance that Luke gave without thinking.

She wasn't sure if it was the lack of air, but she felt faint. With a gasp, she tore her lips away from Nora's. She panted. "I'm sorry. This is not what I wanted to show you."

"Well, it was a lot nicer than being manhandled," Nora said with the teasing smile that was second nature to every prostitute, but the same confusion Luke felt shone in her eyes. When Luke didn't return the smile, her expression grew serious again. "We don't have to do this." Nora used the same words Luke had used before.

"You have to learn how to defend yourself," Luke said. She braced herself. "All right, once again." With more control this time, she held Nora's wrists and pulled her against her body. She took a deep breath, forcing herself not to react to Nora's closeness. "When he holds you like this and tries to kiss you, the best thing to do is bite him. Then you stamp down on his foot as hard as you can, and when he loosens his grip on you... I don't think I need to tell you where to kick a man, do I?" She glanced down at Nora with a grim smile.

Nora's lips were a thin line. "What if I freeze in panic and just can't do it?"

"That's why we're here. You have to practice. So, let's try it with me."

Nora stared up at her. "You want me to kick you?" Her gaze wandered down Luke's body.

Luke swallowed and grinned nervously. She fought against the sudden urge to clasp her hands in front of a certain body part that she didn't really have. A kick between the legs wasn't a pleasant experience, even for a woman. "Maybe you could be so kind as to leave out that last part of the maneuver," she said. "Try the moves, but don't hit me full force. And please skip the lip biting too."

"All right." Nora's chest rose and fell. She looked down, aiming at Luke's foot.

"Don't look down," Luke said. "You have to surprise him. Gazing down could alert him to your plans."

The tip of Nora's tongue stuck out between her lips. She was so obviously trying not to look down that it was suspicious on its own.

Luke said nothing. She didn't want to discourage the younger woman. She grimaced when the sole of Nora's boot scraped along her shin and then almost crushed her little toe. "That's great." She gasped. "You're doing fine. Now hint at that kick. Don't hesitate. You have to kick him as soon as he's distracted by the pain in his foot."

When Nora tried to kick out with her foot, she stumbled.

Quickly, Luke caught her and held on until she had found her balance again. "Don't try to kick out with your foot. It'll make you stumble over your skirts, especially now that your center of balance is shifting." She pointed to Nora's growing belly. "Try to thrust with your knee."

Again, they took their positions, with Luke holding Nora close. Nora's boot scraped over her shin again, and she mentally prepared herself for a day of limping along the wagon tomorrow. Then Nora's foot stepped on her own, and her knee pressed against her in a much softer imitation of a kick.

Luke groaned—not in pain, but in pleasure. She tried to move back, away from the intimate contact, but Nora's foot on her own held her pinned to the place. "That's enough. You can stop now." She took several deep breaths when Nora finally moved away.

"Was that good enough?"

You have no idea. "Yeah. If you use these moves with more force, Brody will be in enough pain for you to make an escape. But just to be sure…" She drew a revolver from her waistband. It wasn't her heavy Walker Colt, but a smaller, lighter model.

Nora's eyes widened. "You want me to shoot him?"

"No. I want you to do whatever it takes to defend yourself. You've got a right to decide who gets to touch you and kiss you."

Nora gazed at her lips, making Luke swallow, but then she hesitantly took the small revolver.

Luke stepped behind Nora and reached around her with both arms so that she could show her how to hold the weapon. She paused for a moment when she noticed how intimate their position was, almost an embrace. "To load it, you swing out the cylinder. You put paper cartridges into each chamber, then place percussion caps on the nipples at the rear of each chamber."

"What are they for?" Nora asked as she tried to imitate Luke's movements.

"When you squeeze the trigger, the hammer snaps down and hits the cap. It explodes, and the resulting spark ignites the powder in the paper cartridge. The explosion discharges the bullet," Luke said. "Try it. Pull back the hammer with your thumb."

Nora did it.

Luke nodded. "Hold on with both hands. Once you really fire the weapon, there'll be a recoil. Now point the revolver at that big stone in the creek."

Nora turned her head to look at her, her gaze full of doubt.

"Go on. It's not loaded. We can't take the risk of alerting Brody or worrying anyone within hearing distance."

Finally, Nora lifted the weapon. She pointed it at the stone, without lifting it to eye level.

Luke smiled. "You've got very good hand-eye coordination."

Nora looked down at her hand. "I do?"

"Yeah, like a first-class gunslinger."

"You're making fun of me." Nora's lips tightened.

Luke turned so that Nora could see the serious expression in her eyes. "No. You could be very good with this weapon with just a little practice."

"Really? You can tell just by me pointing an unloaded weapon at a stone?"

She has no confidence in her own skills. Too many years of only being appreciated for her skills in the bedroom. "Sure," Luke said. "I've taught enough recruits to be able to judge this with a single glance. A few more 'romantic strolls' outside of hearing distance, and you won't have to fear anyone ever again." This would be the biggest gift that she could give Nora. A part of her was almost sorry. Deep down, she wanted to be the one to protect Nora. She reached out to take back the weapon for today.

But instead of handing her the revolver, Nora slid her own hand into Luke's. "Thank you."

Luke swallowed. "You're welcome." She smiled at Nora. "But if you want to use that revolver, we better load it."

Blushing, Nora handed back the revolver.

Parting of the Ways,
July 14th, 1851

"Do you see it?" Luke asked.

Nora shielded her face with her hand, but other than endless, sagebrush-covered plain, there wasn't much to see. "Um, see what?"

"Parting of the Ways." Luke pointed to where the trail in front of them divided. Wagon ruts continued to the left and to the right.

"I say we stay on the main route and take the road to Fort Bridger," Tom Buchanan said, pointing to the left fork. He was low on supplies, and his youngest child was sick again, so Nora couldn't blame him for wanting to choose the safe route that had enough water and made a visit to Fort Bridger possible.

"Do what you want, but I'm gonna take the Sublette Cutoff," Bill Larson said, already steering his mules to the right. "It'll save us over fifty miles."

Nora stared at the road to the right. *Fifty miles?* That would shorten their journey by two or three days—and given her exhaustion, that seemed almost like an eternity to her.

"Yeah, but it'll mean traveling through a desert area," Jacob Garfield said. "Fifty miles with no water, very little grass, but plenty of rough road and alkaline dust."

The emigrants argued back and forth, but no unanimous vote could be reached. Nora looked at Luke, but as usual, her husband didn't voice his opinion. He just stood there, eyeing both trails with a furrowed brow.

Finally, the captain sighed. "Seems like we have to split up. I'll take the shortcut. Those of you who don't want to take the risk go with Tom to Fort Bridger."

Splitting up? Nora bit her lip. *Won't that weaken our defense if we encounter Indians or thieves?* At the same time, hope began to blossom deep inside her. Brody Cowen, the adventurer, would probably take the risky shortcut. If Luke decided to detour to Fort Bridger, as she thought he would, Cowen would be out of her life for good.

Luke stepped closer to her. "What do you think?" he asked, pointing first at the left, then at the right trail.

Nora blinked. Luke knew more about the road ahead than any other emigrant, and he was asking her, a former prostitute who had never been west of Independence before? Most other men hadn't bothered to ask their wives' opinions. "I'm not sure. We've got enough supplies, so a detour to the fort isn't a necessity, but fifty miles through the desert…"

"I think we should risk it," Luke said, his lips a grim line.

"Really?" In the past, Luke had avoided putting her or Amy at risk, and now he decided against the safe route?

"Yeah. Two or three days could mean the difference between you giving birth in the middle of a snowstorm in the Cascade Mountains or safely in a doctor's cabin in Oregon City." Luke directed a glance down at Nora's belly, then up into her eyes.

Nora pressed her palms against her belly. *So Luke's decision is based on our welfare. I should have known.*

The other emigrants gathered in two groups at both sides of the fork.

With longing, Nora looked to the trail on the left. The Garfield family had directed their wagon to this side, preferring the safer route. A glance to her right showed her that Brody Cowen had joined Bill Larson and the captain at the start of the Sublette Shortcut.

"So, which way do we go?" Luke asked once again.

Nora forced her gaze away from the Garfields and looked down at her dusty boots. "Whatever you think is best."

"No. That's not the way I want it to be," Luke said.

Nora turned her head to squint at him. "W-what do you mean?"

"You're not my servant. You're my wife. I don't want you to just follow my orders. I want to hear your opinion. This is something that we have to decide together."

With each step west, Nora discovered not just something new about the land but also about her husband. *Have I been too sheltered in the brothel? Are there other men out there like him, and I just didn't know it?*

"So?" Luke asked.

Nora took a deep breath. "Then we take the shortcut. Giving birth in the middle of a snowstorm is not exactly an appealing thought." It wasn't only that, though. Nora didn't want to take the easy way out, choosing only what was best for her. If it would shorten their journey considerably, she'd pay the price of suffering Brody Cowen's presence a little longer.

"You sure? I know it's gonna be hard for you not to have Bernice nearby, just in case. And then there's…" Luke's gaze traveled over to Brody Cowen and then meaningfully back to Nora.

Nora felt for the small revolver hidden in one of the pockets of her apron. "I'm sure," she answered.

"All right. I'll tell the captain we'll join his group." With a final nod, Luke turned away.

Nora wandered over to the Garfields' wagon.

Bernice's gaze rested on her the whole way. "You're not coming with us, are you?"

"No, we're not." Nora had to fight back tears. Bernice had been the first friend she'd made for herself, almost like a mother or a big sister. "I guess this is good-bye."

"Yeah." Bernice sniffled and engulfed Nora in a warm embrace. "You take care of yourself and the little ones, you hear?" She gently touched Nora's belly.

"Is Jacob really determined to take the detour to Fort Bridger?" Nora asked. She had hoped that Bernice would be with her if she had to give birth on the trail. Sure there were other women who could help, but she hadn't formed close friendships with them. Emeline Larson had enough of her own problems and didn't need to deal with Nora's on top of it.

Bernice squeezed her one last time. "We have to. Our supplies won't last until we reach Fort Hall."

Jacob came over to them. He patted Nora's arm instead of hugging her. "I'm sorry to hear that you won't come with us. We could have used someone like Luke."

Right on cue, Luke wandered over. He shook Jacob's hand and politely nodded at Bernice while Nora hugged the Garfield children.

Amy, who had enthusiastically shared hugs with everyone, began to cry as they walked toward their own wagon and she began to understand that the Garfields weren't going to follow.

Nora bit her bottom lip. She hadn't thought about what their decision to take the shortcut would mean to Amy. Once again, Amy had to say good-bye to people she'd gotten to like. Bernice had been almost like a grandmother or an aunt for Amy, and her youngest daughter was Amy's favorite playmate. Now she would be a lonely child again.

For a second, Nora wanted to turn around and tell Luke that she'd changed her mind, but then she watched Luke urge the oxen forward. He didn't look back, his gaze fixed on the trail that led west. With a sigh, Nora vowed to do the same. Reaching Oregon before the first snow fell was the most important thing; everything else was pure luxury.

BIG SANDY RIVER,
JULY 14TH, 1851

Nora sat with her back against a sack of flour, biting the end of her quill while she thought about what to write in her diary. She had already written down the details of today's travel.

They'd reached the Big Sandy at noon and had decided to camp until nightfall. The wind threw up clouds of dust and made it impossible to build a fire or set up the tents, so each family retreated to their wagon, the covers drawn shut as tightly as possible.

Amy was finally asleep, and Luke had gone with the other men to drive the cattle toward the hills where they would find grass. Nora was alone with her diary and her thoughts. Sitting in the wagon while the wind howled and ripped at the wagon covers, Nora felt isolated and alone as she hadn't for a long time. Bernice, her only friend west of Independence, was many miles away by now. *Only friend.* She stared at her diary. *Is Bernice really your only friend? What about Luke?*

In the last few months, she had learned to trust him as she'd never trusted a man before. He'd held her life and Amy's in his hands more than once on their journey west, and each time, he'd proven worthy of her trust. But she did more than respect his skills and admire his integrity. *Admit it, you like him.*

The cover at the end of the wagon opened, interrupting her thoughts.

Luke climbed into the wagon.

Nora set her diary aside and moved to bring him a plate of bread and cold beans.

"Stay." Luke gestured for her to sit back down. "You don't have to wait on me. Finish your writing."

With a relieved sigh, Nora sank back against the sack of flour. With every day that her pregnancy progressed, her feet were more swollen and her back seemed to ache more than the day before.

A plate in one hand, Luke settled down in the only empty place in the wagon—right next to Nora, leaning against the same sack of flour that served as Nora's backrest. "Can't think of something to write?" he asked after a while and pointed at the diary with his fork.

Nora sighed. It was exactly the opposite. There were too many thoughts going through her head. She closed the leather-bound diary. "The words just don't come tonight. How about I give you that promised reading and writing lesson instead? It's too windy to go out for target practice anyway, so I might as well take my turn at playing the teacher."

Luke chewed thoroughly, taking his time to answer. Finally, he swallowed. "I'm too old to learn this."

"Nonsense. It's never too late to learn. Don't give up before you have even tried."

He took another bite, then set his plate aside. "All right. I'll try."

Carefully, Nora pulled an empty page out of the back of her diary. She scribbled down the letters of the alphabet and then showed them to Luke. "This," she pointed at the first letter, "is an 'a' like in 'apple.'"

Luke took the page from her to study the letters. Their hands touched, and both of them quickly looked away. "Why are there two letters for the 'a'?"

"You use the capital 'A' in names like 'Amy' and at the beginning of a sentence." Nora circled the letter for him.

Luke studied the many unknown symbols on the page. "There's a lot to learn."

"Yes, but there's also a lot of time until we reach Oregon. If you study for an hour or even half an hour each day, you can write the letter, telling your friends that you arrived in Oregon, on your own."

Luke tugged on his bottom lip. "If you don't run out of patience before that."

"You never lost patience with me, so why should I?" Nora held his gaze. "I told you, I dreamed of becoming a teacher, and you can't be worse than an eight-year-old, can you?"

Luke laughed. "Let's hope not. At least I can already count and know how to write the numbers."

"You do?" Nora knew nothing about his past. Had he been born in a poor family that couldn't afford to send him to school? But then why had he learned the numbers, but not reading and writing?

"Keeping count of her money was important to…" Luke paused. "It was important where I grew up."

Nora laid down the quill. "Tell me about it. Where did you grow up?"

Luke pointedly looked at his pocket watch. "Let's get this lesson over with. We won't have the time again until we reach the Green River."

With a sigh, Nora reached for the quill again.

GREEN RIVER DESERT, JULY 15TH, 1851

Luke looked around, making sure that nobody was watching her before she discreetly spat out the dust in her mouth. It might have been a manly gesture, but Luke didn't like the constant spitting. Here, in the middle of the Green River Desert, it was a necessity, though.

They had filled every water casket and every canteen in the Big Sandy and had waited for dusk before they started their journey across the grassless fifty-mile tableland. The boys of the train walked ahead of the wagons, carrying lanterns to show them the way. Traveling by night was cooler, but the wagons still stirred up the alkaline dust and sand.

They'd traveled all night, through deep sand, steep ravines, and dried-up alkali lakes. By sunrise, they still hadn't reached the Green River. Luke knew they weren't lost, though, because the trail was marked by abandoned wagons and the bleached bones of dead cattle.

By noon, the oxen began to slow under the blazing sun. The morning dew that provided some meager fluid for the cattle had long since evaporated. There was no grass for them; even wild sage hardly grew in the sandy soil.

They stopped for half an hour of rest while the sun beat down on them. Luke carefully dipped a tin cup into the water barrel, measuring the amount of water for each animal. She checked their hooves and found that Snow White had lost an ox shoe. The hoof of one front leg threatened to split on the rough trail. Luke used the break to apply hot tar to the hoof, sealing the split.

"Here." Nora came over and offered her a tin can in which two slices of peach remained.

Luke licked dry lips but made no move to take the can. Instead, she held up her hands that were smeared with tar. "I'll eat it later."

"There'll be more sand in the can than peaches if you don't eat it now." Nora stepped around the bucket of tar and held out a slice of peach.

Luke swallowed—not because of the mouth-watering sight of the peach, but because Nora obviously wanted her to eat the slice right out of her hand. "No, I'll—"

"Come on, or it'll go to waste in this heat." Again, Nora held out the piece of fruit.

Reluctantly, Luke bent her head and picked up the slice with careful teeth. Her gaze met Nora's, and she swallowed the peach in one bite, too distracted to chew the fruit. Coughing, she forced it down her throat. "Thanks." She gasped.

Nora turned away with a smile. "You're welcome."

A few hours later, the first wagon began to lag behind. Amy and the other children complained of thirst every few minutes, and Luke started to watch Nora with concern. Her ankles were swollen, and she kept pressing a hand to the small of her back. "Nora," she called to get her attention. "Do you want to ride for a while?" She pointed to Measles who was walking along behind the wagon. The riders had dismounted hours ago to spare the horses the extra weight.

"No, I'm fine," Nora answered.

Just then, the oxen that had plodded on with lolling tongues and glassy eyes picked up their pace. After a few more yards, they broke into a clumsy run.

Luke looked down the bluffs. "Finally, the Green River." A wide, swift-flowing stream lay below them. The water glittered in the sun. It looked clear, and Luke had heard that it was filled with trout and other fish. Cottonwoods lined its banks, and mountain sheep grazed on the lush grass in the valley.

Most of the emigrants broke out in victory dances and hurried down to the river.

Luke followed a bit more slowly. She knew that they had overcome one problem only to be met with another. Unlike most other rivers they had encountered, the Green River was not going in their direction, but bisected the Oregon Trail. They had no choice but to cross the Green River, said to be the most difficult crossing on the way to Oregon. A dozen nearby graves provided testimony to the dangers of the crossing.

"There's a ferry," Bill Larson said.

Luke looked at the raft that carried wagons across on pulleys. A wooden sign announced a price of eight dollars. *Is that per wagon?* "The water's not that high for July," Luke said, gazing down to the river. "I think we should save us the money and hire a guide instead." Every dollar that they saved now would help them start their new lives in Oregon and survive the first, hard winter.

"Trust a dirty Indian with our lives and our wagons? Ha!" Larson spat out, barely missing Luke's shoulder.

Luke stiffened but remained calm. She'd learned not to react to provocations like that. She felt a fleeting touch to her back and straightened further, knowing it was Nora, offering silent support. "The Shoshone are traditionally friendly to us, and they know the Green River better than anyone else. We'd be fools to refuse their help."

"He's right," the captain said. "An Indian guide won't charge as much as the Mormons operating the ferry, and we won't have to wait our turn at the ferry."

Without waiting for Larson's protests to die down, Luke loosened the bolts that fastened the wagon bed to the running gear and propped the bed up, above the reach of the water, with blocks.

Soon, two Shoshones were guiding the double-teamed wagons into the river.

"Do you want to take over?" Nora offered her the whip.

"Do you want me to?" Luke knew they were following a gravel bar so narrow that the smallest misstep by the driver could overturn the wagon and send their provisions rushing downstream. The fear and self-doubt in Nora's eyes told her that she was aware of it too.

Nora's jaw clenched. Slowly, she straightened her shoulders. "I think I can do it—if you trust me to."

Luke didn't hesitate. "You know I do. The boys are playing favorites anyway." She nodded at the oxen. They had gotten used to Nora's gentler, but equally determined approach of handling them.

"All right, then." With a tight grip on the whip, Nora waded into the river, urging the oxen along.

Luke's gaze followed her. She couldn't help the proud grin that curled her lips. It was good to see Nora begin to trust in her skills and in herself. She swung up into the saddle and followed Nora, keeping an eye on her and on Amy, who was peeking out from the back of the wagon.

The river was deep. Amy shrieked when the water ran into the wagon box, but their guides never hesitated, and within an hour, they were safely on the other side.

While they waited for the last of their fellow travelers to cross, Luke took Nora and Amy to the gray sandstone bluff running parallel to the river. Many other emigrants had left their names behind on Names Hill, and Luke had looked forward to carving Nora's name in a place where the younger woman could see it.

Nora watched as Luke worked the sandstone with her knife. "You still know the letters. See, I told you you'd be a good student."

Luke smiled. "I had a good teacher."

Their gazes met and held.

"Come on," Luke said. "Let's go back to camp."

SODA SPRINGS,
JULY 24TH, 1851

Nora looked over her shoulder. Behind them lay steep mountains and clear streams like Ham's Fork. Finally, they had reached the green Bear River Valley. Here, the Sublette Cutoff rejoined the main route from Fort Bridger, but, of course, there was no sign of the other part of their wagon train. The Garfields and their companions were still many miles away, but sometimes, Nora couldn't help looking out for them anyway.

"Mama, it stinks," Amy said from her place inside the wagon.

Nora nodded. A strong rotten egg odor wafted through the air. "Yeah, it does." She pinched her nose.

"That's Sulphur Springs," Luke said, "one of the springs along the banks of the Bear River."

Nora saw the disappointed faces of the other emigrant women. *We won't be able to bathe in that particular spring. That's for sure.* She didn't know whether she should be disappointed or relieved. Since her encounter with Brody Cowen in the hot spring, Nora had mixed feelings about taking a bath. Her tired, pregnant body longed to sink into a tub of hot water, but she was much too scared of Cowen to fully relax. *Maybe it's just as well that we can't bathe here.*

But it seemed as if her conclusion had been rash. They rounded a bend in the Bear River and found themselves in a landscape filled with cones, craters, bubbling springs, and geysers. Some of the springs were cold, some warm, and others hot.

The men gathered around one spring. "Come on over, Hamilton," Larson shouted. "This water tastes like beer."

"No, thanks," Luke said. "I tried it before, and it tastes like rust." He walked away.

Nora gathered their dirty clothes, determined to use one of the hot pools to do their laundry.

"Ah, ah!" Luke blocked her way and took a pile of shirts from her arms. "You're not lugging around heavy, sodden clothes."

"But the laundry needs to be done." Nora wasn't keen on doing the heavy work. The fear of losing her baby was constantly on her mind. There wasn't much of a choice, though.

Now that she no longer had Bernice to help her, she had to do it alone. She vowed to be as cautious as possible.

"Then I'll do it."

Nora stared at him until he began to squirm.

"What?"

"You want to do our laundry?" Nora asked. No other man on the train had ever offered to do a woman's chores.

Luke shrugged. A blush climbed up his neck. "You said it yourself: The laundry needs to be done, and you sure as hell are not going to do it. So that leaves me."

"Do you even know how?"

"You think I never washed my clothes before I met you?" His grin took the sting from his words.

"No, of course I don't." Compared to most other men, Luke was always clean and neat.

Luke dumped the pile of soiled linens into one of the warm pools. "You can watch and correct me if you want."

Nora sat down on a rock and watched. It was hard to sit still while all around her, the other women did their own laundry. Even Emeline Larson, obviously pregnant and with new bruises on her arms, was scrubbing her husband's shirts.

From time to time, one of the other women took a surreptitious glance at Luke. The younger ones giggled as they watched him scrub one of Nora's chemises.

Luke blushed each time, but he never paused in his task. Finally, he hung the wet clothes on a line strung between two wagons.

Nora glanced at Amy, who watched her stepfather. *What kind of woman will she become if she grows up around Luke?* For a moment, she heard her father's scornful words about women who forgot their God-given place in society. Then she straightened her shoulders. *She'll become a woman who doesn't think she's worthless just because she's not the son her father longed for.*

She watched Luke take care of his own chores, checking on the oxen and horses. Not allowed to do any hard work, she felt useless. "I could—"

"Why don't you go and have a bath before all the best hot springs are taken?" Luke said.

Nora gazed with longing at some of the other women heading off with towels and bars of soap. "Maybe later."

"Why not now? Later you'll have to help with the cooking because, frankly, you're a much better cook than I."

Once again, Nora marveled at his ease in complimenting her. No other man had ever praised her for skills beyond the walls of the bedroom. She couldn't help the pleased grin that formed on her lips but then remembered that she still had to answer his question. The smile disappeared from her face.

"Is it..." Luke looked around, making sure no one could hear him. "Brody? Are you afraid that he's gonna catch you bathing alone and helpless?"

He'd guessed her thoughts before she could voice them. Nora felt for the small revolver in her apron. "I'm afraid my bathing suit has no pockets."

A blush inched across his face.

Nora smiled again. *So he knows that my bathing suit consists of nothing but bare skin, huh? I wonder if he's trying to picture me like that.* "I think I better stay here, with you, where he won't try anything. It's not worth the trouble."

"That's just not right." Luke's voice was rough and louder than usual. "It's not right that you have to make sacrifices just because—"

Nora touched his arm. The muscles under her fingers were like stone as he clenched his hands into fists. "It's all right."

"No, it's not." Luke stared at the ground. Finally, he lifted his head and fixed his gaze on her. "Well, you could take your bath while I'm watching. Watching for Brody, that is, not you of course, because I wouldn't... I would never..."

His rambling made her smile. "I know you're a gentleman." *Even in situations when it's not required.*

"So, you want to take a bath? I could sit down on a rock, facing the opposite direction, and, well, there's still today's reading lesson to go over."

Nora hesitated. Finally, she looked down at her dusty clothes and skin and nodded. She wanted a hot bath more than anything else right now, and with Luke standing guard, she was not afraid. The thought of Luke seeing her naked didn't scare her. "All right." She slung a towel across her shoulder, grabbed her bar of lavender soap, and called Amy away from her "conversation" with Measles. Hand in hand, they went in search of the best bathing tub.

Luke followed a few yards behind them, taking care not to intrude even though Nora wasn't even undressed yet.

Without warning, a high-pitched whistle shrilled somewhere in front of them.

Amy jumped and clutched Nora's skirt. "What's dat, Mama?"

"I'm not sure. It almost sounds like..." She turned to look at Luke. "Surely there can't be a steamboat right here in the middle of the wilderness?" The whistle had sounded exactly like that of the steamboat that had brought her to Independence three years ago.

Luke grinned. "No. But you're not that far off. That's Steamboat Springs." He pointed to a large, flat rock in the midst of a grove of trees, right next to the riverbank.

As they walked closer, Nora heard gurgling and hissing sounds from under ground. Curious, she took another step.

"No." Luke caught up with her and held her back with a touch to her shoulder. "Don't go any closer."

A four-foot geyser shot out of a crevice in the rock, emitting the steamboat whistle sound once again.

Amy stared with big eyes and an open mouth, and Nora suspected that she didn't look any more sophisticated than that. "How does this work?"

"I think it's the gas that gathers below the rock," Luke said. "The water recedes for a few minutes, then the pent up gas escapes and the water shoots out. That's what causes the pipe sound."

Three of the wagon train's young boys had gathered behind them and stared at the geyser too. When it receded, they plugged the exit hole with a handful of sod.

The hissing gas blew the grass skyward.

"Ooh!" Amy clapped.

Nora let her watch for a few minutes, then tugged on her hand. "Come on, Amy, let's continue our search for the perfect bathing spring."

"No. Watch!" Amy pulled her hand back. She only had eyes for the small geyser and the game of the boys with the sod.

"All right. One more time." Nora waited until the water bubbled up and then receded once again. "Now..." She tried to get Amy to move away again, but the girl still didn't budge. "Amy, come on."

"No."

It wasn't often that Nora had to be strict with her normally obedient daughter, and she hesitated to force her away from the spring. There were so few entertaining things for a child of her age on the journey, and now that the Garfields were no longer traveling with them, Amy had lost her favorite playmate. Was it fair to pull her away from this fascinating spring just because she longed to sink into a pool of hot water? She gazed at Luke.

"We should go before it gets dark, or you'll get eaten alive by mosquitoes while you bathe," he said.

"Amy..."

"Don't wanna. I watch the spring."

Nora looked at Luke again. "Do you think we could let her stay here on her own?"

For a second, Luke blinked, obviously startled that he had a say in the matter of Amy's upbringing. "It's too dangerous. The water here is very hot."

"Did you hear that, Amy? The spring can be very dangerous for children, so you have to come with us. I promise that we'll visit the geyser again before you have to go to bed, all right?"

Amy didn't look convinced. Her lower lip trembled, her brows knitted, and her arms pressed to her body.

Uh-oh. Nora knew this position. One would rather move a rock than Amy when she was like this. She took a deep breath and prepared to order her daughter away from the spring.

"Amy, did you know that I visited Steamboat Spring before?" Luke's quiet voice surprised her. He was talking to Amy in an adult tone, and it made Amy look up.

She shook her head but didn't answer. Her lips were still pressed together too tightly for that.

"And when I was here, a family was watching the geyser too," Luke said. "They had a little boy not much older than you. While his mama wandered over to see the next spring, he bent down and drank from the spring. Guess what happened?"

Amy was listening intently now. "Don't know," she said with wide eyes. "The boy falled in?"

"No, but he badly burned his tongue, because the water is very hot."

"Uh-oh."

Luke nodded gravely, almost making Nora giggle. She held her breath as she watched them interact.

"Do you know why that was a very bad thing?" Luke asked.

"It hurts."

"Yes, it did. But that wasn't the worst thing." Luke didn't immediately offer what had happened to the boy. He made her wait and ask.

Finally, Amy asked, "What was the bad thing?"

Luke put on his saddest expression. "Because he hurt his tongue, he wasn't able to drink the delicious lemonade his mother made that evening from the carbonated water from another spring. He had to watch the other children drink the lemonade while he couldn't have any."

Amy's body relaxed as she turned to Nora. "Mama, can I have lemonade? Please?"

Nora had to hide a smile. "Well, that depends."

"Please." Amy tugged on Nora's skirt.

"Then you shouldn't risk burning your tongue, huh?"

Amy moved away from the bubbling water of Steamboat Spring. She grabbed Nora's hand. "I go with you now."

As Nora led her away, she grinned back at Luke over her shoulder. "How manipulative of you, Mister Hamilton. How did you learn to handle unruly children like that?" Just three months ago, small children seemed to scare him, and now he had handled the situation as if he'd dealt with Amy's more difficult moments for years.

"Well, let's just say that I learned from the best, Mrs. Hamilton." He winked at her.

"Me?" Nora pointed at her chest, trying hard to look indignant. "I'm not manipulative."

Luke laughed. "Yes, you." *She pretended to be a virgin when we met even though she has a child and is pregnant with another.*

Nora grinned but then sobered. "Luke, I hope you know I never tried to manipulate you just for the fun of it. I just didn't know any other way to—"

"I know," Luke said. While hiding her pregnancy from Luke hadn't exactly been a prime example of honesty, it had only been a lie of omission because Nora feared the consequences.

All thoughts about Nora's honesty vanished as they reached the warm spring of Nora's choice. Nora slipped out of her bodice and skirt without much warning.

Or any warning at all. Luke turned away and fixed her gaze on a nearby cedar, but not fast enough. It was impossible not to register the smooth, fair skin that Nora's clothes normally covered. Nora's belly was more rounded than Luke remembered from watching her bathe in Alcove Springs more than two months ago, but Luke didn't find her unappealing at all. She settled down cross-legged and let her gaze wander over the surrounding hills and trees, everything to distract herself from the sounds of rustling clothes and then the splash of water and the sensuous groan as Nora sank into the warm spring.

As the pregnancy progressed, it had become a bit easier to see Nora as only a mother and try to forget how attractive she was. Now, with even a fleeting glance at her half-naked body, it was impossible to miss that she was still very much a beautiful woman.

More splashing sounds and Amy's excited squeaks came from behind her. "Papa, look."

Luke stiffened. "Very nice, Amy," she answered without turning around.

"Looook," Amy said again.

Luke took a one-second glance over her shoulder, trying not to look at anything but Amy, who had a crown of soap froth piled high on her head. She had to clear her voice before she could speak. "Very nice."

"That's true," another voice said. "Very nice."

Luke whirled around.

Brody Cowen strolled over, his gaze fixed on Nora.

Luke stiffened. She had hoped that Brody would cease his inappropriate behavior toward Nora, now that Luke was aware of it. *Obviously, he's not going to just stop. Nothing in my life can ever be that easy, right?*

Amy began to cry when she saw Brody.

Clenching her jaw, Luke rose to block Nora and Amy from his gaze with her own body. She didn't want to start a fight. All her life, she had avoided getting into trouble. Each argument, each fight held the risk of her getting hurt, possibly leading to her secret being discovered. She had simply walked away from situations that had other officers scramble for their weapons and demand satisfaction in a duel. But now, she couldn't just walk away. There was more at stake here than her honor. "I suggest you turn around and leave." Luke kept her voice as quiet as possible, not wanting to attract the attention of the other emigrants.

"Why?" Brody leered in Nora's direction. "She's more than enough for the two of us. I've seen her service two customers in a row before."

You goddamn bastard. Any residing hero worship she might have felt for Brody vanished in a wave of heat and rage. Without thinking, she took three steps toward Brody before she remembered her rule. *No fistfights.* "I'm not her customer. I'm her husband," she said through clenched teeth. "And I'm not sharing. Now go, or I'll tell the captain and have you banished from the train."

Brody casually folded his arms across his chest. "What'll you tell him? That your beloved wife was the most sought-after whore in Independence? That would get you banished from the train, not me." He laughed.

The worst thing was that he was probably right, at least partially. Revealing Nora's former profession wouldn't get them banished from the train, but there would be negative consequences nonetheless. The women who had formed friendships with Nora would now talk about her behind her back. Some men might even react as Brody had and think they could take liberties with Nora. And Amy would once again be mocked as the bastard child of a prostitute. So, telling the captain was out of the question. Luke had to handle the situation on her own.

"I'll make you an offer." Brody's leering gaze was still fixed on Nora.

Luke cursed the fact that he was a few inches taller than her and could glimpse Nora over her shoulder. *A real man wouldn't let his wife be humiliated like that. A man would have shot him or at least punched him out by now.* "We won't make any deals with you, so move on and leave us alone."

Nora and Amy had hastily dressed, and Luke wrapped a protective arm around each of them and ushered them past Brody, back to camp.

Brody's mocking laughter burned in her ears for hours.

Soda Springs,
July 24th, 1851

Nora stared at the tent's wall. It was well past midnight, and she was tired, but she couldn't sleep. She lay still, trying not to wake up the other occupants of the tent, but her mind was whirling. Thoughts of Brody, her past, and the uncertain future kept her awake.

Weeks of travel were still ahead of them, and that meant she would have to endure Brody's presence in the train for much longer. She'd had cruel customers before who had delighted in humiliating her, but at least they'd always been gone by the next day. Brody would still be there in the morning.

She had hoped to at least be safe when Luke was around, but that didn't seem to be the case any longer. Brody had no respect for Luke, and Luke clearly hesitated to demand that respect by using violence. Nora had never expected him to. She wasn't sure if her slender husband stood any chance in a fight against the more sturdy man. Luke was a hard worker and not exactly weak, but he had none of the other men's rough strength.

Nora liked the gentleness she sensed beneath Luke's aloof surface, but now, it made her worry about him.

The tent's flap rustled.

Nora's head jerked around. Every fiber of her body turned to ice. *Is that Brody, trying to get in?* She peered through the tent, trying to see anything in the darkness.

The flap opened, and a shaft of moonlight fell into the tent.

Nora relaxed. It wasn't Brody, just Luke slipping from the tent. *Probably following the call of nature.* She rolled over and closed her eyes, but sleep still wouldn't come. She waited for what seemed like an hour, but Luke didn't return. The last remnants of sleepiness vanished as she had now something else to worry about.

Where's Luke? What is taking him so long? Her mind's eye showed her pictures of Luke lying in a pool of blood, killed by Brody, who had lurked in the darkness. With a gasp, she sat up. She dressed, knowing she wouldn't sleep until Luke had safely returned. She checked on the still sleeping Amy, tucked the blanket more tightly around her, and then stepped out into the night.

She turned right toward the latrine the men used to relieve themselves. *No Luke.* The area around the hastily dug latrine was empty. *Maybe we passed each other in the darkness.* She turned back around and wandered through the dark camp. Everything was quiet; only loud snoring came from Bill Larson's tent. *Maybe he couldn't sleep and went to visit Measles.*

She walked across the open space in the middle of the circle of wagons, where the horses were grazing or sleeping. Measles snorted a greeting and nuzzled against Nora's apron. "Sorry, girl, no apple tonight. I'm searching for your master. You haven't seen him, huh?" With a sigh, she turned and walked away.

"Stop! Who's there?" A figure sprang up next to the small fire at the camp's edge. It was Elijah Rogers, who was standing guard tonight.

"It's only me, Nora Hamilton, Eli," she called.

Eli Rogers sat back down. "What are you doing up?"

"I couldn't sleep and thought I would take a walk." If she told him she was searching for her missing husband, he might think they'd had a fight. "Is anyone else still up?"

Eli laughed. "Are you kidding? We'll be traveling a very bad road toward Portneuf River tomorrow. Everyone else is getting all the sleep they can."

So he hasn't seen Luke. Where is he? At least it probably also meant that Brody Cowen was asleep and not lurking in the darkness, waiting for her. "All right. I'll take that walk now and then go to bed. Good night, Eli." She slipped past the circle of wagons and tents and headed for the river.

In the silence of the night, something splashed down at the banks, hidden by a small grove of cedars.

Goose bumps broke out all over Nora's skin. She gripped the small revolver in her apron pocket. She longed to be back in the relative safety of her tent, but she took a deep breath and tiptoed forward.

The splashing became louder.

Quietly, she crept closer. She hid behind a cedar, leaning against the rough bark. She counted to three, then peeked around the tree.

Someone was bathing in the river, standing half-naked, facing away from Nora. *Is that Luke? What is he doing, taking a bath in the middle of the night? The water must be freezing.*

When the person turned, she saw the silhouette of a woman. *It's not Luke. So, where is he? And why is everyone out tonight, without the guard knowing about it? What's going on?*

The woman in the river was scrubbing herself, splashing her face with the cold river water. Her shoulders were heaving. Was she shivering in the cold or crying? After a few more minutes, the woman stumbled up the bank and sank to her knees.

Nora heard her sobbing and was just about to step out of her hiding place to comfort her, but another person knelt next to the woman and enfolded her in protective arms.

The woman jerked back with a startled cry.

For a second, Nora saw her face in the moonlight. *Emmy. That's Emmy Larson. With another black eye and a split lip.* She forced down the bile rising in her throat. She had known for some time that Bill Larson beat up on his wife—everyone on the train knew about it, but they all looked the other way because he was her husband and there was nothing they could do about it. Nora had hoped that now, with Emeline being pregnant, Larson wouldn't hit her any longer, but obviously he had no more consideration for his son or daughter than he had for his wife.

Emeline stared at the man kneeling next to her like a deer poised to flee.

He murmured soothingly and wrapped a comforting arm around her shoulder.

Suddenly, there was no doubt in Nora's mind about the whereabouts of her husband. She sensed that it was Luke kneeling in the mud.

For a moment, Emeline's half-naked body froze under his touch, then she fell into his arms and started to sob uncontrollably.

Luke shrugged out of his jacket and hung it around Emeline's shoulders.

Nora could only stare. Her eyes, now used to the darkness, made out the small circles that Luke's hands traced on Emeline's back. He stroked her hair and whispered in her ear until the sobs subsided to an occasional hiccup.

When Nora had to gasp for air, she realized she had held her breath while she watched Luke. Never, not even once in her life, had she seen a man comfort a woman in this way. Emeline seemed to sense that he was different from other men too, because the battered woman relaxed in his embrace. Emmy surely would have run away from any other male. Nora was proud of the way he was consoling Emmy, but at the same time, a spark of jealousy glowed in her belly as she watched Luke hold the half-naked woman close.

When Luke helped Emmy up and led her up the bank, Nora turned around and hurried back to camp, keeping ahead of them so they wouldn't discover her. She slipped into the tent, undressed, and crawled back under her blankets.

Ten minutes later, the tent's flap opened.

Nora tried to feign the quiet breathing of a sleeping person.

Luke stopped at the tent's entrance. He checked on Amy; then his head turned in her direction.

Nora squeezed her eyes shut. She heard him tiptoe through the tent and settle down on his bedroll. Curiosity burned in her chest. She wanted to ask him what had happened to Emmy tonight, why he'd been down by the river, and why he had taken on the role of

Emmy's comforter. Just a few months ago, she wouldn't have dared to ask—a wife was accountable to her husband, but not the other way around. That's what she'd learned and believed in her whole life. But Luke didn't seem to believe in those traditional rules of marriage. He'd encouraged her every day to form her own opinion and voice it.

Nora cleared her throat. "Luke?"

Luke's blanket rustled. "You're awake?"

Isn't it obvious? I've never been prone to talking in my sleep. Nora realized that he was stalling. He didn't want her to ask where he'd been. "Couldn't sleep."

Luke lifted up on his elbow. She felt his gaze rest on her in the almost darkness. "Is it the baby? Is she kicking again?"

Nora's lips curled into a smile. Without realizing it, he always referred to the baby as a "she." "No, it's not that. The baby is quiet for once. I'm just lying awake, thinking."

"Worrying," Luke said.

Nora bit her lip. "Yeah. And then you were gone from the tent for so long."

"Just a quick stroll through the camp to check on Measles," Luke said.

That was an obvious lie. *Should I let him get away with it?* "No," she said.

"No?"

"I checked on Measles when you didn't return to the tent. You weren't with her."

Luke sat up. "Are you accusing me of anything?" His tone of voice wasn't angry, but cautious.

Am I? Other women might have accused him of having an affair with Emeline Larson, but Nora knew that was not it. Luke's embrace had been tender, but without any passion. "No. I just want to know where you've been. This wasn't the first time you slipped away from camp in the middle of the night." Nora remembered the night he had been shot by the guard. She suspected that he hadn't just visited the latrine then, either.

"Where I do or do not go is none of your business," Luke said.

Nora blinked and closed her mouth. *So much for being allowed to voice my opinion.* She rolled away from Luke. She'd thought she was used to being degraded and humiliated, but this harsh rebuke from Luke hurt more than she had expected.

A touch to her shoulder made her flinch.

"Nora, I'm sorry." Luke gently pulled her around. "I'm sorry."

Nora stared up into his eyes. She could read the regret in them. "It's all right."

"No, it's not. It's just..." Luke sighed. "I'm just not used to someone caring about where I am or what I do. I was down by the river. Emeline Larson was there. That damned husband of hers hit her again, and she was in the middle of the river, trying to cool her face and wash the traces of him off her body."

Luke had been honest. *Well, at least partially honest. He still didn't explain why he was out there in the middle of the night.* Nora decided to let it go. She wanted to believe that he would tell her when he was ready. "I know," she said, deciding to return his honesty.

"You know? What? How?"

"When you didn't come back, I was worried, so I searched for you. I saw you with Emmy down by the river." Nora waited with bated breath for Luke's reaction.

Luke frowned. "Why didn't you show yourself? I could have used your help, you know?"

"I guess I didn't want to interrupt. There was something so... From what I could see, you didn't need any help at all." She looked into his face. "You were really good with her. I never thought that she would let herself be comforted by a man, not after what she just went through with Bill."

Luke shrugged. "Anyone with a compassionate bone in his body could have done it."

Yeah, yeah, just try to convince yourself of that. I know you're special, Luke Hamilton.

"Let's go to sleep now. Tomorrow's gonna be a hard day." With a soft squeeze to her shoulder, he retreated to his side of the tent.

SHEEP ROCK,
JULY 25TH, 1851

"Sit down before you fall down, Nora." Luke took the frying pan from Nora and pointed to a fallen log. "You too, Mrs. Larson. I'll take care of this."

She gave Emeline Larson an encouraging nod, but the woman still hesitated, not used to sitting by the fire while a man attended to her. Finally, Nora had to pull her down to sit next to her.

"Beans." Amy's groan said what most of the adults were thinking.

"Well, if you insist, I could shoot one of the 'cute sheep' that we saw earlier." Luke pointed to the rugged mountain called Sheep Rock. Mountain sheep wandered around its base. "Then you wouldn't have to eat the beans."

"Noooo." Amy hastily shoveled down her beans.

Nora giggled, and even Emeline had to smile.

Satisfied, Luke handed out plates of beans and bread to the two pregnant women.

"Thank you," Emeline said in a whisper, not meeting her eyes. "And thank you for last night."

"What the hell does that mean?" Bill Larson's roar made everyone stop eating. He had appeared behind his wife. "Do you think you can cuckold me? You, you joke of a man?"

"Billy, please, he's not—"

Larson pointed a threatening finger at his wife. "Shut up. I'll deal with you later." He whirled around and glared at Luke.

Luke clenched her jaw. She wanted to rip off the finger that he had threatened Emeline with—or even the whole arm. "There's nothing between your wife and me," she said as calmly as possible.

"And just to make sure it stays that way, I'm gonna clean your plow." Larson raised both fists and took a fighting stance. "Come on, Hamilton. Come on, you coward."

Luke knew that she had a good chance of beating him—she'd learned how to fight growing up in seedy neighborhoods and in the barracks of half a dozen forts. But Larson was taller and heavier than she was. If she got injured fighting him, her secret might be discovered. "I'm not the one who likes to discuss things with his fists," she said with a glance at the bruises in Emeline's face.

"What are you implying?" Larson took a step closer, crowding Luke.

Luke held his gaze. "You know exactly what I mean."

"What's going on here?" the captain's voice boomed behind them. "We're moving on, people."

Larson didn't look away from Luke. He pointed a thick finger at her. "I'm not through with you." He stormed off, dragging Emeline with him.

Luke exchanged a quick glance with Nora, who looked worried. *Wonderful.* Luke pressed her lips together. *Now I've got two enemies in the train.* Slipping away from the camp to bathe or tend to other female needs was getting more and more difficult. With a sigh, she turned to reyoke the oxen.

FORT HALL,
JULY 29TH, 1851

"A letter." Nora waved a battered envelope. "I've got a letter from Tess."

Luke grinned, relieved to see Nora smile again. Just an hour ago, Nora hadn't been able to hide her disappointment at reaching Fort Hall and finding out that it was nothing more than a few shabby buildings enclosed in a log wall.

But Amy still trudged over the parade ground with a constant frown. Even the promise of eating fresh vegetables and fruit tonight, something they hadn't had for some time, didn't cheer her up.

"She's just grumpy," Nora said. "We should return to camp so that she can take a nap."

"You mean so that you can read your letter, huh?" Luke smiled at the way Nora clutched the envelope with both hands.

A blush colored Nora's cheeks. "It's just… It's such a surprise. I didn't expect to hear from Tess until we reached Oregon. I don't know how she managed to get a letter to Fort Hall before we got here."

Luke shrugged. "She probably sent letters with every gold digger and officer leaving Independence, hoping one of them would reach you. Men on horses make much better time than our slow-moving oxen with the heavy wagons. A lot of men visit Tess just before they head west." She stopped when she became aware of whom she was talking to. Nora knew better than anyone else how many men visited Tess's brothel. "I'm sorry. I didn't want to remind you of—"

"No. It's all right. I'm not ashamed of what I did while I…" Nora took a sidelong glance at her daughter. "While I lived in Independence. Not anymore."

Luke didn't know what to say, so she just nodded, and they walked back to their tent in companionable silence.

Once they had Amy settled down for the night and all the chores were done, Nora sat down to read her letter. A smile was firmly etched on her face as the opened the envelope.

Luke was glad to hear from her old friend Tess too, but her joy wasn't as unblemished as Nora's. To tell the truth, she was a little worried about the letter's content. Had Tess remembered to refer to her only with male pronouns? Or had she assumed that, after many weeks of traveling together, Luke had long since revealed her secret to Nora?

Not wanting to make her feel as if she was watching her, trying to decipher the words in the letter, Luke forced her gaze away and reached for her newest project. Yesterday, she had started to work on hollowing out half of a yard-long log.

"This is not a new wooden yoke for the oxen, is it?" Nora asked, looking up from her letter.

"No, it's not." Luke scratched her nose, hesitant to admit it. "It's a cradle."

The letter fluttered into Nora's lap. "A cradle? For my baby?" She touched her belly.

Luke shifted the knife from hand to hand. She knew she was sending Nora mixed messages. She had told her to search for another husband as soon as they reached Oregon, and yet she was building a cradle as if she expected a succession of Hamilton offspring to grow up in it. "Well…" She shrugged, trying to play it down. "I figured the little one's going to need it. How's Tess?"

Nora looked back and forth between the cradle and Luke's face for a few seconds more before she picked up the letter again. "She's fine, but she complains that business has been dragging since…for the last few months."

Since Nora left. Luke knew enough about life in a brothel to realize that the beautiful, red-haired Nora had probably obtained the highest prices. Luke clenched her teeth and forced her thoughts in another direction. She always avoided thinking about the talents that Nora had possessed in her former profession. "But otherwise Tess is fine?"

"Yes." Nora slid her thumb over a paragraph in the letter. She glanced at Luke, then quickly back down. "She asked…"

Luke let go of the knife. She wanted to avoid cutting herself if Tess had somehow managed to get her in trouble with a question. *I just hope she didn't give my secret away.* "What?" she asked after several seconds of hesitation.

"She asked how our marriage is going." Slowly, Nora looked up from the letter.

Luke's mouth grew dry. She desperately wanted to know the answer to that question. What did Nora think about their marriage? Did she regard it as the farce it was? "What will you write her?"

"What do you want me to write?"

That was not the way Luke wanted things to be between them. She didn't want to be anything like Bill Larson, who tried to control everything his wife did, said, and even thought. "The truth," she said.

Nora kept eye contact. "Then I'll write that you're hardworking, gentle, a good father to Amy…and even more afraid to trust someone than I am." Finally, Nora lowered her gaze, as if afraid that she'd said too much.

I can't trust you fully, Luke thought. *Not with the truth about myself. You wouldn't have anything complimentary to say about me any longer if you knew.*

When Luke didn't answer, Nora was the one to break the silence. "Tess also wanted to know how you reacted to the fact that I'm with child again."

Luke stiffened. Tess would immediately know that she hadn't fathered the child, so she might have asked Nora who the baby's father was. She hoped it wouldn't make Nora suspicious.

"Maybe you want to answer that question for Tess?" Nora said.

"My writing is not good enough yet." Luke's emotions regarding the baby were much too conflicted to give a clear answer. Sometimes, when she lay awake at night, she dreamed of settling down with Nora, Amy, and the baby, building a happy little family, but then, in the light of day, she reminded herself that it could never be.

Nora accepted that answer with a sigh. She became engrossed in the letter again.

Relieved, Luke reached for the knife and started to carve out the cradle.

"Lucinda," Nora said.

The knife slipped. It sliced across Luke's palm, but she hardly felt the pain as she stared at Nora. *What...? How does she know?*

"You're bleeding," Nora said.

Luke still stared at her. She didn't even blink, too shocked at the name that she hadn't heard in many years. "What?"

Nora pointed at her palm. "You cut yourself."

Why is she talking about my palm? Why is she so calm? She was almost too breathless to speak, but she managed a "What did you just say?"

Nora's gentle fingers lifted her hand and pressed a cloth against the cut. "You cut yourself." She dabbed at the wound.

"No, not that. I mean that...that name that you..."

"Lucinda?"

Hearing that name again was more painful than the cut on her palm. Lucinda had been the name of a helpless girl with no prospects in life while, at least to the world, Luke was a man who could do whatever he set out to do. "Yeah."

"Tess asked me if I'd already thought of a name for the baby," Nora said, still cradling Luke's hand. "You seem to assume that it's gonna be a girl, so I thought maybe we could name her Lucinda—or Lucas junior if it's a boy. What do you think?"

Nora's fingers trembled against Luke's equally unsteady hand. She relaxed as she realized that Nora had no idea that Lucinda had once been her own name. The question still possessed its own dangers, though. Naming the baby after her would mean agreeing to raise it as her own son or daughter—and not just being a temporary second parent. Luke bit her lip as she considered the dilemma. She didn't want to disappoint Nora now that she had just started to trust her, but she also didn't want to give her any false hopes. She didn't know how long she would stay with Nora and her children, but one thing she knew for sure: She didn't want to hear the name Lucinda shouted through the house. Not only would it remind her of a time in her life that she would rather forget, but she also didn't want to risk reacting to the name that had once been her own. But, of course, she couldn't very well tell Nora that. "Is there no one in your family that you'd want to name the baby after? Your father or your mother?"

The pressure that Nora applied on the wound increased. "No."

"No one? No brother, sister, cousin…?"

Nora shook her head. "I've never been close to anyone in my family."

It was hard to believe for Luke that someone could have a family and still not be close to anyone. Growing up as a neglected only child, she had often dreamed of having loving parents and siblings.

"You don't want the baby to be named after you, do you?" Nora's voice held a defeated tone.

Luke took the piece of cloth from Nora and stalled by inspecting the cut. "It's not that."

"But?" Nora asked.

"I'm not that fond of my name. There are other, much nicer names."

Now Nora seemed to relax a bit. "Do you have a favorite?"

Oh, no. I'm not naming this baby when I'm not sure if I'll be around to see it grow up. "No, not really."

"What about Nathaniel, Nathan, or Natalie?" Nora asked.

Luke's fingers tightened around the cloth. It was the one name in the world that held a personal meaning for her. Was it just luck, a simple coincidence, that Nora had suggested those of all names? "Why that name? Does it mean anything to you?"

"It means something to you," Nora said. "You sometimes call out for a Nate in your sleep. Is he a friend of yours?"

For a few moments, Luke considered not answering. She had never told anyone about Nate. But Nora had earned her trust. She couldn't tell her the most basic truth about herself, her biggest secret, but she could tell her this. "He was my friend, yes. We fought together in Mexico. He didn't make it home." *Nate's whole life, reduced to three short sentences.*

"I'm sorry. If he was a good man and a good friend, then it would be a good name for the baby, wouldn't it?" Nora gently touched her sleeve.

Luke wrestled with herself. She closed her eyes, then exhaled. "Yes," she said.

"All right." Nora looked down at her belly with a smile. "Did you hear that? Your name's gonna be Nate or Nattie."

Amy began to murmur and sigh in her sleep. She tossed and turned, throwing off the blanket in the process.

Luke, sitting closer to the girl than Nora, reached out to tuck the blanket back around Amy. "Nora?" she said with a frown. "Have a look at Amy. She's not always this hot when she sleeps, is she?"

The letter was forgotten as Nora rose to check on her daughter. She laid a hand on Amy's forehead. Her eyes widened. "She's burning up with fever. Her shirt is soaked through."

Hot and cold waves raced through Luke's body. She didn't know how to deal with a sick child. "What should we do?" She looked down at Amy's flushed face.

Amy struggled against the blanket as a cough racked her small body.

For a moment, the same panic that Luke felt glimmered in Nora's eyes, then she straightened her shoulders. "Let's try to give her some tea and a little onion syrup."

"Tea. All right." After wrapping an improvised bandage around her hand, Luke scrambled to her feet, grabbed a pot, and rushed from the tent.

The camp lay in silence. Bill Larson and some of his friends were still sitting in Fort Hall's small saloon, and most other emigrants were already asleep in their tents and wagons. Luke had never missed Bernice Garfield as much as at this moment.

She hurried down to the Snake River and dragged a pot of water back to the camp. Without a comment, she hung the pot over the fire that the guard had already burning.

"What are you doing?" At the sound of the guard's voice, Luke realized it was Brody Cowen.

"I need hot water. Amy's sick." Luke didn't have the patience to deal with him now. *God help him if he tries to stop me now.*

But Brody settled back down. He made no move to help Luke, but he also didn't try to stop her.

With the hot water, Luke rushed back to the tent.

Nora was still kneeling next to Amy. She had changed her into a dry sleep shirt and covered her with an extra blanket.

"Here's the hot water," Luke said, lowering her voice to an almost whisper. "What kind of tea do you want? Sassafras?"

"Yeah. But I need some sugar to sweeten it—she won't drink it otherwise."

Luke didn't hesitate. Once again, she raced to their wagon and returned with some sugar. She poured a generous spoonful into the cup that Nora held out in her direction.

Nora settled Amy on her lap and pulled her against her chest to raise her up a bit. She blew across the tea's surface before she patiently poured it into Amy's mouth.

Hours went by with preparing tea, changing cold compresses, and trying to get Amy to swallow some of the onion syrup. When the sun came up, Amy fell into a restless sleep.

Nora looked up at Luke with red-rimmed eyes. "She can't travel like this. It would be her death."

Luke gazed through the half-open flap to the mountains in the distance. The snow-capped peaks reminded her of the need to continue their journey as quickly as possible. If they lost too much time now, they would find themselves still on the trail when the first snow fell.

"Maybe I can stay in Fort Hall until Amy is better," Nora said when she didn't answer. "I could try to get some work in the saloon or—"

"No," Luke said. "You'll never have to work in a saloon or a brothel again. I promised you that when I married you, and I still mean it. We'll both stay here with Amy until she's well enough to travel."

Nora blinked. Tears trembled on her eyelashes. "But the wagon train... The others won't wait for us, will they?"

"No, probably not. But maybe we can join another train in a few days. Amy's health is all that matters now." Luke rose to tell the captain about her decision.

Fort Hall,
August 5th, 1851

Nora cried uncontrollably. Her whole body shook with her sobs. "God, I never thought—"

"Don't cry. I thought you'd be happy to see me again." Bernice used the edge of her apron to wipe away Nora's tears.

Nora laughed through her tears. "I am happy. It's just... I thought I would never see you again, and then Amy got so sick, and we had to stay behind when the others left." She took a deep breath, trying to calm herself.

The other emigrants had left Fort Hall almost a week ago, leaving behind only the three Hamiltons and the Larsons. Bill had been too hungover to travel. To Nora's discomfort, Brody Cowen had decided to also stay behind. Just when she had thought that she would be forced to continue the journey in the company of only two men she hated, their old friends who had chosen the longer route via Fort Bridger had arrived at Fort Hall.

"The little darling is all right now, isn't she?" Bernice asked with almost grandmotherly concern.

Nora turned to look at Amy, who was resting next to the fire, cuddled up in Luke's protective arms. "Yeah, she's fine now." She closed her eyes and sent a silent prayer of thanks to heaven.

"Has Luke been sick too?" Bernice asked.

Nora's gaze wandered from Amy to Luke. He'd lost some weight in the last few days, and the dark circles under his eyes told of many sleepless nights spent sitting next to Amy's bedroll. Luke had tried to keep his emotions hidden behind a mask, but Nora knew him well enough by now to see through this act quite easily. She knew he had been as worried about Amy as she had been. "It was a hard week for all of us," she said.

Jacob rose from his place by the fire and held up his cup of coffee in a silent toast. "We've just taken a vote," he said. "Luke, you were elected captain of our small wagon train."

"What?" Luke raised one hand in a gesture of protest. "I didn't even run for captain."

Jacob laughed and clapped him on the shoulder. "Congratulations."

Luke's shoulders slumped. "I really don't know about this." His gaze searched out Nora's.

"You'd make a wonderful captain," Nora said. "The men trust you to make the right decisions." She did too.

Luke tapped his fist against his lips. "All right." He straightened his shoulders. "I'll lead this wagon train to Oregon, if it's the last thing I'll do."

AMERICAN FALLS,
AUGUST 8TH, 1851

Slowly, Nora made her way through three-foot-high sagebrush and over razor-sharp rocks, careful not to stumble in the darkness and lose her balance with her growing belly. At a grouping of black lava rocks, she stopped and sat down with a relieved sigh. Lately, she often found herself a little short of breath, and she knew it would only get worse in the last months of her pregnancy.

She peered down the cliffs. The water of the Snake River battered the jagged walls of the lava gorge below.

Luke had led the exhausted oxen down a precipitous path to the river earlier tonight. Nora knew that she couldn't have done it. The day's travel over the worst road since leaving Independence had worn her out. The steep trail led over sharp rocks that cut the oxen's feet. Choking dust and clouds of mosquitoes hung in the air. Not long after noon, oxen began to collapse in front of the wagons. Amy had been inconsolable when they had to leave "Red Rose," one of their oxen, behind.

Now, after stopping for the night, when she would have been able to rest, Nora couldn't. A rhythmic twitching in her belly kept her awake. She smoothed her palm over her belly, hoping the baby's hiccups would stop. She sat and listened to the sounds of the night.

The American Falls roared not far from their camp. Then another sound drowned out the peaceful rumbling of the water. An angry shout, the sound of flesh hitting flesh, and then stifled whimpers. Nora knew only too well where the sounds were coming from. *Emmy. He's beatin' up on her again.* Her jaw began to hurt as she clenched her teeth.

Instead of calming down after a while, as Bill Larson usually did, the sounds from the Larsons' wagon didn't stop; they became even louder. There was a loud snap, as if something heavy had been shoved against the wagon's boards, then a cry of pain.

Nora took a deep breath. She had listened to Emmy's muffled crying more than a dozen times during their journey. As much as she wanted to, she had never intervened, because she always thought she didn't have the right—or the means—to do it. She didn't know why or how, but that opinion had slowly changed over the last months. She no longer believed that their marriage certificate gave Bill Larson the right to terrorize his wife. *It's*

Luke. He set new standards for me. He treats me like a person, not a possession, a slave to order around, or a whore to satisfy his needs.

She touched the small revolver in her apron pocket, reassured by the feel of cold metal against her fingertips. With a pounding heart and wobbly knees, she made her way toward the Larsons' wagon.

"Hello, luscious," a voice from the darkness stopped her. "What are you doing out here, all on your own? Been waiting for me?" Brody Cowen stepped out from behind a wagon.

Nora froze. "N-no. I'm just h-heading back to my tent...to Luke. He's waiting up for me."

Brody smirked. "I bet he doesn't even know you're gone."

He didn't. He'd been asleep when Nora slipped from the tent. Her glance darted left and right. Quickly, she tried to step around Brody and escape into the darkness.

Brody's brawny arms closed around her like iron shackles. He pulled her back against his heaving chest.

Nora shivered and started to struggle when she felt his lips on her neck. "Let go of me." She tried to use the tricks Luke had taught her, but Brody only grunted when she kicked his shin. He didn't loosen his hold on her. "I'll call for help."

"Ha! So everyone can learn about your sordid past?" Laughter shook his body.

Nora used the opportunity to get one arm free. She elbowed him in the ribs. When his grip on her loosened, she whirled around. Her fingers dived into her apron pocket and came up holding the revolver. The barrel shook when she pointed it at Brody.

"Nice toy." Brody grinned down at her. "Do you even know how to use it?"

Nora had to swallow before she could speak. "I do."

"And do you also know what it's like to shoot a man? To stand right in front of him and pull the trigger? There's gonna be a lot of blood, and it'll all be on your hands. Think you can do that, huh? Can you look into his eyes while he's dying, knowing you're responsible for it?" His hand shot out and grabbed the revolver, pulling it from Nora's grip. "Yeah, that's what I thought. Now, where were we?"

"Emeline? Is that you?" Bernice's voice sounded from just a few yards away. "I heard someone cry out and—"

Both Nora and Brody froze. He grabbed her hair and roughly pulled her head back until she had to look into his cruel eyes. "You better keep quiet about this, or I'll make sure you regret it."

She stumbled when he let go of her.

"Nora?" Bernice had reached them now. "Did you hear...? What happened to you?" She smoothed a motherly hand over Nora's tangled hair, then fixed a suspicious gaze on Brody.

"What are you doing here, all alone with a young woman who is not your wife, Mister Cowen?"

The protective tone of her voice was a balm to Nora's soul. No one had ever taken a stand for her. *No one but Luke.* It felt good to see a woman have the courage to stand up to a man.

Brody flashed a grin. "Just showing our mutual friend here how to defend herself, Mrs. Garfield." He pressed the small revolver into Nora's hand.

"Nora?" Bernice turned toward Nora. "Was he bothering you?"

Nora slid the revolver into her apron pocket and held her breath. Now she had to make a decision about the way she would live her life. Since marrying Luke and setting out for Oregon, she hadn't really had to make any decisions. The captain, Luke, and the other men decided which road they would take, when to stop for their noon break, and where to camp. She had limited herself to what she did best—making sure that she and her daughter would survive. The easiest thing to ensure survival would be to keep quiet and suffer in silence until she reached Oregon and Brody would be gone from her life.

But now other things were important to her. Merely surviving wouldn't be enough any longer, not when it meant sacrificing her dignity. If she ever wanted to leave her former life as a prostitute behind, she would have to stop men like Brody Cowen from treating her like one. "Yes," she whispered.

"Yes?" Bernice tilted her head as if she wasn't sure if she had understood correctly.

"Yes, he was bothering me," Nora said a little more loudly.

Bernice put her hands on her ample hips. "I think you better leave, Mister Cowen, before I decide to wake up my husband—and hers." She pointed at Nora.

Brody smirked. "Oh, don't worry. She's used to being 'bothered,' isn't that right, Fleur?" Not waiting for an answer, he winked at Nora and then strolled away.

Bernice stared at him until he had disappeared into the darkness. Then she turned and directed a confused gaze at Nora. "What's going on? What is he talking about?"

"It's nothing," Nora said. To her, Bernice was the epitome of a respectable woman, and she didn't want to lose her friendship by telling her about her past.

"Why did he call you Fleur?"

Nora had hoped that Bernice had missed that, but, of course, she hadn't. She pressed her lips together, searching for something to say.

Bernice stared into her eyes. "You're not on the run from the law, are you?"

"No." A tired smile flitted over Nora's face. She just didn't have the energy to lie to her friend any longer. "Fleur was the name I used in my former profession."

"Profession?"

Nora sighed. She had hoped she wouldn't be forced to say it out loud. "I worked in a brothel."

The normally imperturbable Bernice stared at her. Both of her eyebrows lifted until they nearly reached her hairline. "And Brody Cowen?" She gestured but didn't find the words to ask.

"He was one of my customers, yes." Nora closed her eyes. She didn't want to see the expression of disgust on Bernice's face. "And now he thinks he can still take those liberties with me."

Bernice was silent for a long time. "And your husband? Does Luke know about...that you lived in a brothel?" she finally asked, her voice almost a whisper.

"Yes, he knows. That's where I met him." Nora opened her eyes to see Bernice's reaction.

Bernice's eyes widened. "He was one of your...?"

"No," Nora said quickly. Defending Luke's honor was more important than defending her own. "He refused my advances, but then he came back and asked me to marry him."

"Even knowing what you did for a living?" Bernice asked. "It must have been love at first sight."

Nora knew it hadn't been, but she said nothing. How could she explain why Luke had married her when she didn't understand it herself? She looked at Bernice, waiting for a reaction to her revelation, but none came. Bernice continued to look at her with the same warmth as before. "You're taking this awfully well," Nora finally said.

Bernice laughed. "What did you expect me to do? Yell and turn my back on you?"

"Well, yes," Nora said.

"Who am I to pass judgment on what other people had to do in order to survive?" Bernice shook her head. "You are a good mother, a hardworking wife, and a loyal friend. You deserve a chance to start anew, without people like Brody Cowen interfering."

Nora stumbled as her knees turned to jelly.

Bernice caught her in a motherly embrace. "You were really worried about my reaction, weren't you?"

Nora nodded, her face pressed against a rounded shoulder. "I was so glad to have you in my life again, and I didn't want to risk losing your friendship. You've been more like a mother to me than my own mother ever was."

"Lord, you make me feel old."

The comment made Nora chuckle, and she finally relaxed.

Bernice looked down at the enlarged belly that was pressed against her in their embrace. "The baby," she said with wide eyes. "And Amy? They're not...?"

"Luke's?" Nora bit her lip. As much as she wanted to believe otherwise, they weren't. "No, they're not." She didn't add that a customer had fathered her baby, knowing Bernice would guess it anyway.

Bernice shook her head. "You'd never know it watching him with Amy. I've never seen a man care that way for a child that wasn't his own flesh and blood."

Quiet, dragging steps interrupted Nora's answer. She let go of Bernice and reached for the revolver in her apron pocket.

She didn't need it. Instead of Brody Cowen, Emeline's pale face appeared in front of them. She stumbled forward, bent over, clutching her stomach.

"Emmy!" Nora called out to her.

Emeline sank to her knees, then rolled onto her side. When she reached out pleading hands, Nora saw that there was blood on them. "My baby." Emeline whimpered. "It hurts so much."

"Let's take her to the tent," Bernice said.

Holding up the bleeding woman between them, they stumbled through the darkness, heading for the closest tent.

Luke sat up when they entered, already dressed—one of her husband's little quirks. He always seemed to sleep fully dressed. "What happened?" he asked with a sleep-roughened voice.

"I think she's losing the baby," Nora whispered, her thoughts going back to the night when she'd almost miscarried.

Luke's gaze met hers, and they silently shared the terrifying memories of that night. Then Emeline's moans pulled Nora from her thoughts.

As she knelt down, she felt Luke's warmth at her back. "What can I do to help?" he asked.

Nora opened her mouth, about to tell him to just stay out of their way, but then she stopped herself. Luke had been so good with her when she had almost lost her baby. He'd been the solid rock that she clung to, and he had comforted Emmy down by the river. He was not the average man, who mostly stood by, looking helpless and uncomfortable. "If she lets you, you could try to calm her down some."

Luke turned and stared at the canvas wall while Nora helped the still sobbing woman undress and covered her with a blanket.

Bernice picked up the half-asleep Amy. "I'll get the cramp-stopping herbs and leave Amy with Jacob."

"Thank you," Nora said. She didn't want Amy to see this. When Nora looked up, Luke had turned back around and crouched at the end of the tent, where he wouldn't be in the way. He held Emeline's hand, wiping her sweaty face with a wet piece of cloth.

The three of them worked for almost an hour, but neither the labor pains nor the flood of blood coming from between Emeline's legs stopped. The contractions were coming faster and faster until Emeline let out a piercing cry. After a few endless seconds, she collapsed back against Luke.

With tears in her eyes, Nora looked at the much too small, lifeless bundle in Bernice's arms.

Luke directed a questioning gaze at her.

Biting her lip, fighting not to break down into sobs, Nora shook her head.

"My baby," Emeline whispered. She tried to sit up to get a look at her child but then fell back weakly.

Luke caught her and held her in a gentle embrace.

"I'm sorry," Nora whispered. "It was much too soon. It wasn't ready to be born."

Emeline's wails broke the silence of the night.

The tent's flap was flipped back.

"Goddamn, woman, shut up," Bill Larson slurred, apparently still drunk. "How am I supposed to sleep with all that noise? What the hell is goin' on here?" From his position in front of the tent, he stared down at his heartbroken wife and his dead baby without showing any emotions.

"What's going on? What's going on?" For the first time in her life, Nora didn't think about her own survival; she didn't think about how defenseless she was against the violent man. She was too angry to think at all. "Your wife just lost the baby, thanks to you and your drunken beatings!"

Larson took a threatening step forward, into the already crowded tent. He shook a meaty fist at Luke. "Shut your wife up, or I'll do it for you."

Nora swallowed, for the first time realizing that her angry words had put her and Luke in danger.

Gently, Luke disentangled his hand from Emeline's. He stood and blocked Larson's way, preventing him from coming any closer. Larson was half a head taller, but Luke looked him in the eyes as if Larson were nothing more than dirt beneath his boots. "My wife can say whatever she wants to, and neither you nor I have a right to stop her. Not that I'd want to, because she's right. And now go."

There was nothing weak in Luke's soft tone. A deathly danger lurked just beneath his composure. His normally gentle gray eyes were like sharp steel now.

"What?" Larson stared at him with an expression somewhere between amusement, anger, and confusion.

"Pack up your tent, take your wagon, and go. You're not welcome in this wagon train any longer," Luke said, still not raising his voice.

Larson laughed. It sounded like the roar of an animal. "That's not your decision to make, weakling. I'll stay for as long as I want to."

Luke slowly shook his head. "It is my decision. I'm the captain of this train now. Go."

"Who's gonna force me to, huh? You?"

"I'd say Mister Garfield's shotgun is more than up to the task." Luke pointed to something behind Bill Larson.

When Larson whirled around, Luke followed him with two quick steps, pulled the revolver from the drunk man's holster, and hit him over the head with the barrel.

Larson went down with a groan, only his feet sticking into the tent, the rest of him outside.

Nora stared at her normally gentle husband, who calmly looked down at his fallen enemy. They were still alone in the tent—with no sign of Jacob Garfield or his shotgun.

Luke reached for a rope and dragged the unconscious man outside.

"What are you doing?" Nora asked.

"I can't just leave him to sleep it off," Luke said, "or he'll kill me as soon as he wakes up."

Nora trembled as she realized Luke had just made a mortal enemy.

"Come on." Bernice nudged her. "We have to get Emmy's bleeding stopped."

Nora wrenched her gaze away from Luke, who was tying Larson's arms, and knelt down to help Emmy. From time to time, her gaze darted away from Emmy to the place in front of the tent. *What will he do once he wakes up?*

"Amen," Jacob said, his voice barely audible over Emmy's loud sobs.

Luke and the other men put their hats back on and shoveled earth onto the tiny grave.

"Your little one is in a better place now," Bernice said, wrapping one arm around Emmy. "And you're still young enough to have other children."

Emmy continued to cry.

Nora embraced her from the other side.

Leaning on his shovel, Brody Cowen nodded toward the camp where Bill Larson had been sleeping it off for the last ten hours. "You didn't really ask him to leave, did you?"

Luke straightened. "Yes, I did. He's a drunkard, and he killed his own baby. I won't have him travel with us any longer."

"Oh, come on. It was an accident."

"Accident?" Luke's voice rose. "No, Brody. It would have been an accident if Emeline lost the baby being run down by an ox team. A man beating his wife is not an accident."

"He must have had a good reason," Brody said. "It's his right as her husband to do whatever he thinks best to discipline her."

Stony-faced, Luke looked at him. "Then it's my right as a captain to do whatever I think best to discipline him. He has to leave."

Brody crossed his arms over his chest. "What if he doesn't want to?"

"We'll reach the Raft River tomorrow," Luke said. "The roads to Oregon and to California split there. The wagon train behind us is heading for California. I'll ask them to take Larson with them and only let him go when we're far enough away."

Emeline's sobs became even louder. "Please don't do this. He'll take it out on me."

"He won't be able to—you're coming with us," Luke said. Then he stopped and looked into Emeline's eyes. "That is, if you want to."

"B-b-but how will I survive? I'll never make it to Oregon on my own, and even if I do, I'd never survive the first winter without a husband to take care of me." Emeline covered her face with both hands and cried.

"You're not on your own. You've got friends on this train." Luke nodded at Nora and Bernice, then, reluctantly, he pointed at himself too.

Tears leaked through Emeline's fingers. "You'll all be busy building your own homes."

"Yeah, that's right," Luke said. "Building a horse ranch is gonna be a lot of work. I could use some help. What do you say, do you want the job? I can't pay much, but…"

Emeline stared at him, and Nora found herself doing the same. He'd repeatedly told her that he was taking on the role of father and husband only temporarily and that she should find herself another husband as soon as they reached Oregon. *And now he's taking on the responsibility for yet another woman?*

Brody Cowen stared at him. "You're crazy. You can't just take another man's wife away from him."

"It's Emeline's decision," Luke said. He directed his gaze at Emeline.

"Why are you doing this?" Emeline whispered.

Luke looked at Nora as if he would find the answer there.

Is he doing this for me? He knows I could have easily been in Emmy's place. If Luke hadn't turned out to be the kind and gentle man he is, it could have been my baby, dying before it was even born.

Luke shrugged. "A woman being left to the mercy of her abusive husband, without anyone to intervene… It's just not right."

"You shouldn't be doing this," Emeline said, her voice still a whisper. "You're putting yourself—all of you—in danger, just because of me. It would be better if I just stayed with Bill. Maybe I can convince him not to follow you and take revenge."

"That's what I'm saying," Brody said. "It's none of our business how a man treats his wife. It's his God-given right. No one else has the right to get involved."

Just a few months ago, Nora would have said the same thing. She had suffered the cruelties of customers in silence because she'd known no other way. But since they had left Independence, so many things had changed. Luke had taught her not only the skills to fight back, but, more importantly, he'd made her believe that she had a right to do it. "Emmy." She reached for the pale woman's hands and looked her right in the eyes. "Do you want to stay with Bill?"

"It's for the best."

"Do you want to?" Nora repeated, her gaze even more intense.

Emeline looked away. Tears were leaking from the corners of her eyes. "No."

"Then you won't."

Some of the emigrants shook their heads while others nodded. "Come on," Eli Rogers said to his wife. "Let's go back to camp. I want to stay out of this."

The emigrants dispersed and wandered back to their wagons. Bernice and Jacob led Emmy toward their wagon. Only Brody Cowen, Nora, and Luke stayed behind.

"Listen to my words, young man," Brody said, pointing his index finger at Luke as if it were a revolver. "You might regret this one day." Not even giving Nora a fleeting glance, he strode toward the camp.

Thousand Springs,
August 17th, 1851

Luke shifted in the saddle, trying to get a better view of her surroundings.

On the other side of the river, multiple small waterfalls spilled from the canyon wall, forming a line of white, foaming cascades along the dark lava rock. Luke wasn't sure where the seemingly thousands of waterfalls were coming from; the land around them was barren for many miles around.

But the picturesque waterfalls were not what Luke was on the lookout for. Since leaving Bill Larson with a group of emigrants heading for California, she hadn't slept for more than two hours at a stretch. Constant worrying kept her awake. The days grew shorter, and their oxen and mules were losing their strength. The responsibility for the small wagon train rested heavily on her. But the struggle against time was not the only thing worrying her.

Here, near the Salmon Falls, Indians were all around them. They had put up their lodges near the river and were fishing. Most of them, the Shoshone in particular, were friendly and even traded fresh and dried salmon. But the Bannocks, who also settled along the Snake River, eyed the white emigrants with suspicion. Now that their group was so small, a few angry braves could become dangerous to them. As a result, Luke was constantly on the lookout for hostile Indians while at the same time keeping an eye out for Bill Larson, who might be following them. In quiet moments, Luke admitted to herself that she might have bitten off more than she could chew. *Why on God's green earth did you volunteer for the role of patron saint of helpless women? You've driven yourself into a trap of responsibilities that you can't escape from. What the hell became of "Never get involved"?* She'd lived with that philosophy for many years, making neither friends nor enemies who could discover her secret. But since leaving Independence, she'd broken that personal law more often than she could count.

She'd made the two-thousand-mile trip to Oregon three times, but this time, the journey had become one of discoveries—not about the landscape, but about herself. All her life, she'd thought of herself as a man, but on this journey, she'd discovered hidden female characteristics about herself. She empathized with Nora's and Emeline's situations more than the other men on the train. Even the thought of taking care of a small child didn't scare her any longer. Spending time with Amy had become one of her day's highlights. *Isn't it ironic? Now that I'm married and a "father," more of a man than I've ever been in the eyes of the world, I'm discovering that there are still some female traits left in me.* Sometimes, she worried that being with Nora had softened her, weakened her tough exterior so much that she'd give her secret away someday.

Nearing hoofbeats made her turn around, a hand already on the butt of her rifle. She relaxed when she recognized Tom Buchanan, whose horse fell in step with Measles.

"I wanted to have a word with you," Tom said, his expression serious.

Luke nodded, warily waiting for what he might have to say.

"It's about Emeline Larson."

Luke had waited for this moment. She'd suspected that some of the men in the train would criticize her meddling in the Larsons' marriage, as Brody Cowen had. "Yeah?" Luke was as determined as ever to defend her decision.

"Neither you nor Jacob can take care of Mrs. Larson," Tom said. "You've got enough mouths to feed already."

Luke straightened her shoulders. "I'm not sending her back to her husband, if that's what you're trying to achieve."

Tom held up his hands. "It's not. I'm not too fond of Larson myself. But I think I have a better solution."

"I'm listening."

"Well, I'm a horrible cook, and I need someone to do the laundry and look after my children. I've lost my wife, and Mrs. Larson 'lost' her husband." Tom gazed at her expectantly. "So, what do you think?"

Luke had to chuckle. "Are you asking me for Emeline's hand in marriage?"

"No." The forty-year-old man blushed. "No, of course not. She's still married after all. It would just be a mutually beneficial business relationship."

Business relationship. That's what I told Nora at the beginning too. Just business, nothing more. "It sounds like a good idea, but it's not my decision to make," Luke said. "You have to ask Emeline."

Tom gave a short nod. "All right."

"Good afternoon." Tom Buchanan tipped a finger to his hat. "Mrs. Hamilton. Mrs. Larson."

Nora flicked the whip to keep the oxen moving, then studied him. She had seen him talk to Luke. What was going on? "Good afternoon," she answered while Emeline just gave him a shy nod.

The young woman was sitting next to Amy on the wagon seat, still too weak to walk along all day.

"What can we do for you, Mister Buchanan?" Nora asked when he didn't break the silence.

"I just spoke to your husband, Mrs. Hamilton." He stopped and turned toward Emeline. "I have a proposal for you. You need someone to protect and provide for you, and I need someone to run my household and take care of the children."

Emeline's eyes widened. She fiddled with the strings of her apron and directed a questioning gaze at Nora.

Nora immediately recognized the gaze. She had looked at Bernice more than once in that way, silently asking for advice. Now she was the mentor. *Come on, you can do this. It's not that different from bargaining with a customer.* "You realize that Emeline is still a married woman, don't you? If she agrees to your proposal, you won't have any conjugal rights."

Tom pulled his hat from his head and kneaded it between his hands. "Of course. I didn't think—"

"You'll give her a place in your tent while you sleep in the wagon?"

"I can do that, yeah," Tom said.

"And when we reach Oregon? What will become of her?" Nora asked.

"I'll still need a housekeeper. She can stay with me, of course."

Nora nodded. "Then you'll pay her for her work?"

Tom reached under his collar with a finger as if the shirt had become too tight. "I can't pay her much, but I should be able to set aside a small amount for her."

"All right." Nora turned to Emeline and studied her pale face. "What do you think? You're free to agree or refuse. Whatever you want to do is fine with us." She hoped Emeline would agree. Taking care of Tom's children would help her to get over the loss of her baby, and the wages Tom paid her would afford her a certain independence. But she remained silent, not wanting to take the decision away from Emeline.

Emeline hesitated for a long time. Then she shyly looked from Nora to Tom. "I accept."

Two Island Crossing,
August 23rd, 1851

Another difficult decision—and I'm the one who has to make it. Luke crossed her arms over the saddle horn and looked down at the Snake River from the hill the wagons had stopped on.

The river made a bend and briefly escaped from its high canyon walls at this point. This would be the only chance to cross to the northern bank, allowing them to travel the direct route to Fort Boise with ample drinking water. If they didn't cross here, they would be forced to follow the southern route around the bend through a dry, barren wilderness.

Luke gazed at the two small islands lying side by side in the river, dividing it into three branches. On her last expedition to Oregon, the islands had been covered with grass, but since then it had all been eaten off by the oxen and horses of other wagon trains. They could use the islands as stepping stones to cross the river, but it still wouldn't be easy.

"What is it?" Nora stepped next to her and touched one of the forearms that still rested on the saddle horn. "You're frowning."

Luke looked down at the hand on her arm. She resisted the urge to cover the fingers with her own to keep them in place. Her whole life, she had shied away from other people's touches, but her body seemed to have given up its resistance when it came to Nora. "I'm not sure if we should risk a crossing," she said, directing her gaze back to the river.

"It doesn't look that bad."

Luke nodded. "Yeah, but it's a lot worse than it looks." The Snake River was a clear stream that didn't look as challenging as some of the rivers they'd had to cross. Its clarity was deceptive, though, making it appear much shallower than it actually was. Combined with the swift current and its uneven riverbed, the Snake River was considered the most treacherous river crossing on the entire Oregon Trail.

"Still, I don't like the alternative," Nora said. "You said there's no water along the southern trail."

Luke agreed. Just this morning, one of their cows had died, and the dry southern route was sure to kill many more. She patted Nora's hand, glad to finally hear her voice her opinion. "Yeah. Let's try to cross it."

Their wagon was the first to cross. The hundred yards to the first island were covered pretty easily even if Luke had to hold on to the yokes to keep from being swept away by the swift current. After a moment of rest, Luke drove the oxen into the second, seventy-five-yard-wide stream.

This time, the oxen had more of a struggle. The riverbed was uneven, with many holes and uneven water's depths. The lead pair of their five yoke of oxen was swimming, up to their necks in water, while the last yoke was still plodding through shallow water.

When they reached the second island, Luke raised the wagon bed another few inches and put another yoke of oxen in front of the wagon. The last stretch was not only the longest, but also the most difficult part of the crossing.

They fought for every single inch against the rapid current. Luke, breast-deep in water, felt the oxen slow. The current beat against the wagon until it tilted to one side. Cursing, Luke sent a quick glance inside, preparing to pluck Amy from the wagon should it overturn.

Just then, a few men from a wagon train that had crossed before them appeared on the opposite bank. Two of them waded into the river and attached ropes to the wooden yokes while their comrades on the bank began to pull.

Luke blew out a breath when the wagon finally rumbled up the bank. She immediately extended her hand to the closest of her saviors.

The young man with the auburn hair shook her hand and smiled. There was something oddly familiar about him, but Luke was sure she had never met him before. "Luke Hamilton," she said with a grateful nod.

"Ben Macauley."

Luke had to grip a yoke again to stay on her feet. *Macauley?* Now she realized where she had seen that smile and those green eyes before. *Lord, he's Amy's father.* She had always assumed that Amy had been fathered by a customer too, but clearly they were sharing not only the same smile and eye color, but the same last name too. *Nora never told me she's divorced. If she's divorced. Maybe she just ran away from him.*

At that moment, Nora pulled back the wagon cover and climbed out of the wagon. She froze when she saw the man standing next to Luke. "B-ben?"

The man stared as if he'd seen a ghost. "Nora? Is that you?"

They both hesitated, rooted to the spot.

The stranger took a slow step forward, but Nora still eyed him without moving. Luke had seen the flash of joy in her eyes before it had been replaced with wariness. Her own feelings were more than just wary. It wasn't just her damp clothes that made the fine hairs all over her body stand on end. Was this what jealousy felt like?

The feeling grew more intense as the wagon cover rustled and Amy peeked out.

Ben Macauley stared at the girl, then his gaze traveled back to Nora. He clearly recognized how much the two resembled each other. There was no mistaking them for anything but mother and daughter.

Luke realized that her jealousy didn't stop at Nora; it extended to Amy as well. Up until now, she had been the only father that Amy had ever known, but now there was someone who could claim that title and role in Amy's life.

"Is that…?" Macauley was still staring at Amy.

Nora helped Amy out of the wagon and drew her protectively against her body. "Yes, this is Amy. My daughter."

"And you…?" Ben Macauley gestured at Nora's swollen belly.

"I'm with child," Nora said and lifted her chin. "Again."

Ben Macauley finally looked away from Amy to glance at the wagon train. "You're not with Raphael Jamison, are you?"

"No. But I am married," Nora said. She groped for Luke's arm, searching for support. "This is Lucas Hamilton, my husband. Luke, this is Benjamin Macauley, my brother."

Brother? He's not Amy's father? Luke coughed. "Nice to meet you," she said belatedly while she studied Nora out of the corner of her eye. She hadn't even known Nora had a brother. Why weren't they in each other's arms now, celebrating their reunion?

"Luke!" Tom Buchanan's shout made her look up. The second wagon had reached the middle of the river and was in need of a little help.

She turned to Ben Macauley. "If you're camping anywhere near us tonight, you're welcome to come over and have dinner with us," she said, not wanting to miss the opportunity to learn more about Nora's family and give her a chance to reconnect with her brother.

Macauley nodded and handed her the rope. "I'll be there."

"Why did you do that?" Nora asked as soon as the last wagon had safely reached the other side.

Groaning, Luke bent down, pulled off her boots, and poured out the water. From her place perched on the back of the wagon, she looked at Nora, who was standing with her hands on her rounded hips. Luke frowned. "What did I do?"

"You invited my brother."

"Yes?" Luke failed to see how this could be a problem.

Nora stamped her foot, reminding Luke so much of Amy that she had to suppress a grin. "You didn't even ask me if I wanted to have him over. You're always telling me that I should say what I want, and now that it matters, you're not even asking me."

Luke set her boots down. She stared at the wet leather, not knowing what to say. "I'm sorry. I didn't know. I thought you'd be happy to spend more time with your brother." During her lonely childhood, Luke had always wished for a sibling, and she couldn't imagine not wanting to see a brother.

With a sigh, Nora sank down on the wagon's backboard next to Luke. Her anger seemed to dissipate and was replaced by an expression of resignation.

"You didn't get along with your brother?" Luke asked.

"We didn't spend enough time together to not get along. My brothers mostly ignored me—except, of course, for when they bullied me around or paraded me around in front of their friends when it was convenient for them." Nora shrugged, feigning nonchalance, but the bitterness in her voice told Luke that there were still hurt feelings.

Luke wrapped one arm around Nora's shoulder. "I'm sorry they treated you like that. How many brothers do you have?" she asked to keep Nora talking.

"Three, but not one of them sided with me. They all stood by when my father chased me out of the house."

"What happened?" Luke asked before she could stop herself. She bit her lip, realizing that she didn't have the right to ask about Nora's past when she was unwilling to reveal her own. "You don't have to answer that. Not if you don't want to."

Nora looked directly into Luke's eyes.

Luke barely held herself back from squirming under her intense gaze.

"Well, seeing that it was what led to my working for Tess and marrying you, I figure you've got a right to know," Nora said.

Luke shook her head. "No. Your past is just that—your own. You don't have to tell me if you don't want to."

Nora looked down at her hands resting on her swollen belly. She gazed up at Luke from under half-lowered lashes. "I never told anyone but Tess, and even she doesn't know the details."

"If it hurts you to talk about it—"

"I trust you," Nora said, finally looking up.

God, did she have to say that? Luke wanted to run away, to escape from Nora's trusting gaze. She couldn't return that trust, not when it would most likely destroy the life that she'd built for herself.

"You never asked about Amy's father." Nora's voice was almost a whisper, so low that no one else in the busy camp around them could hear.

Luke plucked at the damp fabric of her pants that were clinging to her thighs. "I assumed you didn't know or didn't want to tell me."

"I know exactly who fathered Amy. I wasn't always a prostitute, you know?" A bittersweet smile played around Nora's lips.

Luke had to look away. "Yeah, I know." She was glad to hear that Amy's father hadn't been some stranger, paying to share Nora's bed. Then she froze as another possibility occurred to her. "You…you weren't…? Amy's father didn't…?"

Nora tilted her head. "He didn't what?"

"He didn't force you?" Luke had known several women who had been forced into prostitution after being raped. Their families had disowned them because they no longer considered them decent women. She held her breath, waiting for Nora's answer.

Nora slid her hand over Luke's and squeezed softly. "No, he didn't."

Luke closed her fingers around Nora's. "Thank God."

"His name was Raphael Jamison. He was an adventurer with high-flown dreams and a poor sense of honor." Nora sighed. "My father forbade him from courting me—he wanted me to marry the son of his business partner, not some ne'er-do-well without any means. But Rafe promised me the moon, and I was naïve and in love. I met him behind my family's back. The last time I saw him was the day I told him I was with child."

Luke stared at Nora. "He just disappeared?" She couldn't imagine just leaving a woman like Nora. *Oh, you're a fine one to talk. Leaving her is exactly what you plan on doing once you find her another husband.*

"He said he was not the marrying kind." Nora's voice was hollow. "I spent three months hiding the pregnancy from my family and then trying to get them to accept the child. They didn't."

Luke rubbed her thumb over the back of Nora's palm. "I'm sorry."

"My father told me in no uncertain terms that no daughter of his was having a baby out of wedlock. He had no use for a 'ruined' daughter who he couldn't marry off to one of his influential friends. Even for him, my body, my purity was the only thing of interest. He never cared about me, my opinions, or my happiness."

"I'm sorry. He's a fool." Luke cleared her throat. "What about your mother?"

Nora grimaced. "In seventeen years, I've never heard her voice an opinion that my father hadn't expressed first. She watched with tears in her eyes as he threw me out of the house, but she never said a word."

Luke finally understood that Nora's childhood had been as lonely as her own even if she'd lived with a big family. "Where did you go?"

"My father gave me enough money to travel west on a steamboat—at least if I didn't stay in Boston, my family's reputation wouldn't suffer. That's all they cared about."

"Bastards." Luke gritted her teeth.

"When I ran out of money, I worked as a seamstress in a small town. But when my pregnancy became obvious, the dressmaker threw me out. I was sleeping in a livery stable, begging for food, when I met Tess."

Luke didn't need to ask another question. She understood Nora's situation almost too well. To ensure her survival and that of her daughter, Nora had no choice but to accept the work that Tess offered her in her brothel. "Do you want me to go over to your brother's wagon train and tell him to stay away?"

Nora slid down from the wagon. She turned around to face Luke. "No. He's still my brother, and he helped us with the river crossing today. The least I can do is offer him a warm meal."

Luke looked back and forth between Nora and her brother. The flickering light of the fire made their hair shine like copper. Other than the way they looked, they didn't seem to have much in common. While Nora barely touched her food, Ben Macauley focused on his beans and beef as if they were the only thing worthy his attention.

Neither tried to start a conversation.

Amy, who was perched on Luke's lap, was unusually quiet too. She watched Ben with the vigilance of a hen watching a hawk and pressed her head against Luke's shoulder.

Luke soothingly trailed her fingers through Amy's red hair.

Finally, Nora put down her fork and peeked at her brother. "How is everyone at home?"

Ben swallowed another forkful of beans. "Oh, we're doing great. Father built two new warehouses last year, and we're now delivering goods as far west as Fort Boise. That's why I'm here."

Nora's asking about her family, and he tells her how successful their business is? Luke shook her head.

Nora continued to look at her brother.

"James is in England right now," Ben said. "Courting the daughter of Sheffield Enterprises."

"And Mother?" Nora asked quietly. "How is she doing?"

Ben shrugged. "Good, I suppose. At least she hasn't said otherwise."

Nora swirled her fork through the beans, then pushed her plate away.

"Do you mind?" Ben nodded at Nora's plate and picked it up before she could answer.

Luke gritted her teeth.

"So," Ben looked at Luke across the fire, "I hear the West is a good place for doing business."

"I don't know about that." Beyond having enough to survive, Luke didn't care about money.

"Then why are you emigrating?" Ben asked.

Luke didn't like having to justify herself, but for Nora's sake, she answered, "I was a dragoon officer, but that kind of life doesn't appeal to me anymore. I want a home of my own, and the Willamette Valley is a great place for a horse ranch."

"Horses. Hmm." Ben tapped his fork against his lower lip. "Not bad. Could be useful to us someday." He stood from his place at the fire and directed an expectant gaze at Luke. "Let's take a walk and have a smoke."

Carefully, Luke schooled her face into a calm expression, hiding a grimace. She'd never gotten into the habit of smoking or chewing tobacco. Not that it mattered. She knew Ben wanted to lure her away from the fire to have a man-to-man talk. The irony wasn't lost on her. She lifted Amy from her lap and gently set her down.

Amy ran to the other side of the fire and clung to Nora, keeping an eye on her uncle.

With one last glance at Nora, Luke followed Ben to the edge of camp.

"So," Ben stopped to light his pipe, "you are the man who married my sister."

Is this the "what are your intentions toward my sister" talk? It's a little late for that. Luke gave a nod.

"That's a very honorable thing to do. I mean…" Ben gestured with the mouthpiece of his pipe. "To marry a woman who's been with another man and to be willing to raise a child that's not your own."

You don't even know half of it, young man. Luke said nothing. She had no intention of telling Ben that his sister had worked in a brothel and was pregnant with a customer's baby. "She's a good wife and a wonderful woman," she said instead.

Ben shrugged. "Still, I want to thank you in the name of my family. My father took it pretty hard when she told him she was with child, but I think he'll be glad to hear that she married a rancher and former officer instead of that Jamison fellow who was completely without means."

Luke tilted her head. On the one hand, it felt good to be accepted into the family, but on the other hand, she had to force down a wave of anger. The Macauleys still weren't interested in Nora's happiness. They didn't want to know what kind of person she had become; all that mattered to them was that she'd married a well-respected man so that they could keep up appearances.

"I want you to know that you—both of you—will be welcome in our home anytime. Why don't you come with me when I return back east?" Nora's brother asked. "You could take up employment in the family business."

Luke didn't even have to think about that offer. She had long since decided that she didn't want to be a soldier or an employee anymore. In Oregon, she would be her own "man." "That's not my decision to make," she said. "It's for Nora to decide whether she wants to live under her father's roof again."

Ben blinked, clearly not used to men who let their wives make their own decisions. Finally, he shrugged. "All right. You'll let me know?"

Luke nodded and stared at the setting sun. Maybe this would solve her problem about what to do with Nora once they reached Oregon. Now that her father would welcome her back, Nora might want to return with her brother. Somehow, Luke couldn't bring herself to be happy about it.

"What did he want to talk to you about?" All chores were done, and Amy was settled down for the night. Now Nora couldn't keep herself from asking any longer.

"He said we were welcome in your family's home anytime," Luke said. "He even offered me a job in your father's business." His expression was calm and didn't reveal what he thought about that job offer.

Nora thought about it. Three years—or maybe even three months—ago, she would have been overjoyed if she could have returned to her former home, and she would have gladly submitted to her father's rules. Now, after living with Luke for almost four months, she couldn't imagine living under her father's thumb again. Most of all, she would never expose Amy to a life like that. Amy would never be a beloved grandchild for her parents. They would never fully accept her, but always treat her like a barely tolerated bastard. "What did you tell Ben?" she asked.

"Not much. I told him it was your decision."

Nora laughed. "I bet that went over well with Ben."

Luke grinned at her, and for a moment, there was the silent understanding of conspirators between them. "He nearly swallowed his pipe."

Slowly, Nora's smile vanished as she realized that Luke still hadn't voiced his opinion about the offer. "Do you want to take him up on it? My father is one of the richest men in Boston. He could pay you much more than you'll ever make raising horses."

Luke leaned back on his bedroll. "Being rich is overrated."

Her mouth fell open. She stared at him. Then her laughter virtually exploded from her. Never had anyone dismissed her family with all their power and money just like that. "God, you're amazing." Nora leaned over from her own bedroll and gently kissed his cheek. She felt the heat under her lips as a blush shot up his face. For a moment, she was tempted to follow the blush down with her lips, but the stiffness of the body next to her made her move back.

He rubbed his hand over his cheek. "I'm not," he said. "I just don't want your family's money. But that doesn't mean that you can't return to Boston. You could tell them that it's just until I've built a house for us. Then I could have someone send them a letter, telling them that I died. You could live your life as a respected widow."

"You've got it all planned out." Nora didn't know whether to be amused or angry.

Luke shrugged. "Just a suggestion. You can take it or leave it."

"Then I'll leave it, if you don't mind. If I ever return to Boston, it won't be for more than a visit," Nora said.

"All right." He relaxed back against his bedroll.

For a minute, there was silence in the tent, then Nora asked, "What else did he say to you?"

"Not much. He offered me the official gratitude of the Macauley clan," Luke answered.

Nora frowned. Her family didn't even know Luke. What did they have to thank him for? "Why's that?"

"Well, he told me how honorable it was to marry a woman who already had a child and to raise it as my own." Luke rubbed the bump on the bridge of his nose, a gesture that, as Nora had learned, signaled embarrassment.

For once, Nora agreed with her brother. "It was a very honorable thing to do. It still is."

"It's not. Not really. Amy is a good girl." Luke turned to look at the sleeping child. "Any man would be proud to call her his daughter."

Yes, she is. Nora smiled. Every man on the train liked Amy, but agreeing to be a father to her was an entirely different matter. "Yes, but I imagine it could be hard on you if people like Brody Cowen announce to everyone that she's not your daughter and that the baby won't be yours either."

"It doesn't matter. I don't care what people like Brody say."

He'd told her that again and again, but still, Nora found it hard to believe. Knowing that his wife was carrying another man's child would have been hard on any man's pride. "But what if someday we have a child of our own, a child that's your own flesh and blood—"

"That won't happen," Luke said.

Nora sighed. She couldn't let it go. The more the pregnancy progressed, the more she started to worry about the future of her children. "Are you really sure that you won't someday resent Amy and the baby for how they came to be?" she asked in a whisper.

"I won't."

Nora sighed again. The two-word answer didn't really reassure her.

"All right." Luke sat up and turned around to face her. "Listen. I know what it means to grow up as the bastard child of a prostitute. I'm the last person who would ever resent a child for that."

In the silence, Nora could hear her own heart pound. "Your...your mother...?"

"Was a prostitute, yes." Luke tried to sound emotionless, but his voice trembled.

So this is where his vast knowledge about life in a brothel comes from. He grew up in one. His mother was a prostitute. Was, Nora repeated. *So his mother is dead.* That wasn't really a surprise for Nora. She knew better than anyone else that most prostitutes never lived to see the day when they'd finally saved enough to leave the brothel and start a new life. Many were murdered by violent customers or killed during a brawl. A lot of the girls she'd known had died of consumption, syphilis, or as a result of botched abortions. Others literally drank themselves to death or fell prey to laudanum. Nora hesitated to ask.

Still, Luke probably saw the question in her eyes. "She was a drunkard. When she couldn't take it anymore, she killed herself."

Tears burned in Nora's eyes. She wiped them away, instinctively knowing that Luke didn't want her sympathy. "H-how old were you?"

"Twelve."

Much too young to fend for himself. "Who took care of you?"

"No one. I took care of myself," Luke said.

At twelve? "What about your father?"

Luke didn't answer. He didn't need to—his gaze spoke volumes.

His mother was a prostitute, and he has never known his father because he was a customer who didn't care what became of his seed. Nora looked down at her belly, then at Luke. The parallels were obvious. "Is that why you married me?" she asked. He'd taught her to speak her mind, and now he would have to live with the consequences. "So Amy wouldn't have to grow up the way you did?"

"It was one of the reasons, yes." Luke looked directly into her eyes, then quickly away.

As far as Nora was concerned, he had nothing to be ashamed of. "Saving Amy from having to grow up as the bastard of a prostitute was one of my reasons for marrying you too."

Luke's gaze met hers. A smile crept onto his face. "Well, then it seems that we both got what we wanted from this marriage."

I got everything I wanted back then. But now, I want more. Nora blinked. Where had that thought come from? She took a deep breath and forced her thoughts in another direction. "If you grew up in a brothel..." She hesitated. Like every young girl, she had been taught that a lady didn't discuss the physical acts that happened between a man and a woman, not even with her husband. When the time came, she had to quietly submit to her husband's urges, but she never, ever talked about it. But Nora was no longer the lady that her mother had raised her to be. She had grown used to the coarser language of the parlor house girls. "Why would you ever want to set foot inside one?"

"It's not as if I've been there every day," Luke said. "I wasn't a regular. I just went there a few times, mostly when my comrades didn't take no for an answer."

Nora touched his arm. The muscles under her hand were knotted and hard like steel. "There's no need to become defensive. I didn't mean it as an accusation. I just want to understand. I mean, you're kind, honorable, and handsome. You could have easily found a beautiful, unspoiled girl who would have gladly married you and shared your bed." Just three years ago, before she had sworn to herself that she would never again be the naïve girl, blinded by infatuation, she could have easily fallen in love with him. Something about his gentle strength was very appealing, and judging from Emeline's shy gazes and the way Bernice's daughter mooned over him, she wasn't the only woman who thought so. "Why did you visit a working girl after what you witnessed growing up?"

Luke looked away. He plucked at a corner of his blanket. He was silent for so long that Nora thought he would refuse to discuss the topic with her when he finally answered, "I've never been with one of the girls. It's just… It's only ever been Tess."

It didn't come as a surprise to Nora. From the first time that she'd met Luke, she had suspected that he'd shared Tess's bed, and he had never tried to tell her otherwise. But still, knowing it for real still gave her a weird feeling. *It's not that I'm jealous. It's just that imagining my husband and my friend in bed together… It's awkward, that's all.* And it made her wonder why he had repeatedly shared Tess's bed but refused to lie with her. "Are you…? Were you…in love with her?"

Luke picked a few loose threads from his blanket. "She's my friend and a very attractive woman," he said without looking up.

"Is that a yes or a no?" Nora asked.

"It's a no," Luke finally answered. "I knew our roles from the start. There was no room for love in our relationship. At least not romantic love. What she offered was friendship and occasional relief, and that was all I was prepared to accept from her."

Nora understood. As she had, Luke had learned through experience that love was fickle and could hurt you much too easily. He didn't expect to ever find love and certainly not in a prostitute's bed. *And not in mine, either.* With a sigh, she settled down on her bedroll. "Good night."

FORT BOISE,
AUGUST 29TH, 1851

"That's as far as I am going," Ben said. He pointed at the three blockhouses that made up Fort Boise. "I'll deliver the supplies and return to the States. Are you sure that you don't want to come with me?"

Nora didn't hesitate. "No." Boston had long since ceased to be her home. All her hopes and dreams were now in Oregon.

"All right. I'll tell Mother you're married to a rancher and former officer who's also the leader of a wagon train. That should make her happy." Ben reached for the reins of his horse. "Anything else you want me to tell her?"

"Tell her that I have a wonderful daughter and a kind husband." Nora hoped that this would mean much more to her mother than any titles her husband might have. "Tell her I'm happy."

Ben gave a short nod but didn't react otherwise. He shook Luke's hand and took Nora into a stiff, impersonal embrace for a second. Then he bent down to Amy. "Come on, girl, give your Uncle Ben a hug."

Amy threw her small arms around Luke's legs and held on as if her life depended on it. She hid her face against the fabric of Luke's pants and peeked at Ben with one eye.

Ben snorted. He pointed a warning finger at Luke. "If you have a son," he said, nodding toward Nora's belly, "you better make sure he doesn't become such a yellowbelly."

Amy clutched Luke's leg more tightly.

Nora pressed her lips together. His careless words hurt. The men in her family had talked about her in the same way.

Luke bent down and lifted Amy into his arms. "If I had a son," he said, looking right at Ben, "I would be proud if he was as clever as Amy and knew enough to stay away from strangers he's never seen before."

With a timid smile, Amy hugged him around the neck.

Ben frowned, shook his head as if Luke had said something foolish, and spurred on his horse.

Nora's gaze didn't follow him; it remained fixed on Luke. She marveled at his ability to make Amy feel as if she was worth something. He had done the same thing for her since they had left Independence. "Thank you."

Luke turned. Their gazes met. "You don't have to thank me for telling the truth," he said and smiled at Amy. "All right. Why don't we visit the fort now? Maybe they'll even have some candy."

Still gazing at him, Nora followed behind them.

Luke strode across Fort Boise's small parade ground with Amy perched on her arm. The fort had been modeled after Fort Hall but was much smaller. It had been built by the Hudson Bay Company, but since beavers had become rare in this area, the HBC had left the area and the fort fell more and more into disrepair. Today, a few Frenchmen and some Shoshone sat in the shadow of the blockhouses.

"I don't think we'll find any candy here," Luke said.

Amy's lower lip trembled.

"But maybe we can buy you a necklace," Nora said. "Look." She pointed at two Shoshone women selling colorful bead necklaces.

Luke steered them in that direction.

Someone grabbed her shoulder and roughly pulled her around.

"What the h—!" Luke stumbled, fighting not to lose her balance. A kick took her legs out from under her.

Nora screamed.

Tucking Amy protectively against her body, Luke couldn't break the fall with her hands. Air whooshed out of her lungs as she crashed to the ground.

The next kick came as soon as she landed, but this time, Luke was prepared. She grabbed the unknown attacker's boot and pulled until she felt him fall too. This gave her the time to quickly release Amy and usher her over to her mother. When she turned back around, the attacker was already getting to his feet.

Bill Larson!

He swung his meaty fists at her.

Luke rolled to the side.

His knuckles grazed her ear.

She grabbed his arm in midroll and used his momentum to bring him down again.

He scrambled up, snorting like an angry bull. The veins on his neck were bulging. "I'll teach you to stick to your own business, bastard. Did you really think I'd allow you to take my wife away from me?" He threw himself forward again, striking out with both fists at once.

Luke sidestepped the attack. When Larson stumbled past her, she hammered her fist down on the back of his neck.

He collapsed on his belly and sprang up again, now even more furious than before.

Luke carefully circled him. She had to end this fast before he could tire her out. He was stronger, taller, and heavier than her, so her only advantage was her quickness. She sprang forward and back, sidestepped, and ducked under his swings, hooks, and jabs until his face was red from anger and exertion.

"Fight like a man, you coward," he yelled.

Luke didn't react. She had learned a long time ago to keep a cool head while fighting. She feinted left, and when he shifted his weight to block the punch, she took his legs out from under him with a kick.

From his prone position, he lunged at her legs.

Luke met him with a kick to his ribs.

One of his bones snapped audibly.

She hesitated to follow up with another kick.

With a piercing yell, Larson tackled her.

Her head hit the ground. For a second, she could see nothing but bright stars.

Then Larson straddled her, pressing the air from her lungs with his weight. He hit her in the face. Left. Right. Then left again.

Pain exploded in her temples. Warm blood dripped down her nose. She struggled to find purchase with her boots on the ground, trying to dislodge him from on top of her.

The much heavier Larson didn't budge. He lifted his fist again.

She jabbed her fingers at his eye.

When he swung up his arm to protect his eyes, she hit his Adam's apple with all her might.

With a choking sound, Larson grabbed his throat.

Another punch to his already cracked rib and Luke managed to throw him off. This time, she didn't repeat her mistake of showing him mercy. She rolled around and pressed her knees against his chest while she pummeled him left and right. "Do you give up?" She paused with her fist in front of his face.

"Never!" Larson spat blood in her direction.

Luke hit him again, then stopped. Her hands were bleeding and raw, and she had no intention of beating him to death. His ribs and his nose were broken, and he stared up at her with glassy eyes. He wouldn't be much of a threat anymore.

She stood. Her arms felt as if the weighed more than their wagon. Hands dangling limply at her sides, she walked over to Nora, who held Amy in a tight embrace. Her expression was one of pure horror.

"Don't worry," Luke said. Her upper lip was cracked and was starting to swell. "I'm fine. He's—"

"Luke!" Nora shouted. "Behind—"

Something hit Luke's shoulder. *What am I doing on the ground?* Luke thought dazedly. *I won.* Slowly, she gazed down her body.

A red stain was spreading over her shirt.

Someone had shot her. *Funny thing. It doesn't even hurt.* She watched with interest as her blood dripped onto the ground.

Then Bill Larson stepped into her line of sight, a revolver dangling from his bleeding hand. "Thanks, Brody." He indicated the weapon with his chin.

"Don't mention it," Brody said from somewhere behind Larson. Steps approached until Brody entered Luke's field of vision. He stared down at her, his eyes bare of compassion. "Hamilton never should have banned you from the wagon train. He deserves whatever comes to him."

"Yeah." Larson lifted the revolver again until Luke looked directly into its muzzle.

Luke's hand crept up to her holster. Her fingers closed around the worn grip, but the weapon felt as heavy as a cannon. She was so tired. No energy to fight anymore. She closed her eyes.

A click echoed across the fort's parade ground as Larson pulled back the hammer.

"Put the weapon down," a trembling voice came from the right.

Nora. Luke opened her eyes again. *God, please, please, please, stay out of this. Don't make him shoot you too.*

"Or what?" Larson sneered. He didn't even turn to look at her.

"Or I'm gonna shoot you," Nora said. Her voice was quiet, but determined.

Luke weakly lifted her head, trying to get a glimpse of her.

Amy was nowhere in sight. Nora stood alone, holding her small revolver with both hands. The barrel pointed at Larson, but it was visibly trembling.

Despite her own predicament, Luke felt a proud smile flit across her face.

"Oh, don't worry, Bill, she won't pull the trigger," Brody Cowen said. "She doesn't have the balls it takes to shoot someone. When she pointed that toy at me, I took it from her without a problem."

With a nod, Larson lifted his revolver again and aimed it between Luke's eyes.

A shot rang out.

Luke felt no pain. She blinked up at Larson.

He was still standing.

He missed, Luke thought hazily.

Then the revolver fell from Larson's hands. He sank to his knees, his eyes wide with disbelief or pain as he clutched his chest. He swayed for a moment, then fell on his face.

"Damn, Bill!" Brody reached for his revolver.

Nora didn't react. She stood frozen, staring down at Larson.

Luke drew her weapon. Pain zigzagged through her body and light spots danced in front of her eyes, but she ignored it all. Her gaze zeroed in on Brody and the revolver he directed at Nora. Just before her vision dimmed, she pulled the trigger, then the world around her grew dark and silent.

Nora let her still smoking revolver fall from her limp grasp. She stared at Bill Larson's motionless body.

Another shot rang out.

She swiveled around.

Brody Cowen dropped his revolver that he had aimed at her and clutched his stomach. *Oh, Lord. He almost shot me. If not for Luke, I would be dead now.* That thought and Cowen's agonized cries made Nora dizzy. Bile rose in her throat. Her gaze fell on Larson's body. *I killed someone.* She looked down, expecting to see blood on her hands, but they were clean.

The same thing couldn't be said for Luke's shirt. A large, red stain covered his shoulder and chest, and it quickly spread.

Nausea threatened to overwhelm Nora again. She leaned forward at the waist, gasping for breath.

When someone dragged the dying Brody Cowen away, Nora slowly straightened. *You can fall apart later, now help Luke before he bleeds to death.* The mere thought of Luke dying made her stomach lurch again, but this time, she forced down her panic and knelt down next to Luke. "Luke?" she whispered, pressing her apron against his left shoulder to stop the bleeding.

He didn't answer. His eyes were closed. Only the weak rising and falling of his chest revealed that he was still alive.

When she reached for the buttons of his shirt to look at the wound, his eyes fluttered open. "Whadda you doin'?" he slurred.

Nora bit her lip. "Trying to save your life. Now lie still and let me—"

"No."

"What?" Nora stared at him.

"Jus' a scratch," Luke mumbled.

Was he hallucinating? Nora wanted to beat some sense into him. "It's not just a scratch, you damn stubborn idiot! You'll be bleeding to death if you don't let me help you."

Bernice tried to peer around Nora. "How does the wound look? Did the bullet go straight through?"

"I'd know if this stubborn maniac didn't refuse to let me look at the wound." Nora clutched his uninjured shoulder. "Luke, please, let me help you! Please! I have no intention of becoming a widow anytime soon."

Luke tried to lift his head but couldn't. "A' right," he mumbled. "But not here. Wagon."

Jacob, Tom, and some of the other men came running. "Christ, Bernice!" Jacob stared at them. "What happened?"

"No time for explanations," Bernice said. "Help us get Luke settled in their wagon."

With the help of the two men, they carried Luke over the parade ground and to the wagon just outside of the fort.

A few reassuring words to the sobbing Amy, who struggled against Emeline's grip, then Nora climbed into the wagon and knelt down on one side of Luke while Bernice crawled in on the other.

When Nora looked down, she realized he had lost consciousness. She smoothed her palm over his face that was unnaturally pale except for the bruises that were already beginning to form. With a deep breath, she started to unbutton the bloodstained shirt. She eyed his slender, yet strong body, but then she called herself to order. This was neither the time nor the place to ogle Luke's body.

"What's this?" Bernice pointed at the bandages wrapped around Luke's chest. "He was already hurt?"

"No. At least not that I know of." *How typical of Luke to heroically hide whatever injury he might have suffered on the trail.* With a glance at the blood that was still seeping from somewhere beneath the wrappings, she quickly began to undo them. One last tug and the bandages fell away, revealing...

Nora gasped, blinked, then looked again. The image in front of her hadn't changed. Instead of a hairy chest, she looked down at smooth skin and a pair of breasts. The breasts were small but couldn't be mistaken for a man's chest.

"Merciful heavens. W-what's this?" Bernice sounded as shaky as Nora felt. "What's the meaning of this? H-he...he's a...a woman?"

Nora didn't answer. She couldn't. The only thing she could do was stare. *A woman? No, no, no, that's not possible.*

"You didn't know?" Bernice asked.

Nora mutely shook her head.

Both of them looked at the half-naked, bleeding stranger. "Let's try to dress his…her wound," Bernice finally said. "We can talk about this later."

Nora watched as Bernice wiped the blood away and studied the wound.

Bernice gave her a nudge. "Help me turn him…her around. We have to see if the bullet went straight through or is still stuck inside."

Bernice grasped the uninjured shoulder, but Nora hesitated to touch the pale body, almost afraid to graze the bare breasts by accident.

"Come on," Bernice said.

Finally, Nora helped Bernice turn Luke around.

"He…she was really lucky. The bullet went right through without hitting any bones," Bernice said. "Good. Then we don't need to dig the bullet out." She pressed a clean cloth against the exit wound to stop the bleeding.

Luke moaned without waking.

The sound of pain shook Nora from her stupor. Concentrating just on the wound and no other part of Luke's body, she managed to pull herself together. She got their carbolic soap from the wagon box and helped Bernice clean the wound.

When they poured whiskey into the wound, Luke flinched but didn't wake.

Finally, after half an hour, they had a thick bandage in place.

Bernice settled a blanket over the limp body, but Nora still found herself staring at the contours of Luke's chest.

"Now, tell me how this is possible." Bernice leaned back against a keg of pickles. "How did you end up being married to a woman?"

"I don't know," Nora whispered. "I don't know anything anymore. Just when I thought I finally had the life I wanted… I should have known something would happen to take that away from me."

"So I guess there really is no chance that the baby is Luke's?" Bernice asked.

Nora shook her head. "And now I know why he always insisted that we would never have children together." She couldn't stop the bitterness from showing in her voice.

"You never…?" Bernice gestured between Nora and the unconscious woman. A blush covered her chubby cheeks.

"No. He said he didn't expect that from me." A lot of things about Luke now began to make sense—why he had refused to share her bed and didn't let her see him naked. And Nora now understood why Tess had tried to stop her from marrying Luke, even though Luke was her friend. *And that's why he seemed to understand me better than any man before.*

Bernice stood and straightened with a groan. "I think you need some time alone now. I'm gonna go and tell the others that Luke is still alive."

Nora nodded numbly. Bernice was already climbing from the wagon when something occurred to her. "Bernice!"

"Yes?" The older woman peeked back in.

"Could you…I mean…would you please stay quiet and tell nobody about…about Luke? At least for now. Please?" Nobody was going to believe that she hadn't known her husband was a woman. If their fellow travelers found out the truth, there was no telling what they would do. Maybe some hotheads would try to kill Luke or at least banish her from the train—and Nora wouldn't be allowed to stay either. They would believe that she had committed unnatural acts with the woman who was her husband. Nora realized that she had to hide Luke's secret because her own fate was inevitably interwoven with Luke's.

"All right. I'll keep quiet for now. And I'll take care of Amy tonight."

Then Bernice was gone, leaving Nora alone with her thoughts and a lot of unanswered questions. She stared down at Luke, scanned the calm face for any signs of female softness. It was the same familiar face as ever. Dark lashes rested against a face that was deeply tanned even though it had gone pale now. The best word that Nora found to describe Luke's lips was "sensuous," but the strong jaw and the stubborn chin prevented her from appearing too feminine. The nose was slightly crooked due to an old break. Fine lines around the now closed eyes attested to a life spent working outside under the burning sun. Nora could easily remember how the lines deepened when he smiled.

She, Nora corrected herself again. Slowly, with hesitation, she reached out a hand and touched Luke's cheek with a single finger. The skin was as smooth as her own. *Why did I never notice? I know more about men than most other women. I've been with young men, old men, rich and poor men, fat and thin men, but nobody has ever been like Luke. Why couldn't I tell that she's a woman? I should have known as soon as she refused to share my bed.* Her self-doubts crept up again.

She watched over the unconscious woman for hours, lost in her thoughts and doubts. She had thought that she had gotten to know Luke, that he had started to reveal his innermost self to her, but now she realized she knew nothing about this stranger. *Why did he visit a brothel if he…she's a woman? To bolster her male identity? But why would he want to live as a man in the first place? And why did he ask me to marry him, knowing that it was all a farce? God, what will I do?*

There were so many questions, and she would get no answers until Luke awoke. *If he… she awakes and gets well.* Nora was disappointed and hurt by the betrayal of yet another person in her life, but she didn't wish Luke any harm. A part of her was still convinced of Luke's honorable intentions.

The first gray light of predawn was already lighting the sky when Nora finally fell into a troubled sleep, dreaming about the stunned expression on Bill Larson's face as she had pulled the trigger.

Thump. Thump. Thump. Pain radiated through her body with every beat of her heart. Luke blinked open heavy eyes. It took a few seconds for her to realize that she was resting on her back, lying in the wagon. *Bill Larson. We fought. Nora shot him. And he shot me.* Pain lanced through her shoulder.

Then, with another wave of pain, came the realization that Nora had probably discovered her secret by now. The last thing she remembered was being carried to the wagon. She weakly reached out her right hand and lifted the blanket covering her.

Damn, damn, damn. Her shirt was gone. A bandage covered her left shoulder and half of her chest, but it was not the wrapping that normally bound her breasts. Her breasts were bare, and she quickly tugged the blanket higher to cover them again. *Too late. Nora has already seen what you are.*

Her first instinct was to search for her clothes, run away, and start a new life somewhere else where no one knew that she was not what she appeared to be. But when she tried to sit up, she realized it wouldn't be that easy. A wave of dizziness made her sink back. She closed her eyes as the pain and a feeling of hopelessness overcame her.

A scratching sound next to her made her open her eyes again.

Nora was asleep just a few inches away from her, half hidden between a bag of flour and the keg of pickles. Her face was pale, and a few strands of hair had gotten free of the tight knot at the back of her head. She was tossing and turning as if caught in the throes of a nightmare.

She's still here. What does it mean? Luke didn't dare to hope that Nora would forgive and accept her. She didn't know how to face her.

At that very moment, Nora jerked upright with a cry and opened her eyes.

They found themselves staring at each other.

So many emotions seemed to swirl through Nora's green eyes that Luke couldn't tell them apart. Finally, she couldn't stand the silence between them any longer. "I don't know what to say," she whispered.

Nora didn't seem to know how to open up communication between them either.

"What happened to Brody and Larson?" Luke finally asked. Maybe it would be easier to start with something other than the discovery that must have shocked Nora.

Nora stared at her for long moments before she finally answered, "They're both dead. You shot Brody, and I shot Larson when he tried to kill you."

"Thank you." Luke reached out a hand, intending to squeeze Nora's hand in a gesture of gratefulness, but Nora flinched back before she could make contact.

"Don't thank me," Nora said with a rough voice. "I killed a human being. That's hardly something to be thankful for."

Luke knew from firsthand experience how hard taking a life could be. For her, it had changed everything, even how she had felt about herself. *Add to that the discovery that she's married to a woman, and it's hardly surprising that Nora is one very confused individual.* "I'm not thanking you for killing him. I'm thanking you for saving my life. Of course, now that you know who...what I am, you might not think that my life is worth saving." She studied Nora intently, searching for a reaction.

Nora's face didn't reveal any emotions.

Working in the brothel taught her to hide her feelings.

"You saved my life before and when Brody wanted to shoot me, so it was only fair that I should save yours," Nora finally said.

So she has paid the debt, and now she doesn't owe me anything anymore. Is that what she's saying? "Did you...did you tell anyone?"

"No."

Luke exhaled sharply. So there might be a chance for her to resume her life and the role as captain of the train. At the very least, she had enough time to recover from her wound without an angry mob just waiting until she was healed enough to be chased off. "Thank you."

"I didn't do it for you. I did it to protect myself. And because I promised Tess."

"Promised Tess?" Tess hadn't told Nora anything, had she? "What do you mean?"

"Right before the wedding, she made me promise that I'd never give away any of your secrets." Nora snorted. "She told me you're not like other men. She knew, didn't she?"

Luke nodded. "I'm sorry. I know you must feel betrayed by—"

Nora cut her off with a wave of her hand. "Bernice saw your body when we tended to your wound."

Luke covered her eyes with the back of her hand. *Wonderful.* She groaned. *The whole train probably knows by now.* She propped herself up on her right elbow and tried to sit up.

"What the hell are you doing?" Nora asked.

"Where are my clothes?" Luke tried to look around, but her vision was blurry, and she swayed.

Nora frowned. "They're covered in blood. But it doesn't matter, you don't need them at the moment."

"I do—unless you want me to ride through camp like this." Luke nodded down at her blanket-covered chest.

"I don't want you to ride through camp at all. It would be your death."

Does she still care whether I live or die? Luke's right arm began to tremble as her strength dwindled. Groaning, she fell back onto her bedroll. When her vision cleared again, she looked into Nora's glowering, green eyes. "I know that you must be angry, confused, and—"

Again, Nora didn't let her finish her attempt to explain. "You don't know anything about how I feel. I don't even know what I'm feeling."

Luke sighed. The friendship that had slowly grown between them seemed to be lost. They weren't even able to talk anymore. "You can have the marriage annulled as soon as we reach Oregon."

"I doubt I'll even need an annulment—this marriage wasn't exactly legal." Nora's voice was dripping with bitterness. "But it's not as easy as that. An annulment won't solve the problems you caused. If anyone finds out that you're…" she hesitated, avoiding the word for a moment, "…a woman, it's not only your life and your future that will be destroyed. My reputation will be affected too. No one will believe that I lived with you for four months without realizing that you're not a man. I won't be able to find another husband in Oregon if it becomes common knowledge that I was married to a woman."

"I'm sorry. I never wanted—"

"I don't want to hear it. I can't talk about this right now." With jerky movements, Nora stood and climbed from the wagon.

Nora stared into the clear water of the Boise River. She bent down, carefully keeping her balance that had shifted with the growth of her belly, and picked up a flat stone. She clenched her fingers around it, then raised her arm and threw the stone. It bounced off the water's surface, once, then twice, before it finally sank. Nora stared at the spreading circles on the water, remembering the day when Luke had shown Amy how to throw a stone like this.

Back then, her life had seemed so perfect, but now, her hopes of leading a simple family life were shattered.

"How is Luke…or whatever else her name might be?"

Nora jerked when Bernice stepped next to her. "She was awake half an hour ago. I think she'll survive." It still took conscious effort to call Luke a "she."

"What did she say? Did she tell you why—?"

"We didn't talk much," Nora said. To tell the truth, she didn't even want to talk to Bernice right now.

Bernice stepped around a small willow so she was face-to-face with Nora. "Aren't you curious at all? Don't you want to know why she lives in disguise? Why she asked you to marry her?"

Nora considered it for a moment. Yes, she was curious, but she had other feelings that ran so much deeper. "What would it change if I knew?"

Bernice's brown eyes narrowed. "Change?"

"Yeah. What he…she has done, is done. Nothing that Luke or I say or do will change the fact that she can never be the husband that I dreamed of." It occurred to Nora that she was basically grieving. Luke had survived the shooting, but Nora had still lost her husband.

"It's unbelievable." Bernice shook her head. "I always thought Luke was the perfect husband."

Nora bit her lip until she tasted blood. It had all been an illusion.

"Do you want me to talk to her?" Bernice asked.

"No." Nora knew Luke didn't want anyone to see her in her weak, half-dressed condition. She grimaced as she noticed that, after all that had happened, she still felt protective of Luke. "I'll go and see how she is."

She tried not to make any noise as she climbed back into the wagon, hoping that she would find Luke asleep. It was easier facing a sleeping woman than to have these familiar gray eyes staring at her.

Luke's eyes were closed.

Nora breathed a sigh of relief. She silently sat on a trunk at the end of the wagon and stared at the pale face.

Luke moved in her sleep and moaned. The blanket slid down a bit, baring a shoulder that was smoothly muscled but not as bulky as most men's.

Nora stared at the fair skin and the bandage covering part of it. *I should change her bandage before she wakes.* She knew Luke would feel uncomfortable letting her see her body while she was awake, and Nora wasn't exactly at ease with it either.

Slowly, not touching her more than absolutely necessary, Nora turned down the blanket. Her hand still gripped the edge of the blanket while she stared down. Living in a brothel, she had seen scantily clad girls every day, but for some reason, looking at Luke was different. Only when the fair skin of Luke's chest broke out in goose bumps and her nipples stiffened in the cool air did Nora shake herself from her stupor and began to move again. She lowered her hand to Luke's bandaged shoulder.

"W-wha…?" At the first slight contact, Luke jerked back from Nora's touch, one hand gripping the blanket while the other searched for her revolver. Luke's reflexes were astonishing for a woman who had nearly died last night.

"It's only me," Nora said.

Luke sank back but kept her tight grip on the blanket. "What were you doing?"

Nora felt the blood rush to her cheeks. *Great. Now she thinks I was ogling her.* "I need to change your bandage," she said as matter-of-factly as she could.

"I-I can do it," Luke stammered.

All the other times when Luke had refused to let her dress a wound now made sense. "I've already seen your body," Nora said. "There's no need to be shy about it any longer. I worked in a brothel, so I've seen it all before."

Still, Luke lowered the blanket with obvious reluctance, peeling it back just enough to grant access to the bandage.

Nora concentrated solely on her task. When she unwrapped the bandage, the body under her fingers was stiff and unmoving. "Breathe," she said. "I don't need you to pass out on top of your other injuries."

Luke took a sharp breath, then grew still again. "How does it look?"

Nora studied the wound. The area around it was swollen and discolored, but there were no signs of infection. She averted her eyes when she noticed that her gaze had followed one of the bruises that disappeared under the blanket. "Better than I expected."

"Papa?" a small voice called from outside the wagon.

Oh, God. Nora and Luke stared at each other. Busy treating Luke's wound and then trying to cope with her own feelings, Nora hadn't thought about what this would mean for her daughter.

Wood creaked, indicating that Amy was trying to climb into the wagon.

"No!" Luke's eyes widened. "Quick! Help me. I don't want her to see me like this."

Nora couldn't even imagine what it would do to Amy if she found out that her beloved "papa" was a woman. She quickly rewrapped the wound and drew the blanket more tightly around Luke's shoulders.

"Papa!" Amy pulled herself up and scrambled over various piles of supplies in her haste to get to Luke.

"Please be careful, sweetheart," Nora said. "Luke has an owie." She couldn't quite bring herself to call Luke "Papa."

Amy stopped and stared at the half-reclining woman. "Is it a bad owie?"

"No, not bad at all," Luke said. "I'll be healed in no time."

She's the best liar I've ever met—and Lord knows, I've met quite a few good cheats in Tess's establishment, Nora thought but said nothing. For once, she was glad about the small lie because Amy tended to worry too much for an almost four-year-old. She didn't need to fear for her "stepfather's" life on top of that.

"I kiss it and make it better," Amy said. Before Luke could stop her, she stepped forward and gripped the blanket, wanting to lift it so she could reach enough bare skin to press a healing kiss to it.

Nora was the first one to react. Quickly, before the blanket could reveal Luke's bosom, she pressed the blanket down and held it in place. When Luke grew very, very quiet, Nora realized that her hand was resting on the upper swell of Luke's breast. She wanted to tear her hand away in a spurt of panic, but then Amy would lift the blanket and see more of Luke than Nora wanted her to, so she kept her hand where it was. "Sorry," she mouthed.

"It's all right," a red-faced Luke mouthed back.

"Do you see this big bruise on Luke's cheek, sweetie?" Nora pointed at one of the marks that Bill Larson's fists had left behind on Luke's face. "I think you should kiss him there because I'm sure that bruise hurts a lot." It wasn't all that hard to remind herself to use male pronouns when referring to Luke, but still, it felt like a lie now that she knew.

Finally, Amy let go of the blanket and kissed Luke's cheek. "There. All better," she said as she had heard from Nora before.

"Thank you, darlin'." Luke reached out a trembling hand and gently smoothed back an unruly strand of Amy's hair.

Everything else about her might have been a lie, but Nora believed Luke's feelings for Amy to be genuine. She knew exactly what faked affections looked like, and this wasn't it.

"I'll pick pwetty flowers for Papa," Amy said and climbed back down from the wagon.

Nora jerked her hand away from Luke's chest. "I don't even know your name."

"Yeah, you do," Luke said. "My name is Luke Hamilton."

"Your last name might be Hamilton, but parents don't name their little girl 'Luke,'" Nora said.

"My mother did. Well, she named me…" Luke lowered her voice to a whisper. "Lucinda, but most people called me Luke anyway. There are no pleasant memories tied to the name Lucinda."

Nora nodded slowly. Growing up as a girl in a brothel wasn't a pleasant experience. "So that was why you didn't want me to name the baby Lucinda?"

"Something like that, yes. I left that part of my life behind, and I didn't want to be reminded of it."

She studied Luke. Her gaze was open, without guile. Finally, Nora felt calm enough to ask. "Why do you live like this? Hiding your true self away behind a disguise?"

Luke looked down at herself. "My true self? Disguise?" She shook her head. "There's no other life for me. This is how I feel most comfortable."

After thinking about it for a while, Nora found a few parallels between their lives. Working as a "lady of the evening," Nora had to pretend and hide away parts of herself too. But this was where the similarities ended—Nora couldn't imagine voluntarily choosing a life where she constantly had to hide. Luke seemed to prefer living her life as a man, though. "Do you..." She swallowed. "Do you think of yourself as a man?"

Luke shrugged, then groaned and clutched her shoulder as the movement tugged on her wound. "I guess, for the most part I do. I just know I'm not like other women."

"No, you're not." There was no disgust in Nora's voice. "But you're also not like other men."

Luke hung her head. "Look, I know I shouldn't have married you, and you have every right to—"

"Why did you?"

Luke blinked. "What?"

"Why did you marry me?" Nora asked. Why did a woman marry another woman, knowing full well that it was a sin before God's eyes? "Was it because you can claim twice the amount of land as a married man?"

"No. The land had nothing to do with it. That was merely a nice side effect," Luke answered without hesitation. "I knew that having a wife and a child would help to make the people on the wagon train assume that I'm a man. And, most of all, I didn't want Amy to grow up the way I did. I could see that you are a caring mother, and I wanted to give you the chance at a new life that my mother never took."

If that was true, then Luke really was the honorable person that Nora had thought her to be. "How long have you lived like this?"

"Since I was twelve."

Twelve? God, no wonder she's so convincing. She practically grew up as a boy. Nora thought back to the conversation about Luke's mother that they'd had just a week ago. A week that felt like an eternity. "Since your mother died?"

"Yeah. I was on my own, with no family or friends to provide for me, and I knew no one would employ a twelve-year-old girl—except maybe as a girl of the night," Luke said. "So I dressed as a boy and told them I was fifteen. I worked as a stable boy, then as a ranch hand, and four years later, I joined the dragoons."

"So you disguised yourself as a man to avoid ending up as a prostitute?" Nora could certainly understand that. She wished it had been an option for her four years ago, but she could have never hidden her pregnancy.

"Yes. And no," Luke said. "It's not just a means to an end. It's how I feel most comfortable."

Nora still didn't fully understand. How could Luke feel comfortable living a lie?

Luke sighed. "I'm weird, I know. I've been told before."

Nora lifted her head. "Who else but Tess knew?"

"Just Nate."

"Nate? That friend of yours who died in the Mexican War?" *The one I've wanted to name the baby for.*

Luke nodded.

"Did you tell him?" Nora asked.

"No. He found out the same way you did. I was injured, and he tried to help." Luke tucked the blanket more tightly around herself as if wanting to protect herself from the memory.

So another person has been in the same situation? Well, maybe not the exact same situation, but still... Nora wanted to hear more. Maybe it would help her cope with this unusual situation. "How did he react?"

"After a few weeks, he got used to it," Luke said. "He realized that nothing had changed just because he now knew my true gender. I was still the same friend that he had known before."

Is that a message for me? Friend. Nora tried to picture Luke and another young man in uniform, fighting, eating, and sleeping side by side. *A man and a woman living in close quarters during wartime?* She knew from experience that war often seemed to intensify emotions and fuel passions. "Nate and you...were you ever...?"

Luke looked up at her with one raised eyebrow. "What?"

"Lovers?" Nora asked softly.

Luke coughed, then clutched her wounded shoulder.

Nora waited until the coughing spell had passed. "I'm sorry. I shouldn't have asked that."

"No, no, it's all right. You've got a right to know these things about me. You know my biggest secret and you didn't tell anyone, so I should trust you with everything else, right?"

Trust? Is there really any trust left between us? There had been too many lies between them from the start. Just when they had built a reluctant relationship, one of them had shattered the other's trust and they had to rebuild it again. *How many times can we continue to do that until we can't put the broken pieces back together any longer?*

"Nate was my best friend," Luke said into the silence that had fallen between them like a chasm. "The only friend I ever had other than Tess. He was like a brother to me, but no, there was never anything else between us." Luke seemed to be genuinely surprised that she would assume that, as if she had never even considered that possibility.

"But if he was the only one who knew your secret, does this mean you've never been with anyone?" More and more, Nora had the feeling that Luke had led a life that was even lonelier than hers had been. At least, she had Amy, Tess, and a dozen other young women who were her friends. And sometimes, she had shared her bed with a customer who had been gentle and truly seemed to care about her.

Luke turned her face away and stared at the wagon's cover, but Nora could still see the blush rising up her face. *Her life has also been a lot more sheltered than mine.* Nora hid a grin. After a few weeks in their line of work, prostitutes stopped blushing about carnal matters.

"I didn't say that," Luke finally mumbled.

Nora blinked. She fell back against the keg of pickles. "You mean...? You really had relations with Tess? You didn't just say that to bolster your manly image?"

Luke still didn't meet her gaze. "Everything I told you was the truth. I just lied about my gender, but not about anything else."

Nora chewed on her lower lip. She didn't know what to say to that revelation. She had worked as a prostitute, so there wasn't much about carnal pleasures that was a foreign concept to her. She had heard that there were people who preferred the company of their own sex, but she hadn't given it much thought. It had been just a theoretical possibility that didn't matter in her everyday life. She studied Luke with curiosity. "So you paid Tess for—?"

"No. Money was never an issue between us," Luke said. "I was her friend, not a customer."

"Did Tess know who and what you are when you first came to her bed?" Nora couldn't keep herself from asking. The sudden revelation had thrown her thoughts and assumptions into a turmoil, and she wanted to put them back into order and make her head stop spinning.

Luke sighed. "She knew, yes."

And still she invited Luke into her bed, without even taking her money. Nora knew that as a madam of a brothel, Tess was a clever businesswoman first and foremost. She never did anything she didn't want to unless she profited from it in some way. *She took Luke to bed because she wanted to. But why did she send me upstairs with Luke? Did she think that I'd like it too?* Instead of clearing up her thoughts and feelings, their conversation made her even more confused.

"I know this must seem strange and shocking to you," Luke said, her gaze still directed at the wagon's cover, "and it's not something I'm particularly proud of, but that's the way I am, and I can't change that. Believe me, I've tried."

Nora looked at the clenched jaw, the rigid back, and the averted face. Luke Hamilton was a picture of shame. Still, Nora was not ready to let her off the hook and change the topic of conversation. She wanted to understand this. "Did you always prefer the company of women, or do you think it's because you lead the life of a man?"

Luke shrugged. "I'm not sure. I've lived in male apparel since I was old enough to be aware of carnal desires. I can't imagine being with a man…that way." She shuddered.

Studying Luke's features, Nora tried to imagine Luke in bed with a man, but the mental pictures just wouldn't come. She had gotten so used to thinking of Luke as a man that it somehow seemed wrong to picture her with a man. Instead, a mental image of Luke in a passionate embrace with Tess popped into her mind. Now it was Nora's turn to blush.

Someone cleared her throat just outside of the wagon, announcing her presence. "Nora? Luke?" It was Bernice's voice. "Are you…decent?"

Luke stuffed the blanket more tightly around herself, trying to hide any signs of her femininity.

Nora stuck her head out of the wagon. She knew Luke would be more comfortable if Bernice stayed outside. "Where's Amy?"

"She's with Jacob," Bernice said. "He took the children down to the river to watch the wagons cross. Listen, we have to break camp and move on. We can't wait any longer."

Nora knew she was right. It was almost September, and the emigrants worried that the snows would come early and they'd get stranded in the mountains. Every man and woman on the trail had heard of the Donner Party, who had frozen to death or resorted to cannibalism because they were stuck in the snow. That thought followed the travelers as they continued west.

"What will you do?" Bernice asked, nodding at the wagon where Luke rested.

"I don't know." Nora looked forlornly at her friend. For the first time since the beginning of their journey, it was "you" and not "we" as if she was no longer a part of the wagon train. "I'm not sure if Luke is strong enough to travel." And she also wasn't sure if the other emigrants would still want her to travel with them.

"You're always welcome to join us, you know? We could make room for you and Amy in our wagon," Bernice said with her trademark kind smile.

For me and Amy, but what about Luke? At first, she had never wanted to see Luke again, but now her anger had faded, leaving behind only grief, confusion, and fear about her uncertain future. Her life's path had seemed so clear to her just a few days ago. She had dreamed of raising her children with a kind husband and loving father. Now that dream had been shattered.

Still, she couldn't leave Luke behind, wounded and helpless as she was. That was the only thing she knew for sure; everything else about her future seemed uncertain and frightening. She couldn't imagine a future without Luke, knowing that she couldn't provide for Amy and the unborn child on her own. But what kind of future could two women and two small children have together? It would be obvious to everyone they met that they were not a family. Her children would be bastards just the way they would have been if she had continued to work in a brothel.

Then Nora remembered. *Nobody knows we're two women. Everyone still thinks Luke is a man. Everyone but Bernice.* She looked at her friend. "I can't just leave her behind, Bernice," she whispered, very aware that Luke was listening just inches away from them. "She saved my life and Amy's more times and in more ways than I can count, and I—"

"I could talk to the others," Bernice said. "Maybe if Jacob puts in a good word for her, they'll let her stay."

Nora slowly shook her head. "No. She couldn't live that way—and neither could I." She knew what it was like to feel furtive glances and hear the biting remarks that people made behind her back. Luke was used to being an officer and leader, a well-respected man. She wouldn't endure to be looked at as an oddity for long. If their fellow travelers found out that she was a woman, Luke would move on and start a new life as soon as her wounds would allow it.

And Nora and her children would be left behind.

She looked at Bernice with steely determination. "I need you to pretend that you've never seen Luke's body."

"What?"

"Just treat Luke as if she really were the man you thought she was," Nora said.

Bernice shook her head. "But...but...she's not."

Nora closed her eyes. "I know. But it's the only chance we have to start a new life in Oregon. A single woman has no right to claim any land. I would be at the mercy of the men in Oregon City. I would have to marry any man who wanted me." Hoping and praying for a kind man would have been all right a few months ago, but now seemed too high a risk. She wouldn't be that lucky twice. A husband like Luke came along only once. *Oh, Luke.* Nora stared at the woman inside the wagon and sighed. *If only you were the man you pretend to be, you'd be the perfect man.* She sighed again. *The irony of life.*

"Nora, I'm not sure this is a good idea," Bernice said.

"Please. Please, give me that chance." Nora stared into the brown eyes as if that would help change Bernice's mind.

Bernice's brow furrowed. "Is there no other way? Do you really want to keep living with her?"

Nora felt her hackles rise. She didn't like what Bernice's comment was implying. "Luke is still my friend and the leader of this wagon train if nothing else. That hasn't changed, you know?"

"It's not that," Bernice said. "I don't think she's a bad person. It's just... How long do you think this will work? How long until she's found out again—possibly by someone who reacts less tolerantly than you and I?"

"It already worked for a very long time. Luke has lived as a man since she was twelve, and she's only been discovered once before. You have to admit that she's very convincing as a man." Even she, who had more experience with men than most other women, had never even suspected that her husband was a woman. She had sensed that Luke was different from other men, yes, but she had never suspected the true cause of those differences.

Bernice gave a reluctant nod. "Oh, yeah, she is. Lord knows how often I had to listen to my own daughter moon over that dreamy Lucas Hamilton."

"So you'll keep quiet?" Nora asked.

"You'll never find another husband if everyone thinks you're married to Luke," Bernice said.

Nora shrugged. "I don't care." She didn't want another husband. The only thing she wanted was to hold on to the peace she had found living as Luke's wife even if they had never been a couple in the truest sense of the word.

"All right," Bernice finally said. "I just pray that you won't regret holding on to that strange arrangement." With a shake of her head, she walked away.

Nora moved back into the wagon and drew the strings of the cover shut. She hesitated before she turned around to face Luke.

Luke was staring at her, her eyes searching for something in Nora's face. "Why are you doing this?"

Nora froze. "You didn't want me to do this?" It hadn't occurred to her that Luke might not want to continue the life they'd had. Maybe Luke wanted to take this opportunity to get rid of the wife and the two children she had burdened herself with and start a whole new life.

"I didn't expect you to do it," Luke said. "I was convinced that you would run away yellin' and screamin' as soon as you found out that you married a woman."

"Oh, I wanted to do that," Nora said with a small smile. "But that only lasted for an hour or two. Running is not that easy when you're almost eight months pregnant."

Luke nodded. "You're staying because of the baby."

Nora thought about it. *Why am I staying?* "The baby and Amy are a part of it." It would be very hard to rob Amy of the person who was the only father she had ever known. "I'm still angry and confused, but mostly I feel...betrayed. Yes, that's it. I feel like you've cheated me out of the future I could have had as your wife. After a few months as a prostitute, I stopped dreaming of a white knight that would charge in and rescue me from Tess's establishment. Then you came along, and you turned out to be a better husband and father than I ever imagined. And then…this." She bit her lip and gestured toward Luke's body.

Luke looked away.

"I'm staying because I still think that I'll have the best possible future at your side," Nora said. "This marriage doesn't need to be about romance or physical love. Like you said when you proposed to me—we'll be business partners. I'll play the dutiful wife and make people believe that you're the most virile husband in history." She winked at Luke. "And you'll make them believe that I'm a prim and proper wife with a chaste past and two children born in wedlock."

Luke finally looked into her eyes. Slowly, she lifted her hand and offered it to Nora. "It's a deal…partner."

Nora shook the offered hand, feeling the calluses of a life spent doing hard work against her palm.

"Should you ever find a real man, someone you could love, I promise that I won't stand in your way," Luke said when she let go of Nora's hand.

Nora swept the offer aside with a wave of her hand. "Don't worry. That won't happen. Love is not for me."

Luke nodded. "I don't think it's for me either."

Nonetheless, Nora felt obliged to offer her the same deal that Luke had offered her. "If you ever find a…"

When she hesitated, Luke quietly supplied, "A woman."

Nora gave a short nod. "Yeah. If you ever find a woman that you could love, I won't stand in your way either."

A sad smile flitted across Luke's face. "That won't happen."

The sound of braying mules and moving wagons outside made Nora get up with a groan. "Stay put. I'll get our boys yoked."

Inch by inch, Luke lifted herself up into a sitting position. She felt weak as a newborn but could sit up without passing out. Taking it as a good sign, she searched for a clean shirt and pants in her saddlebags. With a quick glance at the closed flap of the wagon covers, she threw off her blanket.

The process of binding her chest, transforming herself into a man, had been a daily ritual for Luke since she was little more than a child. She could practically do it in her sleep. But not today. When she tried to wrap the bindings around her chest, she found that she couldn't move her left arm behind her back without immense pain. She moved her hand back inch by inch, clenching her jaw to stifle a moan. Within seconds, sweat beaded on her forehead, and she rested it against the side of the wagon for a moment while she waited for the pain to recede.

"Luke!" Nora's voice made her jerk and reach for the blanket to cover herself. "What are you doing?"

Luke wiped the sweat off her face with the edge of the blanket. "What does it look like? I'm getting dressed."

"Without much success, it would seem," Nora said. "Come on, lie back down and get some rest."

Luke would have liked nothing better than to do just that, but she couldn't stay in the wagon and let the pregnant Nora do all the work. "No, it's all right. I can do this." She looked at Nora, silently indicating for her to leave so that she could get dressed.

But Nora didn't move. "Luke," she said, using the same tone of voice that she sometimes used to talk to Amy when she was being unreasonable. "You're injured. Go back to bed."

"I will. But first I need to talk to Jacob," Luke said.

"If you really need to talk to him, I'll tell him and he'll come here. You don't have to get up."

Luke gripped the sleeve of Nora's blouse. "That's not a good idea. He can't see me like this." She gestured at her blanket-covered body.

"Oh."

"Yeah." Luke gave her an embarrassed grin.

Nora looked down at her hands. "Well, then…I could help you dress."

Luke froze and stared. "Uh…"

After a few moments of just returning her stare, Nora smiled. "You're not the first naked woman I've ever seen. It wouldn't appall me to see your body."

But maybe it would appall me if you saw me. Luke helplessly shook her head. Not even Tess had ever seen her fully naked. The mere thought of letting Nora see her made her heart thump along with her wounded shoulder.

"Come on. I promise I won't look." Nora took the shirt from Luke's weak grasp.

"Um." Luke cleared her throat. "The shirt is not the problem." She held up the bindings that made her chest look like that of a man.

Nora's eyes widened. "Oh. Right." She took a deep breath. "Well, the offer to help is still standing."

The thought of Nora binding her breasts made Luke's body break out in goose bumps. She shivered but couldn't tell whether it was from fear or anticipation of Nora's touch.

"Come on, we don't have the time for hesitation." Nora pointed outside, where the other emigrants were breaking camp.

Still, Luke sat frozen.

"Luke." Warm fingers covered Luke's, squeezing gently. "You don't have to be afraid. You have never been anything but kind and gentle to me, so I'll treat you with the same gentleness."

Slowly, Luke let go of the blanket covering her bare upper body. "Please, hurry," she whispered, her eyes on the flap that was the only barrier to the outside world.

She was very aware of Nora's gaze traveling all over her upper body. Finally, Nora looked down at the broad strips of fabric that were used to strap down Luke's breasts. "Lift your arms," Nora said.

Luke tried, but she couldn't lift her left arm over her head.

"Stop." Nora's fingers closed around her wrist. "Don't hurt yourself. I'll try it like this." She pressed one end of the bindings against Luke's shoulder blade and held it in place while wrapping the fabric around Luke's chest with her other hand.

The warm hands that repeatedly brushed against the sides of her breasts made Luke sweat and tremble. "Tighter." She grunted. Her voice was hoarse, but she knew that pain had nothing to do with it. Luke cursed her traitorous body.

Nora stopped, her hands still resting against Luke, holding the bindings in place. "I'll hurt you if I wrap it any tighter."

"It doesn't matter. It has to be tight," Luke said, her teeth clenched against the dual sensation of pain and pleasure.

"I still don't understand why you choose to do this to yourself every day of your life," Nora murmured. Her thumb rubbed over Luke's upper chest, where the bindings had already left behind a red welt.

Luke covered the hand with her own to hold it still, only belatedly noticing that it drew unnecessary attention to the touch that Nora probably hadn't been aware of.

"Oh. Sorry." Nora withdrew her hand and fastened the bindings.

"It's the only way I can live the life I want," Luke said. She slipped the shirt over her shoulders, but when she tried to button it up, her usually steady fingers were trembling.

Gently, but resolutely, Nora pushed her fingers away and took over the task.

Luke stared down at the nimble fingers buttoning her shirt. It was oddly intimate, like something a wife would do for her husband.

Finally, she was dressed.

"See?" Nora pointed at the row of buttons. "That wasn't so bad, was it?"

It didn't feel bad at all—and that's the problem. Of course, Luke didn't say it out loud. She just nodded.

Nora smoothed a hand over the collar of Luke's shirt. Her gaze slid up and down Luke's body, taking in the transformation. "Amazing," she whispered.

"What?" She squirmed under Nora's intense appraisal.

An embarrassed smile danced over Nora's lips. "I've seen you nearly naked just a minute ago, but I can hardly believe what's beneath your clothes when I look at you like this."

Luke looked into Nora's eyes. "It would be the best for both of us if you forgot it altogether."

"I wish I could." The answer came fast, without thinking, and was accompanied by a sigh of regret.

"I'm sorry," Luke whispered. With a noise somewhere between a sigh and a groan, she pushed herself upward and stood on shaky legs.

Before she could climb out of the wagon, Nora opened the flap and stuck her head outside. "Jacob?" she called out.

"Yeah?" Jacob Garfield's weathered face appeared at the end of the wagon.

"Luke would like to have a word with you," Nora said, then climbed outside and left them alone to talk.

Jacob studied Luke.

She couldn't help wondering if he looked at her any differently than he had a few days ago. *Does he know? Did Bernice tell him?* Bernice was his wife, after all, and she was supposed to keep no secrets from her husband.

But Jacob's expression was neutral and didn't betray his thoughts. "Glad to see you up and about. How are you?"

"I'm fine. It's not me I'm worried about." Luke nodded to the front of the wagon, where Nora was busy checking the oxen's backs for sores. "Jacob, I know you've got plenty to do without me asking for a favor, but I'm probably out of commission for a few days, and Nora can't possibly do it all on her own, pregnant as she is."

Jacob clapped her on her uninjured shoulder. "Don't worry. Wayne and I will help out while you recover."

Luke swallowed. *Bernice didn't tell him. Yet.* If she had, Jacob wouldn't have offered his help so readily. "Thank you."

When Jacob walked away, she sank back down onto her bedroll. For now, she couldn't do anything but recover and pray that Bernice would keep her mouth closed until she was at least halfway healed.

Farewell Bend,
September 5th, 1851

Nora straightened her aching back and shaded her eyes with her hand to catch one last glance at the Snake River. They were leaving the wide river at this point and would be traveling over dusty hills to the dreaded Burnt River Canyon.

Every muscle, tendon, and bone in her body hurt, but she didn't dare to complain, afraid that Luke would jump out of the wagon and take over the task of driving the oxen at the first sound of pain from her.

Luke was acting like the typical ill man—impatient with the healing process, the people who were trying to help her, and with her own weakness. Nora had watched her carefully during the last few days—not only because she constantly had to keep her from getting out of bed, but also because she wanted to see if she could detect changes in Luke's behavior, now that she knew her true gender.

So far, the differences she had noticed had been very small, convincing her more and more that Luke hadn't just pretended to be a man—she had simply acted how she felt most comfortable. Still, Luke's behavior toward her had changed. The aloof distance that had diminished with every mile of their journey was totally gone now. After an initial awkwardness that had followed the discovery of Luke's secret, Luke was now beginning to show a softer, warmer side when it was just the two of them. Nora suspected that it had been there all along, but Luke hadn't dared to show it, afraid of being thought of as unmanly.

The Garfields joined her as she struggled up the hill. "Just a few more days and we'll catch our first glimpse of the Blue Mountains," Jacob said and grinned.

Nora nodded. On the one hand, she shared Jacob's excitement at being so close to the end of their journey, but on the other hand, the thought of having to cross the mountains worried her. Now that they would need their energy most, the pregnancy made her feel constantly tired, and Luke still hadn't recovered from her wounds.

"Oh, don't worry, girl." Jacob patted her arm. "I won't let anything happen to you while your husband can't take care of you and the wagon."

For the last few days, Jacob and his oldest son, Wayne, had helped her with the tent and the oxen. They had been helpful and friendly, but Nora still longed for Luke's return to her duties. Traveling with the Garfield men was nice, but it was just not the same. Sometimes, they took over tasks that Luke had let her handle on her own, trusting her to do a good job. Luke treated her as an equal, and she liked the feeling of being appreciated that she got when she was with Luke.

"Where's Amy?" Bernice asked when Jacob walked back to his own wagon.

Nora pointed at the wagon with the end of her whip. "In there, with Luke. They're taking a nap." It was the only way to get both of them to settle down for some much-needed rest.

Bernice tugged at her sunbonnet. She eyed Nora's wagon. "Don't you have any misgivings about letting Amy spend so much time with Luke?"

Nora gently prodded Snow White to make the ox move more to the left. She still hadn't come to terms with the fact that her husband had turned out to be a woman, but Nora had no reservations about Luke spending time with Amy. "Why should I? Bernice, you've seen Luke with Amy. Do you really think that Amy has anything to fear from her?" She couldn't believe that Bernice would think such a thing.

"What? No, no, I didn't mean it like that. It's just… Aren't you the least bit afraid that Luke is going to influence her? I mean, it's obvious that Amy worships her. What if Amy models herself after her?"

"Then I'd be a happy mother." She didn't want Amy to choose a life where she had to hide a part of herself, but she did want her to become a kind, courageous, and honorable person like Luke.

Bernice lifted her eyebrows.

"I grew up with a father who constantly belittled me if he paid me any attention at all—just because I was not a boy. I know that Luke would never do that to…" Nora stopped herself. She had almost said "our children." She rubbed her face to chase away the blush. "…to Amy or the baby."

"You're really planning to let them grow up thinking that Luke is their father?" Bernice shook her head.

"I don't know. At this point, I don't have a plan," Nora said. She had avoided thinking about her long-term future. She hadn't thought further than reaching Oregon City. *And how could I when I don't even know what Luke wants? The most important thing in Luke's life is to be regarded as a man. I don't think she's willing to risk that by sharing her life with two children who don't understand the importance of keeping a secret.*

Bernice pointed at Nora's swollen belly. "Then I think it's time to make some plans. This baby is not gonna wait until you figure it all out."

Nora groaned and covered her face with both hands for a moment. "I know, I know."

"Nora?" Luke stuck her head out of the wagon. "Are you all right?"

Nora let her hands drop and looked up at Luke. "Uh, yeah, I'm fine."

"Are you sure?" Luke's concerned gaze traveled down to Nora's belly. "I'll take over with the oxen, and you—"

"No. I told you, I'm fine. Is Amy still sleeping?" Nora asked. Her usually active daughter was suspiciously quiet since she had climbed into the wagon with Luke.

"No. We're reading a story," Luke said, giving her a crooked grin.

Nora stared at her. "You are reading to her?" She wasn't sure what she found more amazing: That Luke was willing or that she was able to do that.

"Well, what I can't read, I improvise. Amy doesn't mind." Luke rubbed her shoulder.

"Stop scratching," Nora said for the hundredth time that day.

"But it's itching like h—" With a quick glance over her shoulder at Amy, Luke stopped herself. "It's itching very much."

Nora nodded. "That means it's healing, and your scratching will only disturb the healing process. I'll check the wound as soon as we stop for the night."

Without another word, Luke disappeared inside the wagon again.

"For a woman who didn't even want to touch Luke when she was bleeding to death, you're taking this awfully well," Bernice said. "As often as you check the wound, hers must be the best-treated wound ever."

Nora gazed down, hoping that her sunbonnet would cover her blush. *She's making it sound as if I like treating the wound...seeing Luke half-naked.* "I just want to prevent the wound from getting infected, that's all," she said. "If left to her own devices, Luke would change the bandage once a week and be done with it." Each time, it took longer to convince Luke to take off her shirt than to check and rebandage the wound. Nora still wasn't sure whether Luke was uncomfortable with her own body or only with Nora seeing it.

"In other words, she's the typical man," Bernice said, her gaze resting on the wagon where Luke had disappeared. "It's still so hard to believe that she's not..."

Don't I know it. Sometimes, Nora woke up and when she looked at Luke, who was sleeping just a few feet away, she could almost convince herself that it had all been just a dream. Once or twice, when her disbelief became too intense to handle, she had even touched the cheek of the sleeping woman, finding it as smooth and hairless as her own. Maybe this was one of the reasons why she insisted on a daily change of Luke's bandage— each time, it drove home the reality of who Luke really was.

The hill they were climbing was getting steeper and steeper, and Nora stopped talking and worrying for a while, trying to concentrate solely on driving the wagon.

FLAGSTAFF HILL,
SEPTEMBER 9TH, 1851

The wagons clattered up the stony road. Luke winced every time her shoulder was jostled. When she couldn't stand the stuffy air in the wagon anymore, she pulled up the cover and peeked outside.

All she saw was the back of the Buchanans' wagon in front of them. The wagons were traveling single file over the worst road they had encountered so far.

Curses drifted over from the front of the wagon train, where some of the men were hacking their way through thickets of bush with axes.

Luke gritted her teeth. She was still too weak to help with that.

Water splashed as they crossed the Burnt River for the ninth time, trying to find the best route.

When a wave of water hit Amy, who sat on the wagon seat, she squeaked and leaned a bit too far to the side for Luke's liking.

"Amy, come back here and keep me company," Luke called. At least she could keep an eye on Amy while Nora guided their oxen through the river.

Amy scrambled up from the seat, crawled over a sack of corn, and joined Luke in the back of the wagon. She tugged on Luke's sleeve. "I want a story, Papa."

"A story? You want me to read to you again?" Luke reluctantly reached for Nora's book of fairy tales. She still couldn't read very well, but Amy probably wouldn't be able to tell when she was improvising.

"No." Amy's red curls flew as she shook her head. "You tell me a story."

Luke swallowed. When she had been a child, no one had read her bedtime stories, so she didn't know how to tell one. "Sorry, Amy, but I don't know any stories."

"Please!"

Luke couldn't resist the pleading gaze. "All right." She scratched her neck. What should she tell Amy? The only stories she knew were the war stories her former comrades told around the campfire, but she doubted they were suitable for children. "What kind of story do you want?"

"A horse story." Amy clapped her hands and leaned against Luke, expectantly looking up at her.

Luke wiped her brow. "A horse story. Hmm. Well, let's see." She tried to remember how Nora's fairy tales usually started. "Once upon a time there was a horse."

"Measles," Amy said.

"Um, yes, Measles." Luke mentally apologized to her trusted mare. "Like all horses, she loved to be in the company of other horses and she wanted a family of her own, so she set out to travel across the country to a faraway place called Oregon, where she wanted to raise beautiful foals and—"

The wagon slowed and then stopped.

Oh, thank God. Had they finally reached the summit of Flagstaff Hill, where they would camp for the night? The beautiful valley below would surely distract Amy until she forgot about the story.

"Luke," Nora called from the front of the wagon. Her voice sounded strained.

Luke squeezed past Amy and stuck her head out of the wagon.

Nora stood with one hand pressed to her back while she rubbed her eyes with the other.

"Everything all right?" Luke asked. "Is the baby—?"

"The baby is fine. But Snow White isn't."

Luke climbed down from the wagon and took a glance at the ox.

The animal's flanks were heaving like a pair of bellows. Its legs trembled.

Dammit. Luke trailed her hand along the ox's side and walked around it. Snow White's eyes were dull. Luke looked up and met Nora's gaze. She shook her head. "He won't make it up Flagstaff Hill."

Nora pressed her lips together. "Is there anything we can do to help him?"

Luke shook her head. "Why don't you take Amy and stay with the Garfields for a few minutes while I take care of this?"

The muscles in Nora's neck moved as she swallowed. Then she nodded.

"Tom," Luke called to the wagon in front of them. "Tell the others to stop and wait for us." She helped Amy down from the wagon and watched them walk away. Using just her right hand, she unyoked Snow White and directed him to the side.

The ox took a stumbling step, then, with a groan that sounded almost human, he sank to his knees.

Luke touched the ox's damp neck and looked into the cloudy eyes. "I'm sorry," she whispered. She curled her fingers into a fist, then opened them again. Gritting her teeth, she drew her revolver, aimed carefully, and pulled the trigger.

The shot echoed through the mountains.

Luke stood with her head bent for a moment before she took a deep breath and forced herself to move away. They couldn't afford to waste time.

When she turned, Nora was herding one of their spare oxen toward the wagon. "I left Amy with Bernice," she said, her voice choked. Tears glittered in her eyes as she looked at Snow White's still body, but she didn't let them fall. She yoked the ox, waited until Luke had climbed back into the wagon, and drove the team past their fallen comrade.

Luke watched her, admiring Nora's strength and her compassion in equal measures.

Nora struggled up the hill.

"Want me to take over for a while?" Luke asked.

"No, thanks," Nora said. "You're still recovering." She marched on, not allowing the oxen or herself to rest. Only when they reached the summit of Flagstaff Hill, she paused and looked down at the beautiful Baker Valley, covered with purple sage and colorful wildflowers.

Luke did her best to help with setting up camp. Hours later, she volunteered for guard duty, happy that she had finally found something she could do despite her healing wound. She stared up at the night sky, breathing into her hands to keep them warm.

Everything was quiet in camp. Only a few of the women were still awake.

Emmy Larson lifted a pot of beans for tomorrow's noon meal over the fire.

Luke's first instinct was to jump up and take over the task, knowing that the pot was quite heavy. But Nora had needed to rebandage the wound twice already because Luke wanted to "play gentleman," as Nora had put it, and she wouldn't be amused if she had to do it a third time. So Luke stayed where she was and simply watched the women at work.

Again, it occurred to her that the women didn't need her help. They got up at four every morning—an hour before the men—to cook breakfast, milk the cows, and gather eggs. And every night, they were still working while their husbands already rested around the fire.

Except for her childhood in a brothel, Luke had never lived in close quarters with women before. As a ranch hand and later as a soldier, she had worked and lived with men and had seen women only from afar. During this journey, she had developed a healthy respect for the pioneer women and what they endured without complaining. For the first time, she realized how strong women could be. Women, she realized, were not the weak, helpless creatures that she had feared to become if she ever gave up her disguise. Most of them were tough and courageous, and Luke admired their gentle strength.

And, Luke admitted to herself, Nora was the woman she admired the most.

Even though Nora's feet were swollen, she was still up, preparing tomorrow's meals.

"Stop," Luke said when Nora passed her, carrying a pile of laundry. "If you do one more thing tonight, I'm gonna get up and help you, the wound be damned. Sit down and rest."

"But the laundry—"

"Will still be there tomorrow," Luke said. "You're pregnant, exhausted, and miserable. You need to rest."

With a groan, Nora gave up and sank down next to Luke. She bent down, trying to reach her swollen feet to massage them, but her belly got in the way.

Luke watched her fruitless attempts for a while. "Come on." She waved at Nora's feet. "I'll rub them for you."

"No, no, you don't have to do that."

"You're carrying my child. It's the least I can do." Luke winked at her.

Nora gave her a small smile and lifted one of her feet onto Luke's lap. "Lord," she murmured, "with all the walking I've done during the last few months, this baby is gonna be able to walk when she is born."

"She?" Luke repeated with a grin. She gently pressed her thumbs against the sole of Nora's foot. "I thought you were sure it's gonna be a boy? Or are you having twins?"

Nora crossed herself. "God, no. To have one newborn during the first winter in Oregon is gonna be hard enough."

Luke nodded while she slid her fingers over Nora's ankle and began to knead her calf.

A long moan rose up Nora's chest.

The sound made Luke shiver. She forced her thoughts away from the soft skin under her hands and back to the topic of conversation. "Yeah. One baby is gonna put me in enough of a panic as it is."

"Oh, I don't know." Nora's grin momentarily chased the exhaustion from her face. "Fathering twins—now that would bolster your manly image."

Luke tweaked her big toe. She had to grin, and it occurred to her that this was the first time that someone had made fun of her life in disguise and she had been able to share the mirth. With Nora, it didn't feel like scorn and mockery, but like a shared secret. Instead of driving them apart as Luke had feared, it was beginning to bind them closer together.

"Do you think we'll make it?"

At the whispered question, Luke turned her head to look at Nora.

Nora's smile was gone. The forest green eyes were dark and worried as she glanced west toward the snow-covered Blue Mountains rising up in the distance. Her hands cradled her belly.

Luke fought the impulse to bend down and kiss the foot resting on her lap. Instead, she smoothed her hand over it in a gesture of comfort. "Yeah, we will." She looked directly into Nora's eyes, letting her see her determination.

"How can you be so sure?"

"I traveled the Oregon Trail three times before, and I made it every time," Luke said.

Nora shoulders slumped. "Yeah, but you didn't have a pregnant woman and a small child with you the other times."

"But I also didn't have the kind of motivation to reach Oregon that I have now." Luke had said it before she could stop herself. She hadn't wanted to say anything that would make Nora believe that they would share their lives as a family in Oregon—not when she wasn't sure if it was what Nora wanted or what would be good for her. She wasn't even sure if it was what she wanted. "I mean, this time, I'm the captain. A whole wagon train is depending on me."

"The whole wagon train. Yeah." Nora moved her foot away from Luke's lap. "I'm tired. I'm turning in now."

Luke blinked at the abrupt end of their conversation and watched her walk away. Slowly, one woman after the other went to bed until Luke sat alone at the fire.

Sudden footsteps behind her made her jerk around, her rifle raised.

"Relax, relax. It's only me, Bernice Garfield," the older woman's voice came out of the darkness.

Luke put the rifle down and exhaled. She had been coiled tightly during the last week, constantly on the lookout not only for hostile Indians or nature's dangers but also keeping an eye on her fellow travelers, afraid that they would discover her secret.

Now it was Bernice of all people who was searching her out. Luke had avoided her since being wounded. At first, it hadn't been too difficult since she had been confined to her wagon, but now that she was slowly healing and back on her feet again, it was becoming more complicated to avoid the people who knew her secret. While she had managed to avoid Bernice so far, she couldn't avoid Nora. She had to live every second of every day with Nora's appraising glances. She constantly wondered what Nora was seeing and thinking when she looked at her like that. Trusting someone to protect her secret, her very life, was scary.

Bernice sat down facing her.

Luke held her breath. She met Bernice's gaze across the fire, then quickly looked away.

"What are your plans once you reach Oregon?" Bernice asked, not bothering to open the conversation with small talk about the weather or the country ahead of them.

"I want to establish a horse ranch in a green, hilly area a few miles southwest of Oregon City. I'm going to breed Appaloosa horses, like Measles, you know?" Luke pointed in the general direction of her mare.

Still, the intense gaze didn't follow her gesture. It remained fixed on her. "I'm not talking about horses. I'm talking about Nora and her children. What will become of them? A woman in her condition needs stability, a home, a husband, not this…this whole confusing situation."

Luke shoved a twig into the fire with more force than necessary. "I know."

"Nora is like a little sister to me, and I won't have her hurt by the likes of you," Bernice said.

The likes of me? Luke repeated bitterly. Still, she appreciated Bernice's attempt to protect Nora. "I won't hurt her."

"Just the fact that you're not what you pretend to be is hurting her." Bernice's voice was an urgent whisper, just low enough that no one else could hear.

Luke bit her lip. "That's not something I can change."

"Exactly." Bernice studied her through narrowed eyes. "Then why keep on trying? Why keep on posing as a man when you're not?"

"Bernice." Nora stepped into the circle of the firelight, making both Luke and Bernice jump. "I appreciate your concern, but leave her alone. This is who Luke is, and if I can't accept that, I'm better off leaving her and living on my own."

Bernice whirled around. "But you can't. You have a child and another one on the way. You can't survive on your own. She put you in a situation where you have to choose between starving to death and staying in this more than awkward situation."

"There's a third choice. There always is," Nora said. "I could have returned back east with my brother, or I could have made an arrangement with a widower, like Emmy has. It's my choice. Luke's not forcing me to stay."

"Then why do you? Stay, I mean," Bernice said. "I don't understand."

And neither do I. Why didn't she jump at the first chance to leave me? Luke wondered.

"I won't entrust my future and that of my children to a stranger or people who don't care about us," Nora answered.

Bernice stabbed her finger in Luke's direction. "And she's not a stranger?"

Nora didn't raise her voice. She looked her right in the eye. "No, she isn't. I made a decision to trust her when I agreed to marry him…her, and so far, she has given me no reason to regret that decision."

"But…but…but she lied to you the whole time."

Nora turned her head to gaze at Luke. "Yeah, but only because she was afraid that I wouldn't keep her secret."

Luke gave her a relieved nod, glad that she seemed to understand that she had never meant to betray her.

Still, Bernice couldn't let it go. "But she's a woman."

"So am I," Nora said.

"That's not the point. You don't go around marrying other women."

Nora looked down at the ring on her finger. When she glanced up, an impish smile curled her lips. "Well, apparently, I did."

Luke suppressed a chuckle. She didn't want to annoy Bernice any more than she already had.

"Bernice," Nora said, "I know you don't understand the life that Luke has chosen. Frankly, I'm still not sure I understand it myself. But that doesn't change the fact that she's a good person. She saved Amy's life when she fell off the wagon, and she even risked her own life saving Amy from a rattlesnake. She jumped into a raging river to rescue me. She was almost killed because she took on two cruel men who abused helpless women. She's a main part of the reason why we made it this far with far less fatalities than most other wagon trains. And now you act as if all that isn't important any longer, as if she's a cruel person out to hurt me, just because you found out she's a woman?"

Luke had to swallow against the sudden lump in her throat. No one had ever defended her like this. Where she had hung her head in shame and looked away from Bernice's accusing eyes, Nora was fighting for her honor.

Bernice was quiet now, clearly at a loss for words.

"All right. I'm going back to bed now. I just came out to tell you that I forgot to check your wound," Nora said to Luke. "You coming?" With a glance over her shoulder, she walked back to the wagon.

Luke stayed behind for a moment. She turned to Bernice, almost embarrassed at Nora's passionate defense of her. She wasn't sure she deserved being defended like this. Maybe Bernice was right. Her complicated life did indeed have the potential to hurt Nora.

"Dear Lord," Bernice whispered, watching Nora's retreating back. "Who is that woman, and where is the self-conscious young woman who was so afraid to stand up for herself that she let Broderick Cowen torment her for weeks?"

"She grew up and learned to trust in herself," Luke said. She gently touched the stricken-looking woman on the shoulder. "And I think you made an important contribution to that."

Bernice closed her eyes, and when she reopened them a moment later, the angry accusation was gone from her expression. "No, you did. She learned to believe in her own worth because you treated her with respect."

"I'm really not out to hurt her, Bernice," Luke whispered. "If there ever comes a time when my presence in her life will harm her, I'll just disappear and leave her the ranch. If I'm ever found out again, I'll leave. I won't let her live in shame."

Without an answer, Bernice turned and walked toward her own wagon.

GRANDE RONDE,
SEPTEMBER 12TH, 1851

And I thought the ascent was hard, Nora thought, too exhausted to voice her complaint out loud. The climb up this rocky hill had been long and tedious, but the descent was even more murderous. The trail was so steep and rocky that they had to tie the wagons to a tree and slowly zigzag their way to the valley below.

Only when their wagon had safely reached the bottom did Nora take the time to admire the idyllic valley of Grande Ronde. Here, at the foot of the Blue Mountains, they had finally left the sandy sagebrush plains behind. This was more like the Oregon that Nora had imagined. Pine-covered mountains surrounded the lush valley, and a clear stream, lined by willows, alders, and cottonwoods, coursed through it. Judging from Amy's smeared face, berries grew in the vicinity. Indians swarmed around the wagon train, offering food and horses in exchange for clothing and other articles.

Nora smiled when she saw Luke gazing at the handsome ponies that resembled Measles with their spotted flanks. What she wanted wasn't horses or berries, though. What had kept her going for the last few miles had been the thought of letting her heavy, pregnant body sink into one of the numerous springs, creeks, and waterfalls all over the valley. Nora closed her eyes with a dreamy moan. She grabbed fresh clothes and her bar of soap. "Amy?" she called. "Come on. We're taking a bath."

Amy looked up from the berries she was gathering. "No. I'm gonna make a cake."

"Let her stay with me," Bernice said. "I'll give her a good scrubbing with my own brood when we're done with the cake."

"All right." Nora smiled. That meant she could enjoy her bath instead of working to get her berry-smeared daughter clean.

"Nora!" Luke's shout stopped her.

This better be important. Nora wanted to go before all the good bathing spots were taken. She turned around. "What is it?"

"You shouldn't go off alone," Luke said. She pointed at the Indian braves riding through the camp. "The Nez Perce and the Cayuse are friendly tribes, but when you take off your sunbonnet, your red hair is gonna attract them like bees to honey."

"But…" Nora threw a wistful glance at the waterfall in the distance. "My bath." Her shoulders slumped.

Luke rubbed the bump on the bridge of her nose. "I didn't say you couldn't have a bath. Just don't go off without protection."

"Then you'll come with me?" Luke had stood guard once before while she had taken a bath. Back then, she had still thought of Luke as a man. *So letting her see you now shouldn't be a problem, right? Since we're both women.* When she had lived in the brothel, changing or bathing in front of the other girls had been completely normal. But somehow, she knew that Luke's presence would feel entirely different.

"Only if it doesn't make you uncomfortable."

Nora gestured down her heavily pregnant, dust-covered body. "Uncomfortable is what I am right now. I would kill for a bath."

Luke laughed. "No need for that. All right, let's go." She shouldered her rifle and followed Nora to her choice of bathing places, a waterfall with a small basin just out of sight from camp.

When Nora began to unbutton her bodice, Luke turned away and busied herself with checking her weapon. Carefully, Nora stepped over the rocky rim of the basin and slipped into the cool water. "Ooooh."

"Cold?" Luke asked without turning around.

Nora watched her stiff back. "Yes, but it's nice." She let herself sink into the water until it reached her chin. Slowly, her muscles and tendons, which had been overly stressed by the pregnancy and the strains of the journey, began to relax. Still, some tension remained in her body. Luke's presence made her skin tingle, but she ignored it and floated until she felt her fingers start to shrivel. Without opening her eyes, she reached for the soap. Her hand encountered only hard rock and tickling grass. She opened her eyes. The soap was lying next to her clothes, just out of reach. With a groan, Nora prepared to climb out of the water to get the soap.

"Something wrong?" Luke glanced over her shoulder, then quickly away as she got a glimpse of Nora's naked skin.

"No, I just can't reach the soap."

Covering her eyes with one hand, Luke turned around and blindly began to search for the soap with the other.

"Luke!" Nora had to laugh at her antics. "You can open your eyes. If you're not careful you're gonna…"

With a splash, Luke landed next to her in the pool.

"…fall in," Nora said.

"Sorry. I'm sorry." Splashing and sputtering, Luke scrambled to climb back out.

"Luke, calm down." Nora held on to the now wet shirt. "Now that you're already wet, why don't you stay and take a bath too?"

Luke's muscles tensed under her fingers. "You know why that's not a good idea. This is not exactly a remote place. Anyone could see me here."

"Then at least stay and enjoy the water," Nora said. "Your clothes won't get any wetter than they already are. I could even wash your hair for you."

"No." Luke still wasn't looking at her and avoided touching Nora's body with any part of hers.

Is she ashamed, shy, or disgusted? Nora gazed down at her own body. A few months ago, her body had been the asset that ensured her survival. She had taken a certain pride in the fact that she had always obtained the highest prices of all the girls in Tess's establishment. Now her belly was swollen, her breasts heavy and covered with blue veins, and her formerly smooth skin was marred by stretch marks and calluses. Nora realized that men would no longer find her desirable. And Luke, who normally admired the female form, obviously shared their opinion. She sighed. "I look hideous, huh?"

"What?" Finally, Luke turned around to look at her but carefully kept her gaze fixed on Nora's face.

"My body." Nora gestured down. "It's a good thing I don't work in a brothel anymore. No one would pay a dime to look at me, much less anything else. I know that's not something I should regret, but I guess I'm just a little vain."

Luke stopped in her attempts to climb out of the basin. For a moment, her gaze flitted down Nora's body, then just as quickly back up until she looked into Nora's eyes. "You don't look hideous at all. You're beautiful."

"You're not just saying that to comfort a pouting pregnant woman?" Nora doubted that anyone could find her beautiful in her condition.

"No. I was surprised—"

"By what?" Nora asked when Luke stopped midsentence.

Luke shook her head. "Uh. It's nothing. Nothing important."

"I want to hear it."

Luke stared into the swirling water, avoiding Nora's eyes. "I never thought that I'd find a pregnant woman attractive."

Nora held her breath. "But you do?"

Luke nodded silently. She still didn't look at Nora.

"Thank you," Nora whispered.

Luke lifted her head. She blinked. "You're not angry?"

Bernice and every other respectable woman in the train would probably expect her to be scandalized by being complimented by a woman who posed as a man. *A woman who prefers the company of other women.* But Nora was sure that the warm feeling in the pit of her stomach was not outrage. "No, I'm not," she said slowly. She took a deep breath, trying to shake off the confusing feelings. "Could you…" She cleared her throat. "Could you pass me the soap, please?"

Luke pressed her hands on the edge of the pool and heaved her body out of the water in one smooth move. Water rushed down her back and dripped from her clothes. Her shirt and pants clung to her skin.

Nora couldn't help studying the body that the wet clothes revealed. When Luke bent down to pick up the soap, she caught a glimpse of strong thighs and a firm bottom. *What are you doing? Just because she said she thinks you're beautiful doesn't mean you have to return the favor. She's a woman, for heaven's sake, and you're not…like that.* She took a deep breath. *It's just because I've gotten so used to thinking of her as a man.*

"Nora? The soap." Luke's voice brought her back to the present.

"Thanks." She took the soap Luke held out to her. Deeply in thought, she began to scrub her body.

IN THE BLUE MOUNTAINS,
SEPTEMBER 14TH, 1851

"Damn." Luke slipped when she tried to climb into the wagon. Her collarbone bumped against a box of supplies, making pain flare through already hurting muscles.

Since leaving Grande Ronde Valley, they had traveled over trails so steep that in some places, they had to attach up to ten yoke of oxen to each wagon to navigate the steep grades.

In addition, the Blue Mountains were densely wooded. Often, towering pines and firs blocked the narrow trail. They had to make long detours or hack their way through the dense body of timber.

Every single member of the wagon train was footsore, weary, and exhausted, and Luke was no exception. Her still not fully recovered shoulder hurt, and she was so tired that she was afraid that she might fall and never get up again. As the captain of the wagon train, she could have ordered a day of rest, but she knew they couldn't afford it.

Far ahead in the distance, she could make out the snow-covered peaks of the Cascade Range, the white cone of Mount Hood looming above the others. Luke could already feel the bite of winter in the air. The fear of snow that could close mountain passes and trap them made her urge the exhausted emigrants onward.

Their small wagon train had stopped for the night, camping in a tiny clearing. Voices of travelers from other trains echoed through the woods, but they couldn't see them or tell how far away they really were. On the winding roads through the dense forest, they could see only the wagon directly in front of them. Even the sky above them was invisible, blocked out by the tall trees, giving them the feeling of being trapped and closed off from the rest of the world.

Nora huddled at the other end of the wagon, staying close to the already sleeping Amy. She jerked each time gunfire echoed through the dark forest.

"Just another emigrant, hunting for some game," Luke said.

Nora bit her lip and nodded but didn't relax.

Moving carefully to avoid waking Amy or jarring her hurting muscles, Luke sat down next to her. Up close, she could see that Nora was trembling. "Sshh." She reached out a hand, hesitated for a moment, then gently touched Nora's arm. "Don't be afraid."

"I'm not," Nora said. "It's just so cold tonight."

It was. Heavy white frost had settled on the outside of the wagon covers, and by morning, ice would have formed on the water buckets. Still, Luke knew Nora well enough to know that it wasn't just the cold that made her tremble. Very slowly, prepared to stop anytime should Nora flinch away from her, she slid her hand along Nora's shoulder until she held her in a gentle, one-armed embrace. "Better?" she whispered into the golden-red hair.

Nora cuddled into Luke's warm lambskin jacket. "Mm-hm."

Luke lifted her other arm and settled it around Nora too. The movement made her groan in pain as her hurting muscles protested.

"Your shoulder." Nora's sleepy eyes widened. "Did the wound break open again?"

"No, no." Luke held on to her when she tried to move away. "I'm fine, just a little stiff."

Nora raised up onto her knees and pointed to the bedroll that was spread over a couple of trunks. "Take off the shirt."

"What?"

"Take off your shirt," Nora repeated. "I'll rub your shoulders for you."

Luke shook her head. "You don't have to do this. You're as exhausted as I am."

"Then you can return the favor after your back rub." Nora gestured down at the bedroll again.

After nine years as a soldier, Luke knew when she was defeated and had to capitulate. She turned around, and with her back to Nora, she slipped out of her jacket and shirt.

Nora's hand on her shoulder stopped her when she moved to lie down on her stomach. "This too." She tugged on the wrappings around Luke's chest. "I'll rub your skin raw if I try to give you a massage while you wear this thing."

Luke froze. "No. What if Amy wakes up?"

"She was so exhausted when I put her to bed, I'm sure she'll sleep tight till the morning."

"Nora..." Didn't Nora understand how difficult this was for her? Unwrapping the bindings, transforming herself from man to woman, was something she did in privacy. She closed her eyes, trying to find the words that would make Nora understand that the bindings weren't just another article of clothing for her. "Undressing in front of someone... it's not as easy for me as it might be for you."

"But I'm not just 'someone.' I'm your wife."

"That's what the marriage certificate says, yes, but we both know that our relationship is not that easily defined."

Nora tilted her head and studied her. "Then how would you define our relationship?"

Luke had thought about this question a lot during the last few days. "We're...friends." It sounded more like a question than an answer in her own ears.

"Then why don't you trust me? You trusted Tess enough to let her see you, didn't you?" A trace of bitterness reverberated through Nora's voice.

Nora was probably wondering why Luke found her less trustworthy than Tess. At times, Nora still tended to attribute things to her own perceived shortcomings. "That was different," Luke said.

"Different how?"

Luke rubbed her tired eyes. "Tess was not just my friend in the traditional sense of the word. I also shared her bed on a few occasions." She wasn't proud of it, but it had happened, and it gave her friendship with Tess a unique twist.

"Oh." Nora was silent for a few moments. "I forgot about that. Again." A rare blush colored Nora's cheeks.

Nora seemed only too willing to forget that Luke's more passionate feelings were directed toward women. For the most part, Luke was content to let her live in denial, but now she had to clear up a few things before they could forget about it again. *Or at least try to forget, in my case.*

Nora was silent for so long that Luke thought the topic was closed. She slipped her shirt back on and began to rebutton it.

"Does this mean I have to share your bed before I can give you a simple back rub?" Nora asked.

Luke's fingers slipped. She almost tore off a button. "What? No. Of course not." She realized she had raised her voice and looked over at Amy to make sure she was still asleep.

Amy slumbered on peacefully.

"Then unwrap your chest and lie down," Nora said. "If I don't give you a massage now, you're gonna be of no use to this wagon train tomorrow."

Luke covered her face with her hands. "God." She groaned. "Have you always been this stubborn, or is it a recent development?"

"Must have rubbed off on me," Nora said.

Folding her arms over her still bandage-covered chest, Luke stared down at her. "From me, you mean?"

"We've been discussing this massage for longer than it will take me to administer it. I think that speaks for itself, doesn't it?" Nora didn't even try to hide her smirk.

Luke sighed.

"Luke." Nora stopped smirking and looked at her with a serious expression. "I know this isn't easy for you, but we both have to learn to deal with reality. Once we reach Oregon and work to establish a ranch, we'll only have each other. There'll be no doctor, no priest, and no friends anywhere near us. I'll be your doctor, your father confessor, and your friend, and you'll be mine."

Luke didn't want to admit it, but she knew Nora was right. She had to learn to trust Nora in every situation. Wordlessly, she took off her shirt. She waited for Nora to turn around, but when Nora didn't avert her eyes, Luke turned away before she started to loosen the tight bandages that bound her breasts. The cold air and Nora's curious gaze resting on her made her shiver. She quickly settled down on her belly.

Nora knelt in the narrow space next to her. She inhaled deeply as if she had to mentally prepare herself for her task.

Luke opened her mouth to tell her again that she didn't need to do this. She almost choked on the words when she felt Nora's hands on the bare skin of her back.

Nora's skillful fingers found the large knot between Luke's shoulder blades and began to work on it. After a while, her touch moved upward and gentled as her fingers neared the area that had been wounded not long ago. When Nora bent over her, her distended belly rubbed against the small of Luke's back.

Luke's body began to tingle. She clenched her fists around the edge of the bedroll.

"Relax," Nora whispered. Her breath flowed warmly over Luke's ear, making her shiver.

Luke let go of the bedroll and consciously tried to relax. Her attempts didn't last for long, though, because soon, Nora's concentrated kneading became a caress. Her fingertips traced along Luke's spine and explored the shape of her shoulder blades. Warm hands smoothed over Luke's hips and waist, then trailed upward and grazed the sides of her breasts. "Nora!" Luke groaned. She gasped, caught between intense arousal and a panic attack. "What are you doing? I can't relax like this," she said through clenched teeth.

Nora didn't answer. It was almost as if she hadn't heard Luke, too focused on exploring her body. "Your skin," she murmured. "It's so soft. It feels like velvet over steel. Not like a man's at all."

A part of Luke was sure that she was imagining things, but for a moment, she thought she had felt Nora press a kiss to the back of her neck. Confused, she sat up and stared up at Nora. "Nora…"

Nora took in her body.

Quickly, Luke covered her chest with her hands. She hadn't realized that she would expose her breasts to Nora when she sat up.

Nora laid her hand over Luke's. Her fingers were only inches away from Luke's breast. "Don't," she said. "Don't hide your body. Not from me."

"B-but it's…"

"It's beautiful. You're beautiful." Nora made eye contact.

Luke found only sincerity in her eyes. "Nora." It seemed to be the only word in her vocabulary. She wasn't even sure what she was begging for—for Nora to stop or to continue with her gentle touches.

Nora didn't answer. Her lips were otherwise occupied as she leaned forward and kissed Luke's cheek, then her jaw, and finally, her lips skimmed over Luke's own.

Luke forgot about her protests. She forgot all the reasons why this was not a good idea as her body reacted to Nora's closeness and her gentle touches. Her arms slipped around Nora's back, drawing her closer until Nora's belly rested warm and comforting against her side. She caressed Nora's cheek with her thumb until Nora searched her lips again. Inebriated by the feel and taste of Nora, Luke lost herself in the kiss.

"Mama?"

Amy's sleepy voice was like a bucket of ice-cold water that someone had poured out over them. They jerked away from each other.

Luke quickly pulled her shirt up to cover her chest.

Her chest heaving, Nora turned toward her daughter. "Amy, sweetie, why are you awake? You should be sleeping."

"Are you sick?" Amy mumbled around the thumb in her mouth.

Nora stared at her child. "What? No. Why would you think that, sweetheart?"

"You moaned," Amy said. "It waked me up."

Luke felt her cheeks grow hot.

"Everyone's fine," Nora said. "Go back to sleep, sweetie."

While Nora tucked Amy in again, Luke picked up her bindings with trembling fingers. Nora returned after just a few minutes.

"Do you think she saw?" Luke whispered.

"No. I'm sure she didn't." Nora's voice shook. "Come on. Let me help you with that thing."

As soon as Nora had wrapped the bandages around her chest, Luke slipped from the wagon. She would rather stand guard again than having to face Nora tonight. She needed the long hours alone to think about what had happened.

Crawford Hill,
September 15th, 1851

Nora looked at the Umatilla River running west in the distance. They were now very high up in the mountains, but it was not the thin mountain air that made her head spin. Her thoughts were still revolving around last night. Now, in the light of day, what had happened between them seemed almost unreal, but Nora knew it had not been a dream. Luke's behavior proved that it had been very real.

Luke had avoided her all morning, keeping ahead of the wagons under the pretense of finding the best way for the wagon train.

Nora was almost glad about it. It spared her from having to find ways to avoid her. She needed time to think before she was ready to face Luke. She needed to understand her own actions before she could explain them to Luke.

So, why did you touch her body and kiss her? She had tried to seduce Luke before, true, but that had been before she had found out that Luke was a woman. At the beginning of their journey, she had thought that her body was the only thing she could offer her husband in exchange for his protection. Now she knew she had much more to offer. *Keeping Luke's secret, making everyone believe that she's a man—that's your part of the deal. You're not obliged to give her anything else. So why for heaven's sake did you do that? God, if Amy hadn't woken up when she did... Would you really have slept with her?*

Nora didn't understand it. She didn't understand herself. She tried to tell herself that it was just because she was still so used to thinking of Luke as a man. Even now, Luke was acting like a man, so it was hard to relate to her as a woman.

Then she sighed and shook her head. *You've lied to your customers, to Amy, and all the townsfolk for years, but please, don't start lying to yourself.* She had been very aware that Luke was not a man when she had kissed her. She had kissed and touched men only in exchange for their money or their protection. Yesterday, she hadn't thought about money or other selfish reasons. She hadn't thought at all—she had only felt.

And it felt really good. After the unwelcome attentions of her rough, beer-smelling customers, Luke's soft touches had been... Her eyes fluttered shut as she remembered the softness, the gentleness of it all.

"Nora? Are you all right? There's nothing wrong with the baby, is there?"

Nora groaned. Of course, Luke had to choose this moment to finally return to the wagon. She opened her eyes and met Luke's gaze. "No, I'm all right." *At least physically.* She eyed Luke, trying to gauge her mood.

"Oh. Good, good." Luke averted her eyes. With a fleeting nod, she started to walk away again.

Nora hesitated for a few seconds, but she had always met difficult situations head-on. "Luke? I think we should talk."

Luke stopped in midstep. Her shoulders slumped, and she slowly turned back around, still not meeting Nora's eyes.

What does she have to be so upset about? Nora furrowed her brow. *She's shared her bed with a woman before, so how is this any different for her?*

"I should apologize," Luke murmured.

Nora stared at her. It would be so easy to blame it all on Luke, who already seemed to feel guilty, but that would hardly be fair. "Why are you apologizing for something that you didn't even start? I was the one who kissed you first, remember?"

"It was a scary night, closed off from the world in the mountains. You were afraid and overtired, and you wanted to make me feel better—"

"No." Nora couldn't accept the explanations Luke offered even when it would have been so much easier.

Luke's eyes widened. "N-no?"

"Yes, I was afraid and tired, and I wanted you to feel better, but I didn't touch you and kiss you because of that," Nora said.

They stared at each other until Luke asked, "Then why did you do it?"

"Why did you kiss me back?" Now Nora was the one who avoided having to answer.

Luke looked away, intently studying the oxen's backs. "You know that I like women."

"So if Bernice or Emmy came over right now and kissed you, you'd return that kiss too?" It hurt to think that it had been so impersonal for Luke that she could have replaced her with any other woman, but she shoved the thought away. She couldn't imagine Luke kissing anyone else. She didn't even want to imagine her kissing Tess.

"No. No, of course not."

"But you did kiss me," Nora said. She could still feel the soft lips against her own.

Luke sighed. "Yeah."

"Why?" Nora asked again.

"It won't happen again. Let's leave it at that, all right?"

What if I want it to happen again? Nora froze. *Where did this come from? You're not like that. You shared your bed with more men than the rest of the train's women together, remember?* Then another thought occurred to her. *Maybe that's the reason why Luke's lips and hands felt so good. After having to submit to so many men's urges, your body can't relax with one of them anymore.* "No."

Luke stared at her, fear and hope mixing in her gaze.

"Ignoring it won't make this go away," Nora said. "We're planning to build a future together. We can't afford to let this come between us."

"Oh yeah?" Luke crossed her arms over her chest. For the first time, she looked Nora in the eyes, a challenging expression on her face. "You think that we can't afford to ignore this? I have to answer your questions when you still haven't answered mine? You thought I wouldn't notice?"

Nora didn't have to ask what question she was talking about. It was the same question that had kept her awake all night and that had troubled her all day: why had she kissed Luke? "I don't know," she said. "The best explanation that I can come up with is that after all these years working for Tess and then enduring the hardships on the trail..." She shrugged. "I guess for once, I just wanted to do something for no other reason but that it felt good."

"It...it did?"

"You didn't think so?" She had never had any complaints from her sexual partners before. It was the one area where she never doubted her skills, and it felt strange to feel as clueless as a virgin again.

Luke closed her eyes. The dark lashes against the suddenly pale skin of her face made her appear vulnerable and as feminine as Nora had ever seen her. "It felt heavenly," she whispered so quietly that Nora could barely understand.

Nora forced a chaotic wave of emotions back down. Instead, she said, "So, for the record, we both enjoyed it, and we're still determined to build a mutually beneficial life together. Right?"

Luke nodded. She eyed Nora as if she wasn't sure where she was going with this.

"Then there's no reason why we shouldn't extend our deal a bit," Nora said. "We've both had hard lives, so what if we give each other a little comfort every now and then."

Luke clutched the wagon seat with both hands. She stared at Nora, then abruptly turned and walked away.

"Luke." Nora started to hurry after her but then remembered that she was still driving the oxen and couldn't just leave the wagon. "Luke! Did I offend you?"

Luke whirled around and shouted, "If that was what I wanted from you, I could have..." She paused, swallowed, and lowered her voice. "I could have paid to share your bed in Independence."

Nora stared at her over the backs of the oxen. The ox team wasn't all that separated them. A rift had opened up between them.

After long seconds of a silent stare down, Luke turned and walked away.

UMATILLA RIVER,
SEPTEMBER 16TH, 1851

The Indian agency was abandoned. Nora had looked forward to visiting with white settlers, maybe even dining in the first frame house they had seen since leaving Missouri. Instead, they camped in wary distance of a large Indian village, finding only dry grass for their exhausted livestock.

Nora had to fight against threatening tears. She tried to tell herself it was only the dust from the trail that irritated her eyes, but she knew it was not. Her very pregnant body simply was at the end of its strength. The trek through the Blue Mountains had exhausted not only her, but every human and animal in the train. And it hadn't even been the worst stretch of trail that was still ahead of them. To the west, the Cascade Mountains appeared like an impassable blue wall. Mount Hood loomed so high that it looked like a stationary white cloud.

Nora was afraid that they would never reach their new home. On top of that, she had possibly lost the person who had been her main source of strength and encouragement during the whole journey. Luke hadn't talked to her for almost two days, and this time, Nora was afraid to break the silence. She didn't know what to say to rectify the situation. *How could I when I don't even know what Luke wants to hear? I thought she desired me, but she was so angry, so disappointed.*

She settled down on a rock on the banks of the Umatilla River, close enough to the circled wagons to hear Amy should she wake up in the middle of the night, but far away enough to be alone. With hanging shoulders, she stared off into the darkness.

"Nora?"

Luke's quiet voice made her look up. She met the gaze of the turbulent gray eyes for a moment, then lowered her head again.

"Are you all right?" Luke asked. "You look—"

"Exhausted," Nora said.

Luke shook her head. "Sad was what I wanted to say."

Nora sighed but didn't answer.

After a moment, Luke sat next to her on the rock. "I shouldn't have yelled at you or ignored you for two days."

"Then why did you?"

Luke scraped the soles of her boots over the pebbles on the edge of the river. "I don't want to be just another customer for you, buying your physical affections in exchange for protecting and providing for you."

Nora's head jerked up. "You're not."

"You offered to 'extend our deal,'" Luke said.

Nora wearily rubbed her forehead. If she was honest with herself, touching Luke wasn't a part of their deal for her. She had phrased it like a business offer to make it easier for herself to explain why she was contemplating going to bed with a woman. She had tried to convince herself that it wouldn't be any different from sleeping with one of her male customers when, deep down, she knew very well that being with Luke would be nothing like that. Her shoulders sagged, and she glanced up at Luke through half-lowered lashes. "I didn't know any other way..."

Luke stared at her. "To do what?"

"To explain why I want to be...close to you." Nora awkwardly bent down, picked up a pebble, and threw it into the river. She watched the circular waves, anything to avoid looking at the silent woman next to her.

"You...you do?" It sounded as startled and confused as Nora felt. "You want to be close to me?"

Still not turning around, Nora nodded.

Luke sucked in a breath. "You don't need an explanation for that. If you want to be close, that's enough for me." Luke lifted her right arm, silently offering her an embrace.

Nora had to smile. This was not exactly the kind of closeness she had meant. In some respects, the experienced, battle-hardened wagon train captain was still very much an innocent. With an amused shake of her head, she turned and moved into Luke's arms for a careful hug.

After a few moments of holding each other loosely, not allowing too much contact between their bodies, both relaxed and moved a little closer. Nora rested her face against the crook of Luke's neck, deeply breathing in the comforting scent of leather, horse, and something that was just Luke. *God, this is nice.* Nora realized that she hadn't been hugged like this in years.

"This is nice," Luke whispered, voicing Nora's thoughts.

"Uh-huh." Nora hummed her agreement and nestled closer. During the last few years, touching had gone hand in hand with pain and humiliation. The feelings of peace and pleasure that Luke's touch brought were a surprise. She rested her cheek against Luke's upper chest and closed her eyes. The lack of sight intensified her other senses. She felt the hitch in Luke's breathing and the rapid thrumming of her heart. Her cheek was pressed tightly against the roughness of Luke's shirt. Underneath, she felt the tight wrappings, and her mind immediately imagined the slight swell of breasts beneath.

Nora didn't stop to think about her actions. Relaxed and a little sleepy, she acted on pure instinct. She raised her hand and traced the edge of the wrappings in idle curiosity.

When Luke sucked in a breath, her chest lifted, involuntarily pressing even closer against Nora's fingers. "Nora!" Luke groaned.

Nora looked up at Luke. Her hand stilled on Luke's chest but didn't move away. The situation reminded her of the day years ago when she had first discovered the power she held over men. Luke seemed equally helpless under her touch. Only this time, Nora didn't plan on taking advantage of it just to ensure her and Amy's survival. Luke had already promised to give her everything she needed—now she would take what she wanted.

"Nora!" Luke tried to shake off the gently stroking fingers. "I thought we agreed that there's no need for you to do that."

Pulling her hands back, Nora fixed her gaze on the familiar face. "Do you know what I liked about you from the very first day that we met?"

Luke swallowed heavily. She tilted her head. "W-what? What was it?"

Nora looked down at her hands. "You never, not even once, treated me like a prostitute. Please, don't start doing it now."

Luke's eyes flashed. "I'm not. That's exactly why I don't—"

Nora lifted her hand, pressing her fingers against Luke's lips to stop the words. Once again, she was surprised at how soft those lips felt. "If you avoid touching me and being touched by me just because of my past, if you ignore my right to decide with whom I want to share my bed, out of my own free will, then you are treating me like a prostitute." The lips under her fingers moved and trembled, but Luke just stared at her without saying anything. "Don't you think a former prostitute can share her bed—and her body—without it being work?"

"Of course. Of course, they...you can. But..." Luke shook her head. "It's just hard for me to believe that anyone, much less someone as beautiful as you, would want to lie with me without, well, getting anything out of it."

"What about Tess?" Nora pointed out the first thing that came to mind. "She did lie with you, and you never paid her for it either."

Luke sighed. "She got my friendship and my protection instead of money."

"Luke, I know you're proud of the rank you earned, and you should be, but you were just a lieutenant, so how much protection could you possibly offer her? Don't you think she would have slept with a general instead if all she wanted was protection?" Nora shook her head. "She likes you. That was why she invited you into her bed. And that's why I'm doing it too."

Luke's trembling lips began to move again, no doubt to protest once more. Nora had enough of this discussion. Why couldn't Luke, who had been the one to convince her of her own worth as a woman and a human being, realize that she was likeable and desirable too? Nora decided to show her instead. When Luke's mouth opened, she moved back into the embrace and covered Luke's lips with her own.

Luke struggled halfheartedly and gently tried to push her back, but under the determined attack of Nora's skilled lips, her resistance died down. Calloused hands wandered over Nora's back and pressed her closer against Luke's body.

"Nora?"

Nora almost fell off the rock at the sudden sound of another voice behind her. Working in Tess's brothel, she had learned never to lose track of her surroundings while she entertained a customer. Even during the most heated kisses she had always been aware of everything that went on around her. But now, she had been totally oblivious to everything but Luke.

Luke's hands clutched at her; then she jerked back. She had probably been just as caught up in their kiss.

When Nora turned around, Bernice stood behind them, staring at them with her hands on her hips and a hard expression on her normally warm and friendly face. "Can I talk to you for a minute?"

Awkwardly, Nora climbed from the rock. She was in no hurry to have that conversation, knowing that Bernice didn't want to chat about the weather or tomorrow's meals.

"I think I'll head back to camp and see if Jacob needs my help shoeing that ox," Luke said. With hurried steps, she disappeared into the darkness.

Coward! Clenching her hands into fists, Nora turned toward Bernice. She didn't have to wait long for what the older woman had to say.

"What are you doing for heaven's sake?" Bernice roughly shook her head. Everything in her voice and body language signaled disapproval.

For a moment, Nora was transported back to the countless confrontations with her parents. They had found fault in everything she did too. Nothing she ever said or did had found their approval. She squared her shoulders. "I was kissing the person I'm married to."

Bernice stared at her. "Nora!" She reached out and gently shook her as if to wake her up. "She's a woman. Did you already forget that?"

Nora's rebellion died down. "No, I didn't."

"Then why are you acting like this? It's unnatural. A sin." Bernice's dark eyes flashed.

"Unnatural. A sin," Nora repeated, more to herself. Her parents had taught her the same thing. Being regarded as a sinner was nothing new for Nora. It was what the upright citizens of Independence had called her before crossing to the other side of the street. She had always thought that would change should she one day find an honorable, kind person who was willing to marry her—and now that she had, she was still called a sinner.

"Yes," Bernice said. "So why did you let her do this to you?"

Nora grimaced. Of course Bernice would think that Luke had instigated the kiss. In Bernice's eyes, Luke was a strange, unnatural creature, leading a life that she didn't understand, so it was only logical for her to assume that Luke had been the one to make unwelcome advances and Nora merely endured them out of a feeling of obligation. *Nothing could be further from the truth.* "Luke didn't do anything to me," she said.

Bernice folded her arms over her heaving chest. "Don't try to protect her. I know what I saw."

"No, you don't," Nora said and held Bernice's gaze. "You don't know anything about this situation."

"I know enough to see that you're only gonna get hurt. If anyone else but me had seen you kissing her…" Bernice closed her eyes for a moment as if she was picturing the described disaster.

Nora shook her head. "Everyone else still thinks Luke is a man. No one would have thought anything of it if they had seen us kissing each other."

"All right," Bernice said. "But you, you know better. You know it's wrong to share that kind of intimacy with her."

"Do I?" She had told herself the same thing for weeks, but every time she was close to Luke, it felt so very right. For the first time in her life, she had someone who respected her and stood by her, no matter what. Someone who was a loyal friend to her and a wonderful parent to Amy. How could physical affection with that kind of person be a mortal sin while the cruel groping of her customers had been just a minor offence tolerated by society?

Bernice reached out and touched her cheek, directing Nora's gaze to meet hers. "Nora, don't taint your soul with that kind of thing."

"I'm not a saint, Bernice," Nora said. "If my soul is tainted, it has been like that long before I ever met Luke. You know what I was and what I've done. I'd still be doing it if it wasn't for Luke."

"So you're doing this out of gratitude?"

"No."

"What is it, then?" Bernice asked.

Nora sighed. How could she explain something that she didn't understand herself? Why did she have to explain her reasons at all? She shrugged, not wanting to say something that would hurt Bernice. The older woman meant well.

"You're risking perdition without even knowing why? Nora, please, think before you rush headlong into disaster." Bernice folded her hands and shook them. "If not for yourself, then at least think about the little ones." She gently touched Nora's enlarged belly.

That had been the wrong thing to say. For all her insecurities regarding her relationship with Luke, Nora was sure of one thing: Luke was the best second parent for her children that she could ever hope to find. She refused to think that Luke's presence in their lives would hurt them in any way. "I'm going to bed," she said, ending their discussion.

"Not into Luke's, I hope."

Nora abruptly turned back around.

They stared at each other. Bernice seemed as surprised as Nora was about what she had just said.

"I'm sorry," Bernice said after long seconds of silence. "I don't want to nag you. It's just..."

Nora touched the older woman's forearm. "I know you don't understand. How could you when I don't understand it myself. I just know that Luke is my future. I feel like I was supposed to marry her all along."

"A woman?"

"I know, I know. I can't explain it, but that's the way I feel."

Bernice sighed. "Go on, to bed with you, girl."

Nora felt Luke's presence when she slipped into the wagon. Her skin tingled where Luke's gaze rested on her.

"What did she want?" Luke asked. "Did she see us?"

"Bernice is a mother—she sees everything," Nora answered.

"She scolded you, didn't she? I'm sorry."

Nora was at the end of her patience. "Stop apologizing. Why does everyone think they have to take responsibility for my actions? Kissing you was my choice."

"Sorry," Luke said. "I mean, not for kissing you back, but for implying that you couldn't make your own choices."

Nora smiled and gradually relaxed. Very aware of the Garfields' wagon next to theirs, she settled down on her side of the wagon, careful not to come into contact with Luke's body in the close quarters. She closed her eyes but knew she wouldn't be able to sleep tonight.

Fifteenmile Creek,
September 30th, 1851

The exhausted oxen crawled up the steep ravine. With heaving flanks, they stopped as soon as Luke halted and put down the whip. Luke gazed back at the wagon. Its condition wasn't any better than that of the oxen, and their provisions were running dangerously low.

Luke waited until Nora had reached her side. Heavily pregnant now, she was more waddling than walking, and Luke was constantly worrying about her. She pointed to the fork in the road ahead of them. "The one to the right goes to The Dalles and the Columbia, the left one to the Barlow Road. Any preferences?"

The emigrants had already discussed their options at dinner last night. At this point, the Cascade Mountains stopped their journey, so they either had to float down the dangerous Columbia River on crude rafts or overpriced boats or travel around the south side of Mount Hood over the Barlow Road, known as the worst stretch of road on the entire Oregon Trail.

"Just the thought of boarding a raft makes me green about the gills," Nora said. "Not that I like the thought of navigating sixty-percent grades any better."

Luke gave her an encouraging pat on the shoulder, then pulled her hand away when she became aware of Bernice watching them from the wagon behind them. "Great." She grimaced. "You're the best-chaperoned lady on this train."

Nora grinned tiredly. "I'm no lady. That's why Bernice thinks she has to watch me like a hawk."

Despite her frustration, Luke had to laugh. "You are more of a lady than any other woman I know. Acting snobbish is not what makes a lady—a good heart is."

"Come on, Captain." Jacob stepped up to them. "Whispering sweet nothings to your wife is not gonna help us across the Cascades."

His good-natured teasing told Luke that Bernice was still keeping her secret. *Yeah. But for how much longer?* Every time she stood a little too close to Nora, Bernice sent her suspicious glances. Straightening her shoulders, Luke turned to Jacob. "I think the toll road is the better choice. It's strenuous, but not as much of a gamble as the whirlpools of the Columbia."

Jacob nodded and without further discussion, they began the last and hardest part of the journey.

Big Laurel Hill,
October 7th, 1851

Dear God. Nora stared down the almost vertical drop-off. She knew they had to get the wagons down this chute but couldn't imagine how they would do it without them ending up splintered at the bottom. Laurel Hill was so steep that only a few laurels clung to it, giving it its name. To make it even worse, a cold rain was pouring down, which made the road slippery.

The road was cut down so deep that Nora couldn't even see the wagons and oxen at some points, almost as if they were traveling in a dry riverbed. Luke and the other drivers waded through deep mud on the bank, while the women carried their children through the dense brush and over fallen logs next to the road.

"And here we thought Little Laurel Hill was bad," Bernice said next to her.

For Nora, their trek through the Cascade Mountains had been a nightmare. She had struggled down muddy inclines and up steep hills, over roots, branches, fallen trees, mud holes, and frothing streams. Luke had sent her sympathetic glances the whole time but said she didn't dare let the wagon train rest for long in the mountains. If they were caught in a storm, their stock would be killed.

Nora watched as the men chained the wagon wheels and wound ropes around trees to slow down the wagons' descent.

Grim-faced, Luke shook her head. "That won't be enough. We need to tie tree trunks to the wagons for additional braking."

The men cut down a tree and tied it to the end of the first wagon. The branches of the tree gouged deep grooves into the wet soil while the wagon inched down the chute.

Nora clutched Amy's hand and slowly started down the steep road.

This time, their wagon was the last to make the descent, keeping Nora in constant tension. Finally, the wagon reached the end of the scree-covered chute.

"Oh, thank the Lord!" Nora released the breath she had been holding.

A loud snap made her freeze.

With an almost human groan, the wood of one front wheel crumpled. The pots and pans in the wagon clattered, and their one surviving hen cackled in protest as the front end of the wagon came crashing down. The oxen lowed when they were jerked back; then the wagon continued to slide down the hill until it stopped at the bottom. Everything went quiet.

Nora only noticed that she had sunk to her knees when Luke wrapped her arms around her and gently pulled her up and into her arms. "Don't worry," she murmured. "It's not the axle. It's just one of the wheels. I'm sure I can fix it. I just have to unload the wagon and lift it enough so that I can slip the spare wheel on."

Nora relaxed against the comforting warmth of Luke's body. She was glad of Luke's foresight not to abandon the extra wheel somewhere along the road despite the weight it added to the wagon. "Do we have enough time?" she asked. Darkness was already falling. In half an hour, she wouldn't be able to see an inch in front of her.

Luke held her more tightly, then let go. "No. It's gonna have to wait until first light tomorrow morning." She walked over to the Garfields. "Jacob, I want you to take the rest of the wagons and lead them to the Zigzag River. Camp there, rest the stock, and wait for us."

"No." Jacob and the other emigrants around him shook their heads. "We'll stay with you and continue together tomorrow morning."

Nora directed a hopeful glance at Luke. As much as she had sometimes longed for some space and privacy on the crowded trail, now she didn't want to stay behind all alone in the inhospitable mountains.

"I'm sorry," Luke directed her words at Jacob but looked at Nora, "but that's not a good idea. The cattle are exhausted and hungry, and there's not a blade of grass for them right here. We'd have to keep them yoked all night or risk them eating the poisonous laurel that's growing all around here. Zigzag River is a much better camp."

Jacob looked at the weary oxen, at the bushes of laurel, and then back at Luke. Finally, he nodded. "All right. We'll see you tomorrow." He turned toward his wagon.

"Jacob?" Luke called after him. "Do you think you can take Nora and Amy with you?"

"No," Nora said and clutched Luke's sleeve before Jacob could answer. "You can send the others away but not me. Not me. We're your family, and we're not leaving you behind." She sent a defiant glance in Bernice's direction, daring her to object to the term "family."

Bernice met her gaze but said nothing.

Luke studied Nora's face as if gauging her determination. Then she sighed and nodded.

Nora watched as the other wagons slowly continued west. As the last formerly white wagon cover disappeared behind the dense wall of pines and firs, a sense of dread robbed Nora of breath.

"It's just for one night," Luke said and rubbed Nora's shoulder. "All will be fine."

Nora forced a smile. "I know."

∝ρ

"Come on." Luke swung the crying Amy up into her arms, instantly making the tears stop. "Let's build you a nice, cozy nest in the wagon."

The wagon was tilted to one side, standing on only three wheels. The provisions and tools inside had rolled to the side with the damaged wheel, so that left only enough space in the wagon for one person to sleep inside.

Nora put Amy to bed between the familiar contours of the pickle keg and a sack of flour while Luke cut down the branches of an alder to feed the oxen.

Wordlessly, they set up their tent next to the wagon.

Luke unrolled one of the bedrolls and covered it with their blankets and the remaining bedroll. She lay down on the bedroll and patted the remaining space next to her. "Come here. This is the only way of keeping halfway warm tonight."

Nora slipped under the blankets, already shivering with the cold. She sensed the warmth of Luke's skin and moved closer.

Luke's arms settled around her.

Finally, Nora's teeth stopped chattering as she slipped an arm around Luke's waist.

"Maybe it's for the best that the others are miles ahead of us," Luke murmured. "If Bernice saw us, she wouldn't like this."

Nora cuddled even closer, feeling quite at home in the warm embrace. "No, she wouldn't—but I do."

Luke pressed her cheek against the crown of Nora's head. "Hmm, me too."

Nora lifted up on one hand to look into Luke's eyes and noticed that her fingers rested on Luke's chest. She felt the tight bandages that bound Luke's breasts. "Isn't that horribly uncomfortable? To live trapped in those wrappings every hour of every day of your life?"

"It's a small price to pay."

Nora studied the flat chest under her fingers. "Well, it certainly makes your disguise much more convincing. But what about...?" She trailed off, biting her lip.

"What?" Luke's voice rumbled low and intimate right next to her ear.

They had developed that much trust between them that she could ask Luke anything, but still Nora couldn't find the words. Instead, she slid her hand down from its place on Luke's chest, tracing down a muscled abdomen and over a strong thigh. "What do you use to make this look convincing?" She pressed her palm against the area in question.

"Uh." Luke's low moan made goose bumps erupt all over Nora's skin. Luke's hand shot down and covered her own, staying there as if she wasn't sure whether she should snatch Nora's fingers away or press them closer against herself. "Careful." She groaned.

Nora barely resisted the urge to feel around. "Is it some kind of prosthesis?" She had heard a few of the girls in Tess's establishment whisper about such things.

"No. Just a little padding that I sewed into my pants." Nora felt the heat of Luke's cheek against her head as the experienced trail leader blushed like a young girl. "Could you move your hand away, please?" Luke's voice was breathless and husky.

If the bulge that she so artfully displayed was just soft padding in her pants, Nora's touch couldn't have hurt her. So why was Luke sweating and trembling? Nora leaned over her to look into her eyes. The weight of her swollen belly pressed her hand more firmly against Luke.

With a growl, Luke surged forward and captured Nora's lips in a rough kiss. The iron self-control that Nora had always admired finally shattered. With an almost desperate intensity, Luke's mouth robbed her of breath while her hands were trying to be everywhere, do everything at once.

"Slow down." Nora moved back an inch to study the wild expression on Luke's face.

Luke snatched her hands away and sat up, all bodily contact between them gone. "S-sorry. I—"

"Oh, no!" Nora grabbed her shoulder and pulled her back down. "I'm through with this dance of one step forward, two steps back that we've been doing. I'm through with letting Bernice or social conventions dictate my actions. You taught me that I have the right and the skills to decide how I want to live my life—and whom I want to share it with. So this is my decision." She faltered. "Unless, of course, you don't want this…don't want me."

The answer was Luke's lips covering her own again, this time without the desperate urgency, but with a more gentle passion.

At first, Nora reacted with the practiced response of a former prostitute, but Luke didn't let her hide in her usual anonymity. Luke looked intently into Nora's eyes, keeping eye contact as her trembling fingers began to work the tiny buttons of Nora's bodice free.

Years of working in a brothel had left Nora anything but shy about nudity. Her body had been her most powerful instrument. But she hadn't been nine months pregnant then, and she hadn't been with someone whose own body was, in Nora's opinion, as close to perfection as possible. When she had seen Luke's body, she had been wounded and weak, but even then, Luke had reminded her of a picture of Artemis, goddess of the hunt, which she had seen in a book in her father's library. Strong and muscular, with just a hint of softness that prevented her from appearing unyielding and hard. There was something untamed about her, yet tenderness glowed in her eyes.

When Luke stripped her free of bodice and skirt, Nora held her breath, waiting for Luke's reaction.

Luke stopped and hovered over her.

"What is it?" Nora asked.

Luke looked back and forth between Nora's belly and her face. "This won't hurt the baby, will it?"

Nora slipped her fingers into Luke's hair, lovingly fingering the soft, cool strands. She couldn't help being touched by her thoughtfulness. "Don't worry. The baby's fine."

"It won't notice if we…when we…?" Luke awkwardly pointed between Nora and herself.

"I don't think he or she can see through my skin, but if she can feel it, then at least she will know that she'll be born into a loving family," Nora said with a grin.

Luke barked out a surprised laugh.

"Relax," Nora whispered. "Despite whatever Bernice might think about it, I came to believe that there is nothing to be ashamed of about this." She slid her fingers down tense shoulders. "Let me—"

Luke's nervous rigidity disappeared as she rolled around so that she was lying next to Nora, leaning over her on one elbow so she wouldn't press against her belly. Her lips trailed down Nora's neck and over her collarbone, then ghosted over her breasts in a whisperlike touch until they pressed a kiss against Nora's bulging belly through the thin fabric of her chemise.

Nora had never had much patience with the awkward fumbling of her customers, but she found the trembling of Luke's hands as she slipped the skirt down her hips endearing and sweet. How could something she had done so often feel so new and fresh, as if she had never shared her bed and her body with anyone before?

When Luke lifted the chemise over her head, Nora shivered in the cold mountain air. Then, in the next second, heat shot through her when Luke's body pressed against hers again. A strong thigh came to rest against Nora's center, and she stifled a moan.

Luke's long fingers entwined with Nora's smaller ones, stroking a thumb over Nora's palm while her other hand tenderly cupped a heavy breast. She looked at it as if it were an awesome miracle of nature.

Nora followed her gaze, trying to see what Luke was seeing. Pregnancy had darkened the skin around her nipples, and blue veins blemished the normally fair skin.

Then soft lips closed over her sensitive nipple, and Nora instantly forgot her self-critical examination of her own body. Her fingers flexed against the back of Luke's head, pulling her even closer.

Luke's free hand rasped along the underside of her other breast, making her hold her breath in expectation of where that hand would end up. The calluses on Luke's palm, testament to years of hard work, formed an alluring contrast to the gentleness of her touch.

When that hand began a tender massage, Luke pulled her lips away and trailed a line of kisses over Nora's belly. She licked the sensitive spot between Nora's belly and thigh.

Nora arched upward.

Luke's hands followed her lips downward, making heat flash along the same path.

"Luke…" Nora gasped for breath.

"Sssh. Your turn to relax. Don't worry, you're safe with me." Luke's words tickled against her skin. Then Luke moved back a few inches and loosened the ribbon that held back Nora's hair. She stared at the red waves that came tumbling down over Nora's shoulders. "You're beautiful," Luke whispered.

Nora couldn't believe that anyone could find her beautiful with her very pregnant, dust-covered body, but the awe in Luke's voice left no doubt about her sincerity.

Luke gazed directly into Nora's eyes, smoothing an errant strand of hair from her forehead while her other hand drew sensuous circles around Nora's breast. The intensity of her gaze was almost overwhelming, and Nora felt it like a touch. "What do you want me to do?"

Nora blinked. Thinking and answering questions was becoming difficult under Luke's distracting touches. "W-what?"

"How do you want me? How should I touch you?" Luke asked.

Nobody had asked her that for years, if ever. She gave Luke a tremulous smile. "However you want to."

"No. However you want to. What do you like? I can do whatever you want me to. Well, except for certain obvious acts, of course." Luke looked away.

Oh. Nora understood. Luke was referring to the fact that physically she was not a man. Obviously, she assumed that Nora would think their lovemaking inferior to anything that she could experience with a man. Nora reached out and touched Luke's cheek, watching her eyelids flutter shut at the touch. "I got to 'enjoy' that particular act in abundance during the last few years. I'm not going to miss it, believe me."

Luke still hovered over her. "So you don't like…?" She stopped and gestured.

"Luke," Nora stopped the nervous discussion, "all appearances aside, you are still a woman."

Luke stared at her with wide eyes. "Um, yes, I guess. I mean—"

"When it comes down to it, our bodies are basically the same," Nora said. "You know what would feel good to you, so why not just assume that I'd like it too?"

Luke took a deep breath. Finally, she nodded and lowered her lips to Nora's again. Her eyes still locked to Nora's, she slowly opened the drawstring closure of Nora's drawers and slid the undergarment down her hips. When Luke looked down at Nora's naked body, her eyes glittered with curiosity and something else that Nora couldn't identify.

Nora shivered under the intense gaze.

Luke moved closer. The blanket still covering Luke's shoulders settled over both of them, blocking out the rest of the world. Luke tenderly smoothed the tip of her finger down Nora's cheek, then kissed the curve of her neck. The warm touch of Luke's lips explored the arch of her collarbones, then trailed open-mouthed kisses over her chest until she nuzzled Nora's breast, this time without the barrier of her chemise.

Nora shuddered. She clutched Luke's shoulders, holding her close against her.

Luke moved back a few inches and looked up at her. "I'm not hurting you, am I?"

The words, spoken so close against Nora's skin, only increased Nora's shivering. "No," she said, reaching down to smooth back the unruly, dark hair that fell onto Luke's forehead. "But with me being with child, they're very sensitive."

"Oh." Luke softly stroked the side of a breast. "I didn't know that."

"That doesn't mean you have to stop. It feels very nice," Nora said.

A slow smile curled Luke's lips before Nora lost sight of them as the tender touches continued and she closed her eyes.

Luke slowly moved down her body. She stopped at Nora's belly. She laid both of her palms against the swell of her abdomen as if to establish some kind of contact.

Nora had assumed that Luke would ignore her belly and just try to work around the limitations that came with her pregnancy. The reverent kisses that Luke placed all over her belly brought tears to her eyes, and she quickly wiped them away, knowing that Luke would become concerned if she saw them.

Luke laid her cheek against Nora's belly, pressing her ear against her skin.

"What are you doing?" Nora lifted her head from the bedroll. She couldn't help smiling as she looked down at Luke. Physical relations had never been like this for her. With most partners, the sexual act would have been over by now, but Luke hadn't even touched her most intimate areas and seemed in no hurry to do it.

"Hush." Luke's ear was still pressed to Nora's belly, her expression one of intense concentration. "I'm talking to your daughter."

Nora swallowed down the sudden lump in her throat. "What's she saying?" she whispered hoarsely.

Luke grinned. "She's complaining."

"About what?"

Luke pretended to listen again. "She says all that rocking and squirming of her temporary home is keeping her awake."

"Well, tell her it can't be helped." She pulled Luke closer.

"Sorry, little one," Luke whispered against her skin, "your temporary home says it can't be helped. You can get back at her for keeping you up all night later this year." After one final kiss to Nora's belly, Luke moved on, raining kisses across the rounded curve of Nora's hip.

"All night?" Nora gasped when the warm lips wandered down her thigh and then nuzzled the sensitive spot behind one knee.

Luke hummed her agreement against Nora's calf. She rubbed her cheek against the skin of Nora's ankle, reminding Nora of a big, purring cat, then tenderly kissed a blister that had formed on Nora's heel.

The kisses continued until Nora felt that every inch of her had been worshipped. Despite still being fully clothed, Luke made love with her whole body and to Nora's whole body, not just the one part of it that men usually concentrated on. *I wonder if it's always like this with a woman.*

Then all thoughts ceased as Luke's lips found the one spot on her body that they hadn't touched yet. Her eyes snapped open. "Luke!"

Soft hair tickled Nora's thigh as Luke lifted her head and stared up at her. "You don't like it?"

"No. I mean, I think I do…enjoy it, I mean." *Lord, and here I thought I was the experienced one. She's only ever been with one person in her life, and yet she's making me tremble and stammer like a virgin on her wedding night.* Another thought occurred to her.

Luke echoed the smile with one of her own. She moved back up to lie next to Nora. "What are you smiling about?"

Nora kissed her. "Well, it just occurred to me that this could be considered our wedding night."

Luke's body jerked against hers. Then Luke laughed, a sound that rumbled through Nora and made goose bumps break out all over her skin. "Great." She frowned playfully. "Now you're making me nervous."

Nora threaded her fingers through Luke's hair. "You've got nothing to be nervous about. You're doing great," she said and meant it.

They stared into each other's eyes for endless moments. Their lips collided in a deep kiss.

When Luke slipped one hand between Nora's thighs, Nora broke the kiss with a gasp. Her hips surged up to meet the gentle touch.

"Like this?" Luke asked, continuing with the light, slow strokes, barely brushing against Nora.

Dazed, Nora looked up into her face. Luke's question held no trace of the smug teasing of some of her former sexual partners. Luke was asking for guidance. She struggled for breath. "Y-yeah. This is… Good God!" She moaned when Luke's fingers began a circling motion. "It's nice. So good."

Luke leaned closer, pressing her lips against the thudding pulse at the base of Nora's throat. The movement made her fingers dip into Nora.

A moan escaped Nora's parted lips. She bucked against the gently invading fingers, clutching at Luke in wordless desperation.

"All right?" Luke tried to move back to study her face, but Nora held her close.

"Don't stop!" Nora panted. She already felt the pressure grow in the pit of her stomach.

Luke began to move her fingers, still torturously slow, exploring, discovering, in no hurry to drive Nora over the edge.

Nora shook her head back and forth. She moved her hips faster, trying to get Luke to pick up the pace, but Luke was having none of it.

"Relax. Enjoy." Luke's hot breath washed over Nora's ear. "We're not in a hurry." She withdrew her fingers, then slowly eased them back inside.

Nora met the movement with a moan. Her belly and her sensitive breasts rubbed against Luke. Heat shot through her. "Maybe I am. Luke…"

"Hmm?" Luke experimentally smoothed her thumb over the firm nub.

Another wave of heat shot through Nora. "Luke!" She threw her head back.

Luke's lips immediately took advantage. She nibbled on Nora's throat, then sucked at the sensitive spot just under one ear while her fingers continued their unwaveringly slow movements.

Nora squirmed and wrapped a leg around Luke, drawing her closer. "Please!"

All movement stopped for a moment. Luke stared into Nora's half-closed eyes. "Tell me what you want me to do." There was still a hint of insecurity in her voice even though Nora's body insisted that Luke knew exactly what she was doing.

Nora stared up at her, for the first time helpless to voice her desires. She wasn't even sure what she wanted. Luke's slow, gentle touches were driving her crazy, but at the same time, she didn't want it to end so soon.

Her back had other ideas, though. Lying on her back for too long made her lower back hurt. Slowly, she rolled around, careful not to lose the connection between their bodies, until she was straddling Luke. She waited, unsure if Luke would be comfortable with being the one in the more submissive position. *Being on top is the traditionally male position, and if Luke…* Her thoughts and worries died away when Luke began to move her fingers again.

Nora bit back another moan. Sitting astride Luke's muscled hips, she began to rock against the gentle fingers.

Luke brought her free hand up, resting it in the small of her back to steady her and hold her even closer.

Nora leaned forward. She searched Luke's lips with her own, moaning into her mouth. Her hips began to move faster, and this time, Luke willingly followed the pace she dictated. Blood roared through Nora's ears, and she could no longer understand the words Luke whispered to her.

Luke sat up and wrapped one arm around Nora.

The rough fabric of Luke's shirt rasped across her sensitive breasts. Nora gasped and rocked even faster. "Luke." The ball of pleasure in her lower belly began to spread. She groaned and flung her head back.

Then Luke's mouth was on her heaving breast, grazing the tip with gentle teeth.

Nora dug her fingers into Luke's back to anchor herself as the tremors began deep inside her. With a cry, she collapsed, only Luke's steadying hand keeping her from falling.

As if from some distance away, she felt Luke gently ease her down. "Nora," she whispered, over and over, "Nora." It sounded almost like a prayer. She kissed away the droplets of sweat that glittered on Nora's chest and face. "Are you all right?" Luke smoothed damp hair away from Nora's face with the back of her fingers.

Nora could only nod. She lay there, dazedly pressing her flushed cheek against Luke's still covered chest. The frantic thumping beneath her ear matched the rhythm of her own heart. *Lord, that was…* She allowed herself a few moments to revel in those feelings, then shook her head at herself. *What are you, some love-sick young girl? So it was a lot more pleasant than being with a customer, but that's hardly a surprise, is it?*

Being with Luke had been exactly as she had thought it would be—a bit hesitant at first and very, very gentle with just the right amount of passion thrown in. Luke had been the considerate lover she had expected her to be. What Nora couldn't have predicted, though, was her own reaction.

It wasn't only that Luke had managed to bring her to climax—although that had never been a given in the past. But that was just mechanics. What surprised her were the emotions Luke's touch had evoked in her. Gone was the clinical distance she had felt with her customers. For the first time in years, she hadn't been Fleur when she shared her body with someone. She had been Nora.

Luke gently kissed her cheek, almost as if she were unsure whether she was still allowed a more intimate kiss now that their act of physical loving was over. "Was I…was it enough?" she asked, her gaze never leaving Nora's face.

Nora could practically feel waves of insecurity flowing from Luke. She wasn't sure what made Luke doubt her ability to please her in bed—her lack of male "equipment" or the fact that she had so much less sexual experience than Nora. "Enough?" She barely stopped herself from rolling her eyes. "God, Luke, this was so much more than just adequate. Is it always like this with a woman?" Most men she'd met believed that a woman existed solely to provide for their comfort, but Luke had concentrated only on Nora's pleasure.

Luke halted in her self-imposed task of raining kisses down on Nora's face. She smiled. "Well, it's not like I have vast experience with a lot of women. I've only ever been with Tess, and no, it was never like this between us. I enjoyed Tess's…talents, but deep down… There always remained a nagging belief that it's wrong to have relations with another woman. But with you, it just feels so right."

Nora swallowed through a parched throat. The emotion in Luke's eyes was almost too much to bear. "Yes," she whispered. "It felt wonderful."

Nora lay in silence. She felt her heartbeat quieten and her breathing slow. After a while, she pushed up on her elbow, slid the suspenders off Luke's shoulders, and started to undo the buttons of her shirt.

"You don't have to do this," Luke said, her voice husky.

Nora playfully pushed her back down. "Shut up, Mister Hamilton."

Luke lay still and stared up at her. "You know that there's no Mister under these clothes, don't you?"

Nora pressed a kiss to the collarbone she had just laid bare. "I wouldn't be doing this if there was."

"Really?" Luke studied her. "You…you want to touch me because of my body, not in spite of it?"

Nora rested her chin on her hand to stare down at Luke. "Why is that so hard to believe? You prefer touching a female body to that of a man too, don't you?"

"Yeah, but I'm hardly the norm, and you—"

"And I found out that I'm not all that different from you in that regard," Nora said. "I haven't been attracted to a man in so long, and it really surprised me that there was something about my new husband that was so appealing to me." She grinned down at Luke. "Well, I guess now I know what that 'something' was that made you so special."

She reached out to open the second button, but Luke stopped her again. "Nora—"

"Don't do this to me," Nora said.

"To you?" Luke echoed.

"Yeah. You brought me great pleasure, and now I want to touch you too."

Luke squirmed. "I'm not sure I can…or should. What if—"

"Luke, you have trusted me with your revolver, with the oxen, and the wagon. You even trusted me with your secret and your very life. Please, trust me with this."

"Are you sure you want to do this?"

"I wouldn't have initiated this if I wasn't. I'm not some wide-eyed, innocent girl, Luke. I know you, and I know myself." Nora smoothed her hands over tense shoulders. "I will neither be surprised nor abhorred by your body. You don't have to keep up the façade of a man. Not with me."

Luke stared up at her with almost childlike wonder. Then she shook her head. "You want to make love to a woman, but I don't know how to be anything but a man."

"I don't want you to act like a woman or a man. Don't act at all—just be yourself, all right?"

Luke gave her a shaky nod. "I'll try to remember just who exactly that is."

Nora raised herself up on her knees. Her belly rested against Luke's side as she undid button after button. Finally, she slipped the shirt off the strong shoulders. "Lift your arms," she said and then helped Luke to slip the sleeveless undershirt over her barely healed shoulder and over her head.

Then both of them sat and stared down at the coverings around Luke's chest.

Nora's first impulse was to take them off as fast as possible, but then she paused. Luke had let her make all the decisions, had made sure that she felt comfortable at every turn while she had made love to her. Now she would do the same for Luke. "Would you be more comfortable if we leave that in place for now?" She nodded at the thick bandages holding down Luke's breasts.

"Would I be more comfortable? Yeah." Luke let out a shuddering breath. "I've never let anyone touch me there, and I'm not sure I can—"

"You don't have to." Nora lifted one strong hand to her lips and kissed it. "No expectations and no pressure, all right? I'd like to see and touch you, all of you, but if you can't do that, you just tell me and we can find another way."

Luke paused. "I want to give you whatever gives you pleasure. I just didn't expect it to be my body." Slowly, she straightened her shoulders. "I do trust you. Let's take them off."

Nora reached out her hands but then stopped again. "Do you want to do it yourself?" Maybe Luke would feel less nervous if she could control what they did and when they did it.

Luke nodded. She reached around her chest to find the secured ends of the wrappings. Slowly, she peeled back layer after layer of the bandages, uncovering the soft skin beneath.

Nora watched the process without moving. She studied the small breasts, so much firmer than her own. The fair skin of Luke's chest contrasted with her tanned neck, face, and arms. Her gaze wandered over the defined muscles of her abdomen, over powerful shoulders until it reached strong, but gentle hands. Luke was a curious combination of male and female characteristics. Any lover that Luke had would find whatever she wanted in Luke—a gentle man or a strong woman, whatever she preferred. Luke, desperate for some affection, would play every role that her lover expected of her.

In the beginning, Nora had been no different. She had wanted a loyal husband and a kind father, and Luke had been both. Now she wanted to experience making love to a woman, and Luke willingly revealed her female form. Her whole life, Luke had played a role to survive, and she had become so adept at it that she could no longer separate the role and the person behind it.

A sudden determination gripped Nora. She promised herself that she wouldn't try to force Luke to fit into any mold, may it be that of a man or that of a woman. She would accept every part of Luke equally.

When Nora just sat and looked at her, Luke squirmed. She crossed her arms in front of her chest, covering her exposed breasts.

Nora looked away from her body and directly into her eyes. "Don't be afraid," she whispered. "I won't hurt you."

Luke gave her a shaky grin. "I'm not sure if that reassures me or makes me even more nervous. I've always been the protector, never the scared woman."

Nora reached for Luke's hand and pressed a kiss against the palm, then to every one of the fingers that had brought her so much pleasure. Next, her lips caressed the tiny hairs on Luke's forearms and pressed soft kisses to the bend of her elbow. She slid her palms over the tense shoulders, kneading them for a moment before her fingers dipped into the hollow at the base of her throat. This spot seemed so vulnerable, so female, that Nora couldn't help pressing a tender kiss against it. The strong muscles vibrated beneath her hands and lips. Her gaze flickered up to the familiar face. "Tell me if it gets to be too much."

Luke nodded.

Nora traced the arch of Luke's ribs and trailed a single finger over the outer swell of her breast.

Luke stiffened. She was trembling and almost hyperventilating under Nora's touch, and Nora could see that it wasn't just caused by arousal. Being touched as a woman was scary for Luke, and yet she made no move to turn away or hide from her.

Luke's trust took Nora's breath away. "How does this feel?" she whispered, stroking the breast.

"I can't decide if I want to run away or grab your hand and press it against me more firmly," Luke answered hoarsely.

Nora bent down, letting her breath wash over one hard nipple. "Well, I pronounce myself in favor of option number two, but there are other ways to do this if this is too much right now. Just tell me what you want me to do. What did Tess—?"

"No." Luke touched her lips to silence her. "We're not in a brothel. You're not Tess, and I'm not a customer. This is me and you."

Nora nodded. Secretly, she was very pleased with that answer. "So, we're turning over a new leaf?" *New land, new life, new roles.*

"Let's try. I think we could both do with some changes in our lives."

"Well, then let's change you out of these clothes for starters," Nora said, trying to introduce some playful humor into the tense situation. Sexuality hadn't been fun for her in the last few years. It had been a means to an end, sometimes even a matter of life and death. With Luke, it had been wonderful and fun. She had enjoyed the little playful gestures, like the conversation with the unborn baby, that Luke had used to relax her. She would try to do the same for Luke.

Luke held her breath as Nora worked the button on her pants free and pushed them down over Luke's hips.

When the pants pooled around Luke's ankles, Nora pulled them off and eyed the phallus-shaped padding Luke had sewn into the crotch of her pants. "I'm impressed," she said with a little smirk.

Heat suffused Luke's cheeks. "It's not that big."

Nora laughed. "Not with the size of this thing. I'm impressed with your skills as a seamstress."

"Oh, yeah, of course." Luke felt her blush deepen.

"God, you're sweet." Nora smiled. "Lie with me." She waited until Luke had settled down on the bedroll again, then reclined on her side to Luke's right. She curled her body against Luke's side as much as her large belly allowed her to and nestled a thigh between Luke's.

For long seconds, they lay pressed against each other without moving, Luke's finely muscled torso molded to Nora's soft curves. Their breasts pressed against each other, and Luke sucked in a breath. She had never experienced a sensation like that before.

She concentrated on that feeling until Nora's thigh gently nudged her legs farther apart and pressed against her center. She groaned but relaxed a little. This was a sensation that she knew from her encounters with Tess.

But Nora didn't content herself with doing the things that Tess had done to her. Instead, she started to place a long line of kisses down Luke's neck, over her shoulder, and then, in smaller and smaller circles, around one of her breasts. The golden-red hair fell like a curtain onto Luke's chest, blocking out the sight of Nora's lips on her breast.

Quickly, Luke reached out and brushed back the reddish strands. She needed to see to fully realize that this was her body that Nora was making love to.

Nora's lips formed a sensuous O as they wrapped around Luke's nipple. The gentle sucking would have made Luke lose her balance if she hadn't already been lying down. She rolled her head from side to side on the bedroll. "Nora." With Tess, she had always hated that helpless need in her voice because it made her feel vulnerable and out of control. The effect that Nora had on her was even stronger, but she trusted Nora enough to let her see the person behind that tough, in-control exterior.

Nora's nose bumped against the underside of the other breast as she moved over to lavish kisses on it.

The soft sighs and murmurs of pleasure escaping Nora's mouth as she caressed, kissed, and nibbled Luke's breasts were as astonishing for Luke as the touches themselves. She had never imagined that someone could get so much pleasure from her breasts. For Luke, they had always been more of an annoyance. *Jesus!* Luke arched her back as Nora gently bit her nipple. *Guess she's on a mission to change that.*

Nora created a path of heat as she moved downward with sensuous licks, playful nips, and a variety of kisses. She stopped to suck on the skin an inch below Luke's navel.

Luke's stomach muscles tensed. She shivered.

Nora scraped her fingernails over the few fine hairs below Luke's navel. Her fingers stopped when they reached the patch of dark curls. Nora looked up and raised a questioning eyebrow.

Luke's heart raced. She nodded at Nora to continue. With a hint of disbelief, she watched Nora's slender fingers comb through the curly hair between her legs. She had never thought that she would see Nora do that outside of her dreams. She shuddered when the fingers grazed the sensitive flesh beneath. Lifting her head to look at Nora, she took in the expression of quiet wonder on her face. *This is new, scary, and wonderful for her too.* The realization that Nora wanted her, desired her, was overwhelming. Then her head fell back onto the bedroll as Nora touched her a little more firmly.

Nora's lips, warm despite the cold air around them, followed the path of her hands. She nuzzled the dark curls, then kissed the soft skin of a thigh.

Luke gently touched a strand of red hair, needing to connect with Nora.

Nora looked up at her.

Luke's heart began to beat even faster under the heat of that gaze. Tess had always looked at her with affection and told her she enjoyed the change of pace of being with a woman every once in a while, but Luke had never seen the raw desire that she had felt reflected back at her.

Now she did. Nora was not an emotionally unaffected participant in this.

Luke let go of Nora's hair as Nora's lips wandered up her inner thigh, afraid to hurt her should she lose control. She didn't want to do anything that might remind Nora of the experiences she had at the hands of some customers in the brothel. She clutched at the bedroll instead, desperately trying to anchor herself.

Nora took a deep breath. Her nostrils quivered as she breathed in Luke's scene. She hummed, then lowered her head and kissed Luke's most intimate place as she would kiss her lips.

Luke gasped at the incredible sensation.

Experimentally, Nora flicked her tongue over the swollen nub beneath her lips.

The muscles in Luke's legs stiffened. She bucked her hips.

Nora reached out a hand, gently urging Luke's fingers to let go of the bedroll and entwine with hers. She playfully rubbed her nose against Luke's inner thigh. Her warm breath met Luke's center.

"Oh." Luke shuddered.

Nora's tongue slid against her again, tasting her.

Luke's hips began to rise and fall under Nora's mouth. She clutched Nora's fingers, trying to hold on to reality. Her thighs pressed against Nora's ears.

Nora curled her lips around Luke's clit, just holding it for a second.

A gentle pulsing began deep inside of Luke. "Nora!" She groaned. "God, Nora." Her free hand cupped Nora's cheek, neither pushing her away, nor forcing her closer, just establishing another connection between them.

Nora closed her lips over Luke and started to suckle. "Good?" she whispered against Luke.

Luke trembled and quivered under her. "I-it's—Nnnnngh! Nora!" The words died on her lips as Nora's touch continued. A slow pulsing started in her belly. She stiffened, her legs closing around Nora and pressing her even closer against her. With a hoarse cry, she fell back onto the bedroll.

Nora gently kissed the pulsing nub once more, then moved up. Her sweat-dampened body slid against Luke's, making her moan again.

Luke lay still and tried to catch her breath. Her lids seemed to weigh a ton as she forced them open and stared up at Nora. "Nora," she whispered, at a loss for other words.

Nora brushed her lips against Luke's temple and held her close. "Are you all right?"

Luke pulled her even closer, enjoying the feeling of their bare bodies pressing against each other. She nodded shakily, then leaned forward and kissed Nora with languid slowness. When she tasted herself on Nora's lips, she jerked back for a moment before she deepened the kiss. "I love you," she whispered against Nora's lips.

Now it was Nora's turn to jerk back. "Luke," she said slowly, warningly. She moved away from the tight embrace, holding Luke at arm's length. "I can imagine that this was an overwhelming experience for you, and I know that in the heat of passion—"

"The heat of passion is not why I fell in love with you," Luke said. "I experienced the heat of passion with Tess, but I never thought I was in love with her. I don't love you because you shared the bedroll, your body, and this incredible night with me. I love you because..." She thought for a moment, then shook her head. "There are too many reasons to even count. Nora, you are a wonderful woman, and the way you grew into yourself during this journey just takes my breath away. I know in my heart and in my soul that you're the right one for me. Can't you feel the connection between us?" She turned desperate eyes on Nora, silently pleading for a sign that her feelings were returned.

Nora touched her cheek in a calming gesture, and Luke immediately pressed her face into the soft touch. "Of course I do," Nora said. "We formed a very special friendship during the last few months. But love? I thought we agreed that love is not for us? Remember back at the Boise River?"

"I changed my mind. You changed my mind," Luke said. It hurt to know that Nora didn't feel the same. For one second, she'd almost let herself believe that Nora might be able to love her. *You should have known better, you fool. Did you really think that a woman as wonderful as Nora could love someone like you?*

With a pained expression, Nora pressed her hands against her lower belly. "Oww."

Luke's eyes widened. "What's wrong? Did I hurt you earlier?"

"No, of course not. If anything, you should be proud."

"Proud?" Seeing Nora in obvious pain made Luke feel anything but.

Nora gave her a tight smile. "That orgasm was quite intense. I'm still pulsing." She rubbed her lower belly again.

Luke bit her lip and averted her eyes. Being able to bring Nora pleasure had been an amazing experience, but without Nora's love, the pleasure didn't really mean anything. Even though she was still lying wrapped in Nora's arms, she felt lonely. She sat up and put the bandages back around her chest. The familiar protective layers didn't shield her heart from the hurt, though. With a sigh, she pulled the blankets up around them and closed her eyes, trying to drown out her thoughts. She just wanted to sleep, dream of making love to Nora, and forget about everything that had happened afterward.

Nora settled down on her side, her cheek against Luke's shoulder. She closed her eyes too, but Luke felt that she wasn't relaxed at all. "Luke," she said after a few minutes.

Luke didn't want to talk about it anymore, but finally she sighed and answered, "Yeah?"

"I think the baby's coming."

The blanket went flying when Luke snapped upward. "What? You don't mean now?"

"I'm afraid, yes." Nora frowned. "My back aches, and my lower belly clenches rhythmically. I don't think it has anything to do with my orgasm, or it would have stopped by now instead of getting worse."

Luke shrugged into her shirt and tried to close the buttons with trembling fingers. "I'll go for help, bring Bernice back here."

Nora held on to the pants that Luke wanted to pull up. "No. If you go, I'll be trapped all alone in these godforsaken mountains. You'll never find them in the darkness and bring back help in time. I can't do this alone, Luke."

Luke closed her eyes for a moment. She pushed her feelings back into the recesses of her mind. There would be time to deal with what had happened between them later. "Then I'll stay and help you."

"Have you ever helped with a birth?"

"Yeah. More than a dozen times."

Nora blinked. "You have?"

"Mostly, I just sat back and watched, but once or twice I had to reach inside and—"

"Reach inside?" Nora clenched her teeth as another wave of pain started.

Luke pulled up her pants and knelt down next to Nora. "Yeah. When the mare had problems—"

"Mare?" Nora spat out with a pained groan. "What are you talking about?"

"I was a ranch hand and a dragoon for years. I helped when the mares had their foals."

Nora pointed a warning finger at her. "I'm not having a foal."

Jacob had reminded her to never argue with a pregnant woman. Apparently, the same went doubly for women in labor. Luke decided that in this case, discretion was the better part of valor. She quickly changed the topic. "What can I do to help you?"

"Right now, you can only do what you did with your horses: sit back and watch," Nora answered. "Ouch." She groaned and gritted her teeth. Her hands gripped the bedroll.

"Are you sure there isn't anything I can do?" It was hard for Luke to see Nora in pain without being able to do anything to help her. "Do you want a cup of water?" At Nora's nod, she hurried to the wagon. Her fingers trembled when she opened the water barrel, and she had to concentrate not to spill the water on her way back. She knelt down and helped Nora to slowly sip the water.

"Luke, calm down." Nora stroked the fingers that were clenched around the cup. "This is gonna take a while, and I need you calm."

"A while? How long exactly?" Luke asked, fighting against her rising panic. *She should have been safely in Oregon City to give birth or at least with the other women on the train, not here, trapped in the mountains, with only a nervous former soldier to help her.*

Nora shrugged. "When I gave birth to Amy, I was in labor for eighteen hours."

"Eighteen hours?" Luke's voice came out as a squeak.

"Don't look at me like that," Nora said. "Do you think it was my idea? If God had asked me my opinion before deciding on a birthing process, you'd be able to order babies straight from *Godey's Lady's Book*. Besides, I think the midwife said something about it not lasting so long with the second baby."

"You think?"

"I didn't listen all that closely at that time," Nora said. "After those eighteen long hours, I was determined that Amy was gonna stay an only child anyway."

During the next few hours, Luke began to understand that sentiment. For the first time in her life, she was glad not to be a man, because she didn't want Nora to ever have to go through this again. The contractions were getting progressively stronger, longer, and closer together until they seemed to come without any pause between them.

Luke tried everything to make Nora a bit more comfortable. She massaged Nora's lower back, where she seemed to feel the pain the most, and wiped away the sweat beading on her forehead with a cool cloth. She fought her way through the dense forest to gather wood that was dry enough to build a fire.

Then, finally, when the first gray light of predawn lit the sky, the pushing and bearing down began.

Luke was getting more worried by the minute. Nora already seemed exhausted.

Another contraction ripped through her. Nora grunted in pain as she bore down again. When the pain finally eased, she fell back, panting heavily, until the next contraction started. "This is all your fault," she ground out between clenched teeth.

Luke froze, her hand with the cloth suspended in midair. She swallowed. "Me? I didn't father that child."

"No, but you gave me the orgasm that induced labor," Nora said.

"Oh." Luke bit her lip and decided to just shut up.

When the next contraction hit her, Nora let out a loud cry. "God, that burns." She gasped and panted when the wave of pain finally receded. "Please tell me that you can at least see the head by now."

Luke, resting frozen on her knees, numbly shook her head.

"You have to look to see anything," Nora yelled.

With hesitation, Luke pulled back the blanket resting over Nora's bent knees and took a peek. Her eyes widened, and she had to press both palms to the ground not to topple over. "I-I can see the baby's head." She gazed up at Nora, trying her best to look encouraging. "It won't be long now, just a few more pushes."

"Mama? Papa?" Amy's voice came from inside of the wagon.

Panic threatened to overwhelm Luke for a second. She couldn't deal with this at the same time too. Then she straightened her shoulders and gave Nora a reassuring nod. "I'll get her to settle back down. I'll be right back." She took the five steps to the wagon, using the time it took her to hide her nervousness from Amy, and looked down at the girl with a calming smile. "Sweetie, you should be sleeping."

"Why is Mama shouting at you?" Amy asked.

"She wasn't shouting. She was..." Luke trailed her fingers through her hair. "She was just talking loudly. All is fine. I promise."

The worried expression finally faded from Amy's face. "Can I sleep with you and Mama?"

Luke knew she couldn't let Amy leave the wagon. It would scare her to see her mother in so much pain. *God knows it's scaring me.* "Tomorrow, all right? If you go back to sleep, I promise that I'll have a big surprise for you when you wake up."

Amy settled back under her blanket.

"Good girl." Luke breathed a sigh of relief. She pressed a gentle kiss to Amy's forehead and started to turn back around when another pained groan could be heard from Nora.

"Mama!" Amy shot back up.

"No, no, no, little one, you stay right here." Luke gently pressed her back down. "Your mama has a bit of a bellyache, but it will be better soon." *At least I hope it will.*

"Luke!" Nora moaned from inside of the tent.

Luke took one last glance at Amy. "Stay here, please. I'll come and get you as soon as I've helped your mother." She hurried back and knelt down next to a panting Nora.

"How's Amy?" Nora asked in a strangled whisper.

"Just fine. She'll be asleep again in a moment," Luke said, knowing it was a lie. She didn't want to add to Nora's distress. Worrying about one child at a time was more than enough for the moment. She peeked under Nora's blanket again. "You're doing good. The head is almost out. One more push should do it, I think."

Nora dug her heels into the bedroll when the next contraction peaked. Her face started to turn red, and she took Luke's hand in a viselike grip. Her other hand was pressed against her mouth, trying to hold back a scream.

Luke could practically feel her bones grind together. She winced but didn't draw back. She was sure that the pain in her hand was nothing compared to what Nora was going through. She looked under the blanket again. "Nora. Let go of my hand!"

The baby's head was finally out, but it was covered with a sacklike membrane, making it impossible for the baby to breathe. Luke had seen a similar thing with the horses she had helped to deliver. She gently pinched the membrane, which broke and released a fluid. With one of the clean cloths she had prepared earlier, Luke cleaned the tiny face.

"Is the baby all right?" Nora panted between contractions.

"She's fine," Luke said. "Just one more push and you can see for yourself." She steadied the baby's head when the next contraction started and Nora bore down again. With trembling fingers, she guided the first shoulder out and then quickly had to grab the baby when it slipped from Nora's body.

The baby instantly started to cry.

Nora collapsed back onto the bedroll.

Luke tied off the umbilical cord with strips of cotton and cut it, then quickly cleaned the baby and wrapped it in her last clean shirt. She sat back and stared at the tiny bundle in her arms. Tears burned in her eyes. Afraid that she would drop the baby should she try to stand, she moved forward on her knees until she could place the baby in Nora's arms.

Nora caressed the baby's face with the tip of her index finger, tracing the tiny features with the same expression of wonder that Luke felt. She opened the shirt a bit to count her fingers and toes. "A girl," she said, her voice hoarse and shaky. She looked up at Luke.

"Yeah. She's beautiful." *Like her mother.* Even with her blotchy red face and sweat-dampened hair, Nora was beautiful to Luke.

Nora looked down at her newborn daughter. The baby's face was a little bluish but quickly gained a normal color, and she blinked up at her mother with puffy, unfocused eyes. "Yes, she is. Look at all that black hair." She stroked the dark fuzz on the baby's head. "She looks like you."

Luke swallowed but didn't say anything. She wanted so much to be a part of that baby, to be a part of her life, but she wasn't sure if that dream would ever come true.

The newborn began to nuzzle against Nora, and she lifted her to her breast.

Luke watched in awe as the baby began to nurse. She had never seen anything as beautiful as this. "God," she whispered, afraid of destroying the moment should she speak more loudly. "I love you."

Nora closed her eyes. "Luke, don't say that. Not when I can't say it back."

Luke shrugged. She hadn't thought about it—if she had, she certainly wouldn't have made a fool of herself a second time. It had slipped out before she could censor herself. Still, she couldn't deny her feelings even if Nora would never return them.

Someone cleared their throat at the tent's opening.

Luke looked away from mother and child, expecting to see Amy, who had climbed out of the wagon.

Instead, she met Bernice Garfield's disapproving gaze.

"Bernice." Nora grinned up at the older woman. "Look who has decided that she didn't want to wait until we reached Oregon City to be born." She held up the bundle in her arms with a tired, but proud smile.

The steely expression on Bernice's face softened. "I had a feeling something like this would happen. That's why I made Jacob bring me back at the first hint of daylight. I had a bad feeling about leaving you behind all on your own."

"I wasn't on my own," Nora said. "Luke was with me, and he did a wonderful job."

The smile vanished from Bernice's face when she looked at Luke. "Maybe it would be better for this innocent child if you stayed out of her life," Bernice said.

"What's the meaning of this, Bernice?" Jacob's voice thundered behind them. He had come up behind his wife. "You're not making any sense. Of course Luke is gonna be a part of the baby's life. He's her father, for heaven's sake."

Bernice took a deep breath and opened her mouth.

Luke squeezed her eyes shut. With just a few words, Bernice would destroy her life and take away the only family she had ever known.

"Jacob, please, I didn't mean it like that," Bernice said.

Jacob stared her down. "How did you mean it, then?"

Bernice wrung her hands but remained silent.

The older woman went up a few notches in Luke's estimation. Bernice had never left any doubt about her disapproval, but now she was risking her husband's wrath by protecting Luke's secret.

"Explain yourself, wife." Jacob stood with his arms crossed, not moving an inch.

"You heard what Nora said," Bernice said, addressing Luke. "Nora doesn't love you. She—"

"What are you talking about?" Jacob asked. "A blind man could see that she does. The night Nora almost lost her baby, you even told me—"

Bernice gave a reluctant nod. "I know what I said. But back then, I didn't know…"

"Didn't know what?" Jacob asked when Bernice fell silent.

Bernice shook her head, refusing to answer.

Her husband's face took on the color of an overripe tomato.

"What she didn't know back then is that the baby isn't really mine," Luke said before the situation could escalate further. "Nora was already pregnant when I married her." Admitting to that was a small price to pay for keeping her secret safe and helping Bernice out of her desperate situation.

Jacob stared at the baby for a moment, then rested his gaze on Nora before he looked back at Luke. "But you're willing to raise her as your own?"

Luke nodded without hesitation. "I couldn't love her more if I had fathered her myself." She didn't say it just for Jacob's benefit. Holding the baby in her arms for the first time, she had immediately felt the love that she held for the baby's mother extend to the little girl too.

Jacob turned a steely gaze at his wife. "Then what is this nonsense about him staying out of the baby's life? Didn't you once say that you consider the man who provides and cares for a child the father even if he isn't by blood? Does that mean you changed your mind?"

"No, no, that's not… I don't mean that at all. It's just… He…" Bernice gestured at Luke but couldn't explain without revealing Luke's secret.

Jacob didn't even listen. "Then maybe you want me to disappear from Wayne's life too?" His normally calm voice vibrated with emotion.

Luke stared from one Garfield to the other. What was going on between them? Their discussion didn't seem to be about her and Nora anymore.

After long moments of tense silence, Jacob turned to her, his expression like stone. "I didn't father Wayne, but I always considered him mine anyway. I thought that Bernice did too, but it seems that's not the case at all." Without another word, he turned and disappeared into the forest.

Bernice stood frozen to the spot. Tears were running down her face, dripping onto the ground. She pressed a hand to her mouth to muffle a sob.

Luke's and Nora's gazes met over the still nursing baby, but then Luke looked away as a feeling of guilt gripped her. She had always longed for a marriage like the Garfields'. *And now that might be ruined, just because of me.*

"Ow!" Nora winced and held the baby out to Luke. "Take her for a moment."

"What? Why?" Luke stared at the newborn. Before this day, she had never held a baby, and now was not the time to practice it, not when she could easily hurt the baby in her agitated state of mind.

Nora still held out the baby. "Because I'm having contractions!"

"C-contractions? You mean you…you're having twins?" Luke wasn't sure whether she should be elated or taken aback. Mostly, she was just panicked.

Nora laughed for a moment before she grimaced. "No, it's the afterbirth. Take her, please."

"I don't have much experience with babies." *Try none.*

"You won't hurt her," Nora said. "You were wonderful with her earlier. Just support her head and neck with one of your hands."

Luke slipped one of her hands under the baby's head and lifted her into the cradle of her other arm. "Like this?"

"Yeah, that's good." Nora rubbed her lower belly.

"Mama?" Amy called from the wagon.

Luke gazed down at Nora, hesitant to leave her.

"Go," Bernice said and dried her eyes. "I'll help her."

Very slowly and carefully, Luke stood and made her way to the wagon with the baby in her arms. "Amy? Come and meet your little sister."

Amy scrambled up from beneath her blanket and eagerly rushed toward Luke. Then she took one look at the baby and frowned. "But she is so small. I can't play with her. Can I give her back and get a filly?"

Luke bit back the laughter that wanted to bubble up. She was afraid that if she allowed herself to laugh, she would lose control of her emotions and the tears would follow close behind. The night had been a constant up and down of various emotions. Before she met Nora, Luke had led a simple life, feeling very little except for contentment and sometimes a mild annoyance. Now she had experienced the whole spectrum of intense emotions in just one night.

"She'll grow and you can play with her when she's a little older," she said, silently wondering if she would still be a part of the little girl's life when she was Amy's age. Then she forced back the thought because it hurt too much.

She left Amy and the baby with Nora, who was getting cleaned up with the help of a stony-faced Bernice, then went in search of Jacob. *I better ask him for help with the wheel now before Bernice tells him everything and he refuses to help me, leaving me to freeze to death next to my broken-down wagon.*

Luke stalked through the dense forest, enjoying the time away from the small camp where so much had happened in the course of just a few hours. She finally found Jacob sitting on a fallen log, driving his knife into the bark again and again. "Jacob?"

"I don't want to talk about it," Jacob said.

Good, neither do I. I had enough heartache for one night. "Do you think you can help me with the wheel?" Luke asked him. "I want to get Nora and the baby to Oregon City as soon as possible."

Jacob slid from the log. "Let's get it over with."

Nora looked down at the sleeping baby in her arms. Every muscle in her body hurt, and she didn't look forward to traveling in the wagon as soon as Jacob and Luke had finished the repairs. The bumping and jostling would be anything but pleasant, and she could only hope that the baby would sleep through that.

"What are you going to call her?" Bernice asked as she helped Nora slip back into her bodice after nursing the baby.

"Natalie…Nattie," Nora answered with a smile. "We'll name her for Nate, a friend of Luke's who died in the Mexican War."

At the mention of Luke, Bernice's smile vanished. She hadn't said a word to Luke or Jacob for the last few hours, nor had Jacob talked to her.

"I didn't know that Wayne is not Jacob's son," Nora said into the awkward silence.

Bernice sighed. "Nobody knew. No one but me and Jacob."

"Not even Wayne?"

"No." Bernice slowly shook her head. "We never thought it necessary to tell him. Jacob is his father in every way that counts."

Nora looked down at the baby and thought about her own children. Would they someday tell them that Luke was not their father? Would they tell them who and what she really was? Would Luke even stay with them long enough for it to become an issue? Nora had felt the pain that the unrequited declaration of love had caused Luke. It had hurt her too, just to see the pain in Luke's eyes. The worst thing was that Luke would take her rejection as a confirmation that no one would ever love her.

It's not her. It's me. I'm not able to love anymore. Affection, desire, yes, but not unconditional, all-consuming love. She had loved once, and it had nearly destroyed her life. She wouldn't risk that again. She was no longer a naïve young girl; she was a grown woman with children who depended on her. She couldn't afford to put her trust in something as transitory as love and act like a besotted fool again. Her future decisions would be made with a level head, not with an infatuated heart.

She didn't allow herself to think about the consequences that her decision would have for Luke. Forcing her thoughts in another direction, she asked about Bernice's life instead. "How old was Wayne when you met Jacob?" She still couldn't believe that Jacob was not Wayne's father. The boy, almost a man by now, was so much like Jacob in everything but his physical appearance.

"He hadn't even been born yet," Bernice said. "Wayne's father…the man who fathered him, we were engaged, but when I got pregnant, he couldn't disappear fast enough."

Nora nodded and squeezed Bernice's hand. It seemed their experiences had been nearly identical.

"Jacob was our neighbor and an old friend of the family," Bernice said. "He helped me through that time. When he asked me to marry him, I said yes without even having to think about it. It didn't matter to me that I was not in love with him. I had been in love with my betrothed, and look where it got me. All I wanted after that was a friend and a father for my baby."

Nora blinked. *Is she really talking about herself? That could have been the story of my life.* The parallels between their lives were almost eerie. "Then you lived with him, shared his bed, and raised children with him without loving him?" she asked. It almost came as a relief to her because it eased the guilt she felt toward Luke. Here was another woman—a woman she had always thought very highly of—who had lived a content life with her husband, without confessing her undying love for him.

"No," Bernice said, shattering Nora's relief. "That's not what I said. I didn't start out loving him. But today, I can honestly say that I love him more than my foolish younger self ever loved that immature young man who fathered Wayne."

"You've come to love him over the years because he proved to be a good father and a reliable friend," Nora said, almost to herself. These emotions were safe enough, and she could readily admit feeling the same for Luke. It was a tame, friendly kind of love that could easily be controlled.

But once again, Bernice shook her head. "He's both, but my feelings for him are more than just that. He can make me laugh, blush, tear my hair in frustration, and forget about everything else in the world when he smiles at me. I love him from the bottom of my heart, and I know that my life would be over if I lost him." Tears shimmered in her eyes as she looked at her husband, who pointedly had his back to her while he worked.

That's where the parallels between us end. I won't tie my heart, my life, my very soul to one person ever again. The possibility of losing Luke was all too real, and she couldn't afford to stop living if it should happen. Her children were her reason for living, not love. "Did you try to talk to him?" she asked, glad to direct her thoughts back to Bernice and Jacob.

"And just what do you suggest I say? The only explanation he would accept is the truth, and that would turn your life upside down." Bernice looked her in the eyes. "Do you want me to do that?"

Nora averted her eyes. "No."

Bernice stood with a sigh. "They're ready. Let's get you and the little one settled in the wagon."

SANDY RIVER,
OCTOBER 9TH, 1851

Luke woke with a start. She lifted up on her elbow with a groan, listening into the darkness. Her muscles hurt from lowering the wagons down the Barlow Pass. They had been forced to zigzag down the steep slope, which had made it necessary to cross and recross the little stream called Zigzag River again and again until they had reached the Sandy River. The roads were still bad, covered with mud holes after it had rained all night. Nora had endured the constant jostling without complaint, but Luke could see that she was hurting and exhausted.

A whining sound came from the wagon under which Luke had settled down for the night. *The baby. That's probably what woke me up.*

The low whining quickly became louder, turning into a nerve-racking cry.

Luke scrambled out of her bedroll. She looked into the wagon and saw the red-faced baby look back at her. The little girl continued to cry, but still Nora didn't stir, dead to the world due to sheer exhaustion.

Luke stared at the baby, willing her to stop crying, but of course Nattie didn't. Luke had no idea what to do. When Nattie cried, Nora had always taken care of her, and Luke had gladly relinquished any baby-related tasks to her, afraid that she would hurt the baby in her inexperience. But now she was on her own. She didn't want to wake Nora, knowing she was exhausted from the exertions of giving birth. She needed the rest. Luke reached over Nora and carefully lifted the baby into her arms.

The baby was silent for a second, then cried even more loudly.

"Sssh, ssshh." Luke walked away from the wagon with its sleeping inhabitants. She cradled the baby protectively against her chest, shielding her from the cold wind, and studied the tiny face. "Why are you crying?"

Nora always seemed to know. She could easily discern the "I'm hungry" from the "I need my diaper changed" cry, but Luke found herself sadly lacking in that department. After two rounds around the outer perimeter of the camp, she still didn't know why the baby was crying. Finally, she decided to check the baby's diaper. She returned to the wagon and took one of the clean cloths that served as Nattie's diapers. Carefully balancing the baby against her chest, she spread out her bedroll on the sparsely growing grass. Then, steadying Nattie's head as Nora had told her, she laid the baby down on the bedroll.

The crying became even louder, and Nattie's tiny limbs kicked out in protest of being moved away from her warm place against Luke's chest.

Luke unwrapped the soft baby blanket. "Ugh. You definitely need your diaper changed, little one." She pinched her nose. "All right," she said to herself, "you can do this." She had watched Nora change the baby's diaper before, but it had always appeared so easy then. Taking a deep breath, Luke removed the soiled diaper. She wrinkled her nose and tied the ends of the old diaper into a neat ball.

The baby continued to cry. Her face turned red from all the crying.

Luke hurried to get her cleaned up and dressed again. Finally, she lifted up the clean cloth that would be Nattie's new diaper. She struggled to get it under the baby until she remembered that Nora had lifted Nattie up a bit by the ankles. Luke hesitated. She didn't want to hurt the baby. Being responsible for something so small and vulnerable was scary. *Come on. Don't be such a coward. You can't let her lie around half-naked in this weather.* She gently lifted the baby's lower half and slid the cloth under her bottom. After securing the corners of the cloth, she leaned back to admire her handiwork.

It didn't look as neat as Nora's, but it would certainly do. Luke allowed herself a relieved grin before she lifted the baby up again. "Why are you still crying?" She lowered her voice to a soothing level. "You're all nice and clean now, aren't you?"

On the third round around the camp, the baby finally stopped crying and nuzzled against Luke's bound breasts.

Luke's cheeks grew hot. "Sorry, little one," she murmured. "I'm not the parent with your built-in dinner." *Parent.* Luke stopped and looked down at the tiny girl in her arms. The baby and the responsibility that came with it were still scaring her, but she had never been so sure that she loved Nora than when she looked at Nora holding her youngest daughter. She wanted to make a life with them, wanted to be there to see the girls grow up. In some moments, it already seemed so real and attainable that she could see the four of them sitting on the porch of the ranch she would build. But then there were the moments when she saw a man sitting in her place next to Nora, a man Nora could love.

"Luke? Is that you?" Jacob called out from his place at the fire. He had volunteered to stand guard for the second night in a row, making it easier for him to avoid his wife.

"Yeah. Me and Nattie." Luke sat in front of the fire, careful not to get too close to the flames with the precious bundle in her arms.

Jacob leaned forward to peer beneath the baby blanket at the now sleeping infant. There was so much emotion in his eyes that Luke just knew that he was thinking about Wayne at that age.

"Walking around seems to calm her," she said, just to break the silence. "She must have gotten used to the constant walking Nora did while she was pregnant with her."

"Of all my children, Wayne is the one who's most like me in everything he does," Jacob said, not reacting to Luke's words at all. "How do you think that's possible?"

"You're his father," Luke answered. "You taught him everything he knows." She tucked the blanket a little closer around the sleeping baby. The thought that Amy and Nattie would someday be a little like her was wonderful and scary at the same time.

Jacob stared into the fire. The circle of light flickered over the dark shadows beneath his eyes.

He's hurting, and so is Bernice. The guilt settled like lead in the pit of Luke's stomach. The Garfields were good people, and she didn't want to see their marriage suffer just because of her. She had promised herself that she would leave before her secret could hurt Nora or the children, and now she felt that the same promise should hold true for the first friends she had made in years. Only this time, leaving wouldn't resolve the situation. She took a deep breath and opened her mouth, then closed it again. *No. Not without talking to Nora first. This affects her and the children too, and she has a right to be a part of the decision.*

Nora slid one hand out from under her blanket and felt around for the baby. Her hand found only an empty space where Nattie had been. She jerked upright. *Maybe Bernice has taken her to allow me some sleep.* Nora was grateful for it. She gingerly stretched her still hurting body and then checked on the sleeping Amy before she climbed out of the wagon. Still a little sleepy, she wandered over to the Garfields' wagon and peered inside.

Bernice was tossing and turning in her sleep, and one of the children was coughing, but there was no sign of the baby. From one moment to the other, Nora was wide-awake. "Bernice," she whispered urgently.

The older woman opened her eyes.

"Nattie was gone when I woke up. She—"

"Luke has her," Bernice said. "I saw him walk around camp with the baby for an hour before Nattie finally fell asleep. I think he even changed her diaper."

"Oh." Nora hadn't expected that. Luke had been so nervous and awkward handling the baby before.

"She's quite the little daddy," Bernice said, her voice so low that only Nora could understand her words.

Nora felt her hackles rise. "Bernice," she said, a quiet warning in her voice. "You're a kind, warmhearted woman. Why can't you just let it go and accept Luke's role in our lives? You say that Jacob is Wayne's father because he's always been there for him, but—"

Bernice shook off her blanket and sat up. "He was. He's the best father that Wayne could wish for."

"I don't doubt that. I just don't understand why you won't accept that Luke can be a wonderful parent as well."

"It's not the same." Bernice struggled to keep her voice down.

"No? Why not?"

"Because it's unnatural," Bernice said. "It'll only bring you hurt and pain."

Nora looked at her through burning eyes. "At the moment, you are the one hurting me," she whispered. "You didn't let nature dictate the relationship between Jacob and Wayne, why should it prevent me and my children from loving Luke?"

"You said you didn't love her," Bernice said.

Nora closed her eyes. "I-I don't. Not like that." She rubbed her temple. "I think I better go and rescue Luke. She must be a nervous wreck by now, all alone with the baby." She fled from the wagon before Bernice could say anything and hurried through camp, not allowing herself time to think. When she reached the fire at the edge of their camp, she stopped abruptly.

Luke sat next to a brooding Jacob, both of her arms safely wrapped around the bundled-up form on her lap. A tiny hand was sticking out from under the baby's blanket, its fingers curled around Luke's larger one.

Nora smiled. Her daughter was sleeping peacefully, and Luke didn't seem far off either. Her eyelids were beginning to droop. Quietly, Nora walked up to them until she felt the warmth of the fire.

Luke looked up. She pulled the baby a little closer, protecting her with her own body. "Nora! Are you all right?"

"Yeah." She blinked away the tears that had gathered in her eyes at the sight of Luke with the baby. "It's just the smoke. Do you want me to take her?" She nodded down at the baby on Luke's lap.

"No, she's fine. She's finally sleeping," Luke said with a smile.

Jacob stood. "I'm going to turn in now. Can you take over guard duty, Luke? Brian will relieve you in half an hour."

Luke nodded.

Nora watched him go, wondering if her presence had chased him away. She gingerly sat down next to Luke and nodded down at the baby. "I'm sorry I didn't hear her. I must have slept like a log."

"It's all right," Luke said. "It was time that I started to take my turns with her anyway. My diapering skills definitely need practice."

Nora studied the gray eyes, almost like a mirror in the firelight. Luke's willingness to take care of the baby was a relief. She hoped it meant she hadn't driven Luke away and that Luke was still willing to take on a more permanent role in the children's lives. Slowly, she leaned closer, and when Luke didn't move away, she rested her cheek against Luke's shoulder, relieved when Luke allowed the simple contact. She knew she had pushed Luke away, and she had been afraid that Luke would retaliate and not allow her close either. "I'm sorry," she whispered.

"You already apologized," Luke said.

Nora shook her head. "Not for sleeping through Nattie's crying. I'm sorry for hurting you."

Luke shrugged. She didn't look at Nora but kept her gaze fixed on the baby. "You can't force love if it isn't there."

Yeah. And you also can't force it to go away if it is. Nora shoved the thought away. *You were not in love with Luke as a man, so you're certainly not in love with her now that you know she's a woman.* "I just want you to know that it's nothing you did or didn't do. You're very loveable."

Luke snorted.

"You are," Nora said with more force. "You're wonderful just like you are, and you deserve someone in your life who can touch you and look at you with love."

"I thought you did," Luke whispered. "The night Nattie was born…when we made love…" She hesitated, maybe waiting for Nora to object to the word "love" in her sentence.

Nora didn't. She sighed. "It's not that I don't care about you. Please, don't think that. I do care. It's just that I…" She pressed the ball of her thumb against one closed eye, forcing back the threatening tears. "I'll understand if this is not enough for you, but, please…" Her voice failed her.

"Not enough?" Luke repeated. "Nora, this is more than I ever thought I would have. I always thought I would spend my life alone. Now I have a wife, who accepts me, and two beautiful little girls. What more could I want?"

Love. Luke acted as if she had accepted Nora's rejection, but still a nagging feeling of dissatisfaction remained in Nora. She wasn't even sure why she was so upset. *Wasn't this exactly what I wanted? For Luke to stay and be content with what we have rather than expecting blazing, reason-defying love from me?*

"Listen," Luke said when an awkward silence spread between them. "I'm about to make an important, life-changing decision. It will also affect you and the children, so I thought it only fair to ask your opinion before I do it."

A coldness that had nothing to do with the temperature in the mountains crept into Nora's bones. *Now you did it,* she thought with a sinking feeling. *You drove her away with your pigheaded refusal to accept her love. She's going to leave.*

"I don't like the situation between Jacob and Bernice," Luke said. "If something doesn't happen soon, their marriage will fail, there will be more angry shouting and accusations, and it's only a matter of time until Wayne will learn that Jacob is not his father. I won't have that on my conscience."

"What are you going to do?" Nora asked with a sense of dread.

Luke bit her lip. "There's only one thing I can do that'll make any difference."

Anger bubbled up in Nora. "Running away is no solution."

"Leaving is not what I had in mind—although it will probably come down to it anyway." Luke shifted the baby in her arms. "I think I have to tell Jacob why Bernice doesn't want me in the baby's life."

Nora could only sit and stare at her. "But that would mean revealing your identity."

"Yes," Luke said. "That's what it means."

Their gazes met.

They both knew the consequences. Jacob would probably react with the same disapproval that his wife had, and soon every last member of the wagon train would know that their captain was a woman living in disguise. They would feel betrayed, maybe even disgusted, and they would ask Luke to leave the train. Even if they didn't, furtive hostilities would start. Some would eye Luke with suspicion, others with pity as if she had contracted leprosy. Most would keep their distance from Luke and her family or even refuse to help them with the obstacles of their journey.

Nora sighed. "Well, I promised to go wherever you go. There has to be another nice place for a horse ranch outside of the Willamette Valley." She tried to sound enthusiastic but didn't quite make it. After building friendships and a sense of community through long months of shared hardships, it would be hard to leave all that behind and begin anew.

Luke shifted the baby into the crook of one arm. She reached out her free hand and squeezed Nora's fingers in a gesture of silent gratitude. "They'll probably offer for you to stay with them."

Nora began to shake her head, but Luke held up her hand to stop her. "Hear me out first and think about it before you make a decision. I know you made friends on the train that you'd have to leave behind."

"They're not much of a friend if they hate you just for being who you are," Nora said. She would miss her friends, but not half as much as she would miss Luke if she left her behind.

"Then you think I should do it? Tell Jacob?" Luke asked.

"I don't want you to," Nora said, "but it's the honorable thing to do."

Luke squeezed her hand again. "Jacob will probably find out anyway. It's a wonder that Bernice kept the secret for as long as she did. I didn't think she would."

"She doesn't understand, but she doesn't want to destroy your life either."

"And I don't want to destroy hers," Luke answered.

They sat side by side until Brian came to take over guard duty.

"Come on," Luke said. "Let's go back to bed. Tomorrow will come soon enough."

Still holding on to Luke's hand, Nora stood, and they walked back to their wagon.

DEVIL'S BACKBONE,
OCTOBER 10TH, 1851

Luke urged Measles toward one of their milk cows, making the cow catch up with the mixed herd of oxen, cows, and mules that they were driving to a strip of prairie with more grass than right next to their camp.

Brian and Tom were herding their own livestock nearby, but they were out of earshot. Wayne and a few of the other boys had ridden ahead with the horses, giving Luke the ideal opportunity to talk to Jacob. She rode up to Jacob and grunted a greeting in true male pioneer style. Only then did she remember that with what she was about to tell Jacob, there was no sense in proving her manliness anymore.

Jacob looked up. "Ah, the elusive Captain Hamilton. I haven't seen you all day."

Luke bit her lip. She had spent the day in nervous rehearsals of what she would say to make Jacob understand. "Yeah, well, I stayed close to the wagon today. Nora is still not up to driving an exhausted ox team over miry ground and through a million mud holes." It wasn't a total lie. Devil's Backbone, the three steep, muddy hills they had just passed over, was aptly named and difficult to travel.

"I hope everything's all right with Nora and the baby?" Jacob asked.

Luke couldn't help smiling when she thought about the newest addition to their family, but then she reminded herself that she wasn't here to gush about Nattie. "They're fine. Listen, Jacob, can I talk to you?"

"I thought that's what we were doing?"

"Yeah, but there's something in particular that I want to talk about," Luke answered.

Jacob turned to look at her. "And that would be...?"

"Bernice."

Jacob turned in the saddle, away from Luke. "I don't want to talk about her."

"Then don't talk, just listen," Luke said. "Jacob, you know she's a good woman. She didn't mean to make you feel like you're not Wayne's father." Maybe she could talk some sense into Jacob without having to reveal her secret.

"How else am I supposed to feel when she tells you that you're not allowed in the baby's life because you didn't father her?" Jacob's voice became louder. "Was it supposed to make me feel all ecstatic and warm about my role in Wayne's life?"

Luke sighed. He was making it impossible for her to take the easy way out. "What Bernice said to me has nothing to do with Wayne or you."

"Ha!" Jacob snorted and flicked the end of a rope at one of the mules. "Come on, can you honestly tell me you can't see the parallels?"

"Our situations, yours and mine, are not as similar as you might think," Luke said.

Jacob said nothing. The muscles in his jaw looked as hard as stone.

Luke inhaled and then let out a shuddery breath. Hinting at it wouldn't convince Jacob. "The reason why Bernice wants me to stay away from the baby is not because I'm not her father. She truly does believe that the man who cares for and is there for a child should be considered his or her father." She emphasized the word "man," knowing that Jacob wouldn't notice anyway.

"Right." The mule earned another flick from Jacob's rope.

Luke sighed. *I better tell him before the poor animal doesn't have any fur left.* "Do you remember the day I was shot?"

Jacob gave her a hint of a smile. "How could I forget that? It was a great fight, and then your wife standing there like some avenging angel with the revolver in her hands…"

"Then you also remember Bernice tending to my shoulder after I was shot?"

"Of course," Jacob said. "She was in there for so long that we thought for sure you were a goner and she had to comfort your inconsolable widow."

Luke suppressed a frown. *How nice. Let's hope he doesn't stay in this macabre mood when I tell him, or Nora will really become an inconsolable widow.* "What kept her for so long wasn't only treating the wound," she said. "She found something out about me that makes her believe it would be better if I stayed out of the baby's life."

"What reason could there possibly be for that? A child needs a father, and that doesn't change just because Bernice doesn't like some minor thing about you!"

"That's just it. It's not just a minor thing." Luke clenched her fingers around the reins. Here it was, the moment of truth that she had avoided her entire adult life. She mentally prepared herself for every possible reaction. At first, Jacob probably wouldn't believe her. But once he did, he might even try to beat her with the rope or ride back to the camp to tell the others. One last deep breath and she slowly unclenched her jaw. "Bernice found out something very fundamental about me. Jacob, I'm…"

Nora stacked the tin plates into the box attached to the back of the wagon. Her gaze wandered over the cooking utensils, tools, and provisions, making sure that everything was tied down should they need to leave in a hurry. *Is this really the right thing to do?* She looked at the baby in her arms and at Amy, who was sitting on the wagon seat, dangling her feet.

Leaving the wagon train and continuing to travel on their own wasn't really dangerous at this point of the journey. Tomorrow, they would reach Foster's farm, where they could stock up their provisions, and a day or two after that, they would be in Oregon City. They could overcome the remaining obstacles on their own. But still, having friends and helpful neighbors while they struggled to build a new home and survive the first winter would have been nice. She would have liked for the girls to grow up with the other children from the wagon train and for her to have a female friend with whom she could share her daily troubles and successes.

You do have a female friend you can share all that with—Luke. A small grin flitted across her face, and she shook her head. She couldn't imagine Luke giving her advice on cooking and needlework. That had been on her mind a lot lately. When they were forced to leave and start a new life where nobody knew them, would Luke keep up her disguise or decide to live as a woman? Somehow, she couldn't imagine Luke wearing a skirt and riding sidesaddle.

She sighed and double-checked if the tent poles were secured tightly to the side of the wagon.

"Nora?" Bernice's voice came from behind her. "Is everything all right? You seem restless today."

Nora let go of the tent pole and turned around. For a moment, she considered telling Bernice it was just because she was getting used to being the mother of a baby again, but then she decided to tell the truth. At least it would give Bernice and her some time to prepare to say good-bye should it become necessary. "Luke is probably with Jacob right now," she said.

"Yeah, I know. They're driving the cattle to a spot with more grass," Bernice said. "But there's no reason to worry. There's nothing dangerous on the trail."

"I'm not worried about the dangers on the trail. I worry because Luke wants to tell Jacob."

Bernice frowned. "Tell him what?"

Nora shot her a pointed look.

"What? You mean…?" Bernice lowered her voice. "She wants to tell him that she's…?"

Nora nodded.

"Why for goodness's sake would she do that after she went to such ridiculous lengths to keep her identity a secret?" Bernice asked, a puzzled expression on her face.

Nora looked directly into Bernice's brown eyes. "She's doing it for you. She doesn't want your marriage to suffer just because of the way she chose to live her life."

Bernice continued to stare at her. She seemed almost horrified.

"What's the matter?" Nora asked with a hint of bitterness. "Isn't that exactly what you wanted? For Luke to be forced to leave?"

Bernice shook her head. "I wanted her to leave you alone, not take you away from your friends. And I certainly didn't want anything to happen to her."

"Happen?"

"Are you really that naïve, girl? Just because you have that strange fascination with Luke doesn't mean that others will react that way too. Do you really think the worst that could happen is that she's asked to leave the wagon train? She could be killed."

"Killed?" Nora gasped. "Surely Jacob won't—"

"Not Jacob," Bernice said. "He's too levelheaded and gentle for that, but if Brian or one of the other hotheads get wind of it, there's no telling what they might do."

Brian. Nora looked at the Stantons' wagon, where Brian's wife was putting away the last of their washed dishes. Brian was nowhere to be found. *He went with Luke and Jacob, didn't he?* Panic raced along her spine. Her heartbeat hammered in her ears. "Bernice! Take her! Please!" She placed the baby into Bernice's arms and grabbed Luke's rifle from behind the wagon seat.

"Nora!" Bernice called.

She didn't listen. She gathered up her skirts with one hand while the other clutched the rifle. She raced through camp, then panted up the hill, following the tracks of unshod hooves.

"Mary, stay with Amy," Bernice called out to her oldest daughter and hurried after Nora.

Nora didn't wait for her. She stumbled up the muddy slope. Her arms flailed when she almost fell. She stopped, gasping for breath, and bent down with her hands pressed against trembling thighs. *Luke! I have to get to Luke before it's too late,* her mind screamed, but her body, still weak from the exertions of giving birth, didn't listen.

Bernice caught up with her. "Nora! What do you think you are doing? You're not up to running around like this, just two days after giving birth." She grabbed Nora's elbow to steady her.

"Please, please, help me, Bernice! I have to find Luke." Nora looked at the older woman with wild, burning eyes.

Bernice rubbed her forearm. "I didn't mean to scare you so badly. The situation could escalate, yes, but I don't think they'll shoot her on the spot."

She had barely finished her words when a gunshot shattered the silence.

Fear flashed through Nora, making her nauseated. Never in her life had she been so afraid, not even when she'd been alone with her cruelest customers. "Oh, no! No, no, no. Not Luke!" She started to run again. Mud splattered her skirt, and branches scratched her skin. Nora barely noticed in her haste to get to Luke.

"Nora. Nora, slow down, or you're gonna hurt yourself," Bernice called and followed her at a slower pace, still carrying Nattie.

"Hurt myself?" Nora yelled back. "They hurt Luke. Maybe she's already…" She stopped, unable to say the word, afraid that it might become reality if she did. "God, it's all my fault."

Bernice caught up with her. "It's not your fault. Luke is an adult. She made her own choices."

Still marching up the hill, Nora threw her a heated glance. "Almost everything she did on this journey, she did for me. She's telling Jacob because of you, because you're my friend and she knows I don't want to see you suffer."

"Don't be angry with me. I didn't cause this whole mess." Bernice puffed along.

"I'm not angry with you. I'm angry with myself. I was so scared and stupid, and now it might be too late." Nora stumbled up the hill and stopped when she could see into the valley below.

A horse splashed through the creek, racing toward them at full gallop. Nora couldn't identify the rider yet, but she saw the rifle in his hand and gripped her own even more tightly. She had let herself believe that the people on the train were their friends and wouldn't hurt them, but now she was determined to fight for her life if need be. For Luke's life.

"It's Wayne," Bernice said next to her. "Oh, Lord, I hope Jacob didn't get hurt."

The rider had almost reached them now, and Nora saw that it was indeed Bernice's oldest son. The horse slid to a stop in front of them, its flanks heaving.

Wayne tipped his hat back. Blood covered his hand.

Nora lifted the rifle, the barrel shaking as she aimed it at the young man. "What have you done to Luke?"

Wayne's eyes widened as he looked into the barrel. He began to raise his own weapon.

"Wayne, no!" Bernice stepped between them and put a hand on Wayne's rifle. "Where's your father?"

"Back there." Wayne pointed in the direction he had come from.

Nora rushed past him, Bernice hot on her heels.

"Jacob, I'm…" Luke nervously cleared her throat. Measles danced beneath her, probably feeling her rider's tension. "What Bernice found out about me is that I—"

"That he's been in prison," a voice behind her interrupted.

Jacob and Luke directed their horses around. "What?" they said at the same time.

"What's the meaning of all this?" Jacob asked.

Yeah, I'd like to know that too. Luke stared at the two breathless women. Her gaze landed on Nora, who was standing next to Bernice with a tight grip on her rifle. Silent tears were running down her flushed face, and Luke had to force herself not to dismount, go to her, and pull her close.

"When I helped treat the wound, I saw the mark of a convicted criminal that was tattooed into his skin," Bernice said. "He's been in prison because he was involved in a bank raid when he was younger."

Jacob turned his horse toward Luke, gazing at her with blazing eyes. "Is that true?"

Luke hesitated, but there was only one answer that wouldn't turn her life upside down. *What a strange world where being a criminal is better than being a woman.* She sighed. "Yes."

"Why didn't you just tell me?" Jacob looked at his wife.

"I didn't want to destroy the lives that Luke and Nora have built for themselves," Bernice said. "And because of Wayne."

Jacob gave a nod of understanding, but Luke stared at them. How was the Garfields' son involved in this?

"Jacob's little brother, Wayne, was killed when he was just eleven," Bernice said. "The stray bullet from a bank robber hit him in the back. We named our son after him."

"Then why did you tell me now?" Jacob asked.

Bernice hesitated.

"Because I just told her that Luke didn't shoot or threaten anyone," Nora said. "He didn't even have a weapon. He was just a boy who agreed to stay with the horses and hold the reins for the older men."

Slowly, Jacob turned in the saddle and studied Luke. "You did time in prison?"

"Yeah." As far as Luke was concerned, it wasn't really a lie. Her whole life had been a prison, locked in by people's refusal to accept her and let her live her life the way she wanted to. Only Nora's presence in her life had freed her from that prison and made her start living instead of just existing, afraid to form close bonds and be found out.

"All right, then you already paid for what you did, and it's not my place to judge you anymore." Jacob slid off his horse, walked over to Bernice, and looked deeply into her eyes. "Next time, just tell me. And now come on, our son just shot a deer. We're gonna have a feast tonight."

"Just a moment. There's something I have to say before we go," Bernice said, her gaze fixed on Luke. "I still don't understand you and the choices you made in your life, and I don't think I ever fully will, but I have to admit that you're the most decent person I've ever met. You were willing to risk your life for my happiness, and I won't forget that."

Before Luke could think of an answer, Bernice stepped closer and waved at her to get off the horse.

Swallowing, Luke dismounted.

Bernice handed her the baby, silently signaling that she approved of her being a part of the children's lives. Then she took her husband's hand and started back to the camp.

Luke watched them walk away, then turned to Nora with a frown. "What the he—?" She stopped herself with a look at the baby in her arms. "What happened? Why are you running around with my rifle?"

The flush had left Nora's face, and she was deathly pale now. "We heard a shot and thought..." She closed her eyes, and a new tear dropped from her lowered lashes. "I thought they had shot you."

Luke had known from the start that she might be killed if she revealed her true identity, but Nora seemed to have only now grasped that. "Don't cry." It was hard to see Nora cry, especially if she was the cause of these tears. "Please don't cry." With the baby cradled in her right arm, she wrapped the left one, which was still a bit stiff, around Nora.

"I almost lost you." Nora sniffled and leaned against Luke's side. "I have every right to cry."

"Yeah, but everything's fine now. We don't even have to leave the train, and the Garfields made up too." Luke rubbed Nora's trembling back.

"Just one second later and everything could have been very different," Nora said. "I didn't fully realize how dangerous the situation could become until Bernice reminded me what a hothead Brian is. When I heard that shot echo through the valley..."

Luke rubbed soothing circles on the small of her back, the baby held cozily in the cocoon between their bodies. "It was just Wayne, killing our dinner."

"But I didn't know that."

"It was a scary moment," Luke said. "Thank God that Bernice saved the day. I didn't expect her to help me out of that situation." Maybe it was time to trust someone else besides Nora. She didn't plan on revealing her secret to anyone who came along, but Bernice had proved again and again that she could be trusted. She looked at Nora, who was still very pale. "Would you have really shot at Jacob?"

Nora grew even paler. "If he had hurt you, yes."

Luke didn't know what to say. The fire in the green eyes made her body temperature rise. She was worried, confused, moved, and a little bit aroused, all at the same time. Finally, she jolted herself out of her thoughts and into action. "Come on, let's go back and set up the tent. We have to get a good night's sleep to keep up our strength." Reaching Oregon City would only be the beginning of another adventure.

Philip Foster's Farm, October 11th, 1851

Nora wandered through the vegetable garden and the orchards with Luke at her side. She stopped in front of the log house and imagined the sweet scent of the lilac bush that would bloom in the front yard come spring. After two thousand miles through barren country, over steep hills, and through raging rivers, this place seemed like the Garden of Eden to her.

Mary Charlotte Foster, a woman of about forty, proudly walked next to Nora, pointing out the two-story building and the green pastures where their livestock was grazing. "Next year, as soon as spring comes, we're building a school," Mrs. Foster said. "It was high time the government finally gave Philip permission, as we have twenty-eight children living around here."

Nora looked at the children running through the orchard with the children from the wagon train.

"Eight of them are ours," Mrs. Foster added with a smile.

Eight! Nora knew she would never have that big a family. Even if they stayed together, Luke wouldn't have a son to take over her horse ranch.

At Nora's sigh, Luke looked up from whatever Mrs. Foster had pointed out. "There'll come a time when they need a school at whatever place we'll end up in too," Luke said. "And they'll need a competent teacher." She gave Nora a pointed look.

It took a few seconds for Nora to understand. "You mean me?"

"Sure. You had the patience of a saint with me—and you needed it. Teaching a room full of small children should be easy in comparison," Luke said with a grin.

Nora smiled. Teaching would be a dream come true, but she wasn't holding her breath, knowing she'd have so much work on the ranch that she would have no time for anything else. "There'll be no time. You'll need me on the ranch."

"We'll make the time," Luke said. "The ranch will have to do without your loving care for a few hours each day."

Nora allowed her smile to grow. Here she was, thinking gloomy thoughts of how she would never be able to give Luke a son, an heir, while Luke concentrated on the positive things in their future. *Who knows… Knowing Luke, one of my daughters might one day be the first woman to own a horse ranch.* She shifted Nattie into the cradle of her left arm and placed her right hand on Luke's arm.

Luke laid her hand on Nora's and led her toward the Fosters' store.

OREGON CITY,
OCTOBER 13TH, 1851

Nora rolled around to lie on her back. She opened her eyes and stared up at the small room's ceiling. She had been tossing and turning for the last two hours. *How ironic. I longed to sink into the soft feathers of a real bed for months, and now that I have one, I can't sleep.*

They had reached Oregon's capital this afternoon, and Luke had rented a room for them.

Nora was exhausted, not only from all the traveling they had done during the last five months, but also from taking in all the things to see in Oregon City. It was a long, narrow town, right where the Willamette River rumbled through a rocky canyon. The town was bigger than Nora had expected. It even had a church, a newspaper office, a hatter, a silversmith, a cabinet maker's shop, two saloons, and a few tailors. Beyond the town, on the Willamette, boats headed toward the Columbia River, and the Willamette Falls supplied power to lumber and flour mills. It was a growing town with a bright future, and most of their fellow travelers decided to settle down in or around Oregon City.

Nora had known for some time that Luke wouldn't be one of those people. Life in town was not for Luke. The dangers of being a part of a close-knit community were just too high—people were nosing into each other's business, and Luke was too afraid of being found out.

So it hadn't come as a surprise to Nora when Luke had emerged from the Government Land Office with a document that announced Lucas Hamilton as the new owner of one hundred and sixty acres of land at a place called Baker Prairie—according to Luke a beautiful green valley, bordered by rivers and surrounded by gentle hills and gorgeous mountains, just seven miles southwest of Oregon City.

Careful not to wake up the other inhabitants of the small room, Nora sat up and looked around. Next to her, on a small table, lay the documents that held their future. In the moonlight she could make out her name on one of the pages. Luke had filed a claim for another one hundred and sixty acres in her name. Nora had never had a place to call her own. Now she would own half of a ranch.

Still a bit overwhelmed, she looked away from the table and the documents. The baby was slumbering peacefully in the crib that Luke had built for her. Nora reached out and touched the squirrel that Luke had lovingly carved into the wood. Her finger trailed along the bushy tail and touched the point of an ear. Then her gaze wandered over to Amy's bed.

The bed was empty and the blanket abandoned.

Nora swung her legs out of bed and looked around. Just as she was about to panic, she found Amy on the small cot next to Luke.

Amy clutched Luke's shirt as she had often clutched Rosie, her doll that had ended up in the Wakarusa River what seemed like an eternity ago.

Nora blinked away a few tears, moved by the bond that had developed between Luke and Amy. They had grown even closer since Nattie's birth. The baby needed so much of her time and attention that she would have felt guilty if Luke hadn't stepped in. Now Luke was the one who read Amy her bedtime story while Nora nursed the baby, and she often took her with her when she scouted ahead on Measles.

Nora moved closer. Her eyes, used to the near darkness by now, studied Luke's face. Her fingers ached to caress the tiny bump on the bridge of Luke's nose, and her lips wanted to kiss away the lines of exhaustion on the familiar face. *Stop this nonsense. Go back to bed and sleep.* But this time, Nora couldn't bring herself to listen to the voice of reason. She stayed sitting on the edge of her bed, staring at Luke.

Tomorrow, their new lives would begin. *A life at the side of this woman if I want it.* She had decided long ago that she did want it because Luke would make sure that she and her children would always have a roof over their heads and food on the table. Then, a few weeks ago, she had admitted that these materialistic considerations weren't the only reason why she wanted to stay with Luke; it was also because she liked Luke.

Like? Another, softer voice in her head repeated. *You don't panic because someone you like is in danger.* She thought back to the scary minutes at Devil's Backbone when she had thought the men might have killed Luke. She hadn't been worried about losing her protector and provider for her children; she had worried about losing Luke.

Can I really let myself think like this again? Feel like this? Wouldn't it be safer in the long run if I got up now and left? The need to protect her vulnerable heart was overwhelming. After being abandoned by Rafe Jamison, the supposed love of her life, she had learned to erect walls around her heart to survive. And after working as a prostitute, hiding what she truly felt had become second nature, even hiding it from herself.

Slowly, Nora got up.

"Luke?"

Luke knew that voice. Its owner had visited her dreams quite often, so she just smiled and slept on.

"Luke?" the voice came again, a little louder.

"Huh?" Luke worked to open sleep-heavy eyelids. "'s it the baby?"

The cot under her dipped. Fingers combed through her hair, but she wasn't certain whether this was reality or a part of a dream.

"No, the baby's still sleeping," Nora whispered.

Luke shook her head, trying to get rid of the fuzziness in her mind. She rubbed the sleep from her eyes and looked around. Sometime during the night, Amy had bedded down next to her, and Nora was sitting on the edge of the cot, looking down at her. "What is it about this cot that's so attractive to you Macauley women?" Luke asked, forcing a smile. She didn't like the serious expression on Nora's face and what it might mean.

"It's not the cot," Nora said. She stopped and stared down at her hands. "Luke, listen. I've got something to tell you. I made a decision."

Luke was glad that she was already lying down. Every muscle in her body lost its strength. She shivered as coldness gripped her heart. *We're in Oregon City. The journey is over. She doesn't need me anymore. She wants to stay in town and marry the schoolmaster or something.* She clenched her jaw, determined not to yell or cry when the hurtful words were spoken.

"I love you," Nora said.

God, you're already hallucinating from holding your breath. Luke blinked. "What?"

"I love you."

"Just like that?" Luke stared at her. A part of her wanted to accept Nora's declaration of love at face value, but an even bigger part remained skeptical. "You decided to love me? Nora, love is not something you can decide on. It's not here," she pointed at her head, "it's here." She laid a palm over her heart.

Nora placed a hand over Luke's, both of their fingers now covering Luke's pounding heart. "I didn't decide to love you. That happened months ago without conscious thought. But after almost losing you, I decided to take the risk and let myself love you. I always thought it would hurt less to lose you if I made myself believe that I didn't love you. But the second I heard that shot, I knew I was lying to myself."

Luke couldn't stop staring. "W-why tell me now? That incident was three days ago."

"I managed to bury it deep down again. But tomorrow is the beginning of a new life for us, and I don't want to start it with a lie—to myself or to you." Nora swallowed and said more loudly, "I love you, Luke."

Luke closed her eyes, then opened them again. Nora was still sitting there. This was really happening. *To me. This is happening to me.* Luke had always been so sure that she would never truly be loved, but the warm glow in Nora's eyes told her that the unbelievable had happened. "I don't know what to say," she mumbled, her mouth dry.

"An 'I love you too' would have been nice," Nora whispered.

Luke reached over Amy, who stirred but didn't wake. She grabbed Nora's nightdress, pulled her down and kissed her with urgent passion. When they broke apart after long minutes, she said with a breathless laugh, "I do."

Laughter and the thumping of booted feet on the porch made Nora look up from the letter on her lap.

Luke strode toward her with Amy riding on her shoulders, both of them covered in dust, hay, and horse lather.

"Papa, Papa!" Nattie stood from her place, playing at Nora's feet, and raced toward Luke as fast as her short legs would allow. "Nattie ride horsie too."

Luke lifted a laughing Amy down from her shoulders, the five-year-old almost too big for being carried around like that anyway, and swung the smaller, dark-haired girl up into her arms. "Maybe next year, little one." She carried her over to Nora.

"Howdy, cowboy," Nora drawled, putting every ounce of seduction that Tess had once taught her into her voice. She loved the effect that voice had on Luke every time she used it.

Luke put their youngest daughter down and stalked closer. "We don't raise cows," she said, pointing at the small herd of Appaloosa horses prancing around in the corral, "and," she bent down to whisper in Nora's ear, "I'm not a boy."

Nora laughed and kissed her on the lips. It was nice to see how comfortable Luke had gotten with that fact over the last two years. Everyone else still assumed Luke to be male—and she hoped they always would—but in the privacy of their bedroom... Nora grinned. *Later.*

The grin on Luke's face told her that her message had been received. "Letter from Tess?" Luke asked and bent down to take a look at the piece of paper on Nora's lap.

Nora used the opportunity to smooth her fingers over the mussed, black hair. "No. It's a wedding invitation. Wayne Garfield wants us to come over and watch him tie the knot next month."

"Woohoo!" Luke whistled. "They're getting married already? That boy works fast."

"Six months is not that fast. You asked me to marry you three days after we first met," Nora said and grinned.

Luke's eyes crinkled at the corners as she smiled down at Nora. "Yeah, after you tried to seduce me the first time we met."

"I suppose we did things a little backwards," Nora said. They had been strangers when they married, then had slowly become friends, and finally, they had fallen in love with each other.

"Yeah," Luke said, bending down to kiss her again, "but I like where we ended up at the end of our journey anyway."

If you enjoyed *Backwards to Oregon*, you might want to check out the sequel, *Hidden Truths*, and Jae's historical romance *Shaken to the Core*, which features Luke and Nora's granddaughter.

Continue reading for the **bonus short story "A Rooster's Job."**

You can find "A Rooster's Job" along with five other short stories about Luke, Nora, and the other characters from *Backwards to Oregon* in the anthology *Beyond the Trail*, available from many online bookstores.

A Rooster's Job

Hamilton Horse Ranch
Baker Prairie, Oregon
December 1852

A gust of wind rattled the greased paper that covered the windows instead of glass. Snow drifted down the chimney, and the flames flickered and hissed.

Luke stepped around her oldest daughter, Amy, and her herd of wooden horses and laid a fresh log on the fire, thankful for something to do. In the year since she, Nora, and the children had arrived in Oregon, they hadn't had such cold. She was glad to have chopped and dried enough wood for the winter. They could keep warm at least.

"Papa, can you make me a baby horse for Measles?" Amy asked, eyeing the wood at the side of the hearth.

Luke had whittled her a menagerie of animals to mirror the ones on their property, but her five-year-old daughter liked the horses best, especially Measles, who was supposed to have a foal in spring.

"Tonight," Luke said. "I need to—"Another weak cough came from the bedroom. *Oh, Nattie.* The strangled sound made Luke's chest ache as if she had been coughing and wheezing for the past two days. She thought about returning to the bedroom to stand silent vigil with Nora over their sick daughter but then stayed where she was. It hurt too much to watch the tiny chest struggle for breath.

If only they didn't live so far from a doctor. If only the snow melted.

Suddenly, Luke couldn't breathe either. The walls of the small cabin were closing in on her. She grabbed her coat and rushed to the door.

"Papa!" Amy laid down her wooden horses and jumped up from her place next to the hearth. "Can I come too?"

She was used to going everywhere with Luke, and normally, Luke liked to have her around and teach her new things. But not now, not in this weather. She wouldn't risk Amy getting sick too.

"No. Not this time."

"But we could check on Measles and the other horses," Amy said.

"No," Luke said again, more roughly than she had intended. "It's too cold outside. Tell your mother I'm going to take care of the roof." Without another word, she escaped from the cabin.

The cold hit her like a tidal wave, but Luke ignored it and marched toward the stable. After one step, she sank knee-deep into the snow. She struggled through the white drifts, her fists clenched in the pockets of her coat.

When she entered the barn, half a dozen horses trumpeted a hopeful whinny.

Luke bit her lip. She didn't have feed to offer them. As she made her way down the aisle, she forced herself not to look at the empty stalls. She reached over one of the stall doors and rubbed her hand over Measles's shoulder, feeling bones more prominent than ever before. "I'm sorry, girl," she whispered. "I'm so sorry. I'll go out later and get you some more moss from the forest."

But first, she had to knock down some of the snow from the cabin and stable roofs before they caved in under their heavy burden. Oregon's winters were normally mild and rainy, so Luke hadn't built their home with so much snow in mind. The cabin wasn't much more than provisional shelter anyway. Lichen grew on the log walls, and Nora had to sweep mushrooms off the dirt floor every morning.

Luke had planned on installing wood floors in the new, better house she had wanted to build during their first summer in Oregon. But now that summer had passed and with so much else to do around the ranch, she hadn't gotten around to it. "Never mind," Jacob Garfield, their old friend whose family had settled in town, had said. "You'll build a new house next year. You can't do it all at once. After all, you're just one man."

Her callused hand rasped over her burning eyes. *You're no man at all.* In the past year, she had found peace with that fact, but now it started to feel like a failure again. If she were a man, maybe she could have built a better home, one with real windows and a cook stove so Nora wouldn't need to cook over a fire anymore. Maybe then Nattie wouldn't be sick all the time. If she didn't have to hide her secret, they could have settled down in town, with neighbors and a doctor nearby, instead of living isolated from the rest of the world.

Sometimes, Luke feared that Nora was lonely without even a post office from which to send her letters to Tess. Could she really give Nora and her daughters the life they deserved? In moments like this, she doubted it.

The rafters above her creaked warningly.

Dammit. I better hurry. Luke carried a ladder outside, leaned it against the side of the stable, and climbed up. A cold wind tugged on her coat. Her fingers felt frozen as she used a shovel to relieve the stable's roof of its burden. Snow slithered into her coat sleeves and dropped down her neck as she worked, but she ignored it. Every shovelful seemed to weigh a ton, and sweat mingled with the melting snow on her skin.

Finally, she freed the roof of most of the snow and climbed back down. Her arms protested as she dragged the ladder through the deep snow toward the cabin. Despite her exhaustion, she couldn't allow herself to rest. She would need to chop more wood, go out to set traps in the forest, and drag home moss so the horses wouldn't starve.

More white drifted across the ranch yard.

Luke frowned and stopped. *That's not snow. Lord! Are those feathers?*

Then she saw the drops of crimson that marred the treacherous innocence of the snow. The ladder slid out of her nerveless hands. She bent down and touched one of the spots, confirming that it was blood.

Fear clutched at her as she followed the trail of blood around the corner. She already knew where it was leading. *No. Please, no. Not this too.* When she ducked into the henhouse, unusual silence greeted her.

It was empty.

Broken eggshells and tufts of bloodstained feathers littered the floor. On the perch, the battered-looking rooster flapped his wings helplessly.

Luke stared at him. Bile rose in her throat; she forced it down. "You should have taken better care of your family," she said. "That's your job, you stupid rooster."

The rooster just crowed at her.

"Goddammit!" Luke yelled back. She rubbed her palms over her cold face until her cheeks burned.

A coyote had gotten into the henhouse before, but that had been last year, when the winter had been mild. This year had brought the hardest winter that settlers in Oregon could remember. The river was frozen, and eighteen inches of snow covered the pasture. Half their herd and two of their milk cows had starved because they couldn't get to the grass. They had run out of flour a week ago, but the snow blocked the roads and made it impossible to reach town. Even if they had somehow managed to make it to the store, prices had soared, so they couldn't afford to buy more than a few pounds anyway.

All Luke could do was hope for spring to come soon.

She jerked the board that had come loose next to the henhouse's door back into place and waded through the snow to where she had left the ladder. There was no time to think about what losing the hens would mean for them or what Nora would say when she heard about it. The cabin's roof was flat, so the snow wouldn't slide off. If she didn't clear it, it would pile higher and higher until the roof caved in and exposed Luke's family to the merciless elements.

Anger fueled her strength, and she shoveled wildly until she had scraped most of the snow off the cabin's cedar shakes. Then she paused, still clinging to the ladder, and stared down at the snow-immersed corral, the feathers, and the trail of blood.

Nora shoved open the door and tucked her shawl more tightly around her shoulders. "Luke?" she called out into the white, frozen world. What was Luke doing out there for so long? Had something happened?

"Up here," Luke called from the side of the cabin. "Go on back inside. I'll be down in a minute." Her voice sounded strangely hollow to Nora.

Nora furrowed her brow. Was it just the snow, which muffled and distorted all sounds? She didn't think so. "Luke?" Nora called again, with more urgency. She stepped out of the doorway, let the door fall closed behind her, and peered up.

The ladder leaned against the cabin, with Luke perched on top.

Luke scrambled down the ladder, her cheeks flushed with panic. "Is Nattie...?"

"No, no, she's fine," Nora said and waved at Luke to slow down before she could fall and break a leg. "Her fever finally broke, and she's no longer coughing. She'll be just—" The words died on her lips, and she stared at the tears that pooled in the corners of Luke's red-rimmed eyes. Her heart plummeted. "Are you...are you crying?"

In the two years she'd known Luke, through a lot of hard times, she had never, ever seen Luke cry. Even when one of the horses had stepped on Luke's little toe and crushed it, she had bravely upheld her manly image. She had cursed but never cried—until now.

"No," Luke said, quickly wiping her eyes. "Of course not. It's this damn cold. It makes my eyes water."

Her attempts to hide her feelings hurt as much as seeing Luke suffer, but Nora let it go. Right now, making sure that Luke was all right was more important. "What happened?" She touched Luke's hand. The gentle strength of that hand had comforted and loved her for many months now, but this time, Luke didn't curl her fingers around hers in silent communication. They remained frozen.

What's going on? Nora studied Luke more closely. Her eyes widened as she detected the red stains on Luke's coat sleeve. "Lord! You're hurt." Her insides trembled, and she reached for Luke's hand again.

"No." Now Luke intertwined her fingers with Nora's, instinctively soothing. "It's not my blood. It's..." Luke closed her eyes, and when she opened them again, she looked toward the henhouse.

Her silence said it all.

"The chickens?" Nora whispered. "All of them?"

"All but that goddamn useless rooster."

Nora took a deep breath. Then another. "Well," she finally said and forced a smile, "I bet he's not so useless when it comes to preparing chicken fixings. We could have potatoes, steamed squash, and turnips with it." That was about all that was left in their pantry—that and the can of peaches Nora was saving for Luke's birthday.

Her words didn't have the desired effect. Luke didn't smile; she didn't even make eye contact. "As soon as the snow melts away a little, you and the girls should move to town," Luke said. "I'm sure you could stay with the Garfields for a while."

"What?"

"Just until spring." Under Nora's incredulous gaze, Luke shuffled her booted feet. "Just until I can build a better house for us."

A sigh formed a cloud of mist in front of Nora's face. "Luke, we talked about this before. The answer is still no."

"But before, we hadn't lost the hens and two of the cows," Luke said.

Nora was still shaking her head. Now that she had found a home and the love of her life, she wouldn't leave either of them.

Snow sprayed both of them when Luke kicked one of the white drifts. "What else needs to happen before you leave?" The normally gentle Luke was shouting now.

"You'd have to leave too," Nora said without flinching back. "We're either all going or all staying. I'm not leaving you behind. Through the good times and the bad, remember?"

Luke stared down into the snow and mumbled into her coat, "You made that promise when you still thought I was a man who could take care of you and the girls."

"I'm not talking about our marriage vows," Nora said. Back then, she'd had no earthly clue about love. She'd married Luke to give her children a better future in a new home. But somewhere along the two thousand miles from Missouri to Oregon, she had fallen in love. "Do you remember last year, when we stopped the oxen on that hill over there and looked down at this very place? Do you remember what I said?"

Luke's gaze wandered over to the hill hidden beneath the heavy snow cover, then came to rest on Nora. For a moment, her eyes were alight with the memory and a slight smile trembled on her lips. "Of course I do. You told me you'd love me forever, through the good times and the bad, until the end of time."

"That I did. And while this," Nora swept her arm over the frozen landscape, "might look like the Last Days, I'm sure it's not, so my promise still holds true." She reached out and touched Luke's cheek, feeling the dampness of sweat, snow—and, yes, tears. "Luke, what's this about? What's going on in here?" She slid her hand down the thick coat and rested it over one bound breast.

Two cold hands closed around Nora's. "I just want you to be safe. It would be better for you and the girls to live in a real house and have flour and eggs and milk. I can't give you any of that right now." Luke dropped her hands from Nora's and looked away.

"And you somehow think people in town and on the other farms aren't suffering this winter? Most of our neighbors lost more stock than we did." Just a few days before, Luke had found two of the Buchanans' cows dead on their north pasture. At least they would provide meat for both families for a while. "These things are out of your control, Luke. There would be nothing you could do about them even if you were a man. Or do you think that Jacob or Tom would be able to melt away the snow with just the heat of their manly gazes?"

"Of course not," Luke said, but her guarded expression never changed.

Lord. Why did I have to go and marry such a pigheaded person? Nora smiled inwardly. *Maybe because she's also such an honorable and loving person.* "Luke, things aren't that bad. So what if we have to eat potatoes, turnips, and boiled wheat for a few weeks longer? We have more than enough food to survive this winter. It just won't be the most varied of cuisine." She nudged Luke, trying to establish eye contact. "If we run out of beef, you could go out and hunt. I hear the coyotes are well-nourished around here."

The corners of Luke's gray eyes crinkled as her concerned features relaxed into a tentative smile.

"And spring comes early here in Oregon," Nora added. "The snow could be gone by the New Year, and then everything will look different."

The cabin's door creaked open. "Mama? Papa?" Amy's worried voice drifted over to them.

"We're here, Amy," Nora said.

Amy leaned forward, both hands clutching the doorway, and peered at them, her lower body still within the cabin. They had forbidden her from setting one foot outside the cabin without them, and Amy was taking that order very seriously. Her eyes widened. "Papa, are you all right?"

"Yes, sweetie, I'm—"

Nora knew what was coming. She had heard that reassurance a thousand times before. Most of the time, Nora thought a little white lie to avoid worrying the children was fine, but she didn't want Luke to think that she had to pretend all the time. "Papa is sad because the hens are gone," she said before Luke could finish her sentence.

"Oh, no!" Amy's happy little face transformed into a frowning one. "What happened to them?"

"I'll explain later," Nora said. "Now go back inside where it's warm. Be a dear and keep an eye on your sister. We'll be with you in a minute."

After a second's hesitation, Amy closed the door.

Luke and Nora were left standing in the snow, staring at each other. More snowflakes dusted Luke's shoulders, and Nora brushed them away. "You are a hard worker, a wonderful parent, and the best husband I could wish for," Nora said. "But I don't expect you to have all the answers and all the solutions for every problem. I won't think any less of you if you don't know what to do every once in a while. You don't have to be strong all the time."

"But if I don't—"

One finger against Luke's bluish lips stopped the words. "We'll figure it out together, all right?" Nora took her hand away and waited.

Luke exhaled sharply, and the forming cloud mingled with Nora's condensed breath.

The image made Nora smile. She bridged the space between them and pressed her lips to Luke's. "All right?" she asked again.

"All right," Luke whispered against her lips.

Luke leaned in the doorway, one arm wrapped tightly around Nora, and watched Nattie sleep. The rhythmic movements of the covers lulled her heart to a calmer beat. Finally, she let herself believe that everything would be all right. She vowed to get started on the new house as soon as the snow melted away and the ground dried.

"Here, Papa," Amy said next to her. "For you."

Something was slid into her hand, and Luke instinctively curled her fingers around it. She looked down into Amy's earnest green eyes.

"Don't be sad about the hens, Papa. You can have one of my animals."

Luke lifted the wooden animal to study it in the dim light filtering in from the fireplace. It wasn't just any of Amy's carved animals. Her fingers rubbed over the tiny spots on the horse's flank. "Measles," Luke said. Her throat constricted. A soft squeeze from Nora finally propelled her into action. She let go of Nora and knelt down to be at eye level with Amy. "Thank you, Amy," she said. Her voice trembled. *Get yourself together. You can't let her see you—* Then she paused and glanced at Nora's hand resting on her shoulder.

You don't have to be strong all the time, Nora had said. *I won't think any less of you.*

"I can't take your horse from you, sweetie," Luke said.

Amy reached out, about to take her beloved toy horse, but then she stopped and looked back and forth between Luke and the wooden animal. After one last longing glance at the horse figure, she pulled back her hand. "But I don't want you to be sad."

"Know what would make me feel better?"

"A hug?"

Luke nodded. "A big hug from you."

With a squeal, Amy threw herself into Luke's arms.

The trusting warmth of Amy's small body made Luke close her eyes. *Maybe,* she thought as she laid her cheek against Amy's soft curls, *maybe I really am a good father and provider. We must be doing something right if we have a daughter like this.* She opened her eyes and met Nora's smile with one of her own.

For a while, they forgot about the snow, the hens, and the lack of flour. Only love existed in their cabin.

Hamilton Horse Ranch
Baker Prairie, Oregon
April 1854

Nora set the pot on the stove. While she waited for the water to heat so that she could scrub the wooden floor, she watched Nattie from across the room.

Her youngest was curled up in Luke's favorite armchair, a slate on her knees. She didn't know how to write yet, but she moved the piece of chalk over the slate in a fairly good imitation. With her black hair, gray-green eyes, and the frown of concentration on her little face, she looked like a two-and-a-half-year-old version of Luke.

"Where's your sister?" Nora asked. Half an hour ago, before she had gone to sweep the bedroom and wash the windows, she had left Amy with the slate to practice her ABCs. As always, Amy seemed to have lost interest quickly.

Without looking up, Nattie shrugged and mumbled, "With da horses."

It was as good a guess as any. Nora still remembered the last time Amy had disappeared. They had finally found her sleeping next to one of their draft horses.

Outside, their dog started to bark.

It wasn't the furious barking meant to chase off a coyote or an intruder. Nora smiled. She recognized the dog's greeting. Luke was home. "Hush, Bear," Nora called outside.

The sound of Amy's crying drowned out the barking of the dog.

Nora's smile withered. Her heart lurched into her throat. She had rarely heard such anguished cries from Amy. She pulled the pot off the stove and rushed outside.

Luke reined in her horse and dismounted, a frown on her face and a red-faced Amy in her arms.

"What happened?" Nora hurried over and ran her hands over every inch of Amy. She didn't seem hurt, but she was still sniffling.

"She climbed up on the top rail of the corral," Luke said. Her voice trembled.

Nora took one hand off Amy to squeeze Luke's arm. "Did she fall down?" It wouldn't be the first time that happened.

"No," Luke said. "She tried to climb onto one of the yearlings."

"What?" While far from being grown up, the yearlings had the unpredictable energy of adolescents and certainly weren't safe for a six-year-old to ride. "What happened?"

"She got thrown off," Luke said. "Sailed right over the corral rails." The horror of that scene was reflected in Luke's troubled gray eyes.

Once again, Nora's hands flew over her daughter's form. "Did you hurt yourself?"

Her lips pressed together, Amy shook her head.

"She's fine," Luke said, but her voice still shook. "She landed on a patch of grass. I made her move her arms and legs and looked her over before I let her stand up. There's not a scratch on her."

"Then why is she crying?"

"She's not crying because she's hurt." Luke joined Nora in brushing the grass off Amy's clothes. "She's crying because I didn't let her get back on the horse."

Nora stopped in her attempts to dry Amy's tears. She closed her eyes and shook her head. *Where on God's green earth did she get that? Certainly not from me.* Nora had always been careful around horses, even a little afraid in the beginning. When she opened her eyes again, she looked right into Luke's and had to smile. While Nattie might look like Luke, Amy was the one who had caught her horse fever. Then Nora looked at her daughter sternly. "Amy Theresa Hamilton, I know you remember what Papa keeps telling you about the horses."

Amy continued to stare at the ground.

Nora glanced at Luke, waiting for her to deliver the lesson again.

"Horses look tough, but they get scared easily," Luke said without missing a beat. "And they're really big animals, so if they run and you get in the way, you could get hurt."

"But they're my friends," Amy said, sniffling.

"Do you remember the time you bowled Nattie over when the two of you were racing to be the first to pet the puppy when we first got him?" Luke asked before Nora could think of anything to say.

Nora smiled. Two years ago, Luke would have let her handle this while she slunk away to take care of her horse. Now all awkwardness regarding the children was gone. Luke had learned to reason in a way a child could understand.

Amy nodded.

"You didn't mean to hurt your sister, did you?" Luke asked.

"No." Loud sniffles almost drowned out Amy's answer before she finally calmed down enough to talk. "But now she has a bump, like you." She pointed at Luke's nose, looking a little jealous as if that bump were a badge of honor.

"See?" Luke reached down and tapped Amy's nose. "So the horses could hurt you without even meaning to, just because they're so much bigger than you. No going off to see the horses without permission. And especially no riding. All right?"

"All right."

"Promise?" Luke held out her hand.

With a solemn expression, Amy laid her small hand into Luke's bigger one. "Promise." They shook on it.

As soon as the handshake ended, Amy asked, "Can I go check on Measles?"

Luke exchanged a glance with Nora, then nodded. "Yes, but stay outside the stall. Don't get her riled up."

When Amy ran off to greet Measles, Nora stepped closer to say a proper hello to Luke. At the last second, she jerked back. "Eww. I thought it was Amy who reeked like that, but it's you." Instead of the comforting mix of leather, horse, and Luke, the strong smell of manure wafted up from Luke.

Luke pinched a piece of her shirt and pulled it away from her skin. "I dove out of the saddle, hoping to catch Amy. Guess I landed in something not quite sweet-smelling."

"Guess so," Nora said and kissed her anyway. "Now go change shirts, hero."

Carefully breathing through her mouth, Luke slipped off the soiled shirt. She poured water into the washbowl and wet a cloth. Habit made her hurry through her ablutions. They had taught the girls to knock before they entered the bedroom, but a lifetime of getting dressed quickly was hard to forget.

She strode across the room and pulled a fresh shirt from a dresser drawer.

The door swung open without warning.

"Luke!" Nora rushed into the bedroom.

Luke's heartbeat doubled. She pulled up the shirt and pressed it against her bound chest.

Nora stared at her, looking as startled as Luke felt. "Oh. Sorry."

"No, it's all right. Just…" Luke gestured at the door, then at her state of undress. "It's an ingrained reaction. If something startles me, I just can't help it." She forced herself to move slowly as she lifted up the shirt and slipped it over her head. Nora had earned her trust, and that meant not hiding anything from her—not even her body.

Nora's gaze followed the path of the shirt as it slid down.

Over the course of the past three years, Luke had slowly gotten used to Nora studying her body, but now Nora continued to stare. "What?" Luke asked.

Nora's gaze flitted up to meet Luke's. A blush rouged her cheeks. "Sometimes, during the day, I almost forget what's under your clothes," Nora said, her voice low.

With stiff fingers, Luke jerked on the leather lacings that tied the opening of her shirt.

Two quick steps brought Nora within touching distance. Gently, she tucked the tail ends of the shirt into Luke's pants, letting her hands caress the body underneath. "It's not that I want to forget. I know most people would consider it wrong," Nora leaned forward to whisper into Luke's ear, "but I really like what's underneath your clothes."

Warm breath brushed Luke's ear, making her shiver. She slid her hands over Nora's hips and pulled her closer.

Their lips met.

Finally, Nora pulled away, panting. "Oh!" She blinked. "You're so distracting. I came in to tell you that Measles had her foal while we were busy berating Amy for her little adventure."

"What?" Luke ran for the door, for once not bothering to put on the vest over her shirt.

As she bounded off the front porch, two hens hopped out of the way, flapping their wings, and the rooster crowed indignantly.

"I knew it." Luke had suspected that Measles would go into labor the minute she turned her back. Like many mares, Measles preferred to give birth when she was alone. Horses could stop the foaling process for days if they felt uncomfortable with being watched.

Luke bolted to the horse barn, not waiting for Nora who had stopped to pick up Nattie.

A week ago, she had put Measles into the large stall at the far end of the barn, where it was quieter. Today, curious horses poked their noses over the stall doors as Luke hurried down the center aisle.

"Papa," Amy whispered urgently. "Look!" She had long ago learned not to shout around horses, no matter how excited she was. She was clinging to the stall door with both hands, standing on her tiptoes on an overturned bucket so she could see into the stall.

Luke stopped next to her and peeked inside. Her eyes needed a moment to adjust to the dim light, but then she made out the contours of Measles, who was already back on her feet. The mare nosed through the straw, rubbing her soft lips over the foal that lay on its side.

"Look, Papa. The foal got red hair, just like me." Amy fidgeted on the bucket, almost knocking it over.

Luke heaved her up, into her arms. The girl was getting too big to be held like this for much longer. "I see it," she said, not as enthusiastic. While the sorrel coat was nice, she'd hoped for a multicolored foal. Measles's first foal didn't have any spots as far as Luke could see.

Measles nickered softly to her foal and pushed at its rear end with her nose.

Its long, thin legs splayed and trembling, the foal stood.

Luke grinned.

A small white blanket, littered with reddish dots, covered the foal's hind end.

Nora stepped up next to her, balancing Nattie on one hip. Now four pairs of eyes were watching the newborn foal stagger through the stall until it found its mother's teats and began to suckle. "Oh, how beautiful," Nora whispered. "A multicolored foal—just like you hoped for."

Luke's heart sang. She wrapped her free arm around Nora and pulled her close against her side. Could life get any better?

"Papa," Amy's voice broke the comfortable silence. "Can the foal be my horse? I can teach her to be a good horse, like Measles."

Luke nearly choked on her own spit, almost making her drop the girl. "Um." She looked at Nora.

Nora stared back. "Sweetie, you're just six years old. You're too small to take care of a horse, much less train a foal."

Tears glittered in Amy's pleading green eyes.

This was the one thing Luke still hadn't learned: how to face tears from one of her daughters. "You can help me with the foal," she said. "And if you do a really good job, in a few years, when the foal is grown up and has her own foal, that'll be yours and you can train her. All right?"

Their neighbors would talk and shake their heads at Luke for letting a girl train a young horse, but Luke didn't care. She had promised herself that their daughters would be allowed to do whatever they wanted.

Amy threw her arms around Luke's neck in a strangle hold.

"Luke Hamilton! That girl has you wrapped around her little finger," Nora said, but her voice sounded affectionate, not really scolding. She glanced down at Nattie. "Both of them do."

Luke leaned over and kissed her cheek. "All three of them."

"Papa?" Nattie tugged on Luke's sleeve.

"Yes, little one?"

"I want baby," Nattie said.

Nora's groan made Luke chuckle. "You want a baby horse too?"

Nattie shook her head.

"Then what?" For Luke, it was often easier to understand Amy's needs and interests than those of her younger daughter. Never before had she seen two siblings more different than these two.

Amy rolled her eyes. "She wants a baby sister because I don't want to play with her."

Heat shot up Luke's neck and suffused her cheeks. She rubbed the bridge of her nose and shot Nora a helpless glance.

Now Nora, equally red-faced, was the one who chuckled. "That's what you get for spoiling them. Try to talk your way out of this one."

"Thanks so much," Luke mumbled. She looked into Nattie's gray-green eyes, which were watching her expectantly. "Um, how about a kitten?"

Nora laughed so loudly that even Measles looked up from her nursing foal.

"Sssh, Mama!" Amy poked her in the shoulder. "No loud noises around the horses."

"Yes, Mama," Nattie said, quite seriously. Thankfully, she seemed to have forgotten all about her wish for a baby sister—at least for now.

Phew. Luke wiped her brow. A child was the one thing she could never give her family, no matter how hard she worked.

"Hey," Nora whispered into her ear. "Don't look so glum. You think either of us could survive a third little one like this? Let's try raising these two without going crazy, all right?"

She's right. Luke turned, touched her lips to Nora's, and said, "I'll give it my best."

###

ABOUT JAE

Jae grew up amidst the vineyards of southern Germany. She spent her childhood with her nose buried in a book, earning her the nickname "professor." The writing bug bit her at the age of eleven. Since 2006, she has been writing mostly in English.

She used to work as a psychologist but gave up her day job in December 2013 to become a full-time writer and a part-time editor. As far as she's concerned, it's the best job in the world.

When she's not writing, she likes to spend her time reading, indulging her ice cream and office supply addictions, and watching way too many crime shows.

Connect with Jae online

Jae loves hearing from readers!
Visit her website: www.jae-fiction.com
E-mail her at jae@jae-fiction.com
Like her on Facebook: facebook.com/JaeAuthor
Follow her on Twitter @jaefiction

Other books from Ylva Publishing

www.ylva-publishing.com

HIDDEN TRUTHS

(The Oregon Series – Book 3)

Jae

ISBN: 978-3-95533-119-1

Length: 476 pages (157,000 words)

"Luke" Hamilton has been living as a husband and father for the past seventeen years. No one but her wife, Nora, knows she is not the man she appears to be. They have raised their daughters to become honest and hard-working young women, but even with their loving foundation, Amy and Nattie are hiding their own secrets.

SHAKEN TO THE CORE

Jae

ISBN: 978-3-95533-662-2

Length: 368 pages (126,000 words)

Kate Winthrop, daughter of a shipping magnate, is expected to marry a respectable man. But her true passion lies with photography—and with women.

Much to the dismay of her parents, she becomes friends with their maid Giuliana.

Then an earthquake hits San Francisco. Will the disaster shatter their tentative feelings? Or will they be able to save each other's lives and hearts?

Kicker's Journey

Lois Cloarec Hart

ISBN: 978-3-95533-060-6

Length: 472 pages (157,000 words)

In 1899, two women from very different backgrounds are about to embark on a journey together - one that will take them from the Old World to the New, from the 19th century into the 20th, and from the comfort and familiarity of England to the rigours of Western Canada, where challenges await at every turn.

The journey begins simply for Kicker Stuart when she leaves her home village to take employment as hostler and farrier at Grindleshire Academy for Young Ladies. But when Kicker falls in love with a teacher, Madelyn Bristow, it radically alters the course of her tranquil life.

Together, the lovers flee the brutality of Madelyn's father and the prejudices of upper crust England in search of freedom to live, and love, as they choose. A journey as much of the heart and soul as of the body, it will find the lovers struggling against the expectations of gender, the oppression of class, and even, at times, each other.

What they find at the end of their journey is not a new Eden, but a land of hope and opportunity that offers them the chance to live out their most cherished dream—a life together.

Charity

(The Charity Series – Book 1)

Paulette Callen

ISBN: 978-3-95533-075-0

Length: 334 pages (94,000 words)

The friendship between Lena Kaiser, a sodbuster's daughter, and Gustie Roemer, an educated Easterner, is unlikely in any other circumstance but post-frontier Charity, South Dakota. Gustie is considered an outsider, and Lena is too proud to share her problems (which include a hard-drinking husband) with anyone else.

Backwards to Oregon
© 2017 by Jae

ISBN: 978-3-95533-870-1

Also available as e-book.

Published by Ylva Publishing, legal entity of Ylva Verlag, e.Kfr.

Ylva Verlag, e.Kfr.
Owner: Astrid Ohletz
Am Kirschgarten 2
65830 Kriftel
Germany

www.ylva-publishing.com

First edition: E-book 2008 / Paperback 2009
Revised and expanded second edition: E-book and paperback 2013
New edition: October 2017

Credits
Edited by Judy Underwood
Cover Design by Streetlight Graphics